"I am in need of an education. Since you are my guardian *and* an expert on rakes, you are the perfect person to teach me their tricks."

"Let me see if I have this correct. You want me to teach you how to spot a rake?"

Julianne nodded. "Yes, for my own protection."

"What do you want me to say? Beware the red devils sporting horns and forked tails?"

"No, silly. I want you to teach me what rakes say and do to lure their victims. It may require a demonstration on your part."

"A demonstration?" he said.

"Yes. For educational purposes only."

An arrested expression crossed his face. "You want *me* to seduce *you*?"

"*Pretend* to seduce me." She smiled. "Given the urgency of the matter, I believe we should begin immediately."

Hawk's eyes darkened.

"The forbidden excites you, doesn't it?"

She dared not admit it: *I want to be naughty.*

Glowing Praise for Vicky Dreiling's
HOW TO MARRY A DUKE

"In her lively debut novel, Vicky Dreiling has penned a fresh, engaging take on Regency matchmaking that brims with clever wit and repartee. I found myself smiling and laughing out loud on numerous occasions. Here's hoping for more of this promising new author's historical romances!"

—Nicole Jordan, *New York Times* bestselling author

How to Seduce a Scoundrel

VICKY DREILING

FOREVER

NEW YORK   BOSTON

This book is a work of fiction. Names, characters, places, and incidents are the product of the author's imagination or are used fictitiously. Any resemblance to actual events, locales, or persons, living or dead, is coincidental.

Copyright © 2011 by Vicky Dreiling
Excerpt from *How to Ravish a Rake* Copyright © 2011 by Vicky Dreiling
Excerpt from *How to Marry a Duke* Copyright © 2011 by Vicky Dreiling

Forever
Hachette Book Group
237 Park Avenue
New York, NY 10017
www.HachetteBookGroup.com

Forever is an imprint of Grand Central Publishing.
The Forever name and logo are trademarks of Hachette Book Group, Inc.

The publisher is not responsible for websites (or their content) that are not owned by the publisher.

Printed in the United States of America

First Edition: July 2011

10 9 8 7 6 5 4 3 2 1

To Mom for giving me a diary when I was ten years old and for encouraging me to write. P.S. This one has naughty bits in it, too. ☺

Acknowledgments

My sincere thanks to my very talented agent Lucienne Diver (a.k.a. Agent Awesome Sauce) for being, well, awesome. And because you got me at hello.

A big shout-out to my wonderful editor Michele Bidelspach for your amazing insights and for the laughter, too. Working with you is truly a joy. *Merci beaucoup!*

Thanks to some other special people at Forever Romance for your support. Amy Pierpont for all the cheers and retweets, Samantha Kelly for arranging some fabulous promotional opportunities, and Anna Balasi for the cool blog tour and most especially that hilarious Blog Talk Radio interview. What fun!

Thanks to my writing friends at West Houston RWA for all the support and friendship. I wouldn't be here if not for our chapter.

Hugs to my supportive family: Daniel, Regina, Amber, and Jonathan. And to the fur kids: Buttercup, Foxy, Sweetpea, and Pebbles. Love you all.

Most of all, my humble thanks to all the readers who took time out to let me know you couldn't wait to read *How to Seduce a Scoundrel.* xoxoxo

How to
Seduce a
Scoundrel

Chapter One

*A Scoundrel's Code of Conduct: Virgins are strictly forbidden,
especially if said virgin happens to be your friend's sister.*

Richmond, England, 1817

He'd arrived late as usual.

Marc Darcett, Earl of Hawkfield, twirled his top hat
as he sauntered along the pavement toward his mother's
home. A chilly breeze ruffled his hair and stung his face.
In the dwindling evening light, Ashdown House with its
crenellated top and turrets stood stalwart near the banks
of the Thames.

Ordinarily, Hawk dreaded the obligatory weekly visits.
His mother and three married sisters had grown increasingly demanding about his lack of a bride since his oldest
friend had wed last summer. They made no secret of their

disappointment in him, but he was accustomed to being the family scapegrace.

Today, however, he looked forward to seeing that oldest friend, Tristan Gatewick, the Duke of Shelbourne.

After the butler, Jones, admitted him, Hawk stripped off his gloves and greatcoat. "Are Shelbourne and his sister here yet?"

"The duke and Lady Julianne arrived two hours ago," Jones said.

"Excellent." Hawk couldn't wait to relate his latest bawdy escapade to his friend. Last evening, he'd met Nancy and Nell, two naughty dancers who had made him an indecent proposition. Not wishing to appear too anxious, he'd promised to think over the matter, but he intended to accept their two-for-the-price-of-one offer.

The fastidious Jones eyed Hawk's head critically. "Begging your pardon, my lord, but you might wish to attend to your hair."

"You don't say?" Hawk pretended to be oblivious and peered at his windblown locks in the mirror above the foyer table. "Perfect," he said. "Mussed hair is all the rage."

"If you say so, my lord."

Hawk spun around. "I take it everyone is waiting in the gold drawing room?"

"Yes, my lord. Your mother has inquired after you several times."

Hawk glanced out at the great hall and grinned at the giant statue next to the stairwell. "Ah, my mother has taken an interest in naked statuary, has she?"

The ordinarily stoic Jones made a suspicious, muffled sound. Then he cleared his throat. "Apollo was delivered yesterday."

"Complete with his lyre and snake, I see. Well, I shall welcome him to the family." Hawk's boots clipped on the checkered marble floor as he strolled toward the cantilevered stairwell, an architectural feat that made the underside of the stone steps appear suspended in midair. At the base of the stairs, he paused to inspect the reproduction and grimaced at Apollo's minuscule genitalia. "Poor bastard."

Footsteps sounded above. Hawk looked up to find Tristan striding down the carpeted steps.

"Sizing up the competition?" Tristan said.

Hawk grinned. "The devil. It's the old married man."

"I saw your curricle from the window." Tristan stepped onto the marble floor and clapped Hawk on the shoulder. "You look as if you just tumbled out of bed."

Hawk wagged his brows and let his friend imagine what he would. "How is your duchess?"

A brief, careworn expression flitted through his friend's eyes. "The doctor says all is progressing well. She has two more months of confinement." He released a gusty sigh. "I wanted a son, but now I'm praying for a safe delivery."

Hawk nodded but said nothing.

"One day it will be your turn, and I'll be the one consoling you."

That day would never come. "And give up my bachelorhood? Never," he said.

Tristan grinned. "I'll remind you of that when I attend your wedding."

Hawk changed the subject. "I take it your sister is well?" His mother planned to sponsor Lady Julianne this season while the dowager duchess stayed in the country with her increasing daughter-in-law.

"Julianne is looking forward to the season, but there is a problem," Tristan said. "A letter arrived from Bath half an hour ago. Your grandmother is suffering from heart palpitations again."

Hawk groaned. Grandmamma was famous for her heart palpitations. She succumbed to them at the most inconvenient times and described them in minute, loving detail to anyone unfortunate enough to be in the general vicinity. Owing to Grandmamma's diminished hearing, this meant anyone within shouting range.

"Your mother and sisters are discussing who should travel to Bath as we speak," Tristan said.

"Don't worry, old boy. We'll sort it out." No doubt his sisters meant to flee to Bath, as they always did when his grandmother invoked her favorite ailment. Usually his mother went as well, but she'd made a commitment to sponsor Julianne.

A peevish voice sounded from the landing. "Marc, you have dawdled long enough. Mama is waiting."

Hawk glanced up to find his eldest sister, Patience, beckoning him with her fingers as if he were one of her unruly brats. Poor Patience had never proven equal to her name, something he'd exploited since childhood. He never could resist provoking her then, and he certainly couldn't now. "My dear sister, I'd no idea you were so anxious for my company. It warms the cockles of my heart."

Her nostrils flared. "Our grandmother is ill, and Mama is fretting. You will not add to her vexation by tarrying."

"Pour Mama a sherry for her nerves. I'll be along momentarily," he said.

Patience pinched her lips, whirled around, and all but stomped away.

Hawk's shoulders shook with laughter as he returned his attention to his friend. "After dinner, we'll put in a brief appearance in the drawing room and make our escape to the club."

"I'd better not. I'm planning to leave at dawn tomorrow," Tristan said.

Hawk shrugged to hide his disappointment. He ought to have known the old boy meant to return to his wife immediately. Nothing would ever be quite the same now that his friend had married. "Well, then, shall we join the others?"

As they walked up the stairs, Tristan glanced at him with an enigmatic expression. "It's been too long since we last met."

"Yes, it has."

The last time was Tristan's wedding nine months ago. He'd meant to visit the newlyweds after a decent interval. Then Tristan's letter had arrived with the jubilant news of his impending fatherhood.

Hawk's feet had felt as if they were immersed in a bog.

After they entered the drawing room, Hawk halted. He was only peripherally aware of his sisters' husbands scowling at him from the sideboard. All his attention centered on a slender lady seated on the sofa between his mother and his youngest sister, Hope. The candlelight gleamed over the lady's jet curls as she gazed down at a sketchbook on her lap. Good Lord, could this delectable creature possibly be Julianne?

As if sensing his stare, she glanced at him. He took in her transformation, stunned by the subtle changes. In the past nine months, the slight fullness of her cheeks had disappeared, emphasizing her sculpted cheekbones. Even her expression had changed. Instead of her usual impish grin, she regarded him with a poised smile.

The sweet little girl he'd known all his life had become a woman. A heart-stopping, beautiful woman.

The sound of his mother's voice rattled him. "Tristan, please be seated. Marc, do not stand there gawking. Come and greet Julianne."

Patience and his other sister Harmony sat in a pair of chairs near the hearth, exchanging sly smiles. No doubt they were hatching a plot to snare him in the parson's mousetrap. They probably thought he was as besotted as the numerous cubs who vied for Julianne's attention every season. But he was only a little taken aback by her transformation.

Determined to take himself in hand, he strode over to her, made a leg, and swept his arm in a ridiculous bow last seen in the sixteenth century.

When he rose, his mother grimaced. "Marc, your hair is standing up. You look thoroughly disreputable."

He grinned like a jackanapes. "Why, thank you, Mama."

Julianne's husky laugh drew his attention. He set his fist on his hip and wagged his brows. "No doubt you will break a dozen hearts this season, Julie-girl."

She regarded him from beneath her long lashes. "Perhaps one will capture my affections."

Helen of Troy's face had launched a thousand ships, but Julianne's naturally raspy voice could fell a thousand men. Where the devil had that foolish thought come from? She'd grown into a stunning young woman, but he'd always thought of her as the little hoyden who climbed trees and skimmed rocks.

Hope stood. "Marc, take my seat. You must see Julianne's sketches."

He meant to make the most of the opportunity. For years, he'd teased Julianne and encouraged her in mischief. After sitting beside her, he grinned and tapped the sketch. "What have you got there, imp?"

She showed him a sketch of Stonehenge. "I drew this last summer when I traveled with Amy and her family."

"Stonehenge is awe-inspiring," the countess said.

He dutifully looked on as Julianne turned the page. "Those are some big rocks."

Julianne laughed. "Rogue."

He tweaked the curl by her ear. When she swatted his hand, he laughed. She was the same Julie-girl he'd always known.

Heavy footsteps thudded outside the drawing room doors. Everyone stood as Lady Rutledge, his great-aunt Hester, lumbered inside. Gray sausage curls peeked out from a green turban with tall feathers. She took one look at Hawk's mother and scowled. "Louisa, that statue is hideous. If you want a naked man, find yourself one who is breathing."

Hawk's mouth worked with the effort not to laugh out loud.

The countess fanned her heated face. "Hester, please mind your words."

"Bah." Hester winked at Hawk. "Come give your aunt a kiss, you rogue."

When he obliged, she muttered, "You're the only sensible one in the bunch."

Tristan bowed to her. "Lady Rutledge."

Hester eyed him appreciatively. "Shelbourne, you

handsome devil. I heard you wasted no time getting your duchess with child."

Hawk's mother and younger sisters gasped. Patience cleared her throat. "Aunt Hester, we do not speak of such indelicate matters."

Hester snorted and kept her knowing gaze on Tristan. "I heard your duchess has gumption. She'll bring your child into the world without mishap—mark my words."

Hawk considered his wily old aunt with a fond smile. Eccentric she might be, but she'd sought to reassure his old friend. And for that alone he adored her.

He led Hester over to a chair and stood beside her. Her wide rump barely fit between the arms. After adjusting her plumes, she held her quizzing glass up to her eye and inspected Julianne.

"Aunt Hester, you remember Lady Julianne," Patience said, as if speaking to a child. "She is Shelbourne's sister."

"I know who she is." Hester dropped her quizzing glass. "Why are you still unwed, gel?"

Julianne blushed. "I am waiting for the right gentleman."

"I heard you turned down a dozen proposals since your come-out. Is it true?" Hester continued.

"I've not kept count," Julianne murmured.

Hester snorted. "There were so many you cannot recall?"

Noting Julianne's disconcerted expression, Hawk intervened. "Mama, I understand we've a bit of a problem. Grandmamma is claiming illness again, is she?"

His mother and sisters protested that they must assume Grandmamma was truly ill. Finally, Aunt Hester interrupted. "Oh, hush, Louisa. You know very well my sister is only seeking attention."

"Hester, how can you say such a thing?" the countess said.

"Because she makes a habit of it." Hester sniffed. "I suppose you and your girls are planning to hare off to Bath on a fool's errand again."

"We cannot take a risk," Patience said. "If Grandmamma took a bad turn, we would never forgive ourselves."

"She ought to come to town where she can be near the family. I offered to share my home with her, but she refuses to leave her cronies in Bath," Hester said.

"She is set in her ways." Hawk grinned down at his aunt. "Few ladies are as adventurous as you."

"True," Hester said, preening.

The countess gave him a beseeching look. "Will you write William to inform him?"

"I'm not sure of his address at present," Hawk said. His younger brother had been traveling on the Continent for more than a year.

Montague, Patience's husband, lowered his newspaper. "It's past time William came home and stopped raking his way all over the Continent. He needs to choose a career and be a responsible member of the family."

Hawk regarded him as if he were an insect. "He'll come home when he tires of wandering." He'd hoped Will would return for the London season, but his brother hadn't written in over two months.

Montague folded his newspaper. "He'd come home soon enough if you cut him off without a penny."

Hawk ignored his least favorite brother-in-law and returned his attention to his mother. "What of Julianne? Her brother brought her all this way. Mama, can you not stay behind?"

"Oh, I could not ask such a thing," Julianne said. "I can stay with either Amy or Georgette. My friends' mothers would welcome me, I'm sure."

"Her friends' mothers will be too busy with their own girls," Hester said. "I will sponsor Julianne. She will be the toast of the season."

A long silence followed. Hawk's mother and sisters regarded one another with barely concealed dismay. They thought Hester a few cards shy of a full deck, but he knew his aunt was prodigiously clever, if a bit blunt in her manners.

The countess cleared her throat. "Hester, dear, that is too kind of you, but perhaps you have not thought of how exhausting all those entertainments will be."

"I'm never tired, Louisa," she said. "I shall enjoy sponsoring the gel. She's pretty enough and seems lively. I'll have her engaged in a matter of weeks."

Hawk schooled his expression. Julianne married? It seemed so . . . wrong. Even though he knew it was customary for ladies to marry young, the idea didn't set well with him.

Tristan eyed Hester. "Granted, she's been out four seasons, but marriage is for life. I'll not rush her."

Hester looked at Julianne. "How old are you, gel?"

"One and twenty," she said.

"She's of age, but I agree marriage should not be undertaken lightly," Hester said.

Tristan regarded his sister. "I must approve any serious attachments."

When Julianne rolled her eyes, Hawk grinned. He didn't envy any man bold enough to ask Tristan's permission for Julianne's hand. The old boy had kept a tight rein on her for years—as well he should.

"Now that the matter is settled, let us go to dinner," Hester said. "I'm starved."

After the ladies withdrew from the dining room, Hawk brought out the port. His sisters' husbands exchanged meaningful glances. Tristan kept silent but watched them with a guarded expression.

Montague folded his small hands on the table and addressed Hawk. "Lady Julianne cannot stay with Hester. Your aunt's bold manners and rebellious ideas would be a bad influence on the girl."

Hawk met Tristan's gaze. "Join me in the study?"

Tristan nodded.

They both rose. When Hawk claimed a candle branch from the sideboard, Montague scrambled up from the table. "Patience will stay behind and look after Julianne."

"My sister is determined to go to Bath," Hawk said. "She will not rest easy unless she sees our grandmother is well." The last thing he wanted was to expose Julianne to his sister's acrimonious marriage.

"You know very well your grandmother feigns illness," Montague said. "If your mother and sisters refused to go, that would put a stop to this nonsense."

Hawk realized Montague had seized the opportunity to keep his wife at home. The man constantly queried Patience about her whereabouts and upbraided her if she even spoke to another man. "I'll discuss the matter with Shelbourne. Gentlemen, enjoy your port."

He started to turn away when Montague's voice halted him.

"Damn you, Hawk. Someone needs to take responsibility for the girl."

Hawk strode around the table and loomed over his brother-in-law. "You've no say in the matter." Then he lowered his voice. "You will remember my warning."

Montague glared but held his tongue. Hawk gave him an evil smile. At Christmas, the man had made one too many disparaging remarks about Patience. Hawk had taken him aside and threatened to beat him to a pulp if he ever treated her disrespectfully again.

As he and Tristan strode away, Hawk muttered, "Bloody brute."

"Montague resents your political influence, your fortune, and your superior height. He feels inferior and engages in pissing matches to prove he's manly."

Hawk wished Montague to the devil. The man had campaigned for his sister's hand and showered her with affection. He'd shown his true colors shortly after the wedding.

When they walked into the study, the scent of leather permeated the room. Hawk set the candle branch on the mantel and slumped into one of the cross-framed chairs before the huge mahogany desk. The grate was empty, making the room chilly. He never made use of the study. Years ago, he'd taken rooms at the Albany. His family had disapproved, but he'd needed to escape his father's stranglehold.

Tristan surveyed the surroundings and sat next to Hawk. "The study is virtually unchanged since your father's death."

He'd died suddenly of a heart seizure eight years ago, closing off any chance of reconciliation between them. A foolish thought. There was nothing he could have done to change his father's opinion of him.

"Your father was a good man," Tristan said. "His advice was invaluable to me."

"He admired you," Hawk said.

Tristan had single-handedly restored his fortune after discovering his late wastrel father had left him in monstrous debt.

"I envied your freedom," Tristan said.

"I had an easy time compared to you." Hawk's father had never let him forget it, either. Unbidden, the words his father had spoken more than a dozen years ago echoed in his brain. *Do you even know how much it will cost to satisfy Westcott's honor?*

He mentally slammed the door on the memory. "Old boy, your sister may prefer to stay with one of her friends, but I advise you to refuse if she wishes to stay with Lady Georgette. I heard a nasty rumor about her brother. Evidently, Ramsey got a maid with child." No honorable gentleman ever took advantage of servants.

Tristan's face showed his revulsion. "Good Lord. He's disgusting."

"If you prefer, take your sister to Amy Hardwick's mother."

"No, your aunt is right. Mrs. Hardwick should concentrate on her own daughter." Tristan frowned. "I cannot impose."

Tristan probably felt a bit guilty because Amy and Georgette had devoted their entire season last year to his unusual courtship. "My aunt is a cheeky old bird, but she's harmless enough. Hester will enjoy squiring Julianne about town."

Tristan glanced sideways at Hawk. "I've a favor to ask."

A strange presentiment washed over Hawk. He'd

known Tristan since they were in leading strings, because their mothers were bosom friends. At Eton, he and Tristan had banded together to evade the older boys who liked to torment the younger ones. Hawk knew his friend well, but he'd no idea what Tristan intended to ask of him.

Tristan drew in a breath. "Will you act as my sister's unofficial guardian?"

Hawk laughed. "Me, a guardian? Surely you jest."

"As soon as the fortune hunters discover I'm out of the picture, they'll hover like vultures over Julianne. I won't feel easy unless a solid man is there to protect her from rakes."

"But... but I'm a rake," he sputtered. Of course, she'd blossomed into an uncommonly lovely young woman, but she was his friend's sister. Even among rakes, it was a point of honor to avoid friends' sisters.

"You've watched my sister grow up the same way I have," Tristan said. "She's almost like a sister to you."

He'd never thought of her that way. To him, she was simply Julie-girl, always ready for a bit of mischief. He never grew tired of daring her to do something unladylike, but she'd never once backed down. "Old boy, you know I'm fond of her, but I'm not fit to be anybody's guardian."

"You've always looked out for her," Tristan said.

Guilt spurted in his chest. His own family thought him an irresponsible rogue, with good reason. He didn't even know how to locate his own brother. But clearly Tristan had complete faith in him.

Tristan pinched the bridge of his nose. "I should stay in London to watch over Julianne, but I cannot bear to leave my wife. No matter what I do, I'll feel as if I've wronged one of them."

Ah, hell. Tristan had never asked for a favor before. He was like a brother to him. Damn it all. He couldn't refuse. "Anything for you, old boy."

"Thank you," Tristan said. "There's one more thing. You're not going to like it."

He lifted his brows. "Oh?"

Tristan narrowed his eyes. "You will give up raking for the duration of the season."

He laughed. "What?"

"You heard me. There will be no ballerinas, actresses, or courtesans. Call them what you will, but you will not associate with whores while guarding my sister."

He scoffed. "It's not as if I'd flaunt a mistress in your sister's face."

"Your liaisons are famous." Tristan tapped his thumb on the arm of the chair. "I've often suspected you delight in your bad reputation."

He made jests about his numerous mistresses. Everyone, including his friend, believed his tall tales. While he was a bona fide rake, Hawk couldn't possibly live up— or was that down?—to the exaggerated reports about his conquests. "I'll not agree to celibacy," he said.

"You don't even try to be discreet. Julianne adores you. I don't want her disillusioned."

"I'll keep my liaisons quiet," Hawk grumbled.

"Agreed," Tristan said.

He'd better forget the ménage á trois with Nell and Nancy. It rather aggrieved him, since he'd never dallied with two women at once, but he couldn't possibly keep that sort of wicked business under the proverbial covers.

Tristan tapped his thumb again. "Write periodically and let me know how my sister fares."

"I will," Hawk said. "Don't worry. Julianne will grow accustomed to my aunt's blunt manners."

"When the babe is born, bring my sister home to me." He smiled. "Tessa already asked Julianne to be godmother. Will you be godfather?"

A knot formed in his chest, but he forced a laugh. "You would trust a rogue like me with your child?"

"There is no one I trust more than you, my friend."

Hawk cut his gaze away, knowing he didn't deserve his friend's regard.

Chapter Two

A Lady's Secrets of Seduction: When in doubt of his feelings, seek advice from your friends.

The next day at Hester's town house

$\mathcal{N}$o one could resist Hawk. Not even the dogs.

Julianne laughed as the two King Charles spaniels abandoned Hester and the bits of cake she was feeding them. The bug-eyed creatures' tails wagged as they barked and ran circles around Hawk's feet.

Hester clapped her hands. "Caro, Byron, cease!"

They whined and pawed him. "Mind the boots," he said. Then he bent to ruffle their long fur. The two spaniels sat on their haunches, panting with doggy ecstasy.

"You've managed to charm them," Julianne said. "I'm quite jealous, you know. They are not nearly so fond of me."

He looked up and winked. "Ah, but I am."

His words cheered her. After not having seen him for nine long months, she'd worried that things might prove awkward between them. Yesterday, they had been surrounded by so many others, and then he'd spent most of his time closeted in the study with her brother. Today, however, she felt as if the months had melted like snow.

Hester shifted on a red sofa with two horrid, gilded sphinxes rising up from the armrests. "Well, Nephew, do you not have a kiss for your aunt?"

With a slow grin, Hawk straightened his tall, powerful frame and approached her. Naturally, the dogs followed. After he deposited a smacking kiss on his aunt's powdered jowl, she tapped him with her fan. "Your cravat is crooked, and your hair is mussed."

Julianne grinned. Only Hawk could make such careless attire seem boyishly handsome. As always, his unruly mahogany locks looked windblown, a consequence of his tendency to twirl his top hat rather than wear it.

"You've not seen my drawing room since I made it over last season," Hester said. "I've developed a passion for the Egyptian style."

He strolled over to a glass case. Then he regarded Julianne over his shoulder with a devilish expression. "Aunt, is the mummy authentic?"

"It is a reproduction," Hester said. "But the ornamented scrolls on the ceiling are true antiquities."

Julianne bit back a smile at the hideous décor. Golden pharaoh statues, pyramids, and urns cluttered the numerous black tables. Many of the furnishings featured enormous clawed feet. Fortunately, Hester had shown her to a sedate bedchamber early this morning. Julianne had almost wilted with relief. Dear God, she'd feared she would have to sleep among mummies.

"Do be seated," Hester said to Hawk.

The dogs followed him to the sofa where Julianne sat. Hawk regarded the dogs and pointed at the carpet. "Sit."

The spaniels complied and lolled their tongues.

"You've made a conquest of my pets," Hester said.

He slouched beside Julianne. "Alas, I fear Byron has a prior claim on Caro's affections. My heart is broken."

Julianne rolled her eyes, but truthfully, she'd missed his silly jests. During the long months of autumn and winter, she'd held out hope that he would visit her family. He'd never stayed away so long before. She'd agonized over his absence and feared he'd formed an attachment with someone else. Last night, Patience had whispered she hoped to call her *sister* soon. Julianne's hopes had soared, knowing his family would approve.

Hawk's voice startled her. "Your brother left early this morning as planned?"

She nodded. "Your mother and sisters departed at the same time." Of course, her brother had given her all sorts of dire warnings. But when he'd hugged her, she'd known he'd only lectured her because he worried about her.

Hester eyed Julianne. "Will you serve tea?"

She rose and walked over to the tray. Hawk and the dogs followed. When she sliced a generous portion of cake, he broke off a piece and ate it before she could set it on the plate. "Mmmm. Breakfast."

"It's well past noon, you heathen," she said.

"The usual waking hour for a gentleman of leisure." He winked as he sucked a crumb off his finger.

She couldn't breathe. An image popped into her head

of Hawk taking her face in his hands. She imagined his lips descending to hers. More than a few of her beaux had tried to kiss her, but she'd never let them. She wanted to save all her kisses for Hawk.

Her thoughts whirled as she poured tea. Although she had no experience, she'd seen her brother kiss his wife, Tessa, swiftly on the lips more than a few times. Julianne had thought their kissing sweet. Once, however, she'd gone back to the drawing room to retrieve her novel and saw Tessa sitting on Tristan's lap. They were kissing with their tongues. Shocked, she'd fled before they saw her.

Hawk took the teacup from her, drained every last drop, and set it aside. She laughed. "More?"

"No, thank you."

She poured a cup for Hester and took it to her. Hester gave her a piercing look. Julianne stiffened, wondering if she'd somehow displeased Hawk's aunt.

"Come sit with me, Julianne, and let us talk," Hawk said.

The spaniels followed as Hawk led her back to the sofa. He sat next to her again. The dogs perched at his feet, looking up at him hopefully. He stretched out his long legs, drawing her attention. His tight trousers showed off his muscular thighs.

"Julie-girl?" he said.

Her face flamed. Oh, dear, had he caught her ogling him?

His mouth curved in a lopsided grin. "Did your brother tell you he asked me to act as your unofficial guardian?"

"Yes." After Tristan had informed her, Julianne had struggled not to reveal her excitement. However, she suspected her mother would object, but her brother had made the decision. As far as Julianne could tell, Tristan did not suspect her feelings for Hawk. Of course, her mother had guessed. Before Julianne had left home, Mama had privately told her to cease her girlish infatuation. According to her, it was a sure path to heartache.

Julianne meant to prove her mother wrong.

"I promised to escort you to balls and other entertainments," Hawk said. "You needn't worry. I'll not interfere with all the cubs who worship at your feet."

Her stomach clenched. Did he think she preferred the younger men? She must let him know that wasn't true. "I've no interest in boys who stare and stutter."

"They're too awed to be dangerous," Hawk said. "I'll keep the scoundrels far away."

"I know you will protect me," she said. He'd always looked out for her, even when she was a little girl.

Hester regarded her with a warning expression. Julianne bit her lip, fearing Hawk's aunt thought her a shameless flirt.

Hawk gave his aunt a lazy smile. "Be sure to send me a list of Julianne's invitations."

"Ridiculous," Hester said, her voice overly loud. "There's no need for you to dog the gel's heels."

Julianne inhaled. Oh, no, Hester would ruin everything.

"Ah, but a promise is a promise." He tweaked the curl by her ear. "You don't mind, do you, Julie-girl?"

She shook her head and pictured him lying on his side next to her beneath a canopy of trees. He would pull her curl and say, *I want to kiss you.*

The fantasy popped like a soap bubble at the sound of his voice. "Now, I shall leave you ladies to your tea and tittle-tattle."

She rose with him. "Must you go so soon?"

"Afraid so. Au revoir." He quit the drawing room, with Byron and Caro yapping as they scampered after him.

Julianne released a wistful sigh and sank onto the sofa.

"You'll never catch him if you wear your heart on your sleeve."

Hester's voice startled her. "I-I've no idea what you mean."

"Of course you do. You make your tender feelings obvious enough."

She winced. Mama had said the same thing, but Julianne could not help herself. She loved him.

Hester considered her for a long moment. "What you need are lessons in amore."

She regarded Hester warily, unsure what she had in mind. "You are too kind, but I would not impose upon you." She doubted the eccentric Hester would dispense any useful advice and hoped she would forget the matter.

"Nonsense, I shall be happy to instruct you," Hester said.

As a guest, Julianne could not refuse without giving insult. She reminded herself she was only obliged to listen.

Hester pointed her quizzing glass at her. "If you wish to snag my nephew, you must use your wiles."

She didn't know if she had any wiles, but perhaps she should get some.

"First, we must devise a plan of seduction," Hester said.

Julianne froze. Mama had always insisted she must guard her virtue at all costs. "Er, is that not improper?"

"My dear, I've wedded, bedded, and buried five husbands. And I promise you, the way to a man's heart is through his nether region."

A bonfire engulfed her cheeks. No wonder Lady Hawkfield had worried about leaving Hester in charge.

"I see your blushes, gel," Hester said. "Mark me. The only way to tame a rake is to persuade him you'll keep him happier than a courtesan in the marriage bed."

She cringed at Hester's frank speech. "What about love?"

"First comes lust. Then comes marriage," Hester said.

Julianne lowered her lashes to hide her revulsion. In comparison to her dreams of romance, Hester's description of courtship sounded, well, sordid.

Surely it was not wrong to yearn for sweet declarations of forever after. She'd become smitten with Hawk at the tender age of eight. That was the year her father had died. Hawk had arrived at her family's country estate that summer, and his teasing had mended her sorrow. She'd adored him, and then when she'd made her come-out at seventeen, he'd danced with her. She'd fallen madly in love, and every night afterward, she'd dreamed of marrying him.

Hawk had not danced with her since that evening, but she knew he'd thought her too young. He'd waited for her to grow up. She was sure of it, almost positive. And she would not give up her dream. Because the very thought of having anything less than his love scared her witless.

"Now, now. There is no need to look so crestfallen," Hester said. "The trick is to steadily increase a man's ardor."

At the promise of a practical suggestion, Julianne lifted her hopeful gaze.

"Your first task is to practice a come-hither look. Now use those pretty blue eyes to your advantage."

Julianne took a deep breath, imagining Hawk kneeling on bended knee before her. She saw him in her mind's eye, begging her to make him the happiest of men.

"Dash it, gel. You look like a lovesick calf. Pretend you're trying to lure him into the boudoir."

"But I would never!" Oh, Hester's advice was very bad. She must not listen to another word.

Hester snorted. "Of course, you are not to act upon it. You must convey with your eyes that you find him desirable."

Julianne clutched her hands. Her mother would swoon if she knew Hester had advised her to act like a strumpet.

"You suffer from unrequited love. At all costs, you must avoid showing it," Hester said. "If he is secure in your affections, there is no challenge for him."

"If I pretend I do not care, he might conclude I am indifferent."

"You must not demonstrate tender feelings. There is nothing more fearful to a rake than the prospect of matrimony. Rakes value their freedom and their mistresses."

Julianne stared at her lap, trying to hide the pain lancing her heart. She'd heard the rumors about his mistresses, but she'd refused to believe he was as dissolute as others intimated.

"Your face is like a signpost, gel. My nephew is one and thirty. Did you think him a virgin?"

Misery engulfed her. Of course, she'd known there had been other women, but she'd tried to push it out of her mind. She could not bear the thought of him touching and kissing another.

"Now, now. Men are passionate creatures," Hester said. "They are made that way. You'll learn, gel. You need only entice him with the promise of your sensual charms."

Julianne looked at her. "But I don't even know if I have any sensual charms."

Hester chortled. "My dear, your charms are apparent to any man with eyes in his head. But you must endeavor to keep him interested beyond the visual feast."

"How am I to manage when I've no idea what to do?"

"Look at him with desire and tease him. But when he gives chase, you must keep him at arm's length. Doing so will stoke his fire, if you catch my meaning."

Julianne couldn't imagine Hawk chasing her or any other woman for that matter. In truth, women chased him.

"If you play your cards right, you can have him in the palm of your hand," Hester said, closing her fingers into a fist. "Why, Anne Boleyn kept Henry the Eighth on a lusty leash for years."

And got her head chopped off in the bargain.

"Well, gel, do you want him or not?" Hester asked.

She would not play horrid games with the man she loved. Hester's ideas sounded like lessons for a courtesan. Julianne lifted her chin in a defiant gesture, but she wasn't quite brave enough to voice her objections.

Hester gave her a knowing look. "You're determined to woo him your way. When you are ready, you'll remember my advice."

The next night, Hawk strolled about the cluttered Egyptian drawing room while he waited for his aunt and Julianne. Earlier in the day, Hester had sent him the requested list of Julianne's invitations for the week.

After much thought, he'd concluded Julianne did not need him to watch her every move. She was a good girl and would never do anything improper. He planned to escort Julianne and his aunt this one night, but in the future, he would make an appearance, ensure all was well, and make a hasty exit.

The drawing room door sighed open. Hester pressed it shut and marched over to him in a billow of purple skirts. Her tall ostrich feathers waved above a gaudy pearl-encrusted turban. "I must speak to you before Julianne arrives."

"Where is she?" Hawk asked.

"Changing her gown."

Lord help him. "Why?"

"Because she is a female." Hester gave him a measuring look. "Her brother says he won't rush her into marriage, but I've given the matter more thought. Everyone knows he is too protective. He still thinks of her as a young gel. I think he's trying to discourage her because he cannot admit she's a grown woman."

"Aunt, she'll wed when she's ready," Hawk said.

"Obviously you are unwilling to help," Hester said. "The task must fall to me."

"What?" Oh, Lord. His aunt fancied herself a matchmaker.

Hester tapped her chin. "I imagine she would prefer a young cub with an agreeable nature, but I fear she would find him disappointing. A gentleman with a bit of savoir faire would suit her best. The young ones don't know what is what. They tend to fire too soon, if you take my meaning."

The devil. "Aunt Hester—"

"Oh, hush, you know it's true. Of course, her intended should not be above nine and thirty. The older ones tend to wither."

He really could bear no more of his aunt's bawdy speech. "Perhaps you should check on Julianne's progress."

The door opened, letting in a draft. Relieved at Julianne's timely appearance, he said, "Ah, there she is now."

"Forgive me. I am terribly late," Julianne said.

A sheer fabric covered her girlish pink underskirt. She looked every inch the virtuous young lady. He crossed the room and bowed over her gloved hand. When he glanced up at her, she blushed.

He intended to discourage his aunt's matchmaking scheme. Julianne was a woman, but a very young one. She'd turned down multiple proposals, and he suspected she enjoyed being the belle of the ball. Hang society. She had every right to enjoy her youth as long as possible.

Julianne fingered a locket nestled just above her bodice, drawing his attention.

"A new bauble?" he asked.

"My father gave it to me long ago." She unclasped the locket.

He swallowed hard as she showed him the tiny miniature of her father, the father who had ignored her because she wasn't the long-hoped-for spare heir. The wastrel had occasionally bestowed kindness upon his wife, son, and daughter. Just often enough to make them hope he'd changed. It had never lasted long.

"I've only worn the locket once before," she said, her eyes downcast.

At that moment, he wanted to give her the most costly jewel to replace that crumb her father had doled out years ago.

"She is an incomparable beauty, is she not?" Hester

said, her voice booming behind them. "I predict all the gentlemen will fall at her feet."

Julianne closed the locket. Her eyes twinkled as she regarded him. "I shall try not to tread on their prostrate bodies on the way to the dance floor."

Hawk chuckled. She was the same merry Julianne he'd always known. "That's my girl."

My girl. His words echoed in Julianne's mind all during the carriage ride. She continued to savor them as they walked inside the Beresford's Palladian mansion and made their slow way upstairs. While they filed through the receiving line, Hawk smiled at her, making her heart melt. Afterward, Hester claimed weariness and ambled toward the chairs occupied by the matrons and wallflowers.

As Hawk led Julianne along the perimeter of the ballroom, dozens of people marked their progress. A sidelong glance assured her more than a few ladies were watching with curled lips. Let the jealous cats scowl. Tonight she was on the arm of the most handsome gentleman in the ballroom. And before this night ended, she hoped to make him yearn for her as much as she yearned for him.

She glanced at him. In profile, his dark brows and prominent cheekbones gave him a roguish appearance. She knew his face so well, and yet each time she looked at him, she found herself mesmerized.

As he returned her gaze, his full lips curved with the hint of amusement, and then he looked out at the crowd once more.

She'd attended more balls than she could count, but tonight, magic filled the air. Usually she paid scant attention to the décor, but now she noticed every detail. A row of rising shelves covered in crimson serge held dozens and dozens of crystal vases filled with hothouse flowers. Yards of scarlet draperies floated across the mantel and fell in a waterfall across the gold wall sconces. She vowed always to remember the romantic ambience.

Julianne tightened her fingers on his arm. The heat of his body seeped into her. She felt all warm and wobbly inside.

Please let him propose soon.

As they neared the dance floor, she caught her breath, hoping he would request her hand for the next set. An enormous gilt mirror reflected the couples twirling and parting in intricate patterns. Above them, candlelight twinkled starlike among the teardrop crystals in the enormous chandelier. She hoped he would stop to watch the dancers, but he led her over to an alcove displaying a large bust of Lord Beresford.

Hawk glanced at a lanky young man passing by. The skinny boy looked at her and almost tripped over his huge feet.

"There's a perfectly harmless cub," Hawk said. "Let me take you to him. I'll hint he should ask you to dance."

Her face heated. "I do not need your assistance."

"You do not wish to dance?" he asked in a teasing tone.

Clearly he had no intention of asking. Offended, she released his arm. "I'm off to find my friends."

She'd taken only a single step when he caught her arm and pulled her back to him.

"Not so fast," he said. "Tell me what I've done to vex you."

She refused to look at him. "Obviously you think no one but clumsy boys will dance with me."

He scoffed. "From the moment we entered the ball-room, I've seen dozens of gentlemen looking at you. Some of those men have bad reputations. Stay away from them."

He'd spoken in a gruff manner. Perhaps he was jealous of those other men. "I will," she said.

"What? No argument?" He released her and pretended to stagger.

His antics confused her. He'd sounded perfectly serious earlier. Then all of a sudden, he'd made a jest. Of course, he always made a joke of everything. She told herself it was his nature and part of his charm, but an uneasy sensation settled in her chest.

Someone called her name. Her friends Amy Hardwick and Lady Georgette Danforth were approaching. Georgette's eldest brother, Lord Ramsey, followed close behind. Julianne inhaled. She would ask her friends for their opinions as soon as she could speak to them in private.

When her friends reached her, she kissed the air by their cheeks. "Oh, it's been ages since last I saw you."

"I've missed you," Amy said. "Letters are a poor substitute for being together."

Georgette's blue eyes sparkled as she beckoned them both aside. "You have made a conquest of Hawk."

"Not exactly," Julianne said in an undertone. "He is to be my guardian for the entire season."

Her friends gasped.

"Oh, this is wonderful," Amy murmured.

Georgette leaned closer. "I saw the way Hawk looked at you. I predict he will dance attendance on you all evening."

"He'll propose this year. I'm sure of it," Amy said.

Georgette grinned. "How could he resist you?"

Julianne glanced over her shoulder at Hawk. Ramsey said something to him. Oddly, Hawk gave him a freezing look and focused his attention on three other gentlemen. Julianne shrugged off his strange reaction to Ramsey and turned back to her friends. "I need your advice."

After she described Hawk's confusing behavior, Georgette's dimples showed as she smiled. "I think he inadvertently revealed his tender feelings."

Julianne worried her hands. "But why did he pass it off as a jest?"

"He is unsure of your regard, and so he resorted to teasing you," Amy said.

Julianne realized Amy was right. "He's teased me for years. Perhaps all this time he's waited for a sign from me."

"You must show him you welcome him as a suitor," Amy said.

Georgette shook her head. "No, she must make him even more jealous by dancing with other gentlemen."

"I disagree," Amy said. "It would be cruel to wound him. He might conclude she does not care for him. All would be lost."

Georgette released a loud sigh. "Oh, why must matters of the heart be so complicated?"

"Because love makes one vulnerable," Amy said. "We all want to protect our hearts. I think it doubly hard for gentlemen because of their pride."

"It is a wonder anyone manages to wed," Georgette grumbled.

Julianne glanced at Hawk again. She started to turn away when Ramsey looked at her. His eyes gleamed as his gaze dipped lower. The horrid man was ogling her bosom.

She averted her gaze, only to realize she'd missed part of her friends' conversation.

"She should express interest in Hawk and ask him questions so she may get to know him better," Amy was saying.

Julianne frowned. "I've known him forever."

"I doubt he has told you his deepest secrets," Amy said.

Georgette scoffed. "What deep secrets? Hawk is a charmer and a rogue. Nothing troubles his mind. Do you not agree, Julie?"

"I've never seen him brood over anything. Even after his father's funeral, he tried to cheer up everyone else." She sighed. "He has a wonderful ability to make everyone laugh even during trying times."

Amy's green eyes widened. "Watch out. Lord Ramsey is coming this way," she said in a stage whisper.

Julianne winced. Oh, she could not bear to look at him after she'd caught him ogling her bosom.

Georgette groaned. "Papa made him escort me. I think he meant to punish Henry. Of course, Mama would not tell me why he was in trouble."

"He's almost here," Amy said

Upon reaching them, Ramsey bowed. "Lady Julianne, you are as dazzling as the sun."

"I hope you are not seeing spots," she muttered.

Georgette snorted.

Ramsey's rumbling laugh reverberated all along Julianne's spine and made her ill at ease. Then his gaze drifted lower as if he were mentally undressing her. Her ears grew hot.

"May I have the honor of the next dance?" Ramsey asked.

Just as Ramsey made the request, Hawk appeared at her side. "Julianne, I believe this is our dance," he said.

Our dance. She smiled at her friends and relinquished her fan to Georgette. As Hawk escorted her to the dance floor, she felt as if she were walking on air.

Hawk gritted his teeth as he led Julianne away. He'd wanted to smash his fist into Ramsey's face after catching the scoundrel eyeing Julianne's body.

He'd had no choice but to rescue her from the lecherous man. Ramsey was six and thirty, much too old for an innocent like Julianne. And Hawk knew too much about Ramsey's bad character to let him near her.

As they stepped onto the wooden floor, the orchestra struck up the opening bars of a waltz. Julianne's lips parted.

Hawk looked into her stunned blue eyes. "I suppose you're familiar with the steps."

She shook back her glossy curls. "I am."

He lifted his brows. "And your brother approves?"

"He would not object to you waltzing with me."

Hawk wasn't entirely sure of that, but it was too late to back out now. He took her gloved hand and clasped her slender waist. When she just stood there, he murmured, "Put your other hand on my shoulder."

She winced and complied.

"You've never waltzed," he said.

"My brother is overly protective. It is ridiculous."

The music started with a flourish. He kept the steps small for her sake and caught her watching her feet. "Look at me."

She lifted her lashes and regarded him with a mischievous smile. "You are being conservative because you fear I will disgrace you."

"Is that a dare?" Before she could answer, he whirled her round and round in dramatic circles.

A breathless laugh escaped her. "Oh, this is wonderful."

He'd waltzed with more women than he could recall. All of them had told him he danced divine. Not one of them had ever expressed such sincere exuberance. But this was Julianne's first waltz, and she would find it special, unlike the jaded women he ordinarily danced with.

Her flowery perfume drifted to him. He looked into her shining blue eyes and found himself hoping she would never succumb to the cynicism so common among the ton.

"A penny for your thoughts," she said.

He let out a dramatic sigh. "I'm crushed you think my thoughts are so worthless."

"Until you tell me, I cannot be certain," she said.

Her naturally husky voice never failed to captivate him. "I might shock you."

She gave him a saucy grin. "You may try."

He enjoyed teasing her. "You would have to pay me a king's ransom for my current thoughts."

"How much is a king's ransom?"

"A thousand pounds."

"Oh, it must be very shocking indeed."

"That is why I named such a high price." *Because I dare not admit I find you utterly enchanting tonight.*

Her eyes lit with mischief. "What if I call your bluff?"

"In that case, I had better quadruple the price." Then he whirled her round and round again. When he neatly evaded a near collision with another couple, she laughed.

He winked at her. She'd always been a bit saucy, and naturally her family claimed he was a bad influence. But her sweet excitement over her first waltz tugged at him.

The couples whirling past blurred. Her blue eyes softened, and he found himself mesmerized by her long lashes. Gradually, her smile faded, and her lips parted a little. He became all too aware of the soft curve of her waist beneath his hand, and something inside his chest shifted.

As the music wound down, he slowed his steps until the very last note. His blood hummed in his ears. Unable to let her go just yet, he held on to her. He was dimly aware of others walking past. His heart knocked against his chest as he gazed at her lush mouth.

The air between them heated and crackled like the calm before a summer storm. A forbidden thought struck him like lightning.

I want you.

An unnatural silence descended over the ballroom, alerting him. He glanced beyond Julianne to the mirror. In shock, he realized all the other couples had exited the dance floor. The back of his neck prickled as he turned his head. A huge crowd had gathered around. Everyone was staring at Julie-girl and him.

Wild applause broke out.

Chapter Three

A Scoundrel's Code of Conduct: To avoid the parson's mousetrap, lie through your teeth.

In a daze, Hawk led Julianne off the dance floor. His heart still thumped hard. What the devil had happened?

He'd lost his head over Julie-girl.

The crowd pressed closer. Everyone spoke at once and at considerable volume as they squeezed past.

"Did you see the way he looked at her?"

"Dear God, I thought he would kiss her."

"I almost melted into a puddle watching them."

"Oh, my," Julianne said, her voice breathless.

"Keep walking," he muttered. Bloody, bloody hell. Half the damn ton had witnessed him clutching Julianne and gazing into her eyes like one of her many besotted beaux. Damn, damn, damn.

In all her innocence, she'd managed to bewitch him.

He'd fallen under a spell. That was the only explanation for his idiocy. No, it was worse. Far worse. Desire had flooded his veins—for his best friend's sister. For God's sake, he was her guardian. She was forbidden.

He glanced at her sideways. Her dreamy expression made him feel like a cad. Obviously, she was still caught up in the magical experience of her first waltz and probably didn't realize the significance of what had happened.

If the damned scandal sheets hinted at an engagement, they would both find themselves in hot suds. How the devil would he ever explain it to Tristan?

Stupid, bloody fool.

He had to do something to turn the tide. When he spotted his aunt sitting by the wall, he knew he must leave Julianne with her. Then he'd make himself scarce in the card room and laugh off any gibes from the other gents.

Heads turned as he led her through the crowd. He gritted his teeth and did his best to ignore the stares.

He'd not gotten far when Amy Hardwick and Lady Georgette waylaid them. Their excited expressions spelled trouble.

"Everyone is talking about your waltz," Georgette gushed.

"My heart nearly stopped when everyone applauded," Amy said.

He considered leaving Julianne with her friends, but Ramsey cut a swath through the crowd.

"Ah, there you are, Lady Julianne," Ramsey said. "I've come to claim the dance Hawk stole from me."

Hawk stared daggers at him. "She does not wish to dance."

Beside him, Julianne stiffened. Her friends watched with wide-eyed expressions. He didn't care.

Ramsey frowned. "And who are you to answer for the lady?"

"Her guardian."

Ramsey laughed. "Famous. The hawk is guarding the henhouse."

Hawk gave him a freezing look. "You accuse me of having improper designs on the lady?"

Ramsey smirked.

Hawk narrowed his eyes. "Lest you or anyone else harbor the wrong idea, I will set the record straight. Lady Julianne is practically a sister to me."

All around them, heads turned. Several gentlemen chuckled and regarded him with amusement.

Ramsey lifted his sandy brows. "Yet you object to her dancing with other gentlemen."

"I object to *you*." He'd heard another disgusting rumor recently that Ramsey and six of his dissipated friends had sneaked a prostitute into one of the private rooms at the club and taken turns with her. There was no way Hawk would let the vile fiend dance with Julianne.

Ramsey bowed. "Lady Julianne, I must withdraw my request. Your *guardian* objects."

After Ramsey left, Hawk blew out his breath. As the tension slowly drained from his body, he realized Julianne's fingers were trembling on his sleeve. With alarm, he saw her face had turned pale. "Julianne, are you unwell?"

Her lips parted, but she said nothing.

"I had better find you a chair. Can you walk?" Hawk asked.

Amy Hardwick took her arm. "We will escort her to the retiring room, my lord."

He thought Julianne looked ready to faint. "She is ill. I'll fetch my aunt and take Julianne home."

"No." Georgette glared at him. "We will take care of her. She is like a sister to us."

Amy shook her head at Georgette. Then she addressed him. "My lord, we will send for your aunt if Julie does not recover quickly."

As they retreated, Hawk frowned. Damn Ramsey for vexing Julianne. Obviously *he* had offended Georgette by refusing to allow her rakehell brother to dance with Julianne. *Too bloody bad.*

Lady Julianne is practically a sister to me.

In a cold daze, Julianne thrust the horrible thoughts from her mind and stumbled as she entered the lady's retiring room. She could hardly recall walking there.

Amy steadied her. "Have a care."

"There are no chairs available," Georgette said. "She must rest."

Julianne stared about the room, so numb she could barely feel her limbs. Three maids bustled around the women, repairing dangling curls and torn flounces. High-pitched giggling sounded from the window seat. None of it seemed real to her.

One of the maids finished tidying an elderly lady's coiffure and turned her attention to Julianne. The maid's eyes widened.

Georgette beckoned her. "Is there somewhere private we may sit?"

"Yes, my lady. Follow me."

The maid found a candle and led the way. She opened a door to a bedchamber next to the retiring room. Julianne leaned on Amy's arm as they followed the maid. While the maid lit a candle branch with the taper, Julianne sank onto a settee. She clutched her gloved hands in an effort to stop them from shaking.

Amy sat beside her. "All will be well," she whispered.

No, it would not.

The maid dipped a curtsy and addressed Georgette. "Shall I get her something? Poor gel looks sickly."

"Wine," Georgette said. "For all of us."

The maid nodded and left the room quietly.

After the door shut, Amy huffed. "Wine for all of us?"

"I need something to soothe my nerves, too." Georgette sat on Julianne's other side. "Dearest, tell us what we can do to help?"

Julianne covered her face. Despite her gloves, her fingers felt icy. The numbness started slipping away. Hawk's words echoed in her ears again. *Lady Julianne is practically a sister to me.* Oh, God, he did not love her.

"It's natural to cry," Amy said.

"I cannot." Julianne's throat felt thick. "I don't want him to see my splotchy face. Then he will know."

Georgette chafed her arm. "How could he be such a brute?"

"Not now," Amy hissed.

"Well, I am angry on her behalf," Georgette said. "He treated her abominably."

The threatening tears welled in Julianne's eyes. She tried to hold them at bay, but it was no use. Her entire body shook as she wept.

Her friends remained silent until she'd spent her tears.

When Julianne shuddered, Amy gave her a handkerchief. "Lean on me," she whispered.

Julianne rested against Amy's thin shoulder and swiped at her damp cheeks.

"Georgette, there is a pitcher and bowl on the washstand," Amy said. "Will you wet a cloth and bring it?"

"Of course."

Julianne closed her eyes, but his words kept creeping into her thoughts. He didn't even know he'd crushed her. She ought to be grateful, but pride wasn't much of a salve for her wounded heart.

Water splashed into the china bowl. "I shall never understand men," Georgette said. A clinking sounded, likely the pitcher. "He was so attentive on the dance floor, and then suddenly he insisted Julianne was a sister to him."

Julianne started gulping air. She jerked upright. Panic clawed at her chest with every short breath.

"Slowly," Amy said. "Take one breath at a time. I am right here beside you."

Don't think. Breathe. Don't think. Breathe.

Georgette's skirts swished as she approached. "Amy, I'm frightened. She is gasping for air."

"Julie, focus on one breath. Just one," Amy said.

Julianne yanked at the gold chain holding the locket. She had to get it off. Now.

"Hold still," Amy said. "Georgette help me."

Georgette knelt and took Julianne's hands. "Be still so Amy can unclasp the necklace."

As Amy fumbled at her neck, Julianne bent her head. When the locket fell onto her lap, Georgette scooped it up. "Amy, put it in your reticule for safekeeping."

She never should have worn it. Never should have shown him.

"Lean back," Georgette said. When Julianne complied, Georgette dabbed the cool, damp cloth over her face and laid it across Julianne's eyes. "This will help reduce any puffiness."

"I wish it would take away her pain," Amy murmured.

Julianne only wished for numbness.

None of them said anything. Julianne appreciated their silence. For now, it was enough to have them beside her. She would not be able to bear being alone.

After an interminable amount of time, she became aware of an aching in her neck. She removed the cloth and lifted her head.

Georgette took it to the washstand. When she returned, she let out a long sigh. "Better now?"

A hysterical laugh escaped her. "Oh, yes. All my dreams are dashed, but I'm perfectly content."

Her friends exchanged worried looks.

"He was only trying to put my brother off the scent," Georgette said. "Hawk would not admit his feelings before telling you."

Julianne huffed. "Are you deaf? He did tell me his feelings." Then, realizing her harshness, she winced. "Forgive me, please."

"You are wounded," Amy said. "We understand."

"I refuse to believe he isn't halfway to falling in love with you," Georgette said. "When he danced with you, he could not tear his eyes away."

"Georgette, it is no use." Julianne shuddered. "He teased me tonight, the same way he's teased me since I was a little girl."

"Where is your spirit?" Georgette laid her hand on Julianne's shoulder. "You cannot give up so easily."

"Easily? I've waited four years for him. Nothing I do will change his feelings." She hung her head. "I gambled on him. And I lost." She'd convinced herself she could make him love her. The same way she'd tried so hard to win her father's love.

What was wrong with her?

The maid returned bearing a tray with a decanter of wine and three glasses. Amy rummaged in her reticule. Coins clinked in her hand as she followed the maid over to the table, speaking softly. After the maid handed round the glasses, she left the room.

"Her name is Meg," Amy said. "I gave her a shilling."

"Oh, I didn't think of it," Georgette said. "You are always so thoughtful, Amy."

The three of them sat silently, drinking wine. After the first few sips, Julianne felt a tiny bit better. Each time thoughts of Hawk entered her head, she drank some more. After several minutes, she tipped the glass to her lips and frowned. It was empty.

"More?" Georgette asked.

"I'll get it." Her legs trembled a little, but the wine numbed her. She refilled her glass and returned to the settee. "I suppose I shall live." Despite her brave words, sorrow flooded her heart.

Georgette sniffed. "You will make him sorry."

"Georgette," Amy admonished.

Julianne contemplated her glass. "He is a swine."

"Amen," Georgette said.

"Let us talk of something else," Amy said.

Georgette gulped her wine. "All men are swine."

"They all take mistresses," Julianne said, remembering what Hester had said about Hawk. "Even some of the married ones." Like her late father.

Georgette sighed. "Sometimes I think mistresses have all the fun."

Amy made an exasperated sound. "They are poor women who have no choice but to sell their bodies. It must be very frightening to be so dependent."

"But we are dependent," Julianne said. "Men control our lives. They have all the power. We wait and wait for them. All the while, they dally with bad women and put off marriage. We pin all our hopes on them, and then, *poof*, they dance away because they do not want to give up their raking."

"You are right," Amy said. "But do we not give them the power?"

"This conversation is depressing my spirits." Georgette rose. "I need another glass of wine. Amy, I'll pour more for you as well."

"But I'm not done with this one."

"I'll top it up." Georgette snatched Amy's glass, spilling a bit on her skirt. A red stain spread, seeping into the cloth. "Oops."

"You had better dab that damp cloth on the stain," Amy said.

"But then my skirts will be wet." She giggled. "Oh, they are already wet."

They all burst out laughing.

Georgette walked to the decanter and refilled the glasses.

"We should take care not to become inebriated," Amy said.

"Oh, why not?" Georgette gulped her wine. "All the gentlemen are sure to be three sheets to the wind by now."

"But we are ladies," Amy said.

Georgette snorted. "We are foxed ladies."

"Not foxed enough." Julianne sipped her wine. "How shall I hurt him?"

Georgette returned with both glasses and handed one to Amy. "We could put a curse on him."

Amy set her glass aside. "Silly. We don't know any curses."

"I do." Julianne smirked. "Damn."

"Bloody hell," Georgette said, lowering her voice in a bad imitation of a man.

"The devil." Amy snickered.

The three of them planned various, ridiculous tortures for Hawk that included the rack and chains. A few minutes later, Georgette poured the dregs of the decanter into her glass. "Julie, I am still convinced he is in love *wish* you," she said.

"No, he isn't." A hiccough escaped her.

Amy regarded her with a frown. "Julianne, everyone in the ballroom remarked upon the way he looked at you on the dance floor. He continued to hold you even after the music stopped. I think his actions speak louder than his words."

Julianne stilled. He'd teased her, and then he'd gazed at her longingly. "Amy, you're right." She hiccoughed again. "He made me believe he cared. But when he realized everyone was talking about our waltz, he got cold feet. How dare he—*hic*—toy with me?"

Georgette smirked. "We will find a way to make him pay."

"We are not the only ladies who suffer because of those rogues who evade marriage," Amy said. "There must be some way for all the ladies to take the power into their hands."

"How?" Georgette said.

Julianne grabbed Amy's arm. "You are brilliant."

Amy blinked. "But I have no solution."

Julianne grinned. "I do. Thanks to Hester. She told me how to entice a rake, and—*hic*—I foolishly ignored her."

"But do we want to entice rakes?" Amy asked. "Should we not concentrate on the nice gentlemen?"

"What *nish* gentlemen?" Georgette grumbled. Then she polished off her wine.

Amy frowned. "The younger ones are agreeable."

Julianne covered another hiccough.

Georgette scoffed. "The cubs can barely utter a word without *twipping* over their tongues."

"You are both missing the—*hic*—point," Julianne said, revenge on her mind. "We can entice the gentlemen by making them think we desire them. And then we will drop them like hot coals."

"We won't remember this tomorrow," Amy said. "Julianne, you have a terrible case of the hiccoughs. You had better stop drinking."

She hiccoughed again and nearly spilled her wine while setting the glass on the floor. "I remember every word Hester said and will write it down for the two of you."

"If we are to succeed, we need all the single ladies to join us," Georgette said. "Then the gentlemen will *notish*."

Julianne frowned. Georgette was slurring her words.

"We will have to sw-swear all our sisters to silence," Georgette said. "I wager all the other girls are as *disguised* with the gentlemen as we are."

"You mean *disgusted*," Julianne said, noting the glassy look in Georgette's eyes.

"But will we not drive the gentlemen into the arms of those hussies who troll the theaters? Or worse, those married women with no scruples?" Amy asked.

Julianne gave her friends a smug look. "We will be— *hic*—like Anne Boleyn."

"What?" her friends cried out in unison.

"She kept Henry the Eighth on a frustrated leash for years. If she could do it, so can we."

Her friends burst out laughing.

The door opened.

"Meg, you're *jush* in time," Georgette said. "Will you bring more wine?"

"It appears you've had quite enough." Hester strode past Meg.

Julianne hiccoughed and clapped her hand over her mouth.

Hester glanced at the empty decanter and turned to Meg. "Everyone is filing downstairs for the midnight supper. Do not let the girls leave. I shall return directly."

Hawk slouched in his chair at the card table. He assumed Julianne was well enough. Amy Hardwick was a responsible girl and would have alerted his aunt if Julianne had taken a turn for the worse. He wondered about Julianne's sudden illness. Was it his confrontation with Ramsey or had the overheated ballroom made her ill? Hawk had never thought Julianne one of those delicate female creatures, but the devil knew his sisters complained incessantly of mysterious ailments.

Despite his preoccupation, he'd automatically memorized the cards previously played. He visualized the remaining ones, an easy task given that he need only recall by a single suit, in this case hearts. Across the table, Ramsey frowned at his hand, hesitating. The reprobate had joined the game at the last minute. Over the years, Ramsey had taken every opportunity to needle him. Hawk had ignored him for years. Tonight, Ramsey had forced a confrontation.

Hawk covered a yawn, growing bored with the tedious delays. Ramsey made a stupid play. With a smug grin, Hawk threw down his queen, winning the trick and the rubber, in this case, the best three out of five games.

His partner, a young cub with a blade of a nose, crowed. "You're a wizard," Eastham said. "It's almost as if you could see through the discards."

Hawk said nothing. Long ago, he'd learned to calculate the odds at cards.

"The devil." Ramsey's partner, Durleigh, gathered the cards and shuffled.

Eastham leaned across the table, his intent gaze on Hawk. "Do you have a talisman?"

"No." Most gamblers were superstitious and kept all sorts of lucky charms on their person while playing. Far too many lost fortunes and called it capricious luck. He'd amassed a considerable fortune simply by leaving the table when he was ahead. When he'd attempted to use his winnings to pay for a mistake he'd made long ago, his father had refused to take the money. The memory still burned, but he shoved the useless thought aside.

At the approach of a footman, Hawk frowned.

"Lord Hawkfield, your aunt requests you attend her in the ballroom," the servant said. "She asked for Lord Ramsey as well. The matter is urgent."

Hawk's heart drummed in his chest as he shoved his chair back. Julianne could be dangerously ill, and he'd wasted precious time. He strode from the card room, fearing the worst. Ramsey followed close behind.

Hester waited near the door. Hawk noted the other guests were leaving the ballroom, probably for the midnight supper.

"Where is Julianne?" Hawk asked his aunt.

"With her friends in a bedchamber adjoining the lady's retiring room."

Hawk envisioned Julie-girl shivering on the bed. "My God, how bad off is she?"

"All three girls are in a shocking state," Hester said.

Ramsey stiffened. "I'll find Beresford and have him send for a doctor immediately."

Hester shook her head. "That would be unwise." She looked about her as if checking to be sure no one listened. Then she leaned toward them. "They drank an entire decanter of wine."

Silence reigned from the retiring room next door.

"Everyone has gone downstairs for the midnight supper by now," Amy whispered.

"Oh my God, I cannot let my brother see me foshed," Georgette said.

"You mean *foxed*." Julianne hiccoughed again. "I will have to convince Hawk to say nothing to Tristan. Otherwise, my brother will make me return home." The very thought made her stomach roil.

"I have a plan," Georgette said. "We will disappear until their tempers cool."

Amy made an exasperated sound. "Hiding will only postpone the inevitable and make everyone angrier with us."

"Hah! You're not the one who must face the f-firing squad." Georgette lurched to the door and opened it. "Meg, come inslide."

"She means *inside*." Julianne hiccoughed.

After the maid entered, Georgette spoke. "We need to go to the water cl-closet."

Meg looked uncertain. "You had better wait for the lady to return."

"I cannot wait," Georgette said. "Tell Lady Rut-Rutledge to meet us downstairs if we mish her."

"My lady, you'd better stay put," Meg said. "The wine has gone to your head, it has."

"No." Georgette motioned to Julianne and Amy. "Come."

Julianne hesitated. "Georgette, we'd better not."

"I'm going," Georgette said. She walked unsteadily out into the corridor.

Amy rose. "Julianne, we must stop her."

They hurried to the door. "Georgette, come back here," Julianne hissed as her friend weaved the wrong way down the corridor.

Meg followed them to the door. "My lady, come back. The stairs are the other way."

Georgette giggled and continued on.

"I'll fetch her," Meg said.

"Meg, I fear she'll not listen to you," Amy said.

Julianne took Meg's candle. "We'll return quickly, I

promise." She cupped her hand around the candle flame, but it went out as they hurried along.

Georgette's white gown was like a beacon. At the end of the corridor, she stopped and stared at a door.

When they reached her, she swayed on her feet. "There was a noise."

"Come, let us return," Amy said, tugging on Georgette's arm to no avail.

Something started thumping rhythmically against the door. Julianne hiccoughed and stared in horror, fearing whoever was in there would fling it open.

A man grunted again and again.

Georgette frowned. "Is he ill?"

The door thumped harder. A woman started making repetitive high-pitched noises, sounding like a squealing pig.

Julianne frowned. "What are they—*hic*—doing?"

"We must leave," Amy whispered.

The thumping turned into banging, and the man's grunting grew louder. "Feel my mighty sword."

"He has a sword?" Georgette asked.

The woman behind the door screamed.

Georgette gasped, "He killed her."

"I'm coming," the man said.

"Not inside me," the woman said in a curt voice. "I don't want a brat."

Julianne dropped the candle and clapped her hand over her mouth. She'd thought a bed was required. As she stared at the door, she tried to work out how the amorous couple had managed, but she failed.

"We must go," Amy hissed. "Now!"

The three of them lifted their skirts. Shrieking with

laughter, they hurried down the corridor. Julianne sprinted ahead and looked over her shoulder.

"Look out!" Amy cried.

Julianne plowed into something big and male. She gasped as two large hands caught her by the shoulders.

"You are in deep trouble," Hawk growled.

Chapter Four

*A Lady's Secrets of Seduction: Forget your
mother's well-meaning advice and take matrimonial
matters into your own capable hands.*

When the carriage jerked into motion, Hawk slapped his
hat onto the leather seat beside him. He'd never forget the
sight of Julianne and her friends scurrying down the corridor, laughing like wild brats. Damn her. She'd tricked him.

Aunt Hester patted Julianne's hand. "Are you feeling
bilious, dear?"

He couldn't hear Julianne's reply over the clacking of
hooves on the cobbled street. "Do let me know if you feel
sick," he said, raising his voice. "I'd prefer you didn't cast
up your accounts in the carriage."

"Marc," Hester cried.

He'd managed to shock his aunt for the first time in his
life. "Should I have the driver pull over?"

"I am not sick," Julianne said in a seething voice.

He huffed. "You'll have the devil of the head tomorrow morning," he said, projecting his voice to ensure she heard him.

"Marc, leave her be," Hester said.

He would do no such thing. "Julianne, what do you have to say for yourself?"

"You cured my hiccoughs."

"You seem to think the matter amusing," he said in a terse tone. "But I assure you it is not. Did you consider your reputation?"

"Now, now," Hester said. "I'm sure Julianne did not mean to overindulge."

"My apologies. I did not realize her friends poured the wine down her throat," he drawled.

"I refuse to answer such a ridiculous accusation," Julianne said in a bitter voice.

"That's just as well," he said. "I've no intention of discussing the matter until you're in a more sensible state."

She whipped her face to the window.

He could hardly believe her capable of such deceit. But clearly she'd planned to hoodwink him, and she'd succeeded with her ruse. No doubt she believed him a soft touch. If she thought he would turn a blind eye to her rebellion, she would learn differently tomorrow.

The carriage rattled to a halt. Hawk descended and helped his aunt negotiate the steps. As Hester started toward the house, Hawk held his hand out for Julianne. She refused him and wobbled. Damnation! He grabbed her by the waist to prevent a fall and swung her down. When she tried to pull away, he tightened his fingers. "Stop resisting me."

She averted her face. "Let me go."

When the front door opened, Hester turned to look back at them.

"My aunt and the butler are watching. Take my arm," he said.

Julianne took a step away. In one long stride, he caught her arm and marched her to the door. Just before they reached it, he leaned down and growled near her ear, "You'd better be prepared to grovel when I call tomorrow, my girl."

"I'm not your girl." An odd gurgle escaped her. Then she fled inside the house.

An hour later, Julianne dried her face and walked to the bed. Nausea had struck, and she'd gotten horribly sick.

Betty, the maid, had turned down the covers. After Julianne climbed into bed and pulled the covers to her chin, Betty frowned. "Miss, won't you let me call Lady Rutledge? She ought to know you're feeling poorly."

Julianne cleared her sore throat. "Please do not disturb her. A night's rest will see me well."

The sheets smelled sunshine fresh, so at odds with the gloomy shadows in the room. Out of habit, she rolled onto her side and hugged the extra pillow to her chest— the same way she'd done every night since her first dance with Hawk at her come-out ball four years ago. And every night afterward, she'd imagined holding Hawk on their wedding night. Raw grief flooded her heart, and tears stung her eyes. She pitched the pillow aside. There would never be a wedding night for them.

She rolled onto her stomach and sobbed into her pillow. How could she have been so stupid? So blind? She'd worn her heart on her sleeve. Even Hester had noticed.

Damn him. A dozen gentlemen had proposed to her, but she'd turned them down because she'd wanted to wait for Hawk.

She hated him. Hated the man she'd thought of every single day for four years. The man she'd fantasized about night after night. She'd tumbled head over heels for him and made him the focus of her whole life. And tonight he'd cut her heart to pieces.

The door creaked open. "Oh, child," Hester cried out.

When the mattress sank beneath Hester's weight, Julianne peeked out from the pillow. The flame from Hester's candle wavered on the bedside table.

Hester rubbed her back. "Tell me what is wrong?"

Pride kept her silent.

Hester rummaged in the drawer of the bedside table and produced a handkerchief. "Betty came to me because she is worried about you."

Julianne rolled over and blew her nose. "I asked her not to disturb you."

"Now, that is foolish. You must tell me when you are troubled," Hester said.

Julianne swallowed. "I'm sorry about the wine."

"I know." She paused and added, "When you did not return to the ballroom, I suspected my nephew had done something to overset you."

Julianne picked at the covers. He had publicly rejected her. Pain sliced her heart again.

"Will you not tell me what happened?" Hester said.

She swallowed. "I do not want him to know."

"Of course not," Hester said. "Perhaps if you confide in me, I might be able to help."

Her burning eyes welled with tears again. Hester found

a fresh handkerchief in the drawer. Julianne dabbed at her eyes and haltingly told the story.

Hester sighed. "I saw the way he looked at you during that waltz. It is not hopeless, dear."

"I have kept hope alive for four years," Julianne said. "Every time he teased me, I convinced myself he was developing tender feelings. Nothing ever came of it. He does not love me, and he never will."

"He gave plenty of evidence that he desires you tonight. As I told you, that is the first step for a man."

He'd made it clear he didn't want her. The thought sent a fresh jolt of pain to her heart.

"Tomorrow, matters will not look so bleak." Hester stood and drew the covers up to Julianne's chin as if she were a child. "You are wounded, but you are more resilient than you believe. I promise all will work out."

She knew all was lost. "Thank you."

"I always wanted a daughter," Hester said. "So you must allow me to pamper and spoil you."

Though Hester spoke in a light tone, Julianne heard the regret behind the words. "I apologize for all the trouble I caused," she said.

Hester rose. "You are exhausted and need to rest. Good night, dear."

After Hester left, Julianne stared up at the canopy, replaying every single event of the evening. When Hawk had gazed into her eyes, she'd thought he was at last showing his love for her.

He'd humiliated her in front of everyone.

She drew in a shuddering breath and swore to make him pay. Oh, yes, she would play the tease as Hester had suggested. Like Anne Boleyn, she would lead him merry dance and hold him at arm's length. She'd make him mad to possess her, and when the moment was right, she would laugh and claim he was practically a brother to her.

The next afternoon, Julianne crumpled the page marred by ink blots and rubbed her swollen eyes. For the past hour, she'd struggled in her pitiful attempt to record Hester's advice. She'd concluded Amy was right. The other belles suffered the same plight when it came to reluctant bachelors. But her head still ached from the wine, making it difficult to think.

The soft ticking of the bedside clock drew her attention. Earlier, she'd sent missives to Georgette and Amy requesting they call upon her. Julianne feared their parents had refused to allow them to leave their homes after last night's debacle. She recalled the way Ramsey had barely contained his fury upon seeing his sister weaving down the stairs. No doubt Georgette had gotten ill, too. Even the slightest case of nerves made her heave.

Betty brought her a cup of tea. "It's dosed with willow bark and will ease your headache."

"Thank you." After the maid left, Julianne capped the inkwell and sipped her tea. She would try to write later when she felt better.

The knocker banged downstairs, startling her. Her heart thudding, she wondered if Hawk had arrived. She hurried over to the dressing table to check her reflection in the mirror. Despite the frequent application of a cold, damp cloth, her eyes were still puffy. Drat it all. She didn't want him to know she'd cried.

A tap sounded at her door. When she answered it, a

footman informed her Georgette and Amy had come to call. She exhaled in relief. "Show them up to my bed-chamber," she said.

A few minutes later, her friends entered. "I'm surprised your parents allowed you to call upon me," Julianne said.

Georgette, who looked remarkably well, straightened her neckline. "My brother made empty threats, but in the end, he told our parents I had suffered from motion sickness in the carriage. I'm sure he lied because he knew Papa would blame him." She snickered. "They had no reason to doubt his explanation, given my history. Of course, my maid smelled the wine on my breath, but I gave Lizzy one of my straw bonnets from last year."

Amy's lips parted. "Georgette, you bribed your maid."

"What of it? Lizzy will enjoy the bonnet." Georgette's wide smile showed her dimples. "Amy, it isn't as if you told your parents."

Amy winced. "I should have done so, but I feared they would prevent me from seeing both of you today." Then she opened her reticule and drew out Julianne's locket. "I brought it for you."

Julianne flinched. Why had she even kept the necklace? She ought to have destroyed it long ago. "Throw it on the fire."

A slight frown marred Amy's red-gold brows. "I beg you to reconsider. You will surely regret it."

Georgette snatched the locket from Amy, walked to the bedside table, and deposited it in the drawer. "Julianne, you can decide the fate of the locket later. We have more pressing matters to discuss."

Julianne nodded, relieved to put thoughts of her father aside. She bade her friends to join her on the bed.

They kicked off their slippers, hiked up their skirts, and climbed onto the mattress.

"Have you written the advice yet?" Georgette asked.

"I tried, but my headache prevented me. The maid brought me a cup of willow bark tea, so I feel a bit better."

"It's just as well," Amy said. "The wine-inspired scheme is harebrained."

"Last night, you agreed," Georgette said. "It will be such a lark."

"The plan is too risky," Amy said. "If we share the advice with the other single ladies, they will spread the news."

Georgette twirled a blond curl around her finger. "Is that not the idea?"

Amy scoffed. "Georgette, you know very well the other ladies will spread the word, and our reputations will be ruined. Our families would suffer as well. And Julianne cannot risk angering Hawk. He might send her home."

"He's planning to call today." Julianne scowled, remembering his words. "He told me I'd better be prepared to grovel."

Amy tucked a red-gold curl behind her ear. "He is worried about you, Julianne. We are very lucky to have escaped worse consequences."

Georgette rolled her eyes. "Ignore her, Julianne. Write the advice just for us. What fun. We'll steal all the rakes away from the other girls. They will be green with envy."

"Now you are being ridiculous," Amy said.

Georgette lifted her palms. "How else are we to help Julianne win Hawk?"

"I don't want him," Julianne said.

"Yes, you do," Georgette said.

Amy considered Julianne for a long moment. "I know you're wounded, but you love him. Aren't you willing to give him another chance?"

Julianne held her fist to her heart. "If I were to let him inside again, I would be giving him permission to treat me cavalierly, the same way he treated me last night. I am done with him." She'd seen the way her father had begged her mother's forgiveness, only to mistreat her repeatedly. Julianne vowed she would never let Hawk hurt her again.

Georgette peered at Julianne. "You can make him jealous by flirting with other rakes."

"Frankly, I do not understand the appeal of rakes," Amy said.

The minute she uttered the words, a knock sounded, and the door whooshed open. Hester ambled inside, her eyes alight. "Did I hear mention of rakes?"

Julianne cleared her throat. "Amy was reminding us to stay away from them."

Hester smiled knowingly as Amy tugged her skirts over her exposed calves. Then Hester walked over to the desk and smoothed out the crumpled paper.

Julianne hissed in a breath, drawing Hester's attention.

"It seems you wrote down part of my advice. Were you planning to share it with your friends?" Hester asked.

Julianne hesitated. "Perhaps I should have asked your permission first."

Georgette nodded. "We thought about sharing it with the other young ladies, but they might reveal Julianne wrote it, and the gossip would ruin her."

Julianne gave her cork-brained friend a speaking look. "You and Amy would be implicated as well." She, on the other hand, had nothing to lose.

Georgette's eyes widened. "Oh, I didn't think about that."

Amy mumbled under her breath.

"I believe you should share the advice with all the young ladies," Hester said.

"The risk is too great," Amy said.

Hester regarded Amy. "Ah, I heard you were a sensible girl. I concede Miss Hardwick's point about gossip, but I have an idea."

Julianne eased off the bed and walked to the desk. "What sort of plan do you have in mind?"

Hester pulled out the chair. "Be seated," she said, drawing out a fresh sheet of paper. "Now, the way to keep our little secret is to publish the advice anonymously. I have a gentleman friend who will ask no questions. He will make all the arrangements. That way no one will trace the identity of the author."

"It will be a book?" Julianne's heart beat faster. "I am to be an author?"

"I'm envisioning a pamphlet, as we can have it produced quicker," Hester said. "Of course, all of us must keep the secret. As Miss Hardwick said, you do not wish to stain your reputations."

"Amy, even you cannot find fault with that plan," Georgette said.

Amy worried her hands. "I have grave misgivings."

Hester lifted her quizzing glass to inspect Amy. "Your concern is understandable, but in this case, there is no danger to any of you. If matters grow hot, I will take responsibility. One of the advantages of old age is that society excuses one's eccentricities."

Amy frowned. "It still seems terribly risky to me."

"The only thing required of you and Lady Georgette is

secrecy," Hester said. "You must never reveal it to another soul."

"We will keep mum," Georgette said. "Oh, this will be such fun."

Hester uncapped the inkwell, dipped the pen, and handed it to Julianne. "Now the work begins."

"I do not know where to start," Julianne said. "It seems an overwhelming task."

"You need a title, do you not?" Hester said. "It must convey the contents in such a way that others will rush to purchase it."

Julianne furrowed her brows. "*Advice to the Lovelorn*?"

"We need something more provocative," Hester said, waving her hand in dismissal. "Ah, I have it: *The Secrets of Seduction*."

Georgette gasped. "Seduction?"

"Only the suggestion of it, my dear," Hester said. "Teasing and implied promises of secret pleasures make any man wild. I've some experience in the matter."

Since Hester had managed to attract five husbands, Julianne concluded she was an expert. "The title is perfect," she said, scribbling it on the page and ignoring Amy's moan. Underneath, she wrote *By a Lady*. She blew on the wet ink, set the page aside, and considered the blank page Hester handed her. "Now what?"

"An introduction is necessary," Hester said. "You must explain what drove you to conclude that unmarried ladies need a better method of leading gentlemen to the altar."

"Write it as if you're addressing a friend," Georgette said.

"An excellent suggestion," Hester said. "Julianne, let the words flow upon the page."

Julianne dipped the pen again. Excitement filled her as she wrote. When she finished, she read it aloud at Hester's urging.

Dear Desperate Readers,

I am prevailed upon by friends to publish my advice designed to fell even the most resistant of bachelors. My friends and I have observed that far too many single gentlemen put off marriage in favor of unsavory pursuits. Meanwhile, our fair sex waits, often in vain. Ladies, it is time we took matrimonial matters into our own capable hands.

Naturally, as a lady, I must remain anonymous to protect my reputation. Before I delve into the particulars, I entrust my readers to keep THE SECRETS OF SEDUCTION from falling into the hands of our gentlemen admirers. After all, a single lady must use every weapon available in her feminine arsenal.

"A wonderful introduction." Hester drew in her breath as if she meant to say more, but a knock on the door forestalled her. "Come in," she said.

A footman announced that Lord Hawkfield waited in the Egyptian drawing room. Julianne's stomach tightened involuntarily.

When the door shut, Georgette stood and shook out her skirts. "We must leave you now."

"You mean to abandon me?" Julianne said, her voice rising with shock.

"I agree with Georgette," Amy said. "You must face him today, and we will only be in the way."

"You needn't worry. Lady Rutledge will be with you," Georgette said.

After her friends left, Julianne swallowed hard. She dreaded seeing Hawk today. In one night, her relationship with him had been altered forever. She needed more time to adjust to the sudden change, more time to mourn the dream she'd clung to for so many years. More time to heal.

Hester gave her a sympathetic look. "Use your wiles to distract him. I'm sure all will work out as you wish."

She didn't even know what she wished for anymore, but remembering his words last night, she pressed her nails into her palms. Under no circumstances would she grovel. She lifted her chin. "Please inform him that I am not receiving."

"That's the spirit," Hester said. "I shall return directly to report his reaction."

Afterward, Julianne returned to the desk, determined to put him from her mind, but that was easier said than done. Memories of their waltz last evening kept invading her brain.

Stop. She would not let thoughts of *him* distract her from writing the pamphlet. Why should she waste her time on a man who had kept her dangling for years?

The word *dangling* spurred an idea. All too often, gentlemen pretended interest, only to dash a poor lady's hopes with nary a thought to the damage they'd done. The idea of letting those arrogant rogues continue to rule over the ladies infuriated her. She dipped her pen and started scribbling as fast as she could.

A gentleman of sense and education wants nothing more than to marry a gently bred young lady with a pleasing countenance, soft voice, and deferential manners.

Poppycock.

At the risk of shocking my readers, I am compelled to reveal the truth. If you wish to secure a marriage proposal from the gentleman of your dreams, you must forget all of your mother's well-intended advice.

I imagine many of you are gasping at such a scandalous idea, but I submit that we are looking at the matter from only a feminine point of view. In order to understand what a man wants, we must first examine his attitude toward marriage.

Do not misunderstand me. Bachelors know they are expected to wed in order to carry out their duty to their families. However, you will note that most are in no great hurry to renounce their bachelorhood. In fact, they are, by and large, determined to remain single as long as possible. Why?

They do not wish to give up their drinking, gaming, and wenching.

Do not despair. In the following chapters, I will reveal the secrets of becoming irresistible to even the most determined of bachelors.

A knock sounded at the door. When Julianne answered, a footman informed her that Lord Hawkfield requested her immediate presence in the Egyptian drawing room.

She sniffed. "Tell him I am occupied."

After the servant departed, she padded back to the desk with a smug smile. Let him stew.

She read over her words and made several corrections when another knock sounded. In exasperation, she strode over to the door to find the beleaguered footman holding out a silver tray with a note. Julianne retrieved the folded paper and read the message.

My Dear Impertinent Ward,
    Either you present yourself in the drawing room in ten minutes or you will forfeit the rest of the season.
                                     Impatiently yours,
                                          Hawk

"A moment please," she said to the footman. Then she returned to the desk and wrote her reply on Hawk's note.

My Dear Dictatorial Guardian,
    You have obviously forgotten the proprieties. It is a lady's prerogative to refuse a caller. I will receive you another day, provided you present yourself in a gentlemanly manner.
                                       Never yours,
                                       Julianne

After instructing the footman to deliver her missive, she returned to the desk, but the latest edition of *La Belle Assemblée* tempted her. She perused the fashion plates, finding one especially lovely walking gown trimmed with pink ribbons.

The door flew open, startling her. Hester hurried inside, her eyes bright. "My nephew is in a *state*. I must say your reply was quite inventive, but now you must come."

Julianne set the magazine aside and frowned. "I will not bow to his demands."

"You mustn't push him too far. He threatened to return you home if you do not cooperate."

Hawk probably wanted to be rid of her so he could spend all of his time carousing and raking. She wouldn't give him the satisfaction. "Oh, very well."

She followed Hester downstairs. Despite her earlier bravado, Julianne's anxiety grew with each step she took. When they neared the drawing room, she turned a pleading look on Hester. "I do not wish to see him today. It's too soon."

"My nephew will bluster, but you've nothing to fear."

She wasn't afraid of Hawk. She was afraid of herself, because deep inside, a little corner of her heart still ached. But she vowed never to let him see he'd wounded her. Taking a deep breath, she walked with Hester into the drawing room.

Hawk turned away from his contemplation of the faux mummy and clasped his hands behind his back. Naturally the dogs leaped up, barking and wagging their tails. Hawk ordered them to sit and strode across the plush carpet. He wore a hunter-green riding coat and buff trousers that hugged his muscular legs like gloves.

Why was she admiring him when he'd humiliated her last evening? She lifted her chin and gave him a freezing look.

"Ah, now I perceive the reason for your reluctance to greet me," he said.

She regarded him with suspicion. "I beg your pardon?"

"You are looking a bit peaked, no doubt the result of your indulgence last evening. I daresay you're ready to renounce wine forever."

She averted her gaze because she didn't want him to see that his jest hurt.

He chuckled. "You're awfully touchy today."

Hester let out a disgusted sigh and ambled over to the sofa. "Marc, you brute. Do not tease her."

Julianne drew in her breath, determined to pretend she didn't care. "I'm impervious to him." She didn't spare him a glance as she marched over to the sofa directly across from his aunt and perched upon it. For good measure, she covered a yawn.

"You did not sleep well last night?" he asked.

She would never admit it. "On the contrary, I slept like the mummy."

"Julianne, you know why I'm here," he said. "I'll hear your explanation and your apology now."

"Marc, she apologized to me last night," Hester said. "Let us forget this matter."

"An apology won't satisfy him," Julianne said. "He expects me to grovel."

"I expect you to tell me why you tricked me last night," he said.

She huffed. "You act as if I have done you an injury."

"You barely escaped ruining your reputation last night," he said.

"I find it exceedingly hypocritical of you to criticize me when your reputation is firmly entrenched in the mud."

"If you think to divert me, you are sadly mistaken," he said. "Your brother named me your guardian, and I intend to protect you, whether you like it or not."

"He must have been out of his wits."

"I believe that described *you* last evening," he said.

"Now, now," Hester said. "She was only a tad tipsy."

"She was three sheets to the wind," he muttered.

"If you had not acted like an ill-mannered ogre last night, none of this would have happened," Julianne said. He'd all but made a public declaration when he'd gazed into her eyes after their waltz. Then he'd denied any tender feelings for her. He was a heartless cad.

"You blame *me* for your indiscretion?" he said, his voice rising.

The dogs growled.

"You are agitating Caro and Byron," Julianne said.

The dogs growled louder.

"Hush," Hester cried.

The dogs started yapping. Hawk ordered them to cease. They kept barking, making Julianne's temples throb.

"I will see to them." Hester pushed to her feet. Despite her cajoling, the canines refused to obey. Then she grabbed two biscuits off the tea tray, walked to the door, and called out, "Treat, treat."

The spaniels raced out of the drawing room.

After Hester followed the dogs out and shut the door, Hawk took three long strides until he stood at Julianne's feet. "Now you will explain, and don't lie. I'll know."

His words last night pierced her heart anew. *Lady Julianne is practically a sister to me.* He knew that he'd misled her and everyone else at that ball.

"Answer me," he said.

She rose from the sofa, refusing to let him loom over her—not that it did much good since he was a head taller. "You presume I planned to escape the ballroom for mischievous purposes."

"It is fact, not presumption," he said.

"I left the ballroom because you made a scene when Ramsey asked me to dance." Her hand had shaken uncontrollably. If her friends had not intervened, she might have shed tears and disgraced herself.

"I thought you would have the grace to take responsibility for your poor judgment," he said.

"You embarrassed me in front of my friends." *In front of the entire ton.* Misery engulfed her. Everyone had heard his words. Others standing nearby had smirked. And he was so blind he didn't even realize what he'd done to her.

He scoffed. "Ah, I see. You were so disappointed that you ran off to drown your sorrows."

She ought to be relieved he'd not guessed the real reason she'd left the ballroom, but his callousness made the pain far worse. "I needed something to soothe my nerves."

"That, my dear, is one of the sorriest excuses I've ever heard."

She glared at him, tempted to ask him what his excuse was for misleading her and everyone else at the ball. But if she voiced the words, he would know she'd tumbled head over heels for him. She would never give him that satisfaction. "You made a spectacle of yourself. Ramsey is my friend's brother, and you insulted him. You had no right to refuse on my behalf." In truth, she would have claimed weariness to avoid dancing with Ramsey, but she'd no intention of admitting *that* to Hawk.

"I had every right," he said in a low, dangerous tone. "You will stay away from him."

She didn't give two straws about Ramsey, but she would not let Hawk give her orders. "I will not treat my friend's brother as if he were a pariah. If I wish to dance with him, I will."

Hawk's eyes blazed. "If you think to add Ramsey to your long list of conquests, you had better think twice. He is not one of those besotted cubs who hang on your every word. You are out of your depths with him."

"I am not a green girl fresh out of the schoolroom," she said. "And your concerns about Ramsey are ridiculous. He would never do anything to risk his reputation or that of his family."

"I know the man. He's risked scandal repeatedly. His exploits reached his father recently. The marquess is pressuring him to marry in hopes of reforming him—a wasted effort, I might add."

"Now I understand. You object to Ramsey's marital aspirations because the loss of one bachelor could spur a matrimonial landslide. All your dissolute friends would abandon you for their wives. Such a lonely prospect must be terrifying to a rake like you."

"Enough of this nonsense," he said. "Ramsey is the worst sort of devil. He views you as a prize. The unattainable Lady Julianne would puff up his overblown consequence. Trust me. He's unscrupulous enough to put you in a compromising position, and then you would have no choice but to marry him."

"Oh, I'm shaking in my slippers," she said, not bothering to hide her sarcasm.

"Seduction is no laughing matter."

"Goodness, I had no idea," she said.

His jaw clenched. "No, you clearly do not or you would not make light of the matter."

He obviously thought she didn't have a brain in her head. "Even if Ramsey were to attempt to lure me into an indiscretion, which I seriously doubt he would, I am not foolish enough to fall for such a trap."

His voice rose. "You wouldn't even realize what was happening until it was too late. Either you agree to stay away from him or I'll arrange to send you home."

How dare he threaten her? "I will not allow you to run roughshod over me all season."

"Pack your trunks," he gritted out.

Her throat constricted. He meant to send her home in disgrace. Everyone in the ton would gossip about her. It would hurt her family. Something hot welled up inside her. "I'll pack my trunks, and then I will go to Georgette's home. Her mother will welcome me, and I will be free of your tyranny."

"If you think I will let you stay in the same house as Ramsey, you are mistaken."

She scoffed and turned away. "You cannot stop me."

His hands shot out. She gasped as he imprisoned her upper arms.

"You are too innocent to understand," he bit out.

"You think me naïve, but I know how to thwart a man."

"I can prove you wrong," he said, his voice rumbling. His eyes darkened as he snared her with his intense gaze. She felt as if he were pulling her ever closer, mesmerizing her as if she were the prey and he the predator.

When he wrapped his arms around her, she caught her breath. His chest and thighs were pressed against her, making her all too aware of his hard, muscular body. She tried to resist the exhilarating sensations coursing through her veins, but her knees and her resolve weakened.

All the while, he never broke eye contact with her. His breathing grew harsher, faster, and her own breath hitched in her throat. She told herself to look away, to break this sensual spell he'd cast over her, but the subtle scent of starch and something else, something male and forbidden, filled her head.

He lowered his face until his mouth was so close his

breath whispered over her lips. "Do you think your bravado would stop Ramsey?"

His words sliced through the haze in her brain. "You don't scare—"

He claimed her lips.

In her many daydreams, she'd imagined he would kiss her tenderly. She'd not expected the urgency, the sheer hunger of his kiss. Nothing could have prepared her for the way he devoured her lips. She knew she should stop him, but as he continued to kiss her, her wits scattered.

When his tongue traced her mouth, her lips parted involuntarily. He plunged inside, setting a rhythm of advance and retreat. She grasped his lapels, holding on for dear life as her knees trembled. None of her fantasies could compare to the reality of his intimate kiss.

He swept his hand down her spine and cupped her bottom, setting her skin on fire. She reached for his shoulders, needing more support as he pressed her closer. Her blood heated to a fever pitch.

He cupped her breast and, through the fabric of her bodice, circled his thumb around her nipple. An unexpected spurt of pleasure shot through her. As his tongue filled her mouth again and again, she felt something harden against her belly. For a moment, confusion gripped her. Then, in shock, she realized he was aroused.

A small voice told her to stop him, but he drew her tongue into his mouth, and the voice grew silent. She was lost, uncaring about anything except the mindless need coursing through her.

He tore his mouth away, leaving her bereft. A haze swirled through her head as she gazed at him. His eyes were darker, glazed with an expression she'd never seen before.

Chapter Five

A Scoundrel's Code of Conduct: Never let the beast take control.

A dense fog enveloped his brain. His cock strained against the confines of his tight trousers. He was burning up as he pressed her closer. Seconds before he kissed her again, he met her gaze. The innocent blue eyes staring back at him washed over him like a giant ocean wave.

He stepped back, breathing like a racehorse. Bloody hell! He'd kissed and touched Julianne.

Her eyes held a look of wonder as she touched her kiss-swollen lips. She'd probably never been kissed before. His chest burned with shame. He'd lost all control with his best friend's sister. Damn his sorry soul to hell.

Hawk turned his back and clenched his fists, trying desperately to will his erection into submission. For God's sake, he was her guardian. Tristan had trusted him to protect her. And he'd failed miserably.

The memory of his father's denouncement more than a dozen years ago echoed in his head. *You're an immoral blackguard.*

He'd proven his father right repeatedly, but he'd never touched an innocent before. Only the worst sort of scoundrel would take advantage of a young, unmarried lady.

He walked over to the sideboard and splashed brandy into a glass. When he downed the liquor, it burned his throat and made his eyes water. The lust coursing through his veins gradually receded, leaving a dull ache in his groin.

What the hell had possessed him?

He recalled his rising anger at her refusal to take his warnings seriously. Then he'd snapped, meaning to teach her a lesson. All he'd done was show himself to be no better than Ramsey.

He set the glass aside. If anyone had burst in on them, he would have had no choice but to offer marriage. He couldn't even let himself think of Tristan's reaction.

Right now, he had to put aside thoughts of what might have happened and deal with the aftermath. All he could offer her was an apology, but hollow words could never make up for what he'd done to her.

He turned to face her, and the blush staining her cheeks made him wince. "I beg your forgiveness. That should not have happened."

A suspicious sheen filled her eyes, and she averted her face as if she didn't want him to see. "I . . . I let you."

He despised himself. Her first kiss should have been gentle and sweet, but he'd never meant to kiss her. And he'd certainly not counted on the desire that had consumed him the moment their lips had met. "You are not to blame."

She glanced at him with a miserable expression and looked away again.

He walked over to her, wanting to offer comfort, but he stopped short of touching her again. "I am the one at fault."

After uttering the words, he recalled walking in on Tristan and Tessa in the library at Ashdown House a year ago. At the time, he'd thought his friend's guilt overblown. Now he understood exactly how Tristan had felt.

Julianne drew in a shuddering breath. "You won't say anything to my brother about our indiscretion, will you?"

The uncertainty in her voice seared his conscience. "No good would come of a confession." The consequences would ruin his friendship with Tristan and alienate their families.

Julianne blew out her breath as if relieved.

He ought to bow out as her guardian, but then he'd have to explain his reasons to Tristan. What would he say? *Your sister got foxed, and I punished her with a lascivious kiss*?

He'd made a bad mistake, but that didn't change his responsibility as her guardian. If anything, he must tighten the reins to ensure she stayed out of trouble. "We have yet to settle the matter of last night's fiasco."

She clasped her hands and faced him. "We both had lapses in judgment, but we will forget them."

He considered her guileless expression for a long moment and didn't trust her. "To prevent future problems, I will set forth my expectations."

She frowned. "What?"

"As your guardian, it is my duty to make the rules clear in advance. Now, rule number one: You may not accept any invitations until I approve of them."

She muttered something under her breath, but he refused to let her deter him. "Rule number two: No more than one glass of wine or sherry."

"Am I allowed to count the number of brandies *you* imbibe?" she said, her voice rising.

He would not let her divert him. "Rule number three: No flirting."

"Do you plan to sew my lips shut?"

He ignored her sarcasm. "Rule number four: I must approve all your dance partners in advance."

"Do you plan to make them audition?" she said in a sugary-sweet voice.

Her saucy retort irritated him. "It was wrong of me to kiss you, but that leads me to rule number five: If any other man tries, you are to slap him and then inform me so I can kill him."

She rolled her eyes. "I'm not a child, and I do not appreciate you giving me rules."

"I'm not done," he said. "Rule number six: You will have nothing to do with Ramsey."

"How am I to avoid him when he is Georgette's brother?"

"I will keep him away," he said.

She made an exasperated sound. "Next thing I know, you'll tether me in leading strings."

"As long as you follow the rules, there will be no trouble. Now, tonight, I will escort you and my aunt to Lady Morley's literary salon." The last thing he wanted was to waste an evening listening to fops read syrupy verse, but he had no choice. After last night's debacle, he dared not trust Julianne again.

"My mother drummed the proprieties into my head long ago," she said.

Evidently, they had flown out of her head last night. "If you wish to stay in London for the remainder of the season, you had better adhere to the rules," he said. "There will be no more chances for you, my girl."

"I'm not your girl."

No, and she never would be.

Hawk took up a stance near the sideboard in Lady Morley's crowded drawing room and sipped a brandy as he watched the guests milling about. Naturally, half a dozen young bucks surrounded Julianne. He tried telling himself they were young, in awe of her beauty, and therefore harmless. But they were *males*. The second they clapped eyes on a lovely woman, their primitive instincts took over, and their brains conjured up a picture—a naked picture.

Fire sizzled his blood at the thought. Clenching his fists, he moved to rescue Julianne from their lascivious ogling. But Lord Morley, a rotund fellow with florid cheeks, lurched past him. Hawk stepped sideways, sloshing his brandy and barely avoiding a collision. He set the glass aside and took out his handkerchief to dab at his damp sleeve.

Julianne sashayed over to him, her slim brows elevated. "You reek like a brew house. How many brandies have you had?"

He put the handkerchief away. "I am not foxed."

She scoffed. "More evidence of your hypocrisy."

"You violated rule number three."

"Refresh my memory," she said.

"No flirting," he growled.

She huffed. "I spoke to those gentlemen for a brief time. They are very nice."

"Right-oh." Out of the corner of his eye, he spied Ramsey, Georgette, and Amy headed toward them. He knew Ramsey intended to use his sister as a means of engaging Julianne in conversation. Determined to thwart the fiend, Hawk took Julianne's arm and all but dragged her away.

"Let me go," she said.

His hand clamped tightly on her fingers. "No."

She looked over her shoulder. "You did that on purpose."

Well, that was obvious. "I'm taking you to my aunt."

"What next? Do you plan to lock me up?"

"Don't tempt me."

As Hawk passed the cubs who had flirted with her earlier, he gave them a menacing don't-even-glance-at-my-ward look. He smiled evilly at their arrested expressions, certain now they would keep their distance.

A sense of satisfaction swelled his chest. He had complete control of the situation now. Granted, he'd probably go bloody mad with boredom while escorting Julianne and his aunt about town. But he would not renege on his promise to Tristan.

When they reached his aunt, a slim, elderly gentleman with thinning hair approached her with a cup of tea.

"How very thoughtful of you, Mr. Peckham," Hester said. "And here is my nephew and Lady Julianne."

While Hester made the introductions, Hawk wondered where she had met Peckham. Then again, his aunt collected strays wherever she went.

Lady Morley clapped her hands and asked everyone to find seats so that the literary event could commence. Hawk sat next to Julianne, wondering how long the poetry readings would last. His aunt had mentioned a midnight repast. He retrieved his watch, and with an inward groan, he noted it was only a quarter past nine. What a dull way to spend the evening.

Julianne leaned closer to him, filling his head with her light floral scent. The devil. This guardian business was addling his brain.

"If you are so eager to depart, be gone," she whispered. "Your aunt and I can take a hackney home."

He put his watch away. "You wound me. I thought you longed for my company."

She huffed.

Lady Morley smiled. "Now let us begin. Lord Ramsey has graciously agreed to read one of Shakespeare's sonnets."

Hawk snorted.

Julianne elbowed him. "Stop acting like a wayward schoolboy," she said sotto voce.

He grinned. "Must I?"

"Hush."

Ramsey strode to the fireplace, opened a small leather-bound book, and looked directly at Julianne. "Shall I compare thee to a summer's day?"

"How original," Hawk muttered.

Julianne swatted his hand with her fan.

"Ouch," he yelped, shaking his stinging hand and interrupting Ramsey's droning voice.

"Hawk, you rogue," Lady Morley said, affection in her voice. "Will you behave?"

He winked. "I shall try to mend my naughty ways."

When laughter erupted, Ramsey narrowed his eyes. "I will start from the beginning so that we may experience the verse as it was meant to be heard."

No doubt the bard was rolling in his grave at the prospect.

Ramsey cleared his throat. "Shall I compare thee to a summer's day? Thou art more lovely and—"

Lord Morley, who was passed out on the sofa, broke wind. His lady kicked him in the shin. He jerked up, looking round wild-eyed. "What? What?"

Hawk's shoulders shook, knowing the next verse would trip up Ramsey.

Ramsey's jaw worked, but he stubbornly continued reading. "Rough winds do shake..." His face heated as he paused.

Julianne clapped her hand over her mouth.

Hawk bit back laughter and slid down in his chair. This evening was turning out to be far more entertaining than he'd expected.

Ramsey managed to stumble through the rest of the sonnet. When he finished, Lady Morley hurried to the hearth. "Lord Ramsey, thank you for that stirring rendition."

Ramsey stalked off to the sideboard, poured himself a brandy, and tossed it back.

As two more gentlemen read from Thomas Wyatt and John Donne, respectively, Hawk fought back a yawn more than once. Then one of the cubs approached Lady Morley. With a bright smile, she informed everyone that Mr. Charles Osgood wished to read his own verse.

The lanky cub blushed as he withdrew a folded paper from his coat. He affected a lovesick expression, one he must have thought suitably poetic. "It is called 'The Lady of Moonlit Tresses.'"

Hawk cupped his hand round Julianne's ear. "Things are bound to liven up now," he whispered.

"You are incorrigible," she murmured. "He's a very nice young man."

Osgood took a deep breath and said, "The moon upon her raven tresses doth shine. Of her beauty, the stars declare divine."

Hawk reached over and tweaked the curl by Julianne's ear. She glared at him.

Osgood paused to place his hand over his chest. "Alack, my heart is filled with woe."

"Is this the part where he mops his tears with a hanky?" Hawk whispered.

"Shhh," Julianne said. "He will hear you."

Osgood lowered the paper and looked at the ceiling as if beseeching a higher power. "Oh, lunar goddess, all my dreams upon thee I do bestow."

A smattering of applause followed. Osgood's friends were smirking and elbowing one another. No doubt they meant to rib the bad poet mercilessly.

After four more dull readings, Lady Morley once more walked to the hearth. Hawk hoped it was time for refreshments.

Lady Morley smiled sweetly. "Lord Hawkfield, perhaps you would care to read a verse or two."

He grinned. "Very well. I shall recite my favorite. There once was a lady with a penchant for whist, who drank so much ale that she pi—"

"That will be quite enough, you scamp," Lady Morley said.

An hour later in the noisy dining room, Julianne huddled with Amy and Georgette in a corner, apart from the other guests. Hawk sat at the table, wolfing down sandwiches.

Satisfied that he was preoccupied, Julianne turned to her friends and told them about the rules he'd given her.

Georgette pulled a face. "That devil."

Amy sighed. "He *is* taking matters too far. I'm sure he'll relent once he realizes you are abiding by the proprieties."

Julianne thought better of telling her friends she'd already broken every rule of conduct when she'd fallen into his arms. She'd given in to his every kiss and touch as if she were a…a courtesan. The memory heated her face. She unfurled her fan and wafted it to cool her cheeks. "I need your help with the next chapter of the pamphlet. How is a lady to become irresistible to gentlemen?"

"Lady Rutledge mentioned implied promises of, er, seduction," Georgette said under her breath.

Amy shook her head. "Julianne, you must not include such indecent advice."

Julianne ignored Amy's warning. "I suppose the lady could give the gentleman a suggestive look. What do you think?"

Amy's lips parted. "I think your scruples have gone on holiday."

Clearly, Amy would object to every idea, so Julianne directed her questions to Georgette. "What else can a lady do to entice a man?"

"Flirt," Georgette said.

Julianne waved her hand. "Yes, but I need an idea that is unique. The lady must stand out among a crowd of women. What can she do to become an original?"

"Beauty trumps everything," Amy said with a touch of sarcasm in her voice.

Julianne regarded Amy with excitement. "You just

solved the riddle for me. Beauty may be the initial attraction, but beauty alone will not sustain a gentleman's interest, particularly one who balks at marriage."

"That would be all gentlemen," Georgette grumbled.

Julianne continued. "It is said that Anne Boleyn was no great beauty, and yet she charmed every man at court."

"Anne Boleyn is no one to emulate. She was a horrid, conniving woman who committed adultery with the king," Amy said.

"She got the worst of the bargain." Georgette demonstrated by slicing her hand across her throat.

"All the same, she knew how to play gentlemen to make them want her," Julianne said. "I need to include specific examples."

Amy's eyes widened. "Have a care. Lord Ramsey is approaching."

Julianne glanced at the table, fearing Hawk would intervene, but he'd wandered off to speak to a group of gentlemen. She mentally chided herself. What did she care what he thought? She would speak with whomever she chose.

When Ramsey reached them, he bowed. "Lady Julianne, at long last, I have an opportunity to speak to you."

Georgette rolled her eyes. "Henry, can you not see we are engaged in a private conversation?"

He ignored his sister and kept his bright gaze on Julianne. "Am I to be privy to your confidences?"

She blurted out the first thing that popped into her head. "Are you interested in ladies' fashions?"

"I'm interested in ladies, or should I say one lady in particular," he said, his voice rumbling.

Good Lord. Hawk had been right about Ramsey's intentions.

Julianne darted a glance at Hawk. He'd yet to notice Ramsey, but he would soon. He'd been watching her all evening and likely would try to rescue her from Ramsey's supposedly wicked clutches. But she'd no intention of letting him take her away from her friends.

Lady Boswood, Georgette's mother, joined them and took her daughter's arm. "Georgette, you are wanted. Miss Hardwick, there is something I wish to discuss with you as well."

"But, Mama—" Georgette said.

"Do as you're told," Lady Boswood said in a grating tone.

Julianne watched them depart. Lady Boswood's obvious machinations spelled trouble—matchmaking trouble. But Julianne had evaded more than a few unwelcome would-be suitors and meant to do so now. "It has been a pleasure, my lord. Now, if you will excuse me, I must speak to Lady Rutledge."

"Don't go just yet." He smiled at her. "I've waited all evening to spend a few moments with you."

Oh, dear. She didn't want to encourage him. Many gentlemen had pursued her over the past four years, even though she'd always teased any who grew too ardent. She'd hoped to spare their feelings, but some gentlemen were oblivious.

"You are even more beautiful than I recollected," Ramsey said, his voice rumbling in a manner she suspected he'd practiced.

She arched her brows. "Do you often have trouble with your memory, my lord?"

He frowned. "I beg your pardon?"

"You saw me two evenings ago."

He laughed a bit too heartily. "I meant more beautiful than the previous year."

To the best of her knowledge, he'd not taken more than fleeting notice of her then.

"I am very glad you were able to come to London for the season," he said. "When Georgette told me you might stay behind for the duchess's confinement, I could not hide my disappointment."

She'd only exchanged a few polite words with him last year when she had called on Georgette. Yet he'd claimed to be anxious for *her* presence in London. She'd dealt with more than a few smooth talkers and recognized insincerity when she heard it. "You flatter me too much, my lord."

He regarded her through heavily lidded eyes, a rake's trick. "That is impossible, my lady."

She decided to make a graceful exit. "Excuse me, please."

He looked disappointed. "Have I offended you?"

She must tread carefully because he was Georgette's brother. "No, but I wish to—"

Ramsey's lip curled as he looked past her. "Here comes the fool."

Frowning, she glanced over her shoulder to find Hawk striding toward them. Then Ramsey's insult registered. She returned her outraged gaze to him, ready to give him a blistering set-down, but he spoke before she could utter a word.

"Do not worry. I'll not let him come between us," Ramsey said.

"Lord Ramsey, you presume too much."

Hawk commandeered her arm. "Julianne, come with me."

"Well, well, it's the court jester," Ramsey said.

Julianne's jaw dropped. He'd purposely goaded Hawk.

"Jealous?" Hawk said.

Ramsey scoffed. "Of a clown?"

Unnerved, Julianne glanced around the crowded dining room. Thus far, no one had taken notice of the two men staring daggers at each other. But she meant to stave off the confrontation before it went further.

"Gentlemen, may I remind you that we are Lady Morley's guests?" she said. "I insist that you cease bickering and observe the proprieties."

Ramsey bowed. "I beg your pardon, Lady Julianne. I did not mean to distress you."

But he'd meant to provoke Hawk. The animosity between the two men fairly crackled in the air. Of course, there would be no dispute if Hawk had allowed her to manage her own affairs.

"Give up, Ramsey," Hawk said. "As long as I've got breath in my body, you haven't a snowball's chance in hell with her."

Julianne said nothing as the carriage rolled along, but Hawk could hear her harsh breathing. She was furious with him. He didn't care what she thought. Under no circumstances would he allow her to associate with Ramsey.

His aunt remained uncharacteristically silent. Earlier, when they'd departed, Hester had raised her brows upon seeing Julianne's splotched complexion.

The carriage rocked to a halt. Hawk opened the door and descended. After helping the ladies negotiate the steps, he turned to Julianne. "I will call on you tomorrow."

"We will have a discussion tonight," she said. "Hester, will you grant us privacy in the drawing room?"

"Certainly, my dear," she said.

The devil. Julianne was in high dungeon, but he didn't give a rat's arse.

He followed the ladies into the house and up the stairs. When they reached the landing, his aunt regarded him through her quizzing glass. "Keep it civil, Marc."

"I'm not the one stomping about," he said.

Julianne glowered at him.

Hawk regarded his aunt. "Shouldn't you join us for the sake of propriety?"

"I'm weary, and I doubt you wish my maid to witness." After that pronouncement, his aunt ambled up the staircase.

Julianne marched off toward the Egyptian drawing room. Hawk strode ahead. When he opened the door, she whipped past him.

He'd barely shut the door when she whirled around. "You go too far," she said.

He indicated the sofa. "Shall we be seated?"

"No." She strode back and forth in front of the faux mummy, reminding him of her brother, who had a tendency to pace when he was agitated.

"I find it rather difficult to have a civil discussion with a moving target," he drawled.

She halted, her skirts swirling around her ankles. "I am thoroughly put out with you."

"Really?" he said. "What precisely is it I've done to warrant your anger?"

"You know very well. I thought you would engage in fisticuffs with Ramsey—in Lady Morley's dining room!"

When he'd seen Ramsey talking to Julianne, his temper

had nearly exploded. The memory of the debaucheries Ramsey had arranged at a party long ago had flooded Hawk's brain. He'd wanted to plant his fist in the lout's face for daring to go near Julianne. "I will *not* allow Ramsey to pursue you," he said.

She pointed at herself. "It is my decision, not yours."

"Rule number six: You will stay away from Ramsey. I'll see it done, whether you like it or not." That recent disgusting incident at the club had only reinforced his belief that Ramsey hadn't changed a bit.

"Hang your rules," she said.

"You welcome his addresses?" he said, his voice rising.

"Whether I do or not does not signify."

He strode right up to her. "It most certainly does."

"You think because you are my guardian that you have the right to control me."

"I have the right to protect you," he said. *Especially from Ramsey.*

"I don't need your protection, and I most certainly do not appreciate you hovering over me like a…a jealous husband."

He was *not* jealous. "I did not hover over you."

"Oh, yes, you did. This is my fourth season. How do you think I turned away unwanted advances before you came along?"

"Your brother," he said.

"He never shadowed my every move. Never."

"You tricked me at that ball. What did you expect?"

A mirthless laugh escaped her. "You treat me as if I am a child. Open your eyes, my lord," she said, spreading her arms. "I am a grown woman."

Her invitation proved too enticing to ignore. His gaze

traveled slowly down her body. When he reversed his inspection, he lingered at her full breasts before meeting her eyes. "I noticed."

She blushed. "You are impertinent."

"You told me to look." Clearly, she had no inkling how susceptible males were to suggestion, particularly where beautiful females were concerned. Of course, he'd never admit *that* to her. "Be wary of setting a fire you may not be able to douse," he muttered.

She narrowed her eyes. Then she grasped his lapels. "Oh, sir, I am so frightened. Please, I am a virtuous girl. I beg you do not ravish—"

"Hush. The damned servants will hear you."

She let go of his coat. "Mind your language."

He huffed. "Now you complain."

"Admit it. You wish you'd never agreed to be my guardian," she grumbled.

They had reached an impasse. Somehow he had to make her understand. "Let us be seated so that we may talk in a rational manner."

She joined him on the sofa, sitting as far away as possible. "I gave you reason to distrust me at the ball, but we cannot go on like this."

"Trust is earned," he said. "I warned you to stay away from Ramsey, and you broke my trust again tonight."

"He cornered me, and I didn't want to cause a scene."

Hawk speared her with a stern look. "How am I to know you're telling the truth?"

She put her fist to her heart. "I *am* being truthful with you. Despite what you think, I've plenty of experience discouraging unwanted advances. If you had allowed me to manage Ramsey, I could have dissuaded him easily."

"I'm your guardian. It's my duty to see to your welfare."

"By confronting him, you only made him more determined."

"You don't understand. He's a master manipulator." *And far worse.*

She studied his face. "Why do you hate Ramsey so much?"

"I've good reason, and that is all you need to know."

"What has he done that is so terrible?"

He couldn't tell her about Ramsey's revolting history. "You'll have to take my word for it."

She angled her body toward him. "Do you think I am too delicate to hear the facts?"

"I won't sully your ears." He'd been shocked at the debauchery he'd witnessed all those years ago at that country house party. One night, he'd walked into the billiards room, only to find Ramsey swiving a woman on the billiards table in front of a crowd of men cheering him on. He'd rolled his eyes and walked away.

Julianne watched him with furrowed brows. "He is my friend's brother. If I were to snub him, it would be a slap in Georgette's face."

"Stay away from him," he gritted out.

"Do you think he would pounce on me?" she asked incredulously.

His jaw worked with frustration. "He means to lull you. He'll gradually draw you into his web if you're not careful."

"You still think I'm a naïve schoolgirl."

He looked into her beautiful blue eyes. "You are young and inexperienced."

"Do you think I've learned nothing in society?"

He measured his words. "You have lived a sheltered existence. Your brother has protected you, with good reason. There are men and women who are far worldlier than you who would take advantage of your innocence." He'd learned that lesson the hard way.

"Give me credit for having enough sense to avoid schemers," she said.

She didn't understand how vulnerable her lack of experience made her. Long ago, he'd paid a high price for his naïveté. He'd have to live with the consequences in silence for the rest of his life.

"Hawk, is something troubling you?"

"I am trouble," he quipped.

"You can tell me," she said.

He couldn't tell her, literally could not reveal those events to anyone. "My confession would take weeks, months, perhaps years."

"I don't doubt it," she said, smiling.

Even if he wished to bare his soul, he could not. Because there was someone else involved, someone he could never speak about.

She searched his eyes. He looked away, uncomfortable with her scrutiny.

"You worry something bad will happen to me," she said.

"I promised your brother I would protect you from rakes."

She arched her brows. "Does that include you?"

Her words pierced a bleak place inside him. He looked away, but his heart seemed to fall to his stomach as he recalled that awful day his father had confronted him.

Time rolled backward, and once again, his world shattered all around him. His chest burned anew with remembered fear and shame at his father's disgusted denouncement. He could have withstood the remorse if not for the fear that he'd condemned an innocent to a life of misery.

"Hawk?" Julianne asked tentatively.

He drew in his breath, realizing he'd let the mask fall. Out of habit, he planted a grin on his face and wagged his brows. "Beware the big bad wolf lurking in the drawing room."

She held her hands up. "Oh, I'm so afraid."

You should be. "I'd best be off."

She rose with him. He winked and swept her a ridiculous courtly bow.

Her husky laughter reverberated all along his spine. He maintained his grin until he strode out of the drawing room. Only then did he let the clown mask fall away.

Chapter Six

*A Lady's Secrets of Seduction: To become irresistible,
you must be seemingly unattainable.*

"I definitely approve of your first chapter," Hester said the next morning as she perused Julianne's work in the Egyptian drawing room. "Your analysis of male behavior is quite insightful."

Julianne smiled. "I had a bit of help from you."

"Now we must plan your next chapter," Hester said.

"It occurred to me that the first step is to exude confidence."

Hester nodded. "I agree. A lady who is sure of her charms attracts the notice of gentlemen. And if she pretends not to notice them watching her, they will grow more interested. Men are attracted to what they cannot have. They love the chase."

All these years, she'd never made a secret of her feelings

for Hawk. She'd agreed to his every suggestion, laughed at his every joke, and followed him everywhere when he visited her family's country estate. Would he have been more interested if she'd not been so open about her feelings?

She fisted her hands, despising herself for speculating about what she might have done to attract him. Did she have no pride at all?

"Once the chase begins, the lady must use her wit, charm, and vivacity—all of which you possess," Hester said.

Hester's voice snapped her out of her reverie. "You mean flirt?" she asked.

"Teasing and witty repartee will beguile a gentleman, but once again, the lady must not let her true feelings show," Hester said. "Once she secures his interest, she must drift away before *he* becomes too confident of *her* affections."

Julianne thought of all the young men she'd teased over the years. She'd danced and flirted with them, but she'd been certain they'd understood it was all in good fun. Yet, twelve gentlemen had proposed to her. Had she given them the wrong signals?

The same way Hawk had done to her?

Guilt flooded her chest. "Hester, isn't it wrong to mislead gentlemen?"

"All is fair in love and war," she said. "If you give the impression you are elusive, you've done nothing wrong."

Julianne bit her lip. If that were true, why did she feel as if she'd done something wrong?

"Something is troubling you, gel."

"I never meant to wound those gentlemen who proposed to me, but I must have inadvertently encouraged them." She looked at her clasped hands. "Afterward, I always tried to explain that I wasn't ready for marriage, but I wounded them nonetheless." Of course, she didn't mention that she'd been waiting for Hawk.

"Did you ever allow any of those gentlemen to court you exclusively?" Hester asked.

She lifted her chin. "No, of course not."

"Did any of them seek your brother's permission first?" Hester asked.

"No. I think their proposals were rather spur of the moment."

"Oh?" Hester said.

Julianne winced. "The first gentleman proposed after I allowed him to walk with me at a garden party. The next time, I was returning to a musical exhibition when the gentleman stepped outside the drawing room and drew me aside. The third one surprised me while I was walking in the park with my maid. The fourth one—"

Hester chortled. "My dear, you must have grown quite wary of gentlemen popping out of the shadows. You obviously inspired their passions."

She remembered what Hawk had said about Ramsey. "At the time, I didn't understand, but now I suspect they viewed me as a sort of prize to win."

"Whatever gave you that impression?" Hester asked.

"Hawk said that Lord Ramsey is trying to pursue me because I'm supposedly unobtainable."

Hester fingered her quizzing glass. "My nephew is jealous. That is a good sign."

She had no such illusions. "I'm sure he's not. He dislikes Ramsey and told me to stay away from him. Do you know if they had an altercation?"

"If they did, my nephew certainly would not discuss it with me."

Based upon Hawk's words, Julianne surmised something had occurred. He knew something about Ramsey, something he refused to divulge. The mystery niggled at her brain. She wanted to know more, but Hawk had no intention of revealing anything.

"You were angry at my nephew last night," Hester said.

"He insists on following my every move. It is quite provoking," she said. But last night, she'd glimpsed a different side of him. He was truly concerned that Ramsey could prove dangerous to her. Of course, it was silly of him. She could manage Ramsey, whether Hawk believed her or not.

"My nephew is fighting his attraction to you because of the promise he made to your brother," Hester said. "Enchant him and build a slow fire. At all costs, however, you must not let him get close too soon."

Julianne's cheeks heated. She rose and walked to the window to avoid Hester's scrutiny. Of course, she'd failed miserably when she'd let him kiss her. She'd not even tried to resist him, even though he'd made his disinterest clear at the ball. Had she secretly hoped that their kiss meant more than mere lust to him?

"Gel, what is wrong?"

She dared not look at Hester. Mama had always said all her thoughts showed on her face, and Julianne did not want Hester to see her tumultuous emotions. "All I want is to complete the pamphlet so that I may help other single ladies."

"You have given up on my nephew?"

She ought to have given up long ago. He didn't love her, and she would not demean herself in pursuit of his heart. With a deep breath, she mustered her courage and faced Hester. "That door is closed."

Hester gave her a knowing look.

She turned to the window again. Drops of rain pattered the wavy glass. Hester didn't believe her, but Julianne had meant every word. She'd spent too many years wanting and waiting for him. "It will be some time before I'm ready to open my heart again," she said.

Hester sighed. "Ah, the trials of young love. I remember it all so well."

Julianne returned to the sofa. "Tell me about your first beau."

"Well, he was not my beau, though I certainly admired him from afar."

"Did he not return your feelings?" Julianne asked.

"We exchanged words occasionally and longing looks. But he dared not declare himself." Hester regarded Julianne with a bittersweet smile. "You see, he was my father's steward and completely unsuitable."

"Oh, no," Julianne said. "Your heart must have been broken."

"I was to undergo a far greater heartache. Unbeknownst to me, my parents had arranged my marriage—to a man more than twice my age."

Julianne gasped. "You must have been horrified."

"I wept for days, but I had no choice. He wasn't the most attentive of men, and he was displeased that I didn't bear him an heir."

Julianne covered her mouth, realizing Hester must have suffered greatly.

"But three years later, he died of a heart seizure." She smiled at Julianne. "He left me a considerable fortune, and as a widow, I had far more freedom. Back then, I was young and attracted the attention of many a handsome gentleman."

"But you remarried four more times," Julianne said.

"Loneliness, I suppose," Hester said. "Well, that's quite enough of my history. You must work on your pamphlet if you are to finish it in a timely manner."

Julianne hesitated a moment but decided to take a page from Hester and speak frankly. "Is Mr. Peckham the gentleman who will make arrangements for publication?"

Hester shook her finger. "The less you know the better."

Julianne wondered if Mr. Peckham was Hester's first love, but she would not pry about such a personal matter, one that had clearly caused such grief. If Hester wanted her to know, she would tell her.

"Once the pamphlet is published, I can observe the other single ladies for signs they are following *The Secrets of Seduction*," Julianne said.

"Perhaps you should test some of the ideas in advance," Hester said. "To ensure they work properly."

Julianne regarded her clasped hands. She could not tell Hester about her vengeance plan, but her conscience bothered her. Hester had been so kind to her, and she was purposely deceiving her.

Hester patted her hand. "Go along now. You must complete the pamphlet quickly if we are to see it published well before the season ends."

Julianne nodded and hurried upstairs to the desk, determined to scrub thoughts of Hawk from her head. An hour later, she set her pen aside and read her latest entry.

Confidence is the key to becoming irresistible. Sweep away feelings of inadequacy. A woman who is assured of herself exudes a mysterious quality, one that makes her alluring to gentlemen. You need not have excessive beauty. It is said that Anne Boleyn was only moderately attractive, but her vivacity and quick wit drew gentlemen to her side. Her elusiveness made her all the more desirable. It is that inexplicable quality you must convey if you are to attract the attention of gentlemen.

Excitement raced through her veins. She was certain the pamphlet would be a roaring success.

Predictably, the food was cold, and his dining partner, Wallingham's daughter, was tongue-tied.

Hawk recalled the sizzling beefsteak at his club and sighed inwardly. Hopefully soon, the ladies would take their leave. It was a sad commentary on his life as a guardian that he actually looked forward to sipping port while the gents passed round a chamber pot at the bloody table. *A pissing good time,* he thought wryly.

Husky, feminine laughter drew his attention to Julianne. She sat beside the Earl of Wallingham's brash young heir, Edmund, Viscount Beaufort. Hawk noted Beaufort's gaze straying to Julianne's low-cut bodice. The devil. Of course, all the ladies showed off their bosoms in a similar manner, though some, like the silent Lady Eugenia, had little to display.

"Well, Hawk," Lord Wallingham said from the head of the table, "I heard all your family is in Bath with your ailing great-grandmother."

Lady Eugenia finally found her squeaky voice. "I am sorry to hear of her illness, my lord."

"Nothing to worry about," he said. "Just the usual heart palpitations."

Eugenia looked horrified. "My lord?"

"She feigns illness for attention," Hawk said.

"B-but why?" Eugenia asked.

Was she deaf? "For attention."

"Oh." Eugenia once again lapsed into silence.

Hawk forked a bite of congealed potatoes into his mouth and instantly regretted it. He managed to hide his revulsion by washing the food down with a gulp of wine.

Wallingham eyed Hawk. "Now that Shelbourne has taken vows, I expect you'll be on the lookout for a bride. Can't be outdone by the duke."

Hester, who sat farther down the table, smirked at Hawk.

He set his glass aside, suspecting Wallingham had hopes of foisting Eugenia off on him. "I daresay no one can top Shelbourne's spectacular match."

Julianne regarded Hawk with a smile. "Their engagement was truly the event of the decade."

Hawk winked at her. Only he and her family had known ahead of time that Tristan meant to propose to the former Miss Mansfield at a ball last spring.

Lady Wallingham patted her lips with her napkin and spoke up from the other end of the table. "Lord Hawkfield, you must take a bride soon. It is your duty."

"Madam, I assure you my immediate duty is to fulfill my role as guardian to Lady Julianne." Weeks and weeks of guarding her from half the lust-crazed bachelors of the ton. He'd be lucky if he didn't go mad in the process.

"Yes, but that does not preclude you from marrying," Lady Wallingham persisted.

"Well, we have high hopes," Hester said. "He showed some interest in matrimony when he got engaged last year. Unfortunately, it lasted only one hour."

Eugenia dropped her fork onto the plate. "Oh, dear," she murmured.

All the other guests stared at Hawk with astonishment.

Beaufort leaned forward. "The lady jilted you after only one hour?"

Hawk let out a melodramatic sigh. "I fear so. It seems I'm doomed to bachelorhood for life."

Julianne shook her head. "His engagement was a jest."

Noting Wallingham's deep frown, Hawk figured he was safe from any further coercion and sipped his wine.

"Lady Julianne, you must have marital aspirations," Lady Wallingham said.

"Her brother doesn't want to rush her," Hawk said. Julianne could wait another year—when he didn't have to watch.

"But this is her fourth season," Lady Wallingham said. "She is of age and must long to make an advantageous marriage."

"I only long to dance and shop," Julianne said.

Lady Wallingham tittered. "Such an amusing young lady. Do you not agree, Edmund?"

"Oh, yes, very," Beaufort said. "Quite jolly."

Lady Wallingham persisted. "I daresay there may be one young man who will capture her heart. Do you not agree, dear Edmund?"

Dear Edmund looked as if he'd eaten something rotten. "Of course."

Hawk gave Julianne a conspiratorial wink. "Alas, my ward has left a trail of broken hearts in her path. She has stringent requirements for a husband. No man can please her."

Beaufort's shoulders slumped, presumably with relief. He might not mind ogling Julianne, but given his youth, he probably had no intention of giving up sowing wild oats anytime soon.

Lady Wallingham sniffed. "Well, perhaps we should discuss the matter in the drawing room, Lady Julianne."

"That is very kind of you, Lady Wallingham, but I have no wish to monopolize you when you have other guests."

Hawk grinned at the edge in Julianne's voice.

"Nonsense," Lady Wallingham said. "I shall be happy to instruct you."

Julianne stabbed her fork into a stewed partridge.

Hawk cleared his throat to get her attention. "The bird looks dead to me."

She looked at him as if he'd lost his wits. "I beg your pardon?"

He shrugged. "No need to kill it."

Lady Eugenia choked and covered half her crimson face in her napkin. Beaufort laughed, earning him a quelling look from his mother.

After the dessert courses, the ladies withdrew. Wallingham brought out the port and the pot beneath the sideboard.

Hawk leaned back in his chair. *Let the pissing begin.*

When the gentlemen entered the drawing room, Julianne breathed a sigh of relief. For the past hour, Lady Wallingham had made Julianne her *concern* and proceeded to warn her of the dangers of staying single too long. According to her, Julianne was in grave peril of finding herself collecting dust on the spinster shelf. Julianne had borne the lecture with amusement, but the woman had persisted beyond all reason and kept asking her if she agreed. Lady Wallingham had not even waited for an answer before continuing.

Upon setting eyes on the gentlemen, Lady Wallingham beckoned her son. "There you are at long last. Edmund, you must turn the pages for Julianne while she plays the pianoforte."

All too eager to escape the woman, Julianne popped up from her chair. She'd not practiced in weeks, but she didn't care if she assaulted everyone's ears.

The young man dutifully escorted her toward the instrument. She saw Hawk frowning and lifted her chin as she walked past him. *Let him watch,* she thought as she turned a bright smile on Beaufort. At dinner, she'd fallen in with Hawk's jests, but only to divert Lady Wallingham.

Hawk strolled to the sideboard and poured himself a brandy he didn't want. He needed to do something while he tried to sort out what was eating at his gut—besides the potatoes.

At dinner, he'd felt as if he and Julianne were in perfect accord. It had seemed like the old days when she'd readily joined him in a lark. Six days ago, he'd seen her for the first time in nine months. And she'd greeted him with laughter in her eyes.

But everything had changed the night of the ball. He hadn't understood her behavior then, and he didn't now. All he knew was that she'd blown hot and cold ever since he'd refused to let Ramsey dance with her.

When Julianne played a discordant note, he glanced at her. If he'd been the one turning the pages, he would have banged on the keys to divert attention away from her mistake, as he'd done so many times before. In the past, she'd laughed and called him a rogue. Now he wondered if she would glare at him for his antics.

After she played the last note, everyone applauded. Beaufort leaned over her, and she laughed at something he said. The young man's gaze strayed to her bosom again. Hawk stiffened. Every instinct he possessed urged him to stride over there and plant Beaufort a facer for leering at her.

He made himself stand there and do nothing. Because she'd accused him of hovering over her and acting like a jealous husband.

He wasn't jealous. He only wanted to protect her.

But as Beaufort led her over to the window seat, Hawk looked away.

Julianne grew a bit anxious as she sat beside Beaufort on the window seat. Lady Wallingham watched them with a satisfied smile. Clearly she thought to promote a match. The last thing Julianne wanted was to mislead Beaufort. She tried to think of some way to tell him that she wanted only his friendship, but she concluded that saying such a thing would sound presumptuous and conceited. Drat it all. She must say something to discourage him, without giving offense.

She needn't have worried. Beaufort started nattering endlessly about a new curricle he meant to purchase. His eyes gleamed covetously as he described every detail. While he spoke of single axles and the dimensions of the wheels, she turned her thoughts inward to the pamphlet.

Now that she'd finished her chapter on becoming irresistible, she decided her next secret should involve witty banter.

When a gentleman approaches, keep your conversation witty and light. You may be anxious to continue the discussion, but do not linger. Doing so will only make him too confident of your regard, and he may lose interest. Flit about the ballroom and let him see that you are popular with ladies and gentlemen alike.

If only she had pen and paper at her disposal, she could scribble her thoughts immediately. Of course, she could not do so in the drawing room. The moment she returned home, she would record her thoughts. She smiled at the image of all those smug bachelors chasing after the disinterested single ladies.

"I can see you are pleased for me," Beaufort said.

His words made her recollect her manners. "Well, I imagine it is akin to the way I feel when I purchase a new bonnet."

He laughed. "It's a bit more exciting than that."

His arrogance vexed her. Clearly he thought his male interests far superior to hers.

He took her hands, startling her. "If all goes well, I'll make the purchase within a week. Now I must have your promise that you will take a drive with me in the park."

Oh, dear. She couldn't refuse without wounding him. Then an idea popped into her head. She fixed a vacuous expression on her face. "I'm forgetful sometimes. Perhaps you had better ask again after you take possession."

"I will," he said.

Rats. He probably wouldn't forget.

A shadow fell over them. She looked up to find Hawk staring daggers at Beaufort.

Beaufort released her hands.

"We are departing," Hawk said gruffly.

She took Hawk's arm, secretly relieved to have escaped Beaufort, single axles, and wheel dimensions.

Chapter Seven

*A Scoundrel Guardian's Advice: Do not ogle your
ward's bosom, no matter how much of it is on display.*

The next evening, Hawk escorted his aunt and Julianne into Lord and Lady Durmont's crowded ballroom. For the life of him, he couldn't understand why the ladies had accepted an invitation to Lady Durmont's ball when they disliked the woman and her scheming daughter, Lady Elizabeth. But Hester had insisted that everyone who was anyone would be there, and therefore their attendance was necessary.

After his aunt ambled off to gossip with her cronies, he stole another look at Julianne. Her bodice consisted of little more than a silky scrap of fabric. Being a man, and therefore not much better than a beast, he couldn't help noticing the creamy swells of her breasts. He recalled the way she'd fit perfectly in his hand as he'd teased her nipple with his thumb. Naturally he imagined freeing her breasts and suckling...

A blast of heat shot down to his groin. Alarmed that she might have caught him ogling her, he jerked his gaze up. She was craning her head and searching the crowd, completely oblivious. The devil. He knew every buck and rake who darkened her path would mentally undress her.

"Your gown is inadequate," he said.

She frowned at him. "I beg your pardon? It is in the first stare of fashion."

He lowered his gaze to her breasts again, thinking the barely-there bodice was definitely stare-worthy.

She unfurled her fan. "Stop looking at my bosom."

"It's rather difficult to avoid when there is so much of it on display."

"I'm sure you've seen far more in your rakehell career." She sniffed. "I'm off to find my friends."

"I'll help you."

"You're not planning to follow me, I hope."

At that moment, Charles Osgood, the bad poet, caught sight of Julianne. His eyes lit up like twin lanterns as he made a beeline for her.

"I've no intention of following," Hawk said, taking her arm and striding away before Osgood could reach her. "I shall escort you."

"I do not need an escort," she said.

"I meant to the dance floor."

"A gentleman is supposed to ask, not demand."

"Let me rephrase. May I have the honor of the first dance?"

"The only reason you wish to dance is so that you can

keep watch over me," she said with a haughty toss of her head.

He wasn't about to admit it. "It's perfectly correct for a guardian to dance with his ward."

"Oh? What rule book did you consult?"

He winked. "I promise to behave."

She considered his request for a moment, and then her lips curved into a sly smile. "On one condition."

Uh-oh. He knew he wasn't going to like it.

"I will dance with you *if* you take yourself off to the card room afterward and leave me in peace."

"Rule number four: I must approve all your dance partners," he said.

She released a long sigh. "Rule number four is nonsensical. In a country dance, I will exchange partners."

Of course she was correct, but that only reminded him of something important he'd forgotten. "Rule number seven: No waltzing."

"Hah! There were only six rules," she said.

"I reserve the right to add new ones as circumstances change," he said.

"We will discuss that at a later time. For now, however, I am desperate to be rid of you and will accept the bargain."

He didn't like the idea of leaving her alone with a roomful of lascivious men, but if he trailed after her all evening, others might conclude he had romantic intentions. His only recourse was to pop into the ballroom periodically and ensure all was well.

"I will accept, with an addendum," he said. "You must remain in the ballroom, and you will abide by rule number two: No more than one glass of wine or sherry."

"Agreed," she said.

When they reached the dance floor, he stood across from her, along with a dozen other couples. The orchestra struck up a lively tune. He glanced at the top of the line and grimaced at the first gentleman, who pranced forward and back diagonally. The lady directly across repeated the movement. Then the couples alternately clasped hands, turning and switching places in the line.

When his turn came, he merely walked forward. Julianne pulled a face, but he didn't care. He refused to skip like a girl.

Eventually, the movements changed, and he led Julianne to the top of the line.

"You're striding," she said. "This is a dance. You are supposed to move gracefully."

"I do not prance."

They moved forward and back and then turned to each other. "An elegant gentleman shows his refinement while dancing," she muttered.

"Have I ever struck you as refined?"

"You don't even try."

He clasped her hands, turning with her. "I have a bad reputation to maintain."

"I concede the point, my lord."

They faced forward again. *Step forward, step back… egad, this dance is asinine.* "Is this almost over?" he asked.

"I hope so," she said. "You are a terrible dancer."

"I waltz divine," he said.

She scoffed. "You are too modest."

He clasped hands with a new partner, turning and changing sides. Julianne did likewise with an elderly gentleman. Hawk would prefer she dance with only old men, but spry men over the age of seventy were in short supply at balls.

At long last the dance ended. He bowed, took Julianne's arm, and led her away.

She pointed. "The card room is that way."

He clapped his hand to his heart. "You wound me."

"We struck a deal."

He released her arm. "For both our sakes, try to stay out of trouble."

Julianne figured Hawk would return soon and hunt for her. Meanwhile, she meant to test her latest theory in the pamphlet. As she meandered through the crowd, she saw gentlemen watching her, but she pretended not to notice. She greeted others and flitted from group to group. In the past, she'd never given much thought to social pleasantries. Mingling with others had come naturally to her, but now she found herself a bit tongue-tied. She felt ill at ease, because her efforts seemed calculated.

She glanced at the wallflowers sitting with the matrons. They looked so miserable. Lady Eugenia sat among them, her eyes downcast. Julianne decided to ask Eugenia to walk with her. Then she would introduce her to others. Perhaps a gentleman would ask her to dance. Delighted with her plan, she started in that direction.

A familiar, snide voice called out her name. Lady Elizabeth Rossdale, the cruelest belle in the ton, stood only a foot away, surrounded by her flock of sheep. Julianne couldn't ignore them, but she planned to greet them briefly and make a quick escape. "Ladies, I hope you are enjoying the evening."

Elizabeth's particular friend Henrietta Bancroft regarded Julianne with a sly smile. "Wherever is your beau? Oops, I mean your guardian."

The other girls snickered behind their hands.

Elizabeth's green cat eyes gleamed with malice. "Henrietta, dear, you know very well he considers her almost like a sister."

Julianne lifted her chin and turned her back on them, a cut direct. Let them laugh. She despised those rotten girls. Though she told herself she didn't care, humiliation burned through her. She'd known others had overheard Hawk's comment, but having it flaunted in her face hurt.

Immersed in her depressed thoughts, she searched the crowd for Amy and Georgette. She didn't notice Lord Ramsey until he intercepted her.

"Lady Julianne, what a pleasure to see you," he said.

She suppressed a groan. His insufferable pursuit irritated her, but she would fob him off. "Lord Ramsey." She curtsied. "I am looking for your sister and Miss Hardwick."

"I've been searching for them as well and can't find them anywhere." He surveyed the crowd. "It's unbearably warm in the ballroom. Perhaps they stepped out onto the landing. Shall we have a look?"

His request sounded innocent enough, but she'd promised not to leave the ballroom. And she couldn't forget the way he'd goaded Hawk on two previous occasions. "That is unnecessary. I'm sure I'll find them eventually."

When she took a step to walk past him, Ramsey grinned and blocked her path.

"My lord, was there something else?" she said in a cool voice.

"I'm not letting you get away so easily," he said.

We shall see about that. "Excuse me, I must find Lady Rutledge." She turned and walked away.

He caught up to her and smiled. "Ah, the lady wishes to play cat and mouse."

She kept walking. "I'm in no mood for games."

"I mean to catch you."

His overconfident demeanor annoyed her. "You may try, my lord, but you will not succeed."

"I only want to spend a little time with you."

"You know Hawk would not approve."

"He is in the card room and will never know."

She narrowed her eyes. "You are asking me to defy him?" As she spoke the words, she noted several guests watching them.

When he tipped his head, a curly blond lock fell over one brow. "Then let us find a quiet corner so that we may talk."

She realized Ramsey would not relent until she told him in no uncertain terms to desist. But she did not want anyone to overhear her words. "Follow me to the wall niche beyond the pillars," she said.

When he offered his arm, she could not refuse without drawing unwanted attention. But every step of the way, she resented him.

After they reached the wall niche, she released his arm and struggled to rein in her temper. "I have no wish to give offense, but you are placing me in an untenable position."

"Because Hawk has forbidden me to court you," he said.

"He is my guardian, and I must abide by his wishes."

Of course, she didn't welcome Ramsey's addresses, but it was a convenient excuse.

"It should be your decision," Ramsey said. "His objections are unreasonable."

Ramsey's argument sounded eerily like the one she'd made recently, but she knew he had ulterior motives for pursuing her. "Whether they are or not does not signify. It is evident to me that there is animosity between you and Hawk. And it is clear that I am a pawn in your feud with him."

His expression registered shock. "He has persuaded you that I am a scoundrel, but he is the one—"

"Lord Ramsey, I've no intention of arguing the point. As far as I am concerned, you are Georgette's brother. She is my dear friend. For her sake and mine, I ask that you cease your addresses to me. It will end badly if you do not."

"You ask me to forget you, but I cannot." He put his fist to his heart. "My feelings—"

She held up her hand. "Say no more. I have given you no encouragement. I am very sorry, but this must be the end of the matter."

A pained expression crossed his face. "It is as I feared. You hold tender feelings for him."

Shock cascaded over her. "What?"

"That night at the Beresford's ball, everyone remarked upon your waltz with Hawk. He led everyone to believe that he cared for you, and then he denied it all by saying you were practically a sister to him. I saw your ashen face and thought I had caused your vexation. But others said you have held a torch for him for years."

Her heart beat madly. *Oh, dear God. Everyone knew.*

"He is a vile deceiver."

"You have twisted matters when you know nothing," she hissed.

He regarded her with pity. "No matter what he has told you, *my* intentions are true and honorable. Please do not let him keep us apart."

"Good evening, my l-lord." She fled, hating the way her voice had shaken. All she wanted was to put as much distance as possible between herself and Ramsey. When a group of matrons looked at her askance, Julianne immediately slowed her steps. She skirted the perimeter of the ballroom to avoid the worst of the crowd and fanned her hot face.

Her stomach roiled. Elizabeth and Henrietta knew. Ramsey knew. *Everyone* knew. She'd made a fool of herself, because she'd worn her heart on her sleeve.

Julianne wanted to go home, but home was miles and miles away. And what would she tell her brother and mother? She didn't want her family to know she'd humiliated herself before the entire ton.

Her throat clogged. Mama had warned her repeatedly about infatuation. She'd told her to keep her own counsel in society and adopt a tell-nothing countenance. But she'd ignored the warnings, thinking her mother too cautious. All these years, she'd openly adored Hawk and misinterpreted his teasing as a sign he returned her feelings.

He probably knew. How could he not when she'd followed him about like an eager puppy?

Her chest hurt. She'd never been so mortified in her life.

Halfway into her circuit of the ballroom, she happened upon Sally Shepherd and managed a weak smile. "Sally, it's been ages since I last saw you."

Sally's round face lit up. "Have you heard? There is to be an announcement tonight."

"What announcement?" she said, not really caring.

"No one knows for certain," Sally said. "Lady Durmont is keeping mum about it."

"I'm sure we'll find out soon enough." She started to excuse herself, but Amy and Georgette arrived, their expressions excited.

Georgette's blue eyes twinkled. "Something is afoot. Sally, do you know what will be announced?"

"No, but everyone is on pins and needles."

Julianne's chest tightened. How could she bear to mingle among the crowd and pretend nothing was amiss?

While Sally and Georgette continued to speculate about the announcement, Amy walked over to Julianne. "You do not seem yourself tonight," she murmured.

Amy's sensitivity made her keenly aware of others' feelings. "It is nothing. I will be myself again soon," Julianne said.

"If you need someone to listen, you need only ask," Amy said.

Julianne nodded, but the wound was too raw. Only a little over a week ago, she'd rejoiced upon learning Hawk had agreed to be her guardian. She'd been so certain this would be the year he would make all her dreams come true. That night at the Beresford's ball, she'd thought his rejection was the worst thing that could ever happen to her. She'd not known everyone mocked her.

Lord Beaufort and Mr. Osgood joined the group. Sally questioned them, but they knew nothing about the impending announcement.

Beaufort turned his gaze to Julianne. "I say, where is your customary smile, Lady Julianne?"

Evidently her emotions showed on her face. She vowed

to work on adopting a serene expression. "I was merely lost in thought." She would have to pretend for the rest of the evening that nothing was wrong.

Georgette walked over to her. "I can guess the reason for your vexation," she muttered. "Hawk is striding in this direction. Honestly, he is a domineering brute."

Amy frowned and held her finger up to her lips. Julianne glanced around and found Hawk almost upon them. Her throat constricted. How could she even bear to look at him when she'd made such a cake of herself?

Hawk stopped beside her. "A footman interrupted the card games for an announcement."

"We're all anxious to hear the announcement," Sally said. "Do you know what it is about?"

He shrugged. "I've only heard a rumor."

Sally's eyes brightened. "What rumor?"

The orchestra played a short, lively tune, interrupting their conversation. Then Lord and Lady Durmont took up a stance before the musicians. Lord Durmont held up his hands, and eventually, the buzzing voices dwindled.

"As you know by now, my lady and I have an announcement to make tonight." He looked thoroughly pleased with himself.

Lady Durmont simpered. Then her husband turned to Elizabeth. "Daughter, will you and Lord Edgemont join us?"

Julianne's heart knocked against her chest, realizing the significance of his words.

"No," Georgette said, drawing Julianne's attention.

Amy's eyes filled with tears as she covered her mouth.

Lord Durmont's voice rang out. "We are overjoyed to

announce the engagement of our daughter Lady Elizabeth to Lord Edgemont."

As thunderous applause erupted, Lord Edgemont gazed into Elizabeth's eyes. Then he raised her gloved hand for a kiss and said something. Though the words were inaudible, Julianne knew he'd said he loved her.

A stinging sensation rushed up her throat and cheeks. She blinked back her own tears. The most hateful girl in the ton had found love. The irony only made her feel worse. Because Elizabeth had gotten what Julianne had dreamed of since the night she'd danced with Hawk at her come-out ball four long years ago.

Julianne's determined smile made Hawk suspicious.

He wandered about the ballroom, stopping frequently to speak to friends. The entire time, he kept a surreptitious watch over Julianne. She never lacked for a dance partner. Between sets, the younger blades surrounded her, vying for her attention. The cubs were none the wiser, but Hawk realized something was amiss. He knew her too well not to recognize the artificial quality of her pasted-on smile.

When midnight struck, he decided to seek out Julianne and his aunt so that he could escort them to the traditional supper. He pressed through the crowd, nodding genially at the ladies, who eyed him as if he were a haunch of beef they'd like to sink their teeth into.

He spotted Julianne exiting the dance floor with Beaufort and strode in that direction. At last, he caught up to them and addressed Julianne. "I will escort you and my aunt to supper."

"Lord Beaufort already offered," she said in a cool tone.

Beaufort looked uncomfortable. "With your permission, sir."

Sir. The cub made him feel ancient.

Julianne regarded Hawk warily as if she expected his refusal.

· Well, hell. He had no reason to object. "I'll see you downstairs."

Julianne looked taken aback at first, but she turned that artificial smile on Beaufort. The young man bowed and led her away. Hawk watched the pair until they became lost in the crowd heading for the doors. For some odd reason, he felt bereft.

Not long ago, she'd enjoyed his company. Now she only wished him to leave her in peace so that she could dance and flirt with her beaux.

In the not-so-distant future, she would marry and have children. Nothing would ever be the same again.

A hollow sensation settled in his chest.

Later that night, Julianne tossed and turned in bed. Then she punched the pillow. She wanted to weep like an infant over her stupidity, but she'd long since passed the awkward schoolgirl age. If she'd not clung to her girlish infatuation, she could have saved herself from humiliation.

Tonight, she'd paid the price for wearing her heart on her sleeve. The most vicious girls in the ton had mocked her, and Ramsey had pitied her. She'd danced the night away to show everyone she held no tender feelings for Hawk. But the damage was done.

The blame fell squarely on her shoulders. If she'd not been such a fool, she would not be in this predicament.

Not once had she ever questioned her feelings for Hawk. She'd been so certain she was in love, but she'd been in love with the fantasy of him.

She prayed he didn't know, but he probably secretly found her infatuation amusing. Oh, God, how could she face him?

The worst part was that she couldn't avoid him. For the rest of the season, she must meet him on a daily basis. But when the season ended, he would escort her home for the babe's christening. Somehow she must find a way to endure, without letting her wounds show.

A tap sounded, startling her. Hester opened the door. "Ah, you are awake."

She took a deep breath, willing a calm expression. "I hope I did not disturb you," she said, sitting up.

"No, I only wanted to check on you." Hester's frilly wrapper billowed as she crossed the room and set the candle on the bedside table. The mattress dipped when she sat beside Julianne. "You were unusually quiet during the carriage ride."

"I was a bit weary," she said.

"Little wonder. You danced your dainty feet off," she said. "You were the belle of the ball."

"No, that title belongs to Elizabeth." Just when she'd thought matters couldn't possibly grow worse, Elizabeth's engagement was announced.

"You seemed displeased by the news of her engagement," Hester said.

"Elizabeth is cruel. I don't like her or her friend Henrietta."

"Lady Elizabeth claimed the first engagement of the season," Hester said. "It will be much talked of, and the papers will make a fuss over her. Even in my day, the gels always hoped to be the first. But I can understand why you cannot be happy for a disagreeable young lady."

"She has a large group of friends who follow her everywhere. They even dress like her and jump to do her bidding."

"I knew such a girl when I made my come-out," Hester said. "She picked on one poor chit. The others followed her lead, because they feared becoming her victim."

"That is an apt description of Elizabeth and her flock of sheep." Julianne swallowed hard. She couldn't bring herself to tell Hester about their mockery or her conversation with Ramsey.

Hester smoothed the covers. "You are unable to sleep. What troubles you?"

Julianne drew her feet up and wrapped her arms around her shins. "It is so unfair. The most hateful girl in the ton is engaged."

When Hester said nothing, Julianne looked at her. "I know it is foolish of me. Mama would tell me life is not fair."

"No, it is not," Hester said. "But your feelings are understandable. I daresay, you are not the only young lady who felt the pangs of envy tonight."

"Amy and Georgette were particularly distressed. Elizabeth treated them horribly last year." Julianne huffed. "She is spiteful and horrid. I hate her."

Hester tilted her head. "It has been many years since I was a young belle, but some things never change. If you are amenable, I will offer you advice."

Julianne nodded. "I welcome your wisdom. You speak frankly. Mama only tells me to follow the proprieties without question."

"That is because she is your mother and has high expectations of you." Hester paused. "Now for the advice. Tonight, you may vent your feelings, but once they are spent, you must banish them forever."

She rested her chin on her knees. "That is easier said than done."

Hester considered her for a long moment. "Yes, but while you are fuming over Elizabeth, she is probably not giving you a single thought."

Julianne lifted her chin. Her chest rose and fell quickly as Hester's words sank in.

"She is not worth your anguish," Hester said.

Julianne threw her arms around Hester. "Thank you. However did you become so wise?"

Hester patted her back. "The usual way. I learned from my mistakes."

Chapter Eight

*A Lady's Secrets of Seduction: Plant posies in the
drawing room so that your admirers will presume
other gentlemen have called.*

The next morning, Julianne worried her hands as Hester directed two maids to plant flowers on the numerous side tables. "Hester, this seems like trickery."

Hester waved her hand. "You must think of those poor single gels who are desperate to find a husband. Gentlemen hold all the power in matrimonial matters. As you said in your introduction to the pamphlet, most men put off marriage for far too long. Ladies have few advantages. If gentlemen conclude they have competition, they will be more eager to court the ladies."

Julianne still thought the scheme deceptive. "Well, we are presuming gentlemen will call today."

Hester chuckled. "Oh, they will call. You were the most popular lady at the ball last night."

Hester had been right after all.

When the five gentlemen had arrived earlier with posies, they had looked abashed and said they could see their offering was not the first. Hester had given Julianne a smug smile. Although Julianne tried to squelch her guilty conscience by thinking of all the lovelorn ladies, she didn't like deceiving the young men. Mr. Osgood, Lord Beaufort, Mr. Portfrey, Lord Caruthers, and Mr. Benton were amiable and witty. In a spurt of inspiration, she'd honestly been able to say she favored their flowers over all the others.

When the footman announced Hawk, Julianne's stomach fluttered involuntarily. She told herself she had nothing to be concerned about. He probably did not suspect her former feelings for him. Even if he had known, he could not deny she no longer held a *tendre* for him. Feeling a tad more confident, she lifted her chin as he walked inside and smiled serenely—at his cravat. Then, she silently chastised herself for acting like a cowardly ninny and forced herself to meet his gaze.

He arched his brows and then sauntered past. Julianne expected him to glower at the other gentlemen and secretly hoped he would be jealous. But he merely acknowledged them with a nod, headed to the tea tray, and heaped biscuits on a plate. He didn't even spare a glance at the numerous bouquets.

Drat him. He'd taken the wind right out of her sails.

Caro and Byron followed him to a chair. The dogs sat at his feet, looking at him hopefully as he ate the biscuits.

"You can give them a crumb or two," Hester said.

He flicked his fingers and set the plate on the carpet. The dogs greedily lapped the crumbs.

Charles Osgood, the bad poet, grimaced. "Is that, er, sanitary?"

Hawk shrugged. "Best way to clean the plates."

Lord Beaufort elbowed Osgood. "Buffle head," he said, his tone good-natured.

The dogs trotted over to the tea tray, sniffing the carpet. Finding no stray crumbs, they sat on their haunches and stared up at the tray as if expecting someone to serve them.

Julianne tried to think of something witty to say to the younger gentlemen, but Hawk stretched out his long legs, drawing her attention. His tight trousers left little to the imagination. She had no trouble discerning the corded muscles of his thighs.

Fearing he might catch her ogling him, she jerked her gaze away. Did she have no shame? She applied her fan in an effort to cool her embarrassment.

Beaufort's voice pierced the silence. "I say, Hawk, your fencing match this morning caused quite a stir."

Julianne regarded Hawk with parted lips. "I did not know you fence."

"The exercise is invigorating," he said.

"You gave Ramsey no quarter," Beaufort continued.

Julianne stiffened. Oh, dear God. Had Hawk purposely sought out Ramsey?

Osgood leaned forward. "He couldn't match your speed."

Hawk shrugged. "Ramsey lost his focus, let his temper get the better of him early on."

Her pulse raced. Had Ramsey said something to Hawk about his encounter with her last night?

"You had him sweating buckets," Mr. Benton said.

"He's a two-bottle man," Hawk said. "Can't keep fit if you drown yourself in claret every night."

The younger men murmured their agreement. They clearly admired Hawk, and he'd given them sage advice. But the news of the fencing match rattled her nerves. Was Ramsey the reason Hawk had called on her?

"I thought at first he meant to refuse to shake your hand after you trounced him," Osgood said.

Mr. Portfrey nodded. "He did so in a grudging manner."

"It was unsporting," Lord Caruthers said.

Julianne winced. Apparently Ramsey had made an ass of himself in front of his peers.

Hawk glanced at her. "I fear this topic is unsuitable for the ladies."

The younger gentlemen rushed to offer their apologies.

"No apology is necessary," Julianne said. But she meant to question Hawk later and find out if he had challenged Ramsey.

"I rather enjoyed hearing of my nephew's victory," Hester declared.

Osgood looked at the mantel clock. "I say, we've overstayed our welcome."

Julianne rose along with Hawk and the other gentlemen. They bowed to her. Then Beaufort approached. "Lady Julianne, I should be in possession of that curricle by the end of the week. Will you allow me the honor of driving you to the park?"

Oh, no. He would likely rattle on about axles and wheels again, but she must be polite. "Let me know when you've taken possession." There, she'd not refused, but she'd not agreed, either.

"Will you attend the theater tonight?" Beaufort asked.

She shrugged. "Perhaps."

Hawk narrowed his eyes. "No one informed me that the plans changed."

Drat it all. She couldn't tell him that she meant to test Hester's idea for the next chapter: *Be vague about your planned entertainments.*

"It is a lady's prerogative to change her mind," Hester said.

Beaufort laughed. "Well, I hope to find you in attendance, Lady Rutledge."

Hester snorted. "Scamp. You're a bit young, but I shall be happy to receive you—*if* I decide to attend."

After the younger men left, Hawk folded his arms over his chest and regarded his aunt. "When were you planning to tell me the plans changed?"

"We have not decided yet," Hester said.

"Oh? What else did you have in mind?"

"The opera," Julianne said. They had not actually discussed the matter, but she saw no reason to enlighten him.

"Then I'll decide," he said. "The theater."

Julianne shrugged, pretending indifference as she perched on the sofa beside Hester. She refused to let him see that his high-handed manner provoked her.

"Do be seated," Hester said to Hawk. "My neck is aching from looking up at you, and I wish to hear more about this business with Ramsey."

"You've heard the salient points." He slumped back into his chair.

Julianne regarded him with suspicion. He'd called today for a reason, but he'd yet to state it.

"How many beaux have paraded through the drawing room today?" he asked.

"She did not receive all of them," Hester said.

"This is a bit excessive, even for you, Julianne," Hawk said.

"She cannot help it if the gentlemen flock to her," Hester said. "Her beauty and wit draw them."

Hawk gripped the arms of the chair. "Julianne, we need to discuss rule number three. You violated the 'no flirting' rule repeatedly last night."

"Rules?" Hester said. "This is news to me."

Julianne waved her hand. "It's just one of his foolish notions. Do not pay any heed to him."

"You are determined to flirt with every man in the beau monde," he said. "The men will think you are a tease, and the dragons will flay you alive."

"If I did not know better, I would think you are jealous," she said.

"I see what you're about," he said.

She fanned herself. "Really? Enlighten me." Of course, she would never reveal she'd meant to show the ton she no longer had feelings for *him*.

"You wish to increase the number of proposals you have refused," he said.

"That is ridiculous. I have not received a single offer of marriage this season." She meant to be careful not to encourage gentlemen. Somehow, she must be clear that she only sought to dance and be merry.

"You've been here only eight days," he said. "By next week, you'll have half the bachelors in London on bended knee if I do not put a stop to it."

"It's not her fault they fall in love with her," Hester said.

"Julianne, you will cease flirting," Hawk said.

She struggled not to laugh. "What do you consider flirting?"

"You are being purposely obtuse."

"I merely wish to know exactly what I may or may not say to a gentleman."

Hester rose. "I'm weary of this foolish discussion. Julianne, when he grows too tiresome, evict him."

Hawk glared at his aunt as she and the dogs retreated. Once the drawing room door closed, he strode over to Julianne and sat beside her on the sofa. "I meant what I said."

"I have more important concerns. Why did you fence with Ramsey?"

"He challenged me. I accepted."

"You wanted to fight him," she said.

"It was a fencing match, not a fight."

She shook her head. "You say that, but I know there was more to that match than mere fencing."

The gold flecks in his brown eyes glinted. "This is no simple grievance, Julianne. He's a blackguard and a poor sport."

She recalled Ramsey's forceful manners at the ball. Clearly he'd sought a confrontation with Hawk today. But she didn't know if it was because of the bad blood between the two men or because of her rejection last night.

"I hope you aren't planning to defend him on account of his sister," Hawk said.

"No. His poor sportsmanship today was inexcusable." Last night at the ball, Ramsey had importuned her, despite her attempts to deter him. She knew now that he was every bit as manipulative as Hawk had said.

"You will stay away from him," Hawk said.

She wanted nothing to do with Ramsey, but she knew it would be impossible to avoid him entirely because of Georgette. On the other hand, she had told Ramsey to cease his pursuit. Most likely, his pride would keep him away.

"I received a letter from your brother today. He asked how you fared."

The abrupt change in topic startled her. "You answered the letter?"

"Not yet, but I will."

She regarded him warily. "What do you plan to tell him?"

"That you're enjoying the festivities and are as popular as ever," he said.

"What else?" she said, narrowing her eyes.

"I'll not reveal your unfortunate episode with the wine, if that's what you're worried about." He paused and added, "Tristan wondered why neither of us has written."

"It's only been a little over a week," she said.

"You know your brother's tendency to worry. I suggest you write to him and your mother soon."

"I meant to do so, but I've been so busy." She'd spent much of her free time writing the pamphlet. Lord help her if her brother ever found out. But Hester's arrangements would ensure no one would trace *her* as the author.

"Take a few moments to pen a letter to your family once a week," Hawk said. "They're not accustomed to having you so far away."

"I traveled with Amy and her family last summer," she said.

He sighed. "Your brother did not say this, but I imagine he and your mother are a bit concerned about my aunt's influence."

"Hester is too blunt for others, but I appreciate her frank advice," Julianne said.

"What advice?" he said, frowning.

"Nothing that would interest you," she said.

"I'm all ears."

Well, of course she couldn't tell him the truth. "I daresay you have no interest in fashion or receipts for beauty remedies."

"I know my aunt well," he said. "She is tolerated because of her age, but some of her ideas are improper. I depend upon you to use your good sense and fob her off if she concocts one of her outrageous schemes."

She bit back a smile. He'd no idea what was in store for him and his fellow scoundrels. They deserved what was coming to them. All too often, women were at the mercy of men. Julianne meant to even the score with her pamphlet. If all went well, this would be one season where the ladies took control of their destinies.

Hawk released a loud sigh. "I know you resent my interference, but with your family away and my aunt's reputation for bawdiness, the society dragons will be watching you closely."

She huffed. "I've done nothing wrong."

He arched his brows.

"Since the night of the Beresford's ball," she amended. "Really, you worry for nothing. No one has ever questioned my conduct before, and I've done nothing to incite gossip." Of course, the pamphlet would cause a stir, but no one would ever know she'd written it.

"I doubt you've even bothered to count the number of posies you received today."

"It would have been unpardonable to refuse them."

Particularly since Hester had gone to a great deal of trouble and expense to procure them.

"I called today to check on you," Hawk said. "As I expected, you had five cubs worshipping at your feet."

"They are honorable gentlemen, and I would never injure their tender sensibilities."

He scoffed. "Trust me, it's not their tender sensibilities I'm worried about."

"You cannot object to them calling on me."

"I object to you collecting beaux like bonnets," he said.

"You insinuate their behavior was inappropriate, but you are wrong. Every gentleman I danced with last evening observed the proprieties," she said. "Well, everyone but you."

He scoffed. "I did nothing wrong."

"Hah! You grumbled the entire time we danced. Your manners were atrocious."

"There is a difference. I am your guardian. You and I needn't stand on ceremony," he said.

She sniffed and lifted her chin. "That reminds me of another faux pas you committed last evening."

"Oh?"

"You ogled my person."

His shoulders shook with unsuppressed laughter. "I ogled your *bosom*, which you displayed too much of, I might add."

"You are my guardian and should not notice my feminine attributes," she said.

"You are fond of euphemisms." His gaze dropped to her bodice. "I prefer indelicate words."

She made a sound of disgust. "I'm sure you do, but you will not speak them in my presence."

He grinned and inched over on the sofa. "Shall I whisper them?"

"Save your scatological language for your ladybirds," she said with a sniff.

He moved over again, this time right next to her. "I can say them in French and Italian."

His breath stirred the curl by her ear, and her heart beat a little faster. "I am not impressed."

He walked his fingers like a spider up her arm.

She swatted his hand. "You are no better than a naughty schoolboy."

"I'm no boy, but I am bad. Very bad."

She affected a bored look. "And yet you question my behavior. Compared to you, I am an angel."

"You know the rules are different for men and women," he said. "Like it or not, your conduct must be above reproach."

But soon those rules would change, thanks to the pamphlet. A smile tugged at the corners of her mouth as she imagined the fury of all the rakehells upon reading what ladies really thought of their scandalous doings.

"I must go now," he said.

"Wait. Surely Tristan mentioned Tessa in the letter. How is she faring?"

"She is well."

Julianne knit her brows. "That is all he said?"

Some odd emotion flickered in his eyes. "The babe keeps her awake at night kicking."

Julianne smiled. "In less than two months, I will be an aunt—and a godmother. Tristan said you agreed to be the babe's godfather."

Hawk wagged his brows. "I shall try not to corrupt him."

"But what if it is a girl?"

He tugged on his sleeves. "We shall see."

"Oh, I cannot wait to hold the babe in my arms," she said. "Mama is planning a large celebration for the christening. All your family will be invited to attend. It will be such a happy occasion."

He stood. "I will call for you and my aunt tonight."

Her lips parted at his sudden change in topic, but she rose and curtsied.

He strode out the door, as if he were in a hurry to escape.

In the end, Hawk's aunt had insisted upon attending the theater. He'd rather be at his club enjoying a fine brandy, but given the limited choices, the theater was preferable to having his ears assaulted at the opera.

When they entered the box, dozens of ladies across the expanse of the auditorium stared at them. Their tall feathers bobbed as they whispered to those beside them.

He grinned at Julianne only to find her scowling. "See something you dislike?"

"Lady Elizabeth and her lapdog Henrietta."

He laughed. "Sheath your claws, kitten. They are not worth your disdain."

She lifted her chin. "You are correct."

"Oh, ho. You are a dragon in the making," he said.

Julianne swatted his arm with her fan, but her eyes twinkled. "What if I am?"

"Shall I tremble in fear?" he asked.

"I beg you to control yourself. I left my smelling salts at home," she said.

"If I swoon, you may revive me with a swish of your fan."

Her husky laughter called to the beast inside him. As he escorted her to the chairs, he imagined the sound of her raspy voice in a darkened boudoir.

He forced those dangerous thoughts from his head.

After they were seated, his aunt went to visit a friend. Hawk took the opportunity to tease Julianne. "Look at those gentlemen strutting along the aisles of the pit. They are taking seats next to lonely ladies. How kind of them."

She sniffed. "A lady never notices lewd behavior in public places, and you are unmannerly to encourage me to watch."

"Lewd?" He made a mock show of horror.

She wafted her fan. "I'm sure you're well acquainted with such doings."

"I'm shocked," he said.

"That is the worst bouncer I've ever heard."

"No, really, I'm quite astounded." He paused for effect. "I'd no idea you were such an expert on ... what were the words you used? Oh, yes, *lewd behavior.*"

"Rogue," she said.

The curtain rose, and the actors stumbled about the stage as if they were as drunk as sailors. He couldn't recall the name of the play, but it mattered not. No one paid much attention, which was a good thing since the actors kept slurring their lines.

Hawk slouched in the velvet chair and stretched out his legs. He accidentally brushed Julianne's arm. The brief contact made his skin tingle.

He gazed at her, intending to make a jest, but she clutched the rail, seemingly mesmerized by the play. When she leaned forward, the exterior candle sconces illuminated her shining midnight curls. A rope of pearls was threaded through her intricately styled hair. Her complexion was as luminescent as the pearls. Without a doubt, she was the most beautiful woman he'd ever known.

Hawk imagined taking her hand and building a slow fire in her with a secret look. Her preoccupation gave him leave to admire her long, slender neck. He wanted to plant butterfly kisses along her jaw and trail his lips to the pulse point. He could almost hear her low gasp as he suckled her.

When his cock stirred, he made a halfhearted attempt to turn his thoughts elsewhere, but in the close confines, the scent of her flowery perfume fogged his brain. Once more, he glanced at her profile, remembering her passionate response to his kiss.

The memory made him feel like a devil. He'd had no right to touch her, but his guilt hadn't stopped him from continually reliving the taste of her sweet lips.

Knowing she was forbidden made her all the more tempting. Night after night, he'd imagined stripping off her gown and undergarments. He'd formed a picture in his mind of her slim, naked body. And he'd thought of dozens of ways to pleasure her. He wanted to taste every inch of her skin. He wanted to spread her thighs and kiss her intimately until she shattered in ecstasy. He wanted to pin her wrists above her head and make her beg to have him inside her.

His cock hardened. The devil. He was making himself half mad over a woman he could never have.

He ought to take a mistress to dampen the damnable lust coursing through his veins. But when would he ever have time to set one up, much less bed her? He was spending all his time ensuring Julianne stayed out of trouble.

Hell and damnation. He'd sworn to be discreet, but that wasn't even an issue. When he'd agreed to be Julianne's guardian, he'd thought he could pop in to a few balls occasionally and return to his usual carousing. The wine episode aside, he didn't dare leave her without protection, not with Ramsey and every buck and blade in London sniffing round her skirts.

In addition to escorting her to entertainments every evening, he'd decided it was necessary to call on her in the afternoons. After their conversation earlier today, he knew she was entirely too naïve where men were concerned. She'd actually worried about injuring their *tender sensibilities*. Clearly, she had no idea what foul thoughts ran through the primitive male brain.

To her, flirting was nothing more than a merry game. She thought herself experienced enough to avoid seductive traps. Nothing he said would convince her, for he'd already tried. She didn't know that one heedless decision, one stumble, could send her sliding down the proverbial slippery slope.

He knew from experience how easy it was to fall.

No matter how much she resented his interference, he could not let down his guard.

Chapter Nine

*A Lady's Secrets of Seduction: Once you secure his
interest, drift away before he becomes too confident
of your affections.*

When the curtains closed for intermission, Julianne
turned to find Hawk feigning sleep. She'd felt him watching her, but she'd not returned his gaze. The entire time,
she'd pretended interest in the play, but her thoughts had
darted about. She'd tried to think of a scheme to draw him
slowly into her web, but she couldn't risk being obvious.

His pretense at sleep, however, presented an opportunity. She hesitated a moment, unsure if she could be so
bold, but timidity would gain her nothing.

She leaned closer to him and whispered near his ear,
"What are you dreaming of?"

His eyes flew open, and he turned toward her, his
mouth only inches from her lips. The ragged sound of

his breath made her heart beat faster. He was much too close. She recollected Hester's advice to drift away before a gentleman became too confident of a lady's affections and rose quickly. Noting his arrested expression, she bit back a secret smile. "You might as well continue napping. I'm off to visit friends."

He shot up out of his chair and caught her arm. "You are going nowhere alone."

"I only wish to call on Georgette. Amy is with her."

He released her and leaned out of the balcony. "You may forget that plan. Ramsey is there, along with his parents."

"Ah, yes, the danger is clear. He will accost me in front of his family and all of society," she muttered.

He faced her. "I said no and that is the end of the matter."

Julianne considered her next move. Hawk couldn't prevent her from leaving without causing a scene. She meant to thwart him, but Hester entered the box on Beaufort's arm.

"The scamp insisted upon escorting me," Hester said. "No doubt, he meant to charm his way into the box so that he could pay court to Julianne."

Osgood, Portfrey, Benton, and Caruthers followed close behind and bowed. Julianne greeted each one enthusiastically and tried to ignore Hawk's scowl. He leaned his hip against the balcony and crossed his arms over his chest. Clearly he meant to monitor her every word so that he could rebuke her later for flirting.

Julianne invited the gentlemen to take seats and made a point of asking how they liked the play. They declared the acting horrid and admitted they had given up watching.

She found herself laughing at Mr. Portfrey's imitation of one actor's stumbling about the stage.

"Lady Julianne, you have not told us your opinion of the play," Caruthers said.

She smiled. "I could not hear a word for Hawk's snoring."

"I do not snore," he drawled.

She glanced at him and then returned her attention to the younger gentlemen. "I fear I've embarrassed him," she said sotto voce.

"I could never fall asleep in your presence," Mr. Benton said.

"Do not be so certain," she said. "I might bore you with talk of bonnets and balls."

Benton gazed into her eyes. "The mere sound of your voice brings me pleasure."

Hawk pulled a face. Clearly, he thought himself far superior to the younger men, but she liked them. They were amiable and appreciated her conversation, whereas all Hawk ever did was lecture her.

When Amy and Georgette arrived, Julianne brightened. Osgood escorted Amy to the chair next to him. Julianne exchanged a secretive smile with Georgette. The sensitive poet would make a wonderful beau for gentle Amy.

Beaufort stood and approached Julianne, holding up a coin. "A guinea for your thoughts?"

She arched her brows. "Are you out of pennies, my lord?"

"Sadly, yes. Will a bit of magic do?"

"Is it a trick?"

He held out his palm. "Allow me to demonstrate."

She took his hand and stood. Then she darted a glance at Hawk. He regarded Beaufort with an amused expression. Hawk's arrogance irritated her. Perhaps his reaction was a defensive one. She made a mental note to consult Amy and Georgette when they were alone.

Beaufort held the coin up for her inspection. Then he placed the coin in his other palm, closed his hand, and held his fist out to her. She obligingly tapped his hand. When he revealed his empty palm, she cried out, "Where are you hiding it?"

Beaufort reached toward her ear with his other hand and produced the coin. She let out a peal of laughter, and everyone clapped, with the exception of Hawk.

"You must teach me," she said to Beaufort.

"Very well. The magic involves sleight of hand." He positioned the coin between her fingertip and thumb. "Now, the trick occurs when you transfer the coin to your other hand."

"Show me."

"As you pass the coin to your other palm, keep your forefinger straight and close your two middle fingers. He bent her fingers to demonstrate. "Let the coin rest between your two fingers as you pull away."

She tried, but dropped the coin.

He retrieved it. "The motion is similar to snapping your fingers," Beaufort said. "You must be quick. Try again. I'll help you."

As he manipulated her fingers, Hawk cleared his throat. "That is quite enough sleight of hand for one evening."

She frowned at Hawk. How dare he object? They were only having fun. "I wish to practice."

"You've had enough practice," Hawk growled.

Beaufort stepped away. "Perhaps another time."

"Oh, there is Mrs. Rankin." Hester hefted herself out of her chair. "Excuse me, but I promised to call on her this evening."

After Hester retreated, Julianne whispered to Georgette, "I need your advice for the pamphlet. Agree to my suggestion."

Georgette smiled and nodded.

Julianne regarded Amy with a speaking look. "Amy, will you come with us to the retiring room?"

"Yes, of course," she said.

Hawk retrieved his watch and regarded her with a stern expression. "You will return promptly, I'm sure."

He'd meant it as a warning. She refused to let him spoil her evening and decided to ignore him. Instead, she turned her attention to the five cubs. "Do you mind very much if I take my leave of you?"

"We'll wait for you," Beaufort said.

When the other gentlemen agreed, she shook her head. "It is very kind of you, but please do not feel obliged," she said. "I do not wish to keep you from calling on your other friends."

Hawk instantly regretted allowing Julianne to leave the box. The devil only knew what mischief she and her crafty friends were brewing.

Her beaux huddled together, speaking in low tones. When a wicked laugh escaped Beaufort, Hawk narrowed his eyes. That cub bore watching. He'd used the magic trick as a ruse to touch Julianne. Hawk had gritted his teeth the entire time. Unless he missed his guess, Beaufort was a rake in the making.

Hawk turned and gripped the balcony rail. If his aunt had not disappeared again, he would have asked her to accompany Julianne to the retiring room. Damnation. If he'd had any idea this guardianship business would take over his life, he would have insisted his mother stay behind to sponsor Julianne. Of course, he'd never suspected a hellion lurked beneath her sweet façade.

He retrieved his watch. She'd been gone only ten minutes. He'd give her fifteen more minutes, and then he would go in search of her. While he couldn't boldly knock on the retiring room door, he could send a servant to fetch her. And if she wasn't there, he would make her pay for deceiving him. Hawk regarded the restless cubs over his shoulder. The besotted fools obviously meant to stay until Julianne returned. Hawk decided to take pity on them. "You've waited long enough. I'll give the ladies your regrets."

Their rumbling voices dwindled as they left the box. Osgood lagged behind and then stopped at the entrance until his friends disappeared.

Hawk let out an exasperated sigh. "Osgood, you'll not impress the ladies by waiting. Go join your friends."

The young man turned around, his expression anxious. Then he cleared his throat. "Sir, I hoped you c-could advise me."

"Hawk," he said.

"Yes, sir." Osgood's face reddened. "I mean Hawk."

Hawk sighed inwardly. "I'm not in the habit of doling out advice. Ask your father."

Osgood shuffled up to him. "I can't. He'd cane me."

"If you've racked up gaming debts, you'd better confess to your papa. And don't go to the moneylenders. The ruinous interest will make matters far worse," he said.

"It's not about gaming," Osgood said. "I need advice about...w-women."

"If this is about my ward, you'd best forget her. She has no interest in forming an attachment."

Osgood tugged at his cravat. "I have the greatest respect for Lady Julianne, but..."

Hawk's patience was wearing thin. "Just spit it out."

Osgood glanced over his shoulder as if checking for nonexistent eavesdroppers. When he returned his attention to Hawk, he spoke in an undertone. "You've a reputation as a legendary lover. I hoped you could advise me how to solicit a c-courtesan."

Lord help him. "How old are you?"

"Two and twenty next month," he mumbled. "It's dashed embarrassing. The other fellows boast about their conquests." He scuffed the toe of his shoe. "I've never... you know."

Hawk thought of that raucous party he'd attended long ago, but shoved the memory aside. "Braggarts often lie or exaggerate," he said. "I doubt your allowance is sufficient to set up a mistress."

Osgood blushed again. "How do I go about...getting experience?"

"The only reason you came to me is because you're feeling pressured to compete with your peers. That's a bad reason to climb into bed with a woman."

He hung his head. "The other gents are ribbing me."

Osgood was too sensitive for his own good. "They will continue to bully you if you don't grow a tough hide. Learn the art of a raised brow and a bored look."

"It won't help. They know." His jaw worked. "I mean to do something about it."

"What do you plan to do? Have a quick tryst with a street prostitute in an alleyway? If you think that will make you feel manly, you're wrong. It's a filthy business." He'd never sunk that low but feared Osgood might.

The young man winced.

Hawk silently cursed, knowing if he said the wrong thing, he'd crush the lad. "Don't rush your fences."

"You think I should wait until I'm older," Osgood muttered.

I don't want you to regret the first time. "In the next couple of years, you'll mature physically and be more confident. Women will take notice."

Osgood regarded him with a dubious expression.

"They'll make their interest clear, but stay away from other men's wives, unless you want to risk getting shot. An experienced widow will teach you. But don't mistake lust for tender emotions. Enjoy the liaison and make a graceful exit before it grows tedious."

Osgood blew out his breath as if he were relieved.

Then Hawk advised him where to purchase sheep-gut condoms to prevent disease and other undesirable consequences.

"Thank you, sir. I mean Hawk."

"If your friends ask, we were discussing fencing," he said. "I've got a bad reputation to maintain."

After Osgood left, Hawk again gripped the balcony railing and thought of all the things he'd not told the cub. That he'd be scared. That he'd probably humiliate himself. That in the wrong circumstances, a woman might take advantage of him.

The cub was too impressionable. He was likely to cave under pressure. The thought made Hawk's stomach churn.

He'd done what he could to dissuade the young man. The rest was up to Osgood. One way or the other, he'd learn to stand up for himself.

Hawk's gaze strayed to the pit below. People were returning to their seats. Frowning, he took out his watch. Bloody hell. Julianne had been gone for three-quarters of an hour. He strode out of the box, swearing he'd make her pay dearly for defying him again.

"I think Hawk is jealous of your beaux," Georgette whispered.

Julianne sat with her friends on a settee in the retiring room and started to speak, but held her tongue until a group of younger, giggling girls walked past. "Hawk is only watching me because he thinks I'm too flirtatious."

"He seemed displeased when Beaufort taught you the magic trick," Georgette said.

"Nothing I do pleases Hawk," she said.

"You said you need help with the pamphlet. Are you almost finished?" Georgette asked.

"No, I'm about halfway done. I've got to write faster if I'm to publish the pamphlet in a timely manner," she said.

Amy's red-gold brows furrowed. "Julianne, I know Lady Rutledge said she could hide your identity. But are you sure?"

"Stop being a ninny," Georgette said. "Julianne, perhaps you could include advice about dancing."

Julianne wafted her fan. "What should I say?"

"Mama said I should never accept more than one dance from a gentleman," Georgette said.

"Excellent," Julianne said. "If a lady dances more than one dance with a gentleman, he is liable to conclude he's already caught her."

Georgette nodded. "And then he might want to throw her back, like a fish."

Amy laughed. "Georgette, that is silly."

"Hester said men love the chase," Julianne said. "So we have to be seemingly unobtainable."

"But what if that doesn't draw their interest?" Georgette said.

"Hester suggested giving gentlemen a come-hither look," Julianne said. "Of course, a proper lady must keep a gentleman at arm's length."

Georgette twirled a blond curl around her finger. "Should you not call it a *seductive* look? After all, the pamphlet is called *The Secrets of Seduction*."

"Georgette, you're absolutely right," Julianne said.

Amy snapped her fan closed. "Have you lost your wits? There is nothing proper about such risqué advice."

Georgette regarded Julianne with a sly smile. "Perhaps you should practice your seductive look on Hawk—to test it for the pamphlet."

Her face flamed. Even though she'd vowed only to get revenge, she'd been unable to put his heated kisses and touches from her mind. Every night, she'd tossed and turned in bed, recalling the wicked sensations he'd aroused in her. She'd never guessed passion could be so thrilling. Heaven help her. She was a wanton.

Georgette studied her. "Why are you blushing?"

She fanned her face. "It is warm in here."

Georgette looked about and then returned her gaze to Julianne. "Did he kiss you?" she whispered.

Julianne tried to control her reaction but knew she'd failed when Georgette gasped.

"He *kissed* you," Georgette said. "I can tell by the look on your face."

"Swear to me you will say nothing," Julianne said. "I cannot afford for my brother to find out."

"You have our word," Georgette said, excitement in her voice.

Amy's eyes widened. "Oh my goodness."

Julianne eyed the last of the ladies leaving the retiring room. When the maid approached, Julianne assured her they had no need of her services.

After the maid retreated through a connecting door, Georgette turned to Julianne. "Now the coast is clear. Tell us everything."

"The day after the Beresford's ball, we had a terrible row," Julianne said. "And then one thing led to another."

"I'm so envious," Georgette said. "You must describe every detail. Did your knees grow weak? Did your heart race?"

She nodded but thought better of telling her friends that she'd allowed him indecent liberties far beyond a mere kiss.

Amy regarded her with concern. "It's dangerous to meddle with a man, especially a rake like him."

"I know, Amy. Trust me. I'll not let him kiss me again. All I care about is seeing the pamphlet published." She considered telling her friends about her vengeance plan, but she knew it would only worry Amy.

"I fear you are putting your reputation in peril," Amy said.

"I risk nothing," Julianne said. "I will keep matters firmly under my control."

Amy sighed. "Please be careful."

"I will."

"We should return, Julianne. We've been gone quite a while," Amy said.

"Why should she jump to do Hawk's bidding?" Georgette said.

Julianne stood and shook out her skirts. "No, Amy is right. I had better return before he thinks of even more rules."

The door opened. Sally Shepherd rushed inside, her chest heaving as tears spilled down her round face.

Julianne hurried over to her. "Sally, whatever is the matter?"

Sally covered her face. "Elizabeth is s-so c-cruel."

Julianne put her arm around Sally's shoulder and led her to the settee.

Amy produced a handkerchief from her reticule and patted Sally's shoulder. "Do not worry. You are among friends."

After Sally mopped her tears, Amy encouraged her to divulge what had happened. Sally's voice caught several times as she described the way Elizabeth and Henrietta had mocked her in the foyer. "When I walked past, Elizabeth said in a loud voice that my gown made me look fat. Then the other girls made fun of my name by making sheep s-sounds."

"Those horrid girls," Georgette said. "I've a mind to go downstairs and give them the set-down they deserve."

"You'll only make matters worse," Amy said. "If you give them ammunition, you will just encourage them. They enjoy nothing more than tearing others apart."

"Are you advocating we do nothing?" Georgette said.

"Amy is right," Julianne said. "If we provoke Elizabeth and her friends, they will seek out Sally at every opportunity. The best thing is to ignore them."

"I tried that last year to no avail," Georgette said. "You know how horribly they treated both Amy and me. Elizabeth and her friends will torment Sally all season if we do not stand up to them."

"I cannot bear it," Sally said.

"You are welcome to be our friend," Julianne said.

Sally sniffed. "I would like that very much."

"I have an idea," Julianne said. "We will go to the foyer and show those mean girls that Sally is not friendless. We will not, however, lower ourselves to speak to them."

"But the silent message will be very clear," Georgette said.

"Julianne, I like your plan, but you are late already," Amy said. "You do not wish to incite Hawk's anger."

She shrugged. "He's undoubtedly already angry. What difference will a few more minutes make? All of you will come with me to the box afterward, and I'll explain what happened."

"A perfect plan," Georgette said. "Sally, are you ready?"

She nodded. "Thank you. I don't feel so alone anymore."

"We understand," Georgette said. "If it weren't for Amy and Julianne, I could not have borne to stay in the duke's courtship last year."

Sally hung her head. "I do not deserve your friendship. Last year, I heard all of Elizabeth's plans to make you quit the courtship." Sally swallowed. "I didn't like them, but Mama warned me to say nothing lest I jeopardize my chances in the courtship."

Georgette took Sally's arm. "We know you were never cruel to anyone, unlike some of those other girls who followed Elizabeth's example."

As they descended the stairs, many guests were returning to their boxes, but a crowd still milled around the foyer. While they walked along, Julianne thought about all that Georgette and Amy had withheld from her last year. They had not wanted to take advantage of her because of Tristan's courtship. She'd not learned the full extent of what had happened behind the scenes until the day after her brother's betrothal ball.

"There they are in the center of the room," Georgette said.

Sally worried her hands. "Oh, I do not wish to see them."

"Hold your head high like a queen," Julianne said. "We will walk past and pretend not to notice them."

When they drew parallel, Elizabeth's voice rang out. "Oh, look, the wallflowers are taking a stroll."

"I should dearly love to box her ear," Georgette muttered.

"Ignore them," Amy said.

"Poor Julianne," Elizabeth said, projecting her voice. "I wonder how she manages to hide her heartbreak."

Red-hot anger sizzled through Julianne's veins. She halted momentarily, wanting to put Elizabeth in her place once and for all, but Amy's gentle voice forestalled her.

"Do not let her draw you in," Amy said. "A confrontation will only make her more determined."

Julianne drew in her breath. "It is very hard to do nothing."

"Others are looking at her askance," Amy said, peering over her shoulder. "She is her own worst enemy."

"What drives her to such cruelty?" Georgette asked.

"If she were assured of herself, she would not bully others," Amy said.

"I always thought her conceited and haughty," Georgette said.

"Her only friends are those who fear becoming her victim. It is rather pathetic if you think about it," Amy said. "One day, she will pay for her cruelty, but now we must return. The next act will begin soon."

They reversed direction, climbed the stairs, and started down the corridor. Up ahead, a group of gentlemen huddled.

Georgette craned her head. "Oh, there are some of my brother's friends. They are reputed to be rakes." Her dimples showed as she grinned at Amy. "I wish a rake would kiss me."

"Hush," Amy said. "You don't want them to hear you."

Sally giggled. "She is teasing you."

"Hah!" Julianne said. "Georgette is perfectly serious."

As they drew closer, hearty masculine laughter erupted. Julianne's curiosity got the better of her. She glanced at them out of the corner of her eye, only to meet the gaze of a tall, dark-haired man. She looked away and flinched when she heard the man speak.

"I say, is that not Hawk's ward?"

"Leave her be, Archdale," one of the other men said. "She's not for the likes of you."

"I cannot resist this opportunity," Archdale said.

Then he stepped right into Julianne's path and bowed. "Lady Julianne, this is a surprise."

Archdale's friends watched with guarded expressions.

Julianne lifted her brows. "Sir, have we been introduced?"

"It grieves me to think you would have forgotten," he said. "But where is your guardian?"

She didn't like the wicked gleam in his bloodshot eyes. "I beg your pardon?"

Archdale laughed. "I'd marked you as a sweet little confection. Have you escaped the nest, little chick?"

"You are mistaken, my lord. I am neither dessert nor poultry," she said.

When Georgette giggled, Amy elbowed her.

"You have a tart tongue, Lady Julianne," Archdale said. "I daresay you are leading Hawk a merry dance."

Amy snapped her fan closed, drawing his attention.

"Your friend disapproves of me," he said. "But I wager you like a bit of fun, don't you, Lady Julianne?"

She looked at him warily. His bold manners intimidated her more than she'd like to admit.

He drew closer and flashed a crooked smile. "Do I frighten you, little one?"

"No. Do I scare you?" The moment the words flew from her mouth, a hand grasped her arm, eliciting a squeak from her.

"Julianne, you and your friends will come with me," Hawk said in a deadly calm voice.

Her heart raced as she saw the murderous glare he turned on Archdale. A slim man with thinning brown hair urged Archdale to step aside. Hawk said nothing else as he led them past.

Hawk gritted his teeth as he led Julianne and her witless friends down the corridor. She'd been gone almost an hour, and then he'd found her flirting with that roué Archdale. Clearly, she'd not taken his warning seriously, but before this night ended, she would pay for testing his will again.

He stopped outside his aunt's box and watched until Georgette, Sally, and Amy disappeared from sight. Then he took Julianne by the shoulders. "My aunt and her friend Peckham are inside. You will keep quiet. Do you understand?"

"Hawk—"

He tightened his fingers on her shoulders. "Not a word."

Her throat worked, but she said nothing.

When he led her inside, his aunt turned. "Ah, there you are at last. The curtain is rising."

Peckham rose and bowed.

Hawk had no intention of sitting through the rest of the play. "Julianne is weary, Aunt. I regret we must leave."

"I'm sorry, my dear," Hester said. "I hope you are not ill."

"No, only a bit tired," Julianne said. "But I do not wish to interfere with your enjoyment of the play. I'm sure I'll recover once it begins."

A muscle in Hawk's cheek twitched. "But you are fatigued."

Hester regarded Mr. Peckham. "You will excuse me. I must see to Julianne."

"Of course," he said.

"Hester, I do not wish to spoil the play for you," Julianne said. "Hawk may escort me home now, and perhaps Mr. Peckham would be kind enough to bring you home in his carriage when the play concludes."

Hawk narrowed his eyes. He'd meant to include his aunt in a discussion about Julianne's latest incident. Obviously, Julianne had maneuvered matters, thinking to outwit him by escaping inside his aunt's house.

"Are you sure, dear?" Hester asked, concern in her voice.

Julianne nodded. "Oh, yes, a good night's sleep will see me restored."

"You must rest," Hester said to Julianne. "I will check on you later."

When Hawk escorted Julianne out into the corridor, he glared at her. "Not a single word until we are in the carriage," he said. "You don't want to cross me again."

Chapter Ten

*A Lady's Secrets of Seduction: Tell the truth,
but you need not reveal everything.*

The cool wind blew Julianne's pelisse about as they walked to the carriage. "I know I was late, but I can explain."

"Hold your tongue," he gritted out.

His harsh expression chilled her.

After he handed her into the carriage, she scrambled to the seat and huddled next to the window. He followed and sat right beside her. The footman closed the door, and moments later, Hawk knocked his cane on the ceiling.

When the carriage lurched into motion, he turned on her. "You lied to my aunt."

"I did not want to spoil the play for her." She thought better of telling Hawk she'd not wanted to keep Hester from Mr. Peckham. As far as she could discern, Hawk was oblivious to his aunt's feelings for her gentleman friend.

"You thought to evade the consequences," he said.

"Once again, you have jumped to conclusions before hearing me out," she said.

"What were you doing talking to that rake?" he snapped.

"He waylaid us."

"Don't lie. You planned your little excursion, because you wanted to provoke me."

"I wanted to speak to my friends privately," she said. "And then Sally—"

"I don't want to hear your excuses. You were gone nearly an hour."

She glared at him. "How would you feel if I had power over you? How would you feel if I told you where you could go, to whom you could speak, with whom you could dance?" She put her fist to her heart. "You have made me your prisoner."

"So mistreated," he said, his voice full of sarcasm. "Not that you give any thought to the feelings of others."

"That is not true," she cried.

"Oh, yes, it is. You purposely told those young men not to wait for you, knowing damned well they would."

Her jaw dropped. "You think I meant to play games with them?"

"We both know you hoped they would wait, and then you went looking for trouble."

"Your accusations are groundless," she said, her voice rising. "They are my friends, and I would never mistreat them."

"You think you can lead men on a merry chase without consequences, but one day it will catch up to you."

Her throat clogged. "I have never knowingly misled any man."

He huffed. "Twelve men have proposed to you. And you expect me to believe you were entirely innocent?"

"I have never given false hope to any man."

"You won't again on my watch," he said.

"Why do men always blame women, when we have so little power?"

"You have wielded your feminine power since the day you made your come-out," he said.

"You have no idea what women suffer at the hands of men," she said. "We have almost no control over our destinies. Our very futures rely solely on our ability to attract a husband."

"We both know you're not interested in marriage right now."

Because he'd spoiled all her dreams and humiliated her. "You've made it abundantly clear that you loathe your role as my guardian. I wish you had refused," she muttered.

"I did it as a favor to your brother. He made special arrangements so that you could enjoy the season. And you have taken advantage of his absence. If he were here, you never would have dared to flout the proprieties."

She winced because there was enough truth in what he'd said to make her feel guilty. But none of this would have happened if her brother had come to London. "I wasn't flouting the proprieties. We went to the foyer because Elizabeth said cruel things to Sally, and we wanted to show that she wasn't friendless."

"Obviously, you think me an easy mark."

"You have no idea what I think." Of course, she would

never admit he'd crushed her, hurt her so much she didn't know how she would ever be able to risk her heart again. "If I had known you would dictate my every move, I would have begged to stay with one of my friends."

"That brings me to the central problem. I cannot sweep your actions under the rug again. But since you object to me telling you what to do, I shall give you a choice."

She regarded him with suspicion.

"Choice number one," he said. "I take you home to your brother. Then *you* will explain what necessitated this action."

She wanted to throttle him.

"Choice number two," he continued. "You will stay home for an entire week. You will decline all of your invitations. You will receive no one. To ensure you abide by the rules, I will periodically call at different times to check on you. One infraction and you start the week over again."

"May I remind you that you are not my parent," she said, her voice rising.

"No, I'm your guardian. The choice is up to you."

"You know very well it is no choice."

"It's the best offer you're going to get," he said.

She held her wrists out. "Go on. Shackle me."

He laughed, damn him.

The carriage rolled to a halt. "Hawk, you know it is unreasonable to make me stay home. Others will question my absence."

"I'll put it about that you're indisposed," he said.

Use your wiles on him. She laid her hand on his arm. "Please."

"Sorry, Julie-girl. I warned you there would be no more chances, and you chose to test my resolve."

After the driver opened the door and let down the steps, Hawk descended and handed Julianne down. Then he escorted her to the house. When Henderson, the butler, opened the door, she started to pull away, but he smiled at her. "I'm coming inside."

"Why?" she said.

"Because I wish to spend more time with you."

She narrowed her eyes, knowing he had something up his sleeve.

After they shed their outer wraps, he took her arm and led her toward the stairs. She glanced sideways at him. "You don't trust me."

"Whatever gave you that impression?"

"I wish to retire. You may go home," she said.

He shook his head and started up the stairs. "Not until my aunt returns."

"If you wish to admire the mummy in the drawing room, be my guest. I am for bed," she said.

"No, you will entertain me," he said. "You can start by telling me the real reason you decided to leave the box tonight."

"What difference does it make?"

"It might to you. If you tell the truth, I might give you an early reprieve. One day for the absolute truth."

"I already told you I wished to speak to my friends privately."

"I'm afraid that response is not good enough. In order to shave off one day of confinement, you must confess what you spoke about."

"Balls, bonnets, and beaux," she said.

"I may add an extra day for lying," he said as they reached the landing.

"You may go to the devil," she muttered.

He opened the drawing room door. "I probably will."

She whipped past him.

When the door clicked shut, he said, "Ring for your maid."

"Do you think I wish to expose our argument to a servant?"

"It wouldn't be necessary if you hadn't manipulated my aunt."

Fuming, she marched past him. "It's not as if we haven't been alone before." She flounced onto the sofa and kicked off her slippers.

He watched her with a bemused smile. "Nice stockings. Are they perchance silk?"

"I'm sure you're well acquainted with lady's undergarments."

He joined her on the sofa. She moved over. He followed. She moved again, right next to the rolled arm. He slid over, crowding her. Exasperated, she started to rise, but he caught her arm and tugged her back.

"You are irritating me." She pointed at the sofa directly across from them. "Sit over there."

"I prefer close proximity during interrogations," he said.

"What next? Torture?"

"You will answer my questions. No prevaricating, no diversions, no sassy remarks. Did you even go to the retiring room?"

"Yes."

"Why?" he asked. "And this time, I want the truth."

She couldn't tell him about the pamphlet, but she recalled Georgette's words and inspiration struck. "When

Beaufort tried to show me how to perform the magic trick, I couldn't help but notice your disapproval."

Hawk folded his arms over his chest. "What does that have to do with your departure?"

"I didn't understand why you objected, so I decided to discuss it with my friends in the retiring room. Georgette thought you were jealous, but I told her that was ridiculous. After all, you are my guardian."

"Why do I suspect there is more to the tale? Ah, I forgot. You also took a little tour of the foyer, or so you said. All I know for certain is that you chose to flirt with Archdale."

"I don't know why you even bother asking me for the truth when you don't believe anything I say," she said.

"Because you've given me ample cause to distrust you."

A startling realization occurred to her as she stared at him. "You won't forgive my mistakes, but I forgave you."

He reared back as if she'd slapped him.

She leaned toward him. "You don't care about me. All that matters to you is discharging your duty to my brother."

He shook his head. "How can you say that when we've been friends all these years?"

"I don't know what to believe of you anymore." She'd adored him as a little girl and loved him for making her laugh when she was sad. He'd been like a knight in shining armor during her youth when she'd felt the horror of knowing her very birth had disappointed her father. Because she was an unwanted girl.

"Believe this," he said. "I tried to refuse your brother's request because I didn't think I was a suitable guardian. But I agreed because he is like a brother to me."

She averted her face so that he would not see the pain

his unspoken words inflicted upon her. *Lady Julianne is practically a sister to me.*

He released a loud sigh. "I did it for your sake as well. I wanted you to enjoy the season. And I suppose I'm partially to blame, because I've encouraged you in mischief for years. As it is, I am keeping secrets from your brother, because I don't want him to worry. Quite frankly, I resent that you've put me in this position."

What he'd really meant was that he resented having to give up his raking to guard her. He was probably elated at the prospect of regaining his freedom temporarily while she was restricted to his aunt's home. No doubt he meant to spend his nights with a brazen hussy.

Pain flared again, making her furious with herself for caring. But the thought of him in bed with another woman burned.

"Julianne, you will abide by the restriction for the coming week," he said.

Why should she make this easy for him? Thus far, she'd failed miserably to make him want her, with the notable exception of that one kiss. But she would turn the tables on him, starting tonight. "Yes, I understand," she said. "But I am a bit confused."

His eyes narrowed. "About what?"

"Earlier, you claimed I purposely lured gentlemen, but I never knowingly misled them. I only wished to be nice. Obviously, my ignorance is a problem."

"I will protect you," he said. "All you have to do is cooperate."

"But you cannot be with me every hour of every day," she said. "Is it not true that rakes are very cunning? One of them might wait for the perfect opportunity to approach me, which is what happened tonight. Not long ago, you saw the way Ramsey cornered me in Lady Morley's dining room—right under your very nose."

"Are you suggesting I failed you?"

"No, but I am in need of an education. Since you are my guardian *and* an expert on rakes, you are the perfect person to teach me their tricks."

"Let me see if I have this correct. You want me to teach you how to spot a rake?"

She nodded. "Yes, for my own protection."

"What do you want me to say? Beware the red devils sporting horns and forked tails?"

"No, silly. I want you to teach me what rakes say and do to lure their victims. It may require a demonstration on your part." Naturally she must remain unresponsive, but if all went well, he would have trouble resisting her.

"A demonstration?" he said.

"Yes. For educational purposes only."

An arrested expression crossed his face. "You want *me* to seduce *you*?"

"Pretend to seduce me." She smiled. "Since my activities are restricted for the next week, the timing is perfect for my lessons."

"I agree your ignorance is problematic. Certainly, it has led you into more than one scrape," he said.

Triumph surged through her veins. She had him in the palm of her hand. "Given the urgency of the matter, I believe we should begin immediately," she said.

Her heart pounded as he turned to her and lowered his head until his breath whispered over her lips. She'd sworn to keep her desire firmly under control, but she found it difficult when his scent made her dizzy with longing.

His eyes darkened. "You are an eager pupil."

She held her breath, certain he meant to kiss her.

"The forbidden excites you, doesn't it?"

She dared not admit it.

He pinned her wrists against the sofa. A thrilling sensation shot through her. She ought to protest, but she didn't. Because secretly, she liked the way he held her captive.

"You want to flirt with a little danger," he said.

I want to be naughty.

When his gaze dropped to her breasts, her nipples tightened. She wanted to yield to him, wanted him to kiss and touch her again.

"I admit I find your request diverting," he said, his voice rumbling.

Alarm pierced through the sensual haze in her brain.

He turned his head slightly, until his breath tickled her ear. "But there will be no seduction lessons, pretend or otherwise."

He'd meant to teach her a lesson, but he'd come dangerously close to falling for his own ruse. The seductive words he'd spoken had left him half aroused.

The devil. He'd almost kissed her again.

"Let me go," she hissed.

When he released her wrists, she bounded off the sofa and pointed at him as if he were one of his aunt's spaniels. "Stay."

He chuckled and knew he'd succeeded in inflaming her temper when she marched off to the bookcase. She selected a volume and padded over to the sofa across from him. After plumping a cushion, she reclined with her feet on the sofa. Clearly, she'd no idea that in her current position, her flimsy skirts revealed the dimensions of one of her slim thighs. Naturally, he imagined pressing her legs wide, raising her skirts, and exploring her soft folds... making her wet and ready for him.

Hawk shifted on the sofa as his cock stirred. He'd better distract himself. What better way than to tease her? "What are you reading?"

"*Sense and Sensibility*."

"What is it about?" he asked.

She kept her gaze on the novel. "Women who have very little control over their destinies."

"Sounds melancholy," he said.

"The ladies triumph in spite of adversity."

"Are there any rakes?" he asked, hoping to provoke her.

She kept her gaze on the novel. "As a matter of fact, there is one. Poor Marianne falls for Willoughby's wiles. He gives her every expectation that he is in love with her, and then he crushes all her hopes."

"Perhaps he will reform and offer to marry her." That sort of fairy tale would likely appeal to Julianne.

"No, there is a twist in the plot," she said.

"How do you know?"

"I've read it before. Now be quiet," she said.

"Why would you read it again? You already know what happens." Damn, he'd never understand women.

"I adore the story and wish to experience it again. Stop interrupting me."

He thoroughly enjoyed needling her. "But I have nothing to do."

"Go home," she said.

"Not until my aunt returns."

She made an exasperated sound and sat up. "Obviously, you need something to occupy you."

As she marched over to the bookcase again, he admired her bottom through the outline of her skirts. Naturally he imagined sliding his hands down to her derriere so he could press her against his swelling erection. Lord, he'd better think of something dull before she noticed. Such as books about ladies triumphing over adversity.

She selected another book and brought it to him. The overwhelming temptation to pull her onto his lap gripped him, but he didn't dare.

"Read this," she said in a supercilious tone. "You might learn something about women."

"*Pride and Prejudice*? Are there are any rakes in this one?"

"Yes. George Wickham is very bad."

Clearly Julianne had an unhealthy obsession with bad men. "What does Wickham do that is so awful?" he asked.

"Read it and find out," she said. "And for heaven's sake, do keep quiet."

After she returned to the sofa, he opened the novel and read the first page. "The author has a razor-sharp wit."

"You're talking again," she said in an irritated voice.

He continued reading. After a few moments, he glanced over at her. She was thoroughly engrossed in her novel, but of course he couldn't pass up another opportunity to bedevil her. "Miss Elizabeth Bennett reminds me of you."

"Thank you. I shall take that as a compliment."

"This Darcy fellow is a regular prig," he said.

"He redeems himself in the end."

"Bingley, on the other hand, is too cheerful and likes everyone on the spot. A man of his age and consequence ought to be more cautious in his opinions."

"For the last time, be quiet," she said.

Hawk stretched out his legs and continued reading. His cock settled down enough that he could concentrate on the story. He thought the novel would be more interesting if the narrator focused more on Darcy. There was far too much emphasis on the relationship between the two elder sisters, which he found tedious. But he kept reading, mostly because he wanted to see how the author portrayed the rake. And then he would exasperate Julianne by pretending sympathy for the evil George Wickham.

A few minutes later, the sound of deep, even breathing drew his attention to Julianne. The novel lay open upon her chest. Her sweet face was turned toward him.

The room had grown a bit chilly. He thought she might be cold. After he stood, he managed to get his tight coat off. Then he crossed the room and gently removed the book. She twitched but didn't awaken. He placed his coat over her, trying not to wake her.

Her eyes opened. She looked dazed. "Hawk?" Her naturally raspy voice sounded a bit hoarse.

"You fell asleep," he murmured.

"Your coat is warm."

The clock on the mantel chimed. It was one o'clock in the morning. Where the devil was his aunt?

Julianne sat up and handed him his coat.

He struggled with the tight sleeves.

She stood. "Turn your back and let me help."

The brush of her fingers as she assisted him made

his skin tingle. When he faced her, she straightened his lapels. Something inside his chest tumbled over.

He'd kissed her. He'd touched her. He'd whispered in her ear. But for reasons he couldn't understand, her simple gesture felt far more intimate. The sort of thing a wife might do.

He thrust that thought out of his head. "I should stay until my aunt returns."

Julianne shook her head. "We're both tired. Go home."

He escorted her to the landing and watched as she ascended the stairs. Then he hurried downstairs to collect his greatcoat, hat, and gloves.

Fifteen minutes later, he walked inside the set of rooms at the Albany he'd occupied since leaving university many years ago. After his valet helped him undress, Hawk donned a banyan robe, poured himself a brandy, and looked about the spartan bedchamber. No paintings adorned the walls. The shaving stand held the usual accoutrements—brush, bottle of cologne, and razor. An untidy stack of papers and books on his desk showed the only signs that he actually lived here.

It was a refuge, but it wasn't a home.

Even though his father had died years ago, Hawk had never returned to live at Ashdown House. He managed the business of two estates from a distance, because every inch of the properties reminded him too much of his father's disappointment in him.

He knew his refusal to return home grieved his mother and angered his sisters. His brothers-in-law thought him a callous beast for abandoning his mother. But if he returned home, his mother and sisters would hound him daily to do his marital duty. He could fob them off easily on his weekly visits simply by escaping.

They had expectations of him. He was the earl, and therefore it was his duty to produce the requisite heir and spare. They didn't know he never would.

Even his brother Will, the heir presumptive, didn't know. Hawk had thought of telling his brother, but he wanted Will to remain carefree as long as possible. As years went by, his brother would guess the truth. By then, Will would be older and likely would have married.

Hawk snuffed the candles, shrugged off the banyan, and climbed into bed, staring at the dark canopy. Years ago, he'd hoped time would lessen his remorse, and though his regret was no longer acute, he could never forget. Because he could never right the wrong he'd done, and he would bear the guilt in silence always.

While he could never change the past, he would do everything in his power to ensure nothing bad ever happened to Julianne.

He wasn't, nor would he ever be, a constant man. As his father had said, men like him didn't change. And so he'd relieved the loneliness by taking mistresses. There had been many over the years, but none of his liaisons had lasted long. He'd found pleasure and given it. But as the demands for jewels and gowns inevitably increased, he'd always grown bored. The temporary comfort was an illusion. The women did what he paid them to do, until he tired of them.

He'd never thought he'd miss the lack of a wife. After all, he knew dozens of men who ignored their wives and turned to mistresses. But he'd not thought of the little things. Discussing a book late at night. And the simple, domestic gesture of a woman's hands tugging on his lapels.

For the first time, his regrets weren't for the past but for a future he would never know.

Her brief sleep in the drawing room left her restless.

He'd lured her, not with seduction but with his charm. She'd pretended to be annoyed with his teasing while they had read. She'd thought she'd succeeded in showing her disinterest. But then he'd covered her with his coat, the coat that had still held his warmth and his scent. He'd made her believe he cared about her.

She'd been groggy when she'd offered to help him with his coat, but for those few moments, she'd forgotten he didn't want her.

Her chest ached as the knowledge pierced her heart anew. She could no longer deny that she still held lingering feelings for him. But those feelings confused her. She didn't know what she wanted anymore, but she knew what she didn't want. A man who did not love her.

A long-forgotten memory crept into her brain. She couldn't remember how old she'd been, only that she'd been a little girl and hiding by a tree near the lake. Hawk had found her there, crying over the crumpled picture she'd drawn of her father. She'd tried to give it to her papa, but she'd smelled the brandy on his breath too late. He'd bellowed for a footman to summon the governess.

Hawk had held her in his arms for a while. Then he'd offered to teach her to climb a tree, something Mama had never let her do. She'd felt naughty and happy all at the same time. Hawk had helped her up the tree, and she'd trusted him not to let her fall, even though she'd been a bit afraid. She'd adored him from that moment on.

Now all her feelings for him were mixed up with the

past. Her father's rejection and now his. Her mother and brother had showered her with love, but somehow it never seemed enough.

The prospect of ever opening her heart to a man again scared her witless. She would never let another man trample her heart. Because she did not want to be like her mother, pining for a man who would hurt her again and again.

But she could not remain dependent on her brother much longer. Tristan had married, and now his wife, Tessa, was the duchess. In a short time, their first child would enter the world. They were starting their own family.

Julianne knew she would feel like an outsider, but that was nothing new. She'd felt it almost from the beginning of their marriage. Of course they had treated her well, but their open affection had embarrassed her. They touched each other often and exchanged longing looks. Mama had said their love was rare.

Part of the reason Julianne had accepted Amy's invitation to travel last summer was to give Tristan and Tessa privacy after their recent marriage. But then she'd returned home only to learn about the babe.

At first, she'd been excited, but soon she'd grown envious because Mama had clucked over Tessa like a mother hen. All anyone talked about was Tessa's nausea, how she must eat to keep up her strength, and how she must rest often. Julianne had felt ignored and resented her sister-in-law. And she'd felt guilty, too, because she knew Tessa had lost all her family and had been alone for many years.

But it was Tessa who had convinced her brother and mother to let Julianne participate in the season. Tessa had helped her pack and said she knew Julianne would be the belle of the ball. And she'd made Julianne promise to write every week.

The memory shamed her. She was fortunate to have a loving family. When her eyes blurred with tears, she swiped them away. Tristan had brought her to London so she could participate in the season. She'd known how reluctant he'd been to leave Tessa. While he never said anything, Julianne knew he worried about Tessa's health and the impending birth.

Julianne looked deep into her heart and knew her petty jealousy had stemmed from her own fears that Tessa was replacing her in her family's hearts. Her fears were groundless, but she'd always felt the need for reassurance. Because no matter how much they loved her, she would always feel like the unwanted daughter.

She'd come to London determined to give Hawk her heart, but she'd given it to him years ago. She'd failed to win her father's love, so she had set out to capture the heart of the man who had rescued her when she was a little girl.

He didn't even realize he'd hurt her at that ball. As long as she was being completely honest with herself, she might as well admit the truth. She'd done the same thing to those twelve gentlemen who had proposed to her. Over the years, she'd told herself repeatedly that a little flirting never hurt anyone. But even though she'd not set out to wound those men, she'd done it nevertheless.

She'd persuaded herself that Hawk had purposely misled her. In retrospect, she knew she'd made him out to be a heartless cad to protect her bruised heart. He cared about her, but he didn't love her.

Outside the door, a floorboard creaked, signaling someone was walking along the corridor. The sound of a door closing made Julianne frown. She sat up, found the tinderbox, and lit a candle. When she held the candle closer to the clock, she saw it was four o'clock in the morning. She suspected Hester and Mr. Peckham were lovers at long last.

Julianne blew out the candle and lay back on the bed. Her heart ached for the dream that had sustained her over four long years. Inside, she felt empty and dispirited. All winter, she'd yearned to be in London for the festivities, and now the remaining weeks of the season made her feel bleak.

But she was not without purpose. Her heart beat faster as the pamphlet took on a whole new meaning for her. Up until this moment, she'd thought of it primarily in terms of getting even with reluctant bachelors. Instead, she would now focus on the positive aspects. She would help other ladies by providing the honest advice Hester had given her about men.

Chapter Eleven

A Lady's Secrets of Seduction: Guard
your heart from charmers.

"This is monstrous," Hester declared the next day after luncheon. "He cannot deny you the pleasures of the season simply because you returned late to the box. I will not allow him to run roughshod over you."

Julianne sighed. "He means to take me home if I do not cooperate. I believe him to be serious."

"We shall see about that," Hester said, bristling. "I plan to tell him in no uncertain terms that I am in charge of you. He can go hang."

"Actually, I think there is a benefit to staying home. If I receive visitors today and attend entertainments, I shall have no time to write. This week at home will allow me to complete the pamphlet. We still need to see about publication, and if I dally, it will all be for naught. As you said,

I must see it circulated early in the season if the plan is to work."

"Well, I agree, but I still feel he has gone too far," Hester said.

"*You* should still attend entertainments," Julianne said. "There is no reason for you to stay behind when I will be spending all of my time writing."

"Provided my hardheaded nephew doesn't command all of your time when he calls," she said.

"I imagine he will be only too happy to spend his time at his club." Of course, she didn't add her suspicion that he would likely seek a mistress, but Hester had no illusions about men in general or her nephew specifically.

A maid appeared at the door with two more posies, making a total of five bouquets. The butler, Henderson, followed. "As you instructed, I turned away the gentlemen callers, my lady."

"Who called?" Hester asked.

"The five young men who typically visit. They sent the posies." He cleared his throat. "I have also brought the mail."

With a sinking feeling, Julianne watched the maid set the flowers in vases. Oh, dear, what if the five cubs, as Hawk called them, had developed a *tendre* for her? Shame burned through her as she recalled the way she'd flirted and danced with them—all in an effort to show the ton she no longer cared for Hawk.

Hawk had been right. She had mistreated them. Never again, she swore. The next time she saw them, she must make it clear that she only wanted friendship.

Hester sifted through the mail. "Ah, here are two letters for you, Julianne."

She tore open the first one from her mother and

winced. Mama had received correspondence from Lady Durmont, who had described Julianne's waltz with Hawk in vivid detail.

Julianne gritted her teeth. Lady Durmont was the worst gossip in the ton. She delighted in ripping others to shreds. With a huff, Julianne continued reading. She could almost hear her mother's terse voice. The waltz was unseemly enough, it seemed, but drawing a crowd was a severe faux pas. However, her mother had received a letter from Lady Boswood that had given her some peace of mind. Mama was relieved to learn Hawk had publicly proclaimed that Julianne was his ward.

Drat it all. Had every dragon in the ton written to her mother? But guilt flooded her chest immediately. She had done far worse than waltz since coming to London. She'd risked her reputation the night she'd drunk all that wine. As Amy had said, they were very lucky to have escaped worse consequences. But that was nothing compared to the way she'd let Hawk touch and kiss her. Thank God no one had caught them.

She turned the page. Alarm gripped her upon learning Tessa had developed irregular tightening sensations in her belly. Mama said these were caused by false labor and were common. The physician had stated that provided the sensations stopped when Tessa walked, they did not signal the onset of labor.

Julianne's shoulders slumped with relief for Tessa. She quickly sent up a prayer for her sister-in-law's health and continued reading.

Naturally, your brother is beside himself with worry, as you might imagine. Therefore, I have reluctantly decided not to inform him of your lapse in judgment. You will, of course, abide strictly by the proprieties for the remainder of the season.

How could she have been so thoughtless? Poor Tristan was probably beside himself with worry about Tessa, and she'd come perilously close to bringing scandal upon herself and her family. She resolved to be more mindful of the proprieties and turned the page.

There is another matter that came as a surprise to me, of which I have pondered over at some length. Lady Boswood informed me that her son has developed a tendre *for you. While the age difference is somewhat of a concern, I would not be averse to the match. As the son of a marquess, Ramsey is most eligible, and his family is one of the most preeminent in the kingdom. Of course, you would have to endure Lady Boswood's vanity, but I would not discourage you if you truly loved him.*

"Dear God, I must write to my mother immediately," Julianne said.

Hester looked up from her letter. "Whatever is the matter, dear?"

"A disaster." She told Hester about Lady Boswood's letter. "I cannot believe the woman's audacity. And to think Mama believes Ramsey is a suitable match for me. I must inform her that Ramsey is a notorious rake and that I have no tender feelings for him."

"Calm yourself," Hester said. "You have another letter. Read it first, as it may contain important news you should address in your letter."

As Julianne broke the seal, she told Hester about Tessa's false labor pains.

"I am glad to hear it is nothing serious," Hester said.

After unfolding the paper, Julianne read her brother's short letter.

You will have received our mother's letter, but let me reassure you that all is well with Tessa and the babe. I have received a letter from Hawk and understand that you are enjoying the season. While I was a bit concerned about leaving you in London, I realized it would be unfair to make you miss the festivities. Hawk is probably far more lenient than I am, but Tessa reminds me daily that you are a grown woman now.

Julianne snorted. If only her brother knew his friend had proven to be far stricter than either he or Mama had ever been.

I hope you will forgive me when I say that I hope my little sister does not grow up too fast. Your presence is sorely missed, and I look forward to your home-coming.

Her throat clogged. She missed her brother, mother, and Tessa as well. "Hester, please excuse me. I must write to my family."

"Yes, of course, dear." Hester patted her hand. "Do not let vexation overcome you. Lady Boswood cannot force the match, and I distinctly recall your brother saying your family is in no rush to see you wed. In that respect, you are far luckier than most young ladies."

Julianne exhaled. "You are right, as always. I will write to my family, and then I will apply myself to the pamphlet."

Hester toyed with her quizzing glass. "If you have concerns about the pamphlet, say the word. You are under no obligation to finish it, though I truly believe it is impossible for anyone to trace your identity as the author."

"I've gotten this far," Julianne said. "If I can help even one lady find the man of her dreams, then I will consider my work a success." But of course she hoped to help far more than that.

Hawk did not arrive at his aunt's house until early evening. He'd spent a particularly grueling day in parliament and had dealt with problems concerning repairs to the estate in Derbyshire. With regret, he'd turned down a friend's suggestion to dine at the club, because he'd sworn to check on Julianne.

When he entered the drawing room, he found his aunt dressed in evening attire. "You are planning to go out?"

Hester regarded him through her quizzing glass. "I am not under house arrest."

"Where is Julianne?"

"Upstairs. I suppose you intend to command her to make an appearance in the drawing room," Hester said, swinging the quizzing glass on its ribbon.

He folded his arms over his chest. "I wish to speak to her."

Hester rang the bell. When a footman arrived, she sent him to bring Julianne to the drawing room.

Hawk strolled over to the sideboard and poured himself a brandy. "Where are the dogs?"

"In the kitchen," Hester said coldly.

His aunt meant to paint him as a villain. When his empty stomach rumbled, Hester let out a disgusted sigh.

"Julianne intended to dine alone in her bedchamber tonight," Hester said. "But since you're here and obviously hungry, I'll have two trays brought to the drawing room."

"Thank you. May I inquire about your plans for the evening?"

"Mr. Peckham is escorting me to the Hartford's dinner party," she said. "He should arrive shortly."

Hawk sipped his brandy. "You are spending a great deal of time with Peckham."

"Do you dare to question my friendships?"

"It was an idle observation," he said. "Frankly, I thought you would remain at home to keep Julianne company."

"You are the one who imposed the punishment upon her. I disapprove of your harsh measures, but you are her appointed guardian. Therefore, you are the one who should attend her each evening. I have no intention of rearranging my plans because of your asinine strictures."

His aunt had never been one to mince words, but he had no intention of defending his decision. He'd done what he had to do, and that was the end of it.

Julianne padded into the drawing room, curtsied, and sat on the sofa across from Hester. Hawk joined her there. "How have you occupied yourself today?"

"Writing letters to my family and friends," she said, her tone dull.

He glanced at her drawn face. "You look exhausted."

"A little rest will see me well," she said.

"I hope you're satisfied, Marc," Hester said. "You've managed to cause her undo vexation by forcing her to be a prisoner in *my* home."

Julianne sighed but said nothing.

Hawk frowned. Where was the spirited woman who matched him word for word? She seemed to have changed overnight.

Mr. Peckham arrived. Before leaving, Hester informed Julianne that she'd ordered a tray to be brought up for her and Hawk.

"You need not stay," Julianne told Hawk. "I'm sure you would prefer to dine at your club."

"I'll stay."

His aunt took Peckham's arm. "Julianne, promise me you will get extra rest tonight."

"I intend to retire early," she said.

After everyone else departed, Julianne reached for her neck.

"What is the matter?" he asked.

"I sat at the desk too long, I suppose."

"Why?"

She shrugged and winced. "I am woefully behind in my correspondences."

"Turn your back to me."

She frowned. "Why?"

"Let me massage the tight muscles."

"That is unnecessary," she mumbled.

"You're in pain. Let me help," he said.

When she turned her back, he instructed her to lower her head. He used his thumbs to knead her neck. "Tell me if I press too hard."

At first she remained tense, but gradually he could feel

her relaxing. He massaged her shoulders, and a funny little feminine sound, almost a purr, escaped her.

"Feel better?" he murmured.

"Yes," she said. "Actually marvelous."

"You mustn't push yourself to the point of exhaustion. There's no call for it."

"That feels wonderful," she said.

He worked the muscles of her back, realizing she wore short stays. Having undressed countless women, he knew this meant there was no busk. *One less hindrance,* the devil inside him whispered.

The tiny hooks on the back of her gown tempted him. He imagined releasing them and sliding the garment, along with the straps of her stays and chemise, down her arms. Then he would draw her against him, pull down the soft stays, and cup her breasts. Slow heat settled in his groin as he pictured her nipples tightening. He would draw her onto his lap and suckle her until she arched up to him, her hands tangling in his hair. Then he would draw up her gown and undergarments, exposing the dark curls. Then at long last he would explore the damp folds of her sex. He knew how to caress a woman until she shattered.

The erotic images in his head aroused him. He ought to be horsewhipped for even imagining touching her. But no matter how wrong it was, he knew he would continue to fantasize a dozen or more ways to make her writhe, to make her wet, to make her beg him to come inside her.

He forced the erotic images out of his head. "Better?" he murmured near her ear.

"Yes."

When he released her, she sat back. He hoped she wouldn't notice the bulge in his tight trousers.

"Thank you," she said.

The languid expression in her eyes made her look like a woman in the afterglow of lovemaking. He recalled her responsiveness when he'd kissed her and felt certain she would shed her inhibitions in bed. Provided the man had the expertise to arouse her slowly.

Another man, a husband, would be the one to introduce her to the pleasures of lovemaking. The thought seared his brain.

He bounded off the sofa and walked over to the faux mummy so that she wouldn't see his agitation. He couldn't let himself think about another man touching her. Soon she would marry, but not this year. He couldn't let that happen while he was her guardian, because he couldn't bear to watch. Yet, he would have to witness her take vows. Their families were close, and he could not avoid her wedding without giving insult.

He would travel out of the country. Switzerland or Paris. Perhaps India or Egypt. Some place far, far away.

"I received letters from my mother and brother today," she said.

Thank God. A safe topic. He glanced at her over his shoulder. "So that is why you spent so much time writing."

"I had to reassure my mother." Julianne paused. "She knows about our waltz and disapproves."

He stilled, imagining Tristan's anger. "I'd better write to your brother and explain we did not know it was a waltz until we reached the dance floor."

"You'll only cause trouble. Mama did not tell Tristan."

He frowned. "I'm surprised."

She told him about Tessa's false labor and the dowager duchess's wish not to alarm Tristan. "He wrote to me as well and assured me all is well. I think he didn't want me to worry."

Hawk walked over to her. "If you wish, I will take you home tomorrow."

She shook her head. "No. It is a long journey, and there are still many weeks left of Tessa's confinement."

He sat beside her. "Are you afraid for her?"

"The physician said she is in no danger. I will not borrow trouble," she said. "If we return now, it will only make it seem that we are worried, and that might increase Tristan's vexation."

He suspected Julianne did not want to be present when Tessa gave birth. Hawk figured it would only frighten her, and the devil knew he didn't want to be there. But once the babe was born, he would have to take Julianne home. He could not shirk that one last duty to her. However, he would be exchanging that duty for another—a lifetime duty as a godfather.

He couldn't think about that now.

The servants arrived, set up a small table, and lifted the covers off the dishes. It was a simple repast of ham, cheeses, bread, and fruit.

"I fear you are missing a more substantial meal at your club," Julianne said after he seated her. "Since I expected to dine alone, I didn't want to put the servants to more trouble than necessary."

He dismissed the servants and sat across from her. "I don't mind." The intimate setting was a nice change from the frenetic ton entertainments.

While he poured the wine, she prepared a plate for him. There was nothing extraordinary about her serving him, but it pleased him nevertheless. The aroma of warm, crusty bread made his stomach growl. He quickly polished off the thin slices of ham, bread, and tangy cheese.

"You're famished." She refilled his plate and added dried figs and a pear.

After they had eaten, he poured more wine for both of them. As she sipped her wine, her eyes glinted with amusement.

"What are you thinking?" he asked.

"You've forgotten I am allowed only one glass of wine or sherry."

He winked at her. "I'll make an exception tonight since it's only the two of us."

"Are you encouraging me to become inebriated?"

"Let me know when you're feeling tipsy," he said. "I don't want to find you running down the corridor again."

She smiled. "You never asked why we were running."

He leaned back in his chair. "By all means, tell me."

"You may wish to fortify yourself with more wine first," she said, sipping from her glass again.

He grinned. "In that case, I'll top up both our glasses."

They sipped companionably for a few minutes, and then she spoke. "Are you ready?"

"As I'll ever be," he said.

She drank more wine and then set her glass aside. "It involves a door."

He drained his glass. "What about the door?"

"It was thumping."

"You must have been soused if you thought the door was thumping."

Her eyes gleamed wickedly. "We heard other strange noises."

"What sort of noises?"

"I thought a rake like you would work it out."

The wine had slowed his brain. It took him a few minutes to figure out what she meant. "The devil. It was a door banger."

She clapped her hand over her mouth.

He shouldn't have let that slip. "I beg your pardon."

Her low, melodic laugh made him think of a dark bedchamber and tangled sheets.

"I ought not to have told you. The wine loosened my tongue."

"Are you finished eating?" he asked.

She nodded and rose. "Wine is very soothing, is it not?"

He glanced at her glassy eyes. "I think you've had too much."

"I'm just a little tipsy."

He led her over to the sofa and rested his arm along the back.

She grinned at him. "I told you about the door. Now it's your turn to confess something naughty."

"Since becoming your guardian, I've mended my ways."

"Hah!"

"No, it's true. I've spent all my time looking after you. My bad reputation will be in tatters after this season," he said.

"But you corrupted me tonight with the wine," she said. "So now I shall claim a boon. You must answer my questions honestly."

"You can ask. I won't promise to answer," he said.

"Is it true you have a love nest?"

He scowled. "Where the devil did you hear that?"

"The ladies' retiring room."

"Lord help us," he muttered.

"You wanted to know what women do in retiring rooms. Now you know our naughty secret." She glanced at him from beneath her lashes. "What do your mistresses do all day while you're out?"

"I do not have a mistress," he said.

"A likely tale," she said.

"The topic is unsuitable for your tender ears."

She sighed. "I always wondered how those women went about becoming famous courtesans."

He tugged on the curl by her ear. "You have an unhealthy interest in rakes and courtesans."

"Even good girls have bad thoughts," she said.

He chuckled. "What sort of bad thoughts?"

She looked at him from beneath her lashes. "You go first."

"Not a chance," he said.

"Then you must have very bad thoughts."

You have no idea. "All men have bad thoughts."

"Because of your animal passions," she said.

He burst out laughing.

"What is so funny?" she asked.

He touched her nose. "You."

She remained silent for a while. Then she turned to him with an earnest expression. "Why do bachelors put off marriage?"

He shrugged. "Freedom."

"Is that why you haven't married?" she asked.

Her question caught him off guard, but he meant to tease her in an effort to divert her. "Alas, I have not received a single marriage proposal—since the one you gave me."

"What?"

"My heart is breaking to think you have forgotten." He winked. "You were nine years old and begged me to wait for you."

She looked away. "I don't remember."

"The best part was when you got down on bended knee. You looked so solemn. I suggested you ask me again in a dozen years." He wagged his brows. "Now is your chance."

"No, thank you."

"What? You are jilting me?" He clutched his chest.

"I would grant you your second one-hour engagement, but I doubt I can stay awake a full hour to break it."

"Are you unwell? I hope the wine—"

"I'm only tired."

Something was off, but he couldn't put his finger on it. "Until tomorrow."

When he left the drawing room, he brushed off his concerns. She'd been tired when he arrived, and the wine had probably contributed to her fatigue. Tomorrow she would be her old self again.

The next day, Julianne sat at her desk and drew out a fresh piece of paper. The blank page intimidated her. She needed an idea, but her brain froze. Drat it all, she couldn't afford to stall now.

A tap at the door startled her. She looked over her shoulder as Hester entered.

"My nephew has seen fit to call before luncheon. He insists upon seeing you."

"Oh, no. Hester, I must work on the pamphlet. I do not have time to coddle him. Is there not a way to put him off?"

Hester smiled. "I shall tell him you are suffering from a headache."

Considering the copious amount of wine she'd consumed last evening, she figured he would believe that excuse. "Thank you," she said.

After Hester left, Julianne frowned at the blank page. Then the perfect advice leaped into her brain. She dipped her quill and started writing.

Once you have secured a gentleman's interest, do not be "at home" every time he calls. You must not forgo your obligations to charities and to your friends in hopes that he will call.

Hester returned a few minutes later. "My nephew expressed concern for your health." She smiled. "He actually took the blame for your headache and admitted he'd topped up your wineglass one too many times. I find it rather peculiar, given his anger upon finding you tipsy at the Beresford's ball."

Julianne waved her hand. "His reasons are unimportant. However, we do have a problem. He swore to call on me at different times daily. I cannot afford to waste time. I must take advantage of this opportunity to finish the pamphlet."

"That reminds me," Hester said. "My friend approached three publishers earlier this week. Two of them refused on the grounds of impropriety."

Julianne sucked in her breath. No. No!

Hester smiled. "But one of them has expressed interest. He wishes to review a few pages in advance. Now, I suggest that you make a copy of the introduction and the first two chapters today."

"Oh my goodness." Julianne rose and hugged Hester. "It will be published!"

Hester patted her back. "There is no certainty, Julianne. If this particular publisher refuses, then my friend will approach others. Hope for the best, but prepare for disappointment."

She nodded. "I must make the copy straightaway. Will you review it for mistakes?"

"Yes, of course, my dear. Now, I'll leave you to your work."

After Hester departed, Julianne twirled round and round. Her heart leaped with giddy excitement. How would she ever be able to focus on the pamphlet when she could barely contain her elation?

She took a deep breath, knowing that all her efforts would be for naught if she did not apply herself to making the copy. And once that was done, she must redouble her efforts to complete the pamphlet. The soft ticking of the bedside clock reminded her that she had only six days left of the restriction, counting today. With a gasp, she returned to the desk, more determined than ever to finish.

Chapter Twelve

*A Lady's Secrets of Seduction: Never be
where he expects you to be.*

Three days later, Hawk rapped the knocker at his aunt's house. He ground his teeth, knowing he'd probably regret his decision. But what choice did he have?

After Henderson installed him in the anteroom, Hawk paced about. His aunt ought to have admitted him immediately to the drawing room. Doubtless she intended to make him cool his heels for insisting that Julianne pay the price for her defiance.

He looked at the mantel clock and grew increasingly impatient. Of course, he'd not missed her. She was a thorn in his side and responsible for making his life miserable. At first, he'd been glad for the reprieve from his guardian duties. He'd shared a bottle of claret or three with friends at the club two evenings ago, but for reasons that mystified him, he'd grown bored and a bit irritable within a short time.

After much thought, he'd attributed his foul mood to celibacy, and so he'd decided to slake his lust. That had led him to attend the theater—or rather the women's dressing room. Nell and Nancy, the naughty dancers, had welcomed him with open arms and scantily clad bodies. They had renewed their offer for a ménage á trois. He'd convinced himself he could keep the matter quiet, but his lust had cooled upon closer inspection of their face paint. They had smelled of perspiration and cheap perfume. Worse still, an image of Julianne's beautiful blue eyes had risen up in his mind. He'd muttered some vague excuse to the dancers and strode away as if the hounds of hell were nipping at his heels.

A different sort of hell awaited him thereafter. Two nights in a row, he'd dreamed about Julianne—very lewd dreams. He'd awakened half mad with lust both times. No matter how often he'd reminded himself that she was forbidden, he could not shake off his desire for her.

The devil take it. He wasn't made out of stone. Her beauty would tempt any man, but his situation posed a monumental coil. He wanted her badly, but he couldn't have her. Not without marrying her, and that was out of the question.

Worst of all, he couldn't avoid her, even when she wasn't present. Last night at the club, he'd gotten aggravated with the number of ladies and gentlemen who had expressed concern for her health. This morning, he'd encountered her forlorn beaux at the fencing academy. Beaufort had wanted to know all the details of Julianne's sudden illness and stated that he would send her flowers posthaste. Not to be outdone, Osgood had declared he would write a poem in her honor. Portfrey and Benton intended to send sweetmeats. Caruthers said he would arrange to have a basket of fruit delivered.

The five had all sighed and agreed the nightly entertainments weren't nearly as much fun without Julianne's presence. In their estimation, she was a "jolly good sport" and the liveliest single lady in the beau monde.

But that was nothing compared to the mention of her *mysterious decline* in the scandal sheets this morning. Damn it all. The last thing he needed was for Tristan to hear about his sister's supposed illness. The old boy had enough to worry about with his wife's confinement.

Hawk glanced at the clock again and groaned. The devil. He was no better than the cubs. His return to his old life had proven dull, and all he'd thought about was Julianne. Hell, he'd even felt guilty for restricting her activities. But most of all, he'd missed her laughter and even her sassy remarks.

Well, he'd make her happy today.

Moments later, Henderson returned and informed him the ladies would receive him. Hawk told him he could find his way to the drawing room. Then he bounded up the stairs, anxious to give her the good news.

Despite her exhaustion, Julianne could barely hold back her excitement. The publisher had requested the rest of her pamphlet yesterday. His enthusiasm had spurred her to write faster and faster. If she could continue this pace, she would finish the pamphlet before the week ended.

She drew out a fresh sheet of paper, dipped her pen, and started the next chapter: "How to Secure and Keep a Beau."

Once you have a steady admirer, you may be tempted to discover his plans for the evening. Do so at your own peril, for he will surely believe you are rushing him to the altar. On the other hand, he may try to pin down your plans. If you wish to keep his interest, be vague about your planned entertainments. Do not lie about your whereabouts, but you are under no obligation to inform him which invitations you have accepted.

Hester entered. "May I interrupt?"

"Oh, your timing is perfect. I just finished another chapter. Will you read it and give me your opinion?"

"My nephew has called, but he can wait a few moments." Hester lifted her quizzing glass and perused the chapter. "Oh, this is excellent. But now we must attend my nephew. You do not want to arouse his suspicions. Come along and greet him."

Julianne wrinkled her nose. "I'd rather hoped he wouldn't call for the rest of the week. I'm so close to finishing the pamphlet."

"He will likely keep his visit brief," Hester said.

Julianne released a gusty sigh. "Oh, very well."

When they reached the drawing room, Hawk was commanding the dogs to sit. After they obeyed him, he rewarded them with a few crumbs.

Hester lifted her quizzing glass. "And they say you can't teach old dogs new tricks."

Caro and Byron scampered over to Hester. She let them jump onto the sofa beside her and ruffled their fur. Julianne sat on the opposite sofa and tapped her toe, drawing Hawk's attention.

She stilled, realizing her impatience showed.

"I have news that will please you," he said.

"Oh?" Perhaps he meant to leave town. She crossed her fingers in the folds of her skirt.

"I have decided to grant you a reprieve for good behavior," he said.

Julianne's lips parted. "A reprieve?" she repeated.

He nodded. "As of today, you may have visitors, and you may resume attending entertainments."

"Julianne, this is wonderful news. Do you not agree?" Hester gave her a speaking look.

"Oh, yes," Julianne said. "It is just so unexpected." Drat him. Why had he lifted the restriction now when she needed it the most?

He scrutinized her. "I rather thought you would be ecstatic."

"Well, of course she is happy," Hester said.

Julianne desperately sought a way out of her predicament. She considered claiming a sore throat or some other ailment, but if she did, he'd probably send for a doctor.

"She has become accustomed to resting," Hester said. "I think it would be best if she only attended evening events for the next few days—to reserve her strength."

Julianne breathed a sigh of relief at Hester's words. At least her days would be free to write the pamphlet.

Hawk arched his brows. "She was tapping her foot moments ago. That is a sign she is in need of exercise. In fact, a walk in the park would do her good. I'll take her there in my curricle."

Her jaw dropped. He spoke as if she were one of the dogs. "Do you plan to put a leash on me?"

He winked. "An excellent idea."

"I prefer to stay at home," Julianne said. Drat him. She needed every available moment to finish the pamphlet.

He frowned. "I thought you would be happy to be out of doors."

"I have to make plans for this evening," she said. "I've no idea what I shall wear." Upon seeing his dubious expression, she made up yet another excuse. "After so much time indoors, I need a beauty treatment."

He snorted. "You cannot be serious."

"You have no idea the measures ladies must take to ensure their complexions are rosy and clear." Julianne regarded Hester. "I purchased a new concoction. Virgin's Milk is reputed to be one of the finest cures for the complexion."

Hawk burst out laughing and slid down in his chair.

"What do you find so hilarious?" Julianne said.

He kept laughing until his thick lashes were damp. Then he drew in a breath and wiped his eyes. "Julianne, whatever price you paid for this absurdly named concoction, you wasted your coin."

"I did not waste money," she said. "And you insult me to say so."

His golden brown eyes glittered as he gazed at her. "It was not meant as an insult. Quite the opposite. You are easily the most beautiful woman in the kingdom."

Her lips parted at his words. Many gentlemen had complimented her, but he had never done so. She cautioned herself not to fall for his idle flattery, but her heart squeezed. Fearing he would see how much his words meant to her, she stared at her folded hands in her lap. She could not allow herself to take pleasure in his praise, for he would surely make a jest of it in the next moment.

"What entertainment will you attend tonight, Aunt?" he asked.

"Lady Dunworthy is holding a musicale this evening," Hester said. "But we have not decided for certain yet."

"I shall escort you and Julianne," he said. Then he walked over to her and tweaked the curl by her ear. "If you play tonight, I will turn the pages for you."

He'd not even asked; he'd just assumed she would be thrilled by his offer. His arrogance irked her, and she meant to take him down a peg or two. "Perhaps I will grant that privilege to another gentleman."

His eyes filled with displeasure. "Cease fire, Julianne. It was a peace offering."

She almost told him to have enough respect for her to ask in the future, but she suspected he had an ulterior motive for calling on her today. "You did not end my restriction for the reason you stated. I had no real choice in the matter, so my compliance was assured." She gazed into his eyes. "Tell me, Hawk, what was the real reason you granted the reprieve?"

He looked momentarily taken aback, but he recovered quickly. "Why are you so suspicious? I thought you would be pleased."

"You have not answered my question."

His jaw clenched. "I have done you a kindness, and you cannot accept it. If I did not know better, I would think you are purposely goading me so that you can continue with the restriction."

She had to distract him from this line of thought immediately. "If you would only treat me in a delicate manner befitting a gently bred young lady, I would not fall prey to vexation."

He snorted. "Gently bred you may be, but you're no delicate hothouse flower."

"Marc, have a care," Hester said.

He turned to his aunt. "I will call tonight."

Hester sighed. "Marc, it is ridiculous for you to follow her everywhere. I will escort her."

"It is my duty," he said. "I will call at eight sharp." He glanced at Julianne. "Be ready."

"Marc, you forget yourself," Hester said.

He ignored his aunt and kept his gaze on Julianne. "I suspect you've something up your puffed sleeve, but I advise you to forget whatever scheme you've invented."

After he strode out the door, Julianne wished she'd thrown one of the Egyptian statues at his head. "Oh, I could cheerfully stamp on his boot."

"Now, now. You must not overset yourself," Hester said.

Julianne regarded Hester. "His conduct is beyond rude. He treats me as if I am a marionette. I am weary of him pulling the strings at his pleasure."

"Well, then, we must find a way for you to thwart him," Hester said. "We will follow your advice in the pamphlet. Never be where he expects to find you."

That evening, Hawk arrived at his aunt's house and regarded the elderly butler. "I'll save you the bother and see myself to the drawing room."

Henderson cleared his throat. "Lady Rutledge is not at home."

Hawk frowned. "Is she not at home to me or is she literally gone?"

"My lord, I am instructed to inform you that her ladyship is not at home."

Hawk fisted his hand on his hip. "I take it Lady Julianne is not at home, either."

"My only instructions are to inform you that Lady Rutledge is not at home."

Hawk rummaged inside his coat and untied a small purse.

Henderson drew back. "My lord, I cannot accept your...gift."

"We both know it's a bribe. How much for full disclosure?"

"I am not at liberty to reveal anything." After a moment, he added, "My lord."

Hawk respected the butler for refusing the bribe and returned the purse to his coat pocket. It wasn't Henderson's fault that his mistress's staircase didn't quite reach the attic. "Henderson, if I were to tell you that there is an emergency, would you then be willing to answer my questions?"

Sweat beaded on the old man's forehead. "In an emergency, I would make an exception."

"I consider this an emergency," Hawk said. "It is a proven fact that females have smaller brains, and sometimes their thinking is hampered by their inferior ability to apply reason."

"My lord, I have never given thought to Lady Rutledge's brain."

"That is probably for the best, Henderson. Now, did a Mr. Peckham escort my aunt and Lady Julianne?"

"Yes, my lord."

His aunt had said they had not decided for certain to attend the musicale. "Did my aunt happen to mention their destination?"

"No, my lord."

He let out a gusty sigh. "Is there anything else you recall that might be of use in this emergency situation?"

"No, my lord."

"Are you certain you will not accept recompense for your help?"

"I am certain, my lord." He withdrew a handkerchief and mopped his forehead. "Will there be anything else, my lord?"

"Only this. You and I never had this conversation. Do we have an understanding, Henderson?"

"Yes, my lord."

Hawk donned his hat, strode out to the carriage, and gave the driver Lady Dunworthy's address. Upon arrival at the musicale, he walked into the drawing room and winced upon hearing Miss Henrietta Bancroft's off-key soprano. She drew in a lungful of air and screamed out the high notes. He fully expected the crystal teardrops in the chandelier to vibrate and shatter.

The exhibition mercifully ended. Hawk searched the drawing room, and as he'd expected, there was no sign of his aunt, Julianne, or Mr. Peckham.

Lady Dunworthy walked toward him. "Hawk, what a lovely surprise. I did not expect you after Lady Rutledge departed rather hastily."

"That is unfortunate," Hawk said. "Was something amiss?"

Lady Dunworthy drew closer. "Your aunt said she did not wish to damage her hearing by listening to Miss Henrietta Bancroft." Lady Dunworthy sighed. "Her voice is terrible, but she is determined. But now that you are here, perhaps you would turn the pages for one of the other young ladies."

"I fear I cannot," he said. "I have news for my aunt that cannot wait."

"Oh, dear, I hope your grandmamma hasn't taken a bad turn," she said. "At her age, heart palpitations are worrisome."

In truth, his mother had written to inform him that Grandmamma's heart palpitations had subsided, but she now suffered from *sinking spells*. "I do feel an obligation to inform my aunt. Did she happen to mention her destination?"

"No, but it is Wednesday night. You might find her at Almack's."

"Thank you, Lady Dunworthy. You have been tremendously helpful."

Lord help him. Almack's of all the wretched places.

After an interminable wait in a long queue, his carriage halted before that hallowed hall. As he strode toward the doors, he recalled the patronesses insisted men wear breeches. To hell with that. He'd gain entrance even if he had to flirt with Lady Jersey.

Lady Jersey met him and shook her head at his attire. "Hawkfield, you know breeches are de rigueur, not that we've seen you here in years. What brings you?"

"My aunt and Lady Julianne," he said.

"They are not here." She laughed. "Oh, how delicious. You have lost your aunt *and* your ward."

"My aunt is in her dotage and obviously gave me the wrong information."

"I wish you luck finding them." A sly look came into her eyes. "Next week, I hope to see you—dressed appropriately, of course. You have been absent too long from the seventh heaven."

He bowed and strode off. "More like the seventh circle of hell," he muttered.

When he reached the carriage, his driver regarded him with pity. "Where to, my lord?"

"Damned if I know," he said.

"My lord, I heard there will be fireworks at Vauxhall tonight."

"Then let us be off." He figured he'd find his aunt and Peckham in one of the supper boxes, if that was, in fact, their destination. Even so, he couldn't trust Hester to keep a close watch over Julianne. The thought of her wandering along the main avenue with her silly friends made him wild. All manner of riffraff tended to lie in wait for unprotected young ladies. His heart pounded at the possibility of Julianne coming to harm.

Chapter Thirteen

*A Scoundrel's Code of Conduct: Put your foot down, but have
a hanky available in case she turns into a watering pot.*

Julianne admired the beautiful lamps hanging in the
great elms lining the avenue at Vauxhall. She sat in
one of the supper boxes with Hester and Mr. Peckham.
They were partaking of thin slices of ham, tiny chick-
ens, biscuits, strawberries, and wine. Sipping a glass of
wine, Julianne smiled as Mr. Peckham offered Hester a
strawberry. He gazed longingly at Hester, and when she
lowered her eyes, the sweetness of her sudden shyness
touched Julianne's heart.

She averted her gaze to give them privacy. Hester had
never discussed her relationship with Mr. Peckham, but
their feelings for each other were obvious to Julianne.
And she had no doubt Mr. Peckham was Hester's first
love. Tonight the world seemed a better place because of

their reunion after so many years. Hester had suffered too much in her youth, but now she was free to give her heart to the man she'd never forgotten.

Julianne was not completely at ease, however. Hawk would be furious when he discovered they had thwarted him tonight. Her conscience had roared when they had left thirty minutes prior to Hawk's expected arrival. Oh, why should she feel guilty? He had gone too far with his rude insistence that he must accompany them tonight.

"Lady Julianne, you look as if you wish to slay someone."

Beaufort's voice startled her. She looked up to find all five of the cubs in the supper box. "I did not know you would be here."

"We didn't want to miss the fireworks," Osgood said.

"Will you take some refreshment?" she asked.

At that moment, great bursts like gunfire erupted. Julianne squeaked, eliciting laughter from the young men. They drank wine and watched the fireworks display. Then Georgette, Sally, and Amy arrived in the box. Julianne's happiness at seeing her friends faded quickly at the sight of Ramsey following close on their heels. For Georgette's sake, she greeted him politely and turned her attention to the others. But she grew increasingly uncomfortable as she caught Ramsey watching her more than once.

After several minutes, he approached his sister. "Georgette, I'll return shortly to escort you back to our parents," he said.

Julianne breathed a sigh of relief when he departed. Obviously, he'd only meant to escort his sister, along with Amy and Sally. Thank goodness he'd taken her seriously when she'd told him to cease his pursuit.

"I say, it is a beautiful night," Caruthers said. "Shall we take a stroll along the Grand Walk?"

Everyone assented, except Amy. "Georgette," she said, "will your brother be angry?"

Georgette waved her hand in dismissal. "Oh, who cares about him? The gentlemen will escort us. We will be perfectly safe, and Henry will never know the difference."

"Let me discuss the plan with Hester first," Julianne said.

When she approached Hester about the walk, Mr. Peckham frowned. "There are unscrupulous sorts out there."

"But Julianne's beaux will be there to protect the girls," Hester said. "Mind you, stay away from the dark walks."

Julianne laughed. "I promise to steer clear of those paths."

The entire group set off to the accompaniment of popping sounds. The sky lit up again and again with great fanfare. After spending so many days indoors, Julianne enjoyed the invigorating exercise.

Georgette spied an unlit path and halted. "Oh, look. That must be one of the famous dark walks."

Naturally, everyone had to stop and look.

The branches of the tall trees formed a canopy over the dark walk, making it look even more forbidding to Julianne. She imagined a villain grabbing an innocent young lady and dragging her down that secluded path. Chill bumps erupted along her arms.

Sally shivered. "Oh, it looks scary."

Caruthers snuck up behind her and made a bloodcurdling sound.

Sally yelped and everyone laughed. "You rogue," she said, swatting his arm.

Georgette edged closer to the dark walk. Then she turned with a sly grin on her face. "I think we should walk a few paces down the path so that we can say we've actually been on one of the dark walks."

Julianne rolled her eyes at her feather-brained friend. "Georgette, don't be silly."

"It's only a lark," Georgette said. "Let us make a pact never to reveal we walked there."

Beaufort cleared his throat. "Lady Georgette, I cannot allow you to embark on that path."

Julianne bit back a grin, knowing Georgette would consider Beaufort's words a dare.

Georgette giggled, lifted her skirts, and tapped her toe on the path. "Oops, I stepped on the dark walk."

Everyone laughed, except Beaufort. "I think we had better turn back now."

"Oh, very well," Georgette grumbled.

Julianne shook her head at Georgette's antics. As the group turned back, Beaufort took her arm. She told herself his escort was nothing more than a gentlemanly gesture, but something in his manner made her feel as if he'd made a propriety claim on her. As they strolled along, Beaufort gradually slowed his pace until the others were far ahead. Her nerves rattled. "We're falling behind," she said.

He smiled at her. "I wanted to tell you that I've acquired the curricle. Will you take a drive with me tomorrow?"

She couldn't refuse when she'd put him off more than once and led him to believe she would accept as soon as he took possession of the curricle. "Yes, of course," she said.

His smile grew wider. "Excellent. Tomorrow it is."

She turned her gaze away so that he wouldn't see her guilty expression. Now would be the perfect moment to tell him she only wanted friendship from him and the other four young men, but she didn't want to spoil his happiness. Tomorrow she would tell him after he returned her home. No, she would say it to all the young men the next time they called, because she must ensure they understood she wasn't interested in a romantic relationship.

The breeze blew her bonnet ribbons across her face. She pushed them away and thought of the Durmont's ball. That night, she'd flirted with all five of those young men and danced with each of them twice. All because she'd wanted to show the ton that she no longer cared for Hawk.

Shame burned deep inside her. She'd taken advantage of the cubs and thought only about herself.

When they reached the supper box, Julianne's pulse sped up at the sight of Ramsey taking Georgette aside. Julianne couldn't hear them, but she surmised Ramsey was displeased that Georgette had left the box.

A few moments later, Georgette approached, and Beaufort excused himself. After he walked away, Georgette let out a loud sigh. "My brother insists I must return to my parents' box now."

"I suspected he was angry at you for leaving," she said. "Will your parents be angry?"

She snickered. "They will never know. Henry was supposed to stay with me, so he'll say nothing."

"Perhaps you should tell your mother the truth. Let her know we consulted Hester before leaving."

"Julianne, that would not satisfy my mother," Georgette said. "Mama disapproves of Lady Rutledge."

"What?" she said, unable to keep the shock from her voice.

Georgette winced. "I know how much you like her, and I do as well. My mother is a high stickler for the proprieties. Don't let her opinion trouble you." She paused. "I had better inform Amy and Sally that we are leaving soon."

Julianne nodded, but inside she seethed at Georgette's mother. High stickler, indeed. Lady Boswood ought to keep her nose firmly planted in her own concerns—such as her horrid son, who was striding toward her now. She had no intention of letting him corner her again and turned away.

She'd taken only a few steps when he called out her name. With a disgusted sigh, she halted. "Lord Ramsey, I understand you are angry that your sister left, but—"

"I wish to speak to you about that letter you wrote to your mother," he bit out.

"My private correspondence is none of your affair. Now, you will excuse me," she said.

"It is my affair when you make unfounded accusations about my character," he said.

"I made my disinterest clear the last time we spoke. Soon after, I received news that your mother proposed a match between us. Obviously, you applied to your mother to further your suit. I stated my objections previously and have no wish to repeat them."

"You told her I am a dissipated rake. Is that what *he* told you?"

Rapid footsteps sounded behind her. Hawk stepped beside her and stared coldly at Ramsey. "I told you to stay away from her."

Her heart hammered against her chest. She had to prevent a confrontation. "He came to collect his sister."

Ramsey inclined his head. As he walked past them, he left a parting shot. "I'll wait for you, Julianne."

"What did he mean?" Hawk gritted out.

"I've no idea," she said under her breath. But of course she knew. He'd used his own mother to try and press his suit. Even in the face of her refusal, he still persisted.

Beaufort approached. "Lady Julianne, we are leaving. I will call for you tomorrow in my curricle."

After he left, Hawk turned on her. "He is taking you for a drive?"

"Yes. He wants to show off his new curricle," she said.

His nostrils flared. "We're leaving."

"But I came with your aunt," she said.

"She's coming with us," he said, striding toward Hester.

"But her carriage is here and so is Mr. Peckham."

"The driver can take Peckham home and return the carriage. You and my aunt have much to explain."

Hawk stood in front of the mummy case and folded his arms over his chest. "Aunt, you went too far tonight."

Hester sighed. "Marc, if you had not acted in such a high-handed manner earlier, I would have waited for your escort. Let that be a lesson to you."

"You seem to have forgotten that I am her guardian and am in charge of her," he said.

"Yes, yes, but I am also responsible for her. And frankly, I am disappointed that you have so little faith in me."

"I chased after the pair of you for half the evening. And what did I find? Julianne in conversation with Ramsey, when I specifically instructed her to stay away from him."

"Ramsey came to escort his sister back to their parents' box," Julianne said. Then she told him about Lady Boswood proposing a match between her misbegotten son and her. "The only reason Ramsey confronted me was because he was angry that I'd reported his bad reputation to my mother."

"Why didn't you tell me beforehand?" he said, his voice rising.

"I resolved the matter with my mother," she said. "And I made it very clear I do not welcome his addresses. When you appeared, I was on the verge of walking away from him. To be honest, you only goaded him again."

"You blame me?" he said.

"No, I'm only trying to demonstrate that I'm perfectly capable of thwarting him."

He held up his hand. "I've heard enough. Matters are going to change or I will take action."

"What are you suggesting?" Hester said.

"Aunt, I appreciate that you are sponsoring Julianne, but I cannot have you working against me. Ultimately, I am responsible for Julianne's welfare. I am her appointed guardian, and if anything goes awry, I am the one who must answer for it. The schemes must stop immediately or I will make other arrangements for her."

Julianne drew in a sharp breath. "Do you mean to send me home?"

"Perhaps you wouldn't be so concerned if you abided by my rules," he said. "I'll leave the consequences of failure to your imagination."

Hester let out an exasperated sigh. "Marc, do stop with the threats."

"It is not a threat, Aunt," he said. "I've reached the limits of my patience. You delight in playing these games, but I will not tolerate it any longer. There will be consequences if you thwart me again."

Hester pushed up from the sofa. "Insolent puppy to speak to me in such a manner."

He gave her a stern look. "You brought this on yourself."

After his aunt lumbered out of the room, Julianne turned to him. "How could you speak to her in such a harsh manner?"

He sat beside her. "My aunt's judgment is questionable at the best of times. And I don't approve of the influence she is having on you."

"Hester has been very kind to me and given me the benefit of her wisdom. Everyone else may think her too bold, but she speaks the truth, and I respect her for it. She has helped me when I've been confused and sad."

He frowned. "Why did you not come to me?"

"Because you do not listen. You make pronouncements and never realize that your words have the power to wound."

A stinging sensation rippled along his arms. She'd insinuated he'd hurt her. When she dashed her hand beneath her eyes, he swore under his breath.

He offered her his handkerchief. She snatched it and dabbed at her eyes. Then she sniffed and lifted her chin in a gesture that reminded him of her mother.

"We've been at cross purposes too long," he said.

She balled his handkerchief in her hand. "I know I've

given you cause to worry. But you have to change, too. You make autocratic decisions, but I should have a say in my life."

"You want to test your wings and be independent. I understand that need, but I made a solemn promise to your brother. I have to answer to him."

"I will answer for myself," she said tersely.

"It isn't just about you and me," he said. "If I look the other way and something goes wrong, I will be responsible. The damage could lead to a lasting rift between our families, but that pales in the face of what my feelings would be if I failed you."

"Then let me be responsible for my own actions," she said.

"I would if I knew that you would use caution. But you've taken risks that could have ended disastrously. You think you're invincible, that nothing terrible could ever happen to you. But one wrong decision could ruin your life." He paused and added, "I'll be honest. The prospect scares the hell out of me, because I couldn't bear it if something bad happened to you."

She turned away and fisted her hands in her lap. "What do you want?"

"All I ask is that you conduct yourself the same way you would if your mother and brother were present. In return, I promise to listen and give you a say in your life, within reason."

She released a shaky breath.

"Can we start afresh? As friends rather than enemies?"

She moistened her lips. "Yes."

The temptation to tease her was on the tip of his tongue, but he bit back the urge. In the not-so-distant past, he never would have hesitated. He wanted to go back in time when things were simpler between them, but she was no longer the impish girl who had willingly joined him in mischief.

"I will call tomorrow," he said.

Julianne rose with him. She curtsied. He bowed. Their parting was stiff and formal. He walked out, thinking he would prefer divisiveness to this cold chasm between them.

But she'd agreed to friendship. The gray cloud that had dampened his spirits lifted. He would charm her and make her laugh. She would be his friend, not his ward. Then she wouldn't feel this need to rebel against him. For the remainder of the season, he would make the most of their time together. He would win his Julie-girl back, if only for a little while longer.

He bounded down the stairs, only to remember she'd agreed to take a drive with Beaufort tomorrow. Well, hell. He couldn't object to a ride in an open curricle. They would be in full view of everyone who cared to parade around Rotten Row at the fashionable hour. It was perfectly within the bounds of the proprieties.

As he walked to his carriage, Hawk tried to think of a good reason to prevent her from going. Beaufort was a male and therefore a threat. He might turn over his curricle while staring at her bosom. Or drive into a tree while imagining her naked. Damnation, the cub would have to help her up into the curricle. Hawk gritted his teeth at the thought of Beaufort touching her.

Bloody hell, he had no right to refuse. No right to anything except to be her guardian. Because she deserved better than a man with a shameful past.

He climbed into his carriage and slapped his hat on the seat beside him. A few minutes later, the carriage rumbled away. He stared out the window into the darkness. Tonight the hollow sensation in his chest seemed as wide as the Thames.

Chapter Fourteen

*A Lady's Secrets of Seduction: Give your heart only
to a man who truly loves you.*

Julianne rose before dawn and wrote her final chapter.

If you have followed the Secrets of Seduction, but your
beau has still not proposed, you must ask yourself
how long is too long to wait. Only you can answer that
question. But if a man truly loves you, he will not risk
losing you to another. Give your heart only to a man
who loves you so much he cannot live without you.

The first rays of sunlight spilled into the room. Chill
bumps erupted on her arms. She had completed the pamphlet.

From that first fledgling introductory paragraph to the
very last sentence, she had poured out her thoughts and

beliefs. And ended the pamphlet with the only advice that truly mattered.

Her eyes watered a little as she stacked the pages and tied a string around the manuscript. She was almost reluctant to send her work out into the world. Her heart squeezed as she considered the possibility that the publisher might reject it. But she had come this far, and she must have the courage to face the final verdict.

The cheery early morning sunshine disappeared, and driving rain pelted the windows in the afternoon. After a short rest, Julianne walked into the drawing room.

"Ah, there you are, dear," Hester said. "I hope you are feeling refreshed."

"Yes, thank you."

Hester handed her a letter. "A footman brought this for you an hour ago."

Julianne read the short missive from Beaufort and laughed.

"What do you find so amusing?" Hester asked.

She folded the note. "Beaufort apologized for the rain. I'm sure he's disappointed. He was so anxious to show off his new curricle."

"And perhaps a certain young lady?" Hester said.

Julianne sighed. "He's such a nice young man, but I don't have tender feelings for him. And I fear he hopes for more." She regarded Hester. "I don't want to wound him."

Hester patted her hand. "My dear, he is one of five young men, and none of them can claim exclusivity where you are concerned."

"You know my history with men proposing to me. I

didn't realize that my flirting gave those twelve men the wrong impression. But I know better now."

"You do not hold tender feelings for any of them?" Hester asked.

"I consider them all friends," she said, "but friendship is all I can offer."

"Well, then, I have a bit of news. Your manuscript was delivered."

Julianne drew in a long breath and released it slowly. "Now the waiting begins. Is there any indication as to when the publisher will respond?"

Hester shook her head. "No, but in the meantime, you must enjoy the festivities and try to put the pamphlet from your mind."

"I can scarcely think of anything else," Julianne said. "I don't know how I'll bear the suspense."

"The pamphlet has come to mean a great deal to you," Hester said.

"I struggled so hard to find time to write it that I did not stop to consider my feelings," she said. "Now I find myself on pins and needles, hopeful and fearful at the same time."

"No matter what happens, you will always know that you persevered. I know that would not be much recompense in the case of bad news, but I am proud of you."

"Thank you. That means the world to me," she said.

When a footman brought the mail, Hester sifted through it. "There is a letter for you, Julianne."

She caught her breath. "It is from Mama. *Please, please do not let it be bad news about Tessa and the babe.*

Hester broke the seal on a letter. "Is all well at home?"

She breathed a sigh of relief at her mother's first paragraph. "Yes, Tessa is well. Her feet are a little swollen. Mama says Tristan teases her when he finds her walking about barefoot."

"Soon, the little one will enter the world," Hester said. "You will be an aunt."

"I can scarcely believe the time is drawing near." She returned to reading the letter. Of course, she wasn't surprised that her mother had written to Lady Boswood and disapproved of the match with Ramsey.

Truthfully, she was still a bit uneasy about Ramsey, but she'd made her displeasure clear to him more than once. Granted, she couldn't entirely avoid him because of Georgette, but she would make only the required acknowledgments whenever she met him in public. Above all else, she would not allow him to draw her into a private conversation ever again.

She returned her attention to her letter, but her mother's next words made her stomach a bit queasy.

You have shown excellent judgment, daughter. I trust that you will continue to avoid men of disreputable character.

She winced. Hawk had been right about the risks she'd taken this season. If she'd been discovered drunk that first night, the society dragons would have flayed her alive. Her family would have suffered. Hester would not have escaped unharmed, either. In all likelihood, her brother would have blamed Hawk for failing to protect her. Even though Hawk had exasperated her with his rules, she couldn't deny he'd never shirked his guardian duties. In truth, he'd devoted the entire season to her.

Yesterday evening, he'd asked if they could be friends rather than enemies. Of course she'd agreed, but deep down, she knew they could never go back. Everything between them had changed.

She didn't even feel like the same person she had been only a few short weeks ago. That day she'd arrived at Ashdown House with her brother, she'd been so full of fanciful illusions about her feelings for Hawk.

Since that day, she'd discovered there was much she'd not known about him. It was strange how she'd known him for years but had seen only the carefree charmer. Now she knew that was only one facet of his character. She'd learned he insisted on being in control at all times. More than once, he'd expressed fear that something bad would happen to her.

She'd attributed his fear as a direct response to things she'd done, but all along she'd thought his reactions unreasonable. He was particularly obsessive where Ramsey was concerned.

The fine hairs on her neck stiffened. Something bad had happened to Hawk. She felt certain that it involved Ramsey.

One week later

Julianne sat on the window seat with the cubs at Lady Amstead's card party and tried to focus on their witty tales of their misadventures at university. But it was all she could do to contain her joy. This morning, she'd received the wonderful news that her pamphlet would be published in a fortnight.

She glanced over at Hawk. He sat at one of the card

tables, shuffling cards. His long fingers made her think of the way he'd caressed her breast. Remembering the sensations, she became all too aware of her nipples tightening and imagined him touching her again. She gazed at his angular face and those full lips that had devoured her, leaving her hungry for so much more. After he dealt the cards, Hawk returned her gaze from beneath thick black lashes. His seductive expression mesmerized her. She felt as if she were falling under his spell.

A hand waved before her face, breaking the enchantment. Beaufort laughed. "You were miles away."

Her face heated. "You caught me woolgathering." She really must stop thinking such wanton thoughts.

"If the weather holds up, I'm hoping to take you for that ride in the park you promised me," he said.

It had rained every afternoon the past week. "Yes, of course," she said.

Amy and Georgette joined the group. "Sally wanted to come, but she has a cold," Georgette said.

"Little wonder with all this damp air," Amy said.

Georgette gave Julianne a speaking look. "We hoped you would take a turn with us."

She appealed to the gentlemen. "Will you excuse me? I've not seen my friends for days."

After Julianne rose, Georgette took her arm. "Let us find a place where we may have a private coze."

They minced about the room. Julianne saw Ramsey leaning against a pillar, staring at her. Alarmed, she squeezed Georgette's arm. "Let us reverse direction. There is an adjoining drawing room with a pianoforte. We can pretend to be examining the music sheets while we gossip."

"Yes, you have much to tell us," Georgette whispered.

Julianne was relieved that no one else occupied the music room. She and Amy walked over to the pianoforte and set music sheets upon the polished top.

Amy thumbed through the sheets. "This seems overly dramatic to me."

"It's just a precaution," Julianne said.

Georgette closed the door. "Now we can speak without fear of listening ears. Julianne, you must give us news of the pamphlet. Did you finish?"

When she told them that it would be published in two weeks, her friends took turns hugging her.

Amy smiled. "I'm still a bit concerned, but you deserve praise for your accomplishment."

"I wish we could have a glass of champagne to celebrate," Georgette said.

"We cannot celebrate openly," Julianne said. "No one must ever know I am the author."

"We would never breathe a word to anyone," Georgette said.

The door opened. When Lady Boswood entered, Julianne planted a serene smile on her face. Thank goodness, Georgette's mother had not heard them speaking about the pamphlet.

"Girls, what can you mean hiding behind a closed door like this?" Lady Boswood said in censorious tones.

"We only wished to have a private coze, Mama," Georgette said.

"Georgette, do you wish others to remark upon your ill-mannered behavior?"

"No, Mama," she said.

Lady Boswood frowned at the music sheets. "Were you planning to play?"

"Um, we only wished to look at the music," Georgette said.

"Let us tidy up," Julianne said in a rush. "Then we will join the others in the drawing room."

When they finished, Lady Boswood tapped her toe. "Georgette, you and Amy are dismissed. I wish to speak to Lady Julianne."

Julianne grew wary. Oh, dear God. Lady Boswood meant to give her a tongue-lashing for having told her mother that Ramsey was a rake.

Georgette pleaded with her mother. "But, Mama, we have not seen Julianne—"

"Georgette, do as you're told," Lady Boswood said.

When Georgette and Amy left, Lady Boswood shut the door and *invited* Julianne to sit with her on the sofa. She gripped her hands hard. Drat it all, she'd not bargained for this confrontation.

Lady Boswood let out a sigh. "Gel, I mean you no harm."

She did not trust Georgette's mother and knew she must think carefully before speaking. With considerable effort, she forced herself to remain outwardly calm.

"I am concerned about you," Lady Boswood said. "I understand you are courting five gentlemen. I daresay your mother would not approve."

She almost reminded Lady Boswood that she'd allowed her daughter to participate in Tristan's courtship with two dozen other belles but thought better of challenging the woman. "You are misinformed. They are only my friends."

Lady Boswood sniffed. "Lady Rutledge ought to have forbidden it."

"There is no impropriety," she said. "Lady Rutledge is always present."

"Dear girl, you are not ignorant of Lady Rutledge's bold manners. Everyone was shocked to learn that she was to be your sponsor."

"She has treated me very well," Julianne said. She didn't like it when others made disparaging remarks about Hester. Julianne found her honesty and pragmatism far more appealing than the false compliments and snippy barbs of most society matrons.

"Of course, we must respect the elderly," Lady Boswood said. "I'm sure Lady Hawkfield did not know how to refuse when her aunt offered to sponsor you. But as I predicted, matters have taken a turn for the worse."

Say nothing. Do not inadvertently give her ammunition.

"As your mother's friend, I will gladly take you into my home and sponsor you for the remainder of the season," Lady Boswood continued. "What do you say? Surely you will enjoy my daughter's company."

"I thank you for the offer, but I am quite content with my present circumstances," Julianne said. "Now, if you will excuse me, I must return. Hawk will worry if I am gone too long."

"Forgive my plain speech, but Lord Hawkfield is not a suitable guardian for you. His rakish reputation is well known. You cannot be unaware of it."

It was on the tip of her tongue to say that she was fully aware of Ramsey's rotten reputation, but she thought better of introducing that topic. "My brother appointed him," she said. "I do not question *his* judgment." Of course, she'd implied that Lady Boswood had no right to do so, either.

"We all know Hawk is a good friend to Shelbourne.

But Hawk cannot give you the guidance you require, and his aunt is a bad influence. Tomorrow, I will send my carriage, and you will remove to my home."

"No, ma'am, I will not. I beg your pardon, but the matter is settled. If I require your guidance, I will call upon you." *When Satan lobs snowballs in hell.*

"If you fear giving insult to Lady Rutledge, I can easily take care of the matter," Lady Boswood said. "She will understand when I tell her that my daughter begged to have you stay with her."

Lady Boswood had conveniently ignored Mama's disapproval of Ramsey as a suitor. "My mother will not approve, and neither will Hawk."

"He has persuaded you that my son is disreputable, but he bases his opinion on the past. You know young men sow wild oats, but Henry has long outgrown his youthful follies. There are men, however, who never do."

Julianne noted she had stopped short of naming Hawk, but the insinuation was clear. "While I appreciate your concerns, I am perfectly capable of making my own judgments. Now I must beg your leave."

"One day, my son will be a marquess. He is prepared to offer you marriage, but you turn him away based upon Hawk's word."

"He is my guardian, and I am under his protection."

"You do not even give my son a chance. Henry is in love with you."

She knew better, but no good would come of revealing Ramsey's manipulation. "I have given him no encouragement. He deserves someone who can return his feelings."

"So do you, Julianne, but you stubbornly cling to an old attachment. And we both know of whom I speak."

Julianne looked straight ahead, refusing to acknowledge her thinly veiled reference to Hawk.

"You have not called upon Georgette once this season," Lady Boswood said. "Call on me tomorrow. I will take you and my daughter shopping and to Gunter's for ices."

She hesitated. The last thing she wanted was to spend several hours with Lady Boswood, but she could not refuse the offer without seeming rude. While Julianne knew Hawk would not like it, she could not insult Georgette or her mother.

Hawk stood near the adjoining music room, waiting for Julianne to come out. He'd been watching her all evening and had witnessed her escaping there with her friends thirty minutes ago. Then Lady Boswood had followed them inside. When Georgette and Amy had emerged without Julianne, Hawk had known Lady Boswood meant to make a plea for her loathsome son's suit.

The entire time, Ramsey had stood at the back of the main drawing room, his anxious gaze darting to the music room.

Hester ambled over to Hawk, her blue peacock feathers bobbing. "Lady Boswood still keeps her there, does she?"

To hell with waiting. "I'm going to rescue her."

His aunt put a staying hand on his arm. "If you go in there, everyone will remark upon it. Let me take care of the matter. I know how to handle scheming women."

He nodded, knowing Hester was right.

The door opened, startling him. Lady Boswood smiled sweetly as she led Julianne out. "I would ask you to sit with me, but I see that your guardian and Lady Rutledge are desirous of your company," she said.

Julianne's expression turned wary, but she said nothing.

"I look forward to your visit tomorrow," Lady Boswood said.

After she walked away, Hawk turned to Julianne. "What the devil?"

"Marc, lower your voice," Hester said. "Julianne, you are agitated. Did that dragon rake you over the coals?"

Julianne hesitated. "She insisted upon providing me with guidance."

Hester snorted. "I wager she meant to persuade you that her son was a fine suitor."

Hawk met Julianne's gaze. "You are not calling on Lady Boswood. Send your regrets tomorrow."

"I cannot escape calling on Lady Boswood any longer. Georgette is my friend, and there is nothing to worry about."

"I forbid it, and that is the end of the matter."

"I think we had better repair to my home so that we can resolve the matter in private," Hester said.

Hawk had no intention of debating endlessly with his aunt and Julianne.

After they entered his aunt's drawing room, Julianne perched upon the sofa next to Hester. He sat in the chair he ordinarily occupied and folded his arms over his chest. "I will make this brief. Julianne will send her regrets to Lady Boswood tomorrow. She is free to receive Lady Georgette here, but I refuse to allow her to set foot into the devil's lair."

"Marc, you are being unreasonable," Hester said. "I know you dislike Ramsey, but Julianne has every right to call on her friend. She cannot refuse Lady Boswood's invitation without giving insult."

"I don't give a damn," he said. "I forbid it, and that is the end of the matter."

"Julianne has proven she is capable of managing Lady Boswood and Lord Ramsey," Hester said. "She has dealt with them in a polite but firm manner. Any worries you may have are unfounded."

"I will not be persuaded," he said. "The discussion is at an end. She will not go."

"You cannot stop me," Julianne said.

"Yes, I can. I will call my mother home from Bath. You will stay with her at Ashdown House. And to ensure that you abide by my rules, I will take up temporary residence there."

Her lips parted. "How could you be so cruel to your own mother when she is worried about your grandmamma?"

"My sisters can look after my grandmother," he said.

"I see," Hester said. "You do not trust me to care for Julianne."

"I warned you not long ago that I will not tolerate interference with my decisions. You have given me no choice," he said.

Hester turned to Julianne. "I am very sorry, dear, but I am powerless in this matter. He is your guardian, and though he has long been my favorite, I find his treatment of me insupportable." She rose. "Marc, you will inform me when your mother arrives so that I can arrange for Julianne's trunks to be packed and ready."

He stood as his aunt walked out of the room.

"You are despicable," Julianne said.

"You have both pushed me too far."

"Lady Boswood will be delighted. She told me that

Hester is unsuited to be my sponsor." She pointed at herself. "I defended her."

His jaw worked. She insinuated that he had not done the same. "I stated my reasons. The matter is settled."

"You have not considered the consequences. Everyone will know that you dismissed Hester. Others will gossip about her. Would you humiliate her?" Julianne said.

He stood and strode over to the mummy. How did she always manage to make him feel like a devil?

The rustling of skirts alerted him. He turned around to find Julianne walking to the door. "Where are you going?"

"Upstairs to comfort your aunt," she said, her voice shaking. "I never believed you could be so cruel. And I will never speak to you again after this."

"How am I to do my duty when she refuses to cooperate?"

Julianne marched right up to him. "Hang your duty. You ought to take her feelings into consideration. She adores you, and you hurt her."

He pinched the bridge of his nose. Bloody hell. He'd lost his temper.

"Do not bother writing to your mother," Julianne said. "I will not leave Hester. You will have to cart me off kicking and screaming."

He smiled a little. "The servants would find that entertaining."

"You owe your aunt an apology."

"I won't take you away," he said gruffly. "But after what happened tonight, I cannot believe you wish to call on Lady Boswood. She manipulated you, and you know that she did so at the behest of her son. She knew you

would not refuse her request on account of Georgette.
Lady Boswood means to work on you again. Why would
you willingly do her bidding?"

Julianne looked miserable. "I don't want to lose
Georgette's friendship."

"Blame me," he said. "Tell her I'm a strict ogre and
watch your every move."

"She will believe that," Julianne muttered.

He tugged on the curl by her ear.

"Don't," she said.

She used to laugh and swat his hand when he pulled
her curl. But he'd managed to make an ass out of himself
tonight and had hurt his aunt very badly. "Tell Hester I
will call tomorrow." He paused. "I'm sorry, Julianne."

"You were right about Lady Boswood," she said. "I
knew she meant to manipulate me. I will send my regrets
first thing tomorrow."

Chapter Fifteen

A Scoundrel's Code of Conduct: Be prepared to eat humble pie.

The next afternoon, Julianne's nerves grew taught as she sat with Hester in the drawing room. Hester's drawn expression troubled her. She was tempted to reveal that Hawk had no intention of recalling his mother to Richmond, but she held her tongue. It was Hawk's place to tell her.

He had better apologize profusely.

The butler entered and said he'd turned away the five gentlemen who usually called on Julianne. After he left, Julianne turned to Hester with a questioning look.

Hester's lips thinned. "Under the circumstances, I thought it best."

Julianne nodded. "Shall I ring for a tea tray?"

"No, thank you," Hester said. "I imagine this interview will be brief."

The dogs sat at Hester's feet and whined. She patted the sofa. When they jumped onto her lap, she ruffled their fur and murmured to them.

Julianne regarded her clasped hands. Although Hester had a large circle of friends, she lived alone and probably suffered from loneliness on occasion. Of course, she had Mr. Peckham, but Hester was very circumspect about their relationship. In public, she treated Mr. Peckham as a friend, probably because she knew others, especially family members, would disapprove of such an unequal match. Undoubtedly, they would think her too old for love.

Julianne's heart squeezed. It was so unfair, but she would not voice the words. Hester meant to keep the truth of her relationship with Mr. Peckham a secret, with good reason. Julianne recalled the barely concealed horror of Hawk's mother and his sisters when Hester had volunteered to sponsor her. They did not know what a treasure they had in Hester.

But she knew. She'd even begun to think of Hester as her own aunt.

The mantel clock chimed the hour. It was four o'clock.

Julianne twisted her hands. How could Hawk keep his aunt waiting when he knew she was overset? Thoughtless, horrid man to treat Hester so cruelly.

She could not bear the silence any longer. "Hester, I believe we could use some diversion. Shall I read to you?"

Hester petted the dogs. "Yes, thank you."

Julianne padded over to the bookcase and drew out *Pride and Prejudice*. When she returned to the sofa, she started at the beginning. " 'It is a truth universally acknowledged, that a single man in possession of a good fortune must be in want of a wife.' "

She'd reached the part where Mrs. Bennet scolded Kitty for coughing when the butler entered and announced Hawk. Julianne set the book aside and rose.

He held his hands behind his back and approached his aunt with a solemn expression. Then he offered her a single, long-stemmed red rose. He looked a bit abashed as Hester accepted it. "I told the woman not to cut the stem," he said gruffly. "The thorn represents the prick to my conscience."

A sheen of moisture filled Hester's lined eyes. Julianne's throat constricted.

His dark brows drew together. "I have been remiss. It is long overdue, but I am grateful to you for taking care of Julianne. Will you . . . continue?"

"Of course," Hester said.

He hesitated. "Forgive me?"

"Rogue." Her voice cracked a bit.

Their awkwardness made Julianne uncomfortable. Her mother had always said a cup of tea could soothe even the most difficult of moments. She crossed the room to the bell. "I will ring for a tea tray."

He sat in the chair he favored. The dogs abandoned Hester and sat at his feet. "You'll have to wait for sweets," he said.

When they pawed at his boots, he leaned forward to ruffle their fur. Then he glanced at Julianne. "You sent the message to Lady Boswood?"

"Yes," Julianne said. "And I wrote Georgette a short missive, informing her as well."

He nodded. "Very good."

The tea tray arrived. Hester asked the maid to put the rose in a vase and place it in her bedchamber. Julianne poured. He took a dish of tea to his aunt. Her heart turned over as she busied herself placing biscuits on the plates.

Afterward, she sat beside Hester and drank her tea. Hawk finished his biscuits and set the plate on the floor. While the dogs lapped the crumbs, he regarded Julianne with an enigmatic expression. "I expected to find the cubs here."

"I will receive them another day," she said.

He set his cup aside. "What are the plans tonight?"

"*Hamlet* is playing at Drury Lane," Hester said. "Lady Durmont sent an invitation to a dinner party, but I sent our regrets."

Julianne had breathed a sigh of relief when Hester had informed her earlier. The last person she wanted to spend an evening with was that nasty Elizabeth.

"The theater it is," Hawk said.

A footman entered. "A package arrived for you, my lady."

"You may leave it on the sideboard," Hester said.

Hawk stood. "I should take my leave now. I will bring my carriage round this evening to escort you both."

"Your escort is very welcome," Hester said.

Julianne stood. "I will walk with you to the landing."

He offered his arm. The moment she took it, her breath caught at the solid muscle beneath his sleeve. Her knees grew weak at the scent of sandalwood and some other essence, something primitive and male. Something completely and utterly him.

He slanted a sideways glance at her as they stepped outside the drawing room. "You wish to tell me something?"

She looked over her shoulder, and then she met his gaze. "Well done," she whispered.

He frowned. "I deserve no praise."

"You made a mistake and begged her forgiveness. Hester was touched by the rose and the thorn."

He looked away. She suspected she'd embarrassed him. "You made her happy." *And me as well.*

When he returned his gaze to her, a lopsided grin lit his face. "If only I'd known a barbed rose would win you over, I might have brought you one every day."

His joke disappointed her a little, because he'd caused his aunt anguish. But the jest was probably a defense against tender emotions. Men didn't like to show their feelings. And really, there was nothing wrong with using a bit of humor to ease the moment. "You may bring me a rose, but have a care. My thorn might draw blood."

Hawk laughed and tweaked her curl. "That's my girl."

Her smile froze on her face. He'd uttered those same words the night he'd escorted her to the Beresford's ball. The words that had twined round her heart and given her hope only a few short weeks ago. That night, she'd not known the casual endearment meant nothing to him.

She swallowed hard as he took the stairs two at a time. When he reached the marble floor, he turned to wink at her. Then he sauntered off as if he'd not a care in the world.

He was a charmer, through and through, the sort of man who effortlessly enchanted with a wink and a smile and never once realized he'd left behind a broken heart.

Ironically, she'd done the same to a dozen men.

"Julianne?" Hester called.

With a deep breath, she planted a smile on her face. She was learning to mask her feelings, not only for her sake but for others' as well.

When Julianne entered the drawing room, Hester rose, clutching the package she'd received earlier. "Shut the door," she said, excitement in her voice.

Julianne closed it. "Hester, what is it?"

"I'm unsure. Come sit with me, and open the package."

Julianne's fingers trembled as she untied the string. When she opened it, she found a small bound pamphlet. "Oh, my stars!" she cried. Tears welled in her eyes.

"Let us admire your printed words together," Hester said.

When Julianne turned the page, she ran her fingers over it. "I do wish my name could be on it."

"It is unfortunate, but necessary," Hester said. "But let us not dwell on that. Will you read it aloud?" Hester said.

While Julianne read, she marveled that she'd actually written the words. She'd worked so hard, but now it almost didn't seem real, even though she held the pamphlet in her hands.

When Julianne finished reading, Hester proposed a private celebration with Amy and Georgette. "We had better not include Miss Sally Shepherd," Hester said. "I'm sure she's a sweet young lady, but the fewer people who know the better."

"I agree," Julianne said.

"It is important that we remind your friends to remain silent about the pamphlet," she said.

"Yes, we must tell them to pretend ignorance of its existence," Julianne said. "I shall tell them not to give any opinions about it whatsoever."

Hester nodded. "The less they say, the less likely they are to accidentally reveal something that might give away your secret. It is only a cautionary measure. As I said before, if the worst happens, I will take responsibility for writing it."

Not long ago, Julianne had accepted that reassurance, but now she knew she could never let Hester take the blame. All of Hawk's family thought Hester too brazen. If they suspected Hester had authored the pamphlet, they would denounce her.

Julianne shook off her concerns. Only three people knew she was the author, and none of them would ever betray her.

Hundreds of voices created a veritable din at Drury Lane Theater.

Julianne sat beside Hawk and straightened the sedate bodice of her gown. She had almost worn a scandalously low-cut gown that Hester had encouraged her to have made up. But at the last moment, she'd changed her mind. The fabric had barely covered her nipples, and she knew she'd worry the entire time.

Not long after they were seated, Hester spotted some of her friends and ambled off to greet them.

"My aunt must know everyone in the blasted ton," Hawk said. "She is always wandering off."

Julianne bit back a smile. She suspected Hester had made arrangements to meet Mr. Peckham.

She glanced at Hawk from the corner of her eye. "You look perfectly satanic all in black."

"I thought it was red devils with horns and twitching tails that intrigued you."

"No ordinary demon would suit me," she said. "I prefer Hades, king of the underworld."

He scoffed. "Hades abducted Persephone."

"But he made her a queen, and she chose to stay by eating the pomegranate seeds."

His golden brown eyes darkened, and he looked at her from beneath his lashes. As he drew her in with his intent gaze, she wondered why the mention of the pomegranate seeds had led him to look at her in such a wicked manner. His lips parted, and as his breathing grew heavy, she found herself unable to tear her gaze away from his mouth.

Thunderous applause erupted. Hawk sat back, interrupting the spell. She released her pent-up breath and reminded herself to act like a proper lady.

When the curtains opened, the applause dwindled. An actor wearing a white robe walked out onto the stage, his face painted an unearthly pale shade. As he paced about, the watchmen cringed in obvious terror. The younger actor playing Hamlet entered the stage. At first, she thought the ghost silly, but when the apparition spoke to Hamlet about murder and revenge, Julianne shivered.

"Scared?" Hawk murmured.

A shaky laugh escaped her. "A little. I know it's silly. I've seen the play before."

He made a low, scary noise in his throat.

"Stop that," she said.

He leaned toward her. "You're not afraid of the real devils, but you're afraid of ghosts."

"How do you know they're not real?"

"I believe what my eyes and ears tell me."

"You once told me there was one in our attic."

He chuckled. "I had to clamp my hand over your mouth to stifle your scream."

She returned her gaze to the stage. "You were always incorrigible."

"But you liked it when I encouraged you in mischief."

"You were very bad to do so," she said. "I was only an impressionable little girl."

"My three elder sisters boxed my ears when I tried to taunt them. You, however, were ripe for teasing and adventure."

"Well, then, you can blame yourself for all of my transgressions this season."

"Ah, so I'm to reap what I've sowed."

"I'm afraid so," she said.

"I admit I was a bad boy," he said, his voice rumbling.

"You still are."

He grinned at her. "I've not done a single bad thing since becoming your guardian."

"You have a faulty memory," she said.

"I do not."

"I can prove you wrong," she said, repeating the words he'd said the day he'd kissed her.

He was silent a moment. "Are you referring to our kiss?"

She was skating on thin ice now, but she meant to keep their banter light. "Thank you for supplying the evidence. I'd forgotten."

"Liar," he said. "You haven't forgotten."

"Neither have you, apparently."

He paused and when he spoke again, his voice was serious. "I shouldn't have touched you."

She didn't want to spoil the fun of bantering with him, so she decided to keep the conversation light. "I apologize for seducing you."

"I kissed you," he said.

"I kissed you back."

"True," he said. "Liked it, did you?"

Her shoulders shook. "I've no basis for comparison. For all I know, you're a bad kisser."

"I am incomparable," he said.

"You take all the credit, but you know I acquitted myself quite well, despite my lack of experience."

"You benefitted from my expertise," he said.

His conceit encouraged her to make a bold move. She leaned toward him, accidentally brushing her sensitive breasts against his arm. He inhaled sharply as she cupped his ear and whispered, "How do you know?"

He turned toward her. The subtle scent of his spicy cologne and something else indefinable curled through her senses. "You abandoned yourself completely to me," he said in a rough voice.

Her breath caught, but she refused to let him win this sensual battle. "So did you."

He angled his head until his lips were inches from her own. Her heart thumped hard as he closed the scant distance.

Applause broke out among the crowd. He inhaled and turned away.

Her head was spinning. Dear God, they'd almost kissed in full view of the ton.

She gulped in air, but the scent of him still enveloped her. He was much too close, making her all too aware of him. He was breathing through his mouth—as if he'd run a race.

Julianne unfurled her fan and applied it near her hot cheeks. Her tingling skin and rapid heartbeat frightened her. Not because of the desire, but because she feared that in a moment of weakness she would let him back inside her heart.

• • •

The curtain closed, signaling the end of the first act. When Hester returned with Mr. Peckham, Hawk walked over to the balcony and gripped the rail. The lingering ache in his groin reminded him how close he'd come to kissing her—in public, for God's sake.

Was he mad? Of course he was mad—madly in lust with a woman he couldn't touch. He wasn't quite sure how matters had taken a decidedly seductive turn, though he'd felt the tension almost from the beginning. That was nothing new.

The sound of feminine voices interrupted his thoughts. Hawk looked over his shoulder to find Julianne greeting her friends, Amy and Georgette. Hester asked the footman to bring a round of champagne for everyone. Hawk left the balcony railing and joined them. A few minutes later, Hester held her glass aloft and proposed a toast. "To the incomparable Julianne," she said.

Why the devil had his aunt proposed a toast? Then again, who knew where his aunt got her strange notions. He clinked glasses with everyone else and started to turn away, but Georgette's voice stopped him.

"Well done," she said.

Hawk regarded Julianne with lifted brows. "Have I missed something?"

The silence following his question increased his suspicion.

His aunt laughed. "Have you not heard that the ton has proclaimed Julianne the most incomparable belle of the season? Did you not see it in the papers?"

He ought to have known it was something ridiculous. "I do not read the scandal sheets."

Julianne lowered her lashes. "Oh, you are all embarrassing me. Truly, I've done nothing to deserve such praise."

He was monumentally relieved that none of her scrapes had reached the blasted papers.

After Hawk returned to the balcony, Julianne took her friends aside. "Georgette, you nearly gave me away," she whispered.

Georgette winced. "I'm sorry. The words just popped out."

"You've got to be more careful. I don't want Hawk to suspect anything," Julianne said under her breath. "If it is ever discovered I authored the pamphlet, I will be ruined."

"I knew this was a bad idea," Amy whispered.

Hester joined them. "Girls, you look concerned, but everything is fine. He took the bait."

"I feel horrible." Georgette hung her head.

"Chin up. A guilty look will cause suspicion," Hester said. "Julianne is not the only one who will suffer if word ever got out."

"Wh-what do you mean?" Georgette asked.

Hester sighed. "I believe Julianne mentioned this the first day we discussed the pamphlet. As her particular friends, you and Miss Hardwick will be implicated as well if Julianne's identity is ever uncovered."

Georgette covered her mouth. Amy winced.

Julianne now thought that possibility rather remote. If it happened, she would tell her friends to deny any knowledge of the pamphlet. She started to voice the words but held her tongue when Hester gave her a speaking look.

"There is no need to be fearful, however," Hester said.

"Just keep in mind your reputations, and that will prevent you from making a slip of the tongue."

After her friends departed, Julianne eyed Hester. "You exaggerated the danger to them in order to ensure Georgette's silence."

Hester nodded. "I thought you would catch on, for you're a clever girl. I hope you're not angry with me, but..."

"What is it?" Julianne murmured.

"Oh, it's silly," Hester said, waving her hand.

"You can tell me anything, Hester. I'll never judge you."

Hester looked a bit abashed. "I just feel this sudden motherly urge to protect you. I know it's silly, for you are grown."

Julianne squeezed her hand. "It's not silly. You have given me wonderful advice."

Hester swallowed. "I shall miss you when the season ends."

She linked arms with Hester. "Spring is a beginning, and you will always be the aunt of my heart."

The next day, Julianne sat in Hester's drawing room with the five cubs and knew it was past time to make her intentions, or lack thereof, clear. "There is something I've been meaning to discuss with all of you," she said.

"Is something wrong?" Beaufort asked.

"No, not at all," she said. "I've been thinking about friendship and how much I've enjoyed getting to know all of you."

"You're the best girl in the ton," Charles Osgood said.

"Thank you, Charles, but I am only one of many young ladies who are out in society."

"Yes, but you are an incomparable," Beaufort said.

Beaufort worried her more than the other four. "Your friendship means a great deal to me. We are all close in age and ought to enjoy ourselves," she said.

"I'll drink to that," Caruthers said, lifting his teacup.

The other gentlemen laughed.

Julianne realized she was not making herself clear. "In a few short years, we will have greater responsibilities. For now, let us dance, have fun, and be light of heart. With no expectations other than friendship."

"As we do now," Portfrey said. He lifted his teacup. "To Julianne."

"To Julianne," the other four echoed.

She breathed a sigh of relief, because she truly liked the young men and didn't want to mislead them.

Chapter Sixteen

*A Lady's Secrets of Seduction: Some secrets
really should go to the grave.*

Lady Dunworthy shook the pamphlet in the air. "Who-ever wrote this filthy advice ought to be burned at the stake."

Julianne's cup rattled on the saucer as she imagined flames licking at her slippers right in Lady Dunworthy's elegant drawing room. Her nerves threatened to overwhelm her as numerous society dragons ranted about the scandalous pamphlet.

Hester, on the other hand, watched the proceedings with a bemused smile. "Lady Dunworthy, have you read the pamphlet?"

"Only parts of it," she said. "It is appalling. The author exhorts young ladies to ignore their mother's advice."

Lady Boswood shuddered. "Well, I shall ensure my Georgette never reads a word of it."

When Georgette snorted, Amy elbowed her.

Lady Wallingham sighed. "The worst part is that everyone is rushing out to purchase it because of the vulgar title. I heard most of the customers are men." She sniffed. "They obviously are hoping to learn new seduction techniques. We must protect our innocent daughters."

"I agree," Mrs. Shepherd said. "I certainly do not want my dear Sally exposed to such horrid advice."

Sally leaned closer to Julianne and whispered, "I bribed my brother to buy me a copy. I hid it under my bed."

Julianne's eyes widened "Have you read the pamphlet?"

Sally snickered. "Yes. I shall have to try the author's suggestions to catch a husband."

"Girls, this is no laughing matter," Mrs. Shepherd said.

"I beg your pardon, Mama," Sally said.

Julianne was secretly delighted Sally had found the pamphlet helpful. Hopefully other young ladies would as well.

Lady Wallingham produced a sheet of paper. "I suggest we all sign a petition to have this wretched pamphlet banned."

Julianne sucked in her breath. Oh, no. Her precious pamphlet was in danger of imminent extinction.

"That would be akin to shutting the barn door after the horse has bolted," Lady Morley said. "I heard the publisher is rushing a third printing.

Julianne covered her mouth. Her pamphlet was succeeding beyond her wildest dreams!

"I see Lady Julianne is shocked," Lady Boswood said. "I am sorry to expose you to this awful publication, but I feel it necessary to warn you. I will of course write to your mother and assure her that you would never read such rubbish."

Georgette hid all but her laughing eyes behind her fan. Julianne shot her a warning look.

Meanwhile, Lady Wallingham was perusing the pamphlet. "Oh, dear God. The author advises ladies to entice gentlemen with a seductive look."

Georgette lowered her fan. "Oh, my. Does the author explain how to achieve such an expression?"

Lady Boswood made a choked sound and grew limp. "Oh, dear, where are my smelling salts?"

Mrs. Hardwick and Mrs. Shepherd produced vials to revive Lady Boswood.

Lady Dunworthy walked over to a desk and opened an inkwell. "Ladies, let us sign the petition, and I will see it delivered to the publisher."

As the women and their daughters formed a queue, Julianne pulled Hester aside. "I cannot," she whispered.

"Julianne, dearest," Hester said in a loud voice. "You are very pale. I must rush you home to bed."

Lady Boswood clasped her hands to her heart. "Poor Julianne. I fear this has been too much strain for your delicate nature."

Julianne obligingly leaned on Hester's arm. "I do feel a bit light-headed."

A few minutes later, they reached the carriage. Once it rolled away, Hester erupted into guffaws.

Julianne regarded her from the other seat. "I knew it would be controversial, but I never guessed others would vilify it."

Hester sighed. "Ah, but it is a roaring success."

Julianne looked out the window and frowned. She

would consider it a success only if it helped young ladies attract husbands. At the moment, she suspected it was only attracting those who wanted to read something scandalous.

Three days had passed since that meeting in Lady Dunworthy's drawing room. Julianne had finally gone for a drive with Beaufort two days ago. The entire time, she'd imagined someone would point a finger at her and declare her the wicked author of *The Secrets of Seduction*. It was a ridiculous fear, but she'd been a bundle of nerves ever since.

When Amy and Georgette called to celebrate the publication of the pamphlet, they hugged and congratulated her. Then the maid brought in a tea tray with scones and clotted cream, Julianne's favorite. The dogs trotted over to the tray. With a smile, Julianne crumbled a bit of scone on a plate for them.

After the maid left, Hester walked over to the sideboard and returned with the pamphlet. "Perhaps Julianne will agree to read select passages."

"Oh, yes, please do," Amy said.

"Very well," Julianne said. As she read, she recalled different events that had taken place while she was writing.

Georgette regarded her with amazement. "Julianne, you have a rare talent with words."

"I agree," Amy said. "You portray the concerns of single ladies very well."

Julianne shook her head. "My phrasing is not eloquent, but plain speech is better suited for the purpose." Then she regarded Hester and her friends. "I will always remember sharing this special day with all of you."

After tea and scones, Julianne could not resist opening the pamphlet again. She turned the pages and found herself amazed all over again to see her words in print. "I fear you will think me vain for admiring my work."

"You deserve to be proud," Hester said.

Henderson arrived to announce Hawk had called. Julianne hid her pamphlet beneath the sofa cushion and put her finger to her lips to warn her friends. When Hawk sauntered inside, they all rose and curtsied. Seeing her friends' frozen expressions, Julianne imagined Hawk would notice something was afoot immediately.

"I beg your pardon," he said. "I did not mean to interrupt."

Amy bobbed a curtsy. "We were on our way out, my lord."

After they left, Julianne released her pent-up breath. "I will ring for a fresh pot of tea."

"No, thank you," he said. "It's a fine day. I thought you might wish to take a drive with me."

"What a lovely idea," Hester said.

Julianne kept her gaze on Hawk. Had he suggested a ride as a pretext to speak to her privately? The fine hairs on her neck stiffened. What if he'd somehow guessed she'd written the pamphlet? But if he knew, he would have confronted Hester as well. She smiled at him and agreed to the drive, but she suspected Hawk meant to tell her something he didn't want his aunt to hear.

The wind blew her bonnet ribbons about as Hawk steered the curricle through the crowded streets. He said nothing during the drive, but the noise of clacking hooves, rumbling wheels, and shouts from street vendors precluded conversation.

When they entered Hyde Park, he drove along the deserted path for a bit. The fashionable hour wouldn't start for another three hours. At last he halted the vehicle, jumped down, and strode around to her side. He grasped her by the waist, lifting her as if she weighed little more than a child. A thrill raced through her blood, but she mustn't let him know.

After he set her down, he offered his arm. "Shall we walk?"

She clasped his sleeve, noting he adjusted his stride to accommodate her slower pace. They strolled along the path, a mixture of gravel and bark. He led her to a wrought-iron bench beneath the canopy of a great oak. She clasped her hands on her lap, but her stomach clenched. Something was wrong.

The wind rustled the leaves. He drew in his breath and looked at her with a solemn expression. "I brought you here so that we could talk privately."

She swallowed. "I know."

He leaned forward, his elbows on his thighs. "Beaufort called upon me this morning."

She frowned. "He took me for a drive at Rotten Row two days ago. But why would he call on you?"

Hawk looked at his boots. "I told him I could not grant permission."

A stinging sensation rippled along her arms. "For what?"

Hawk's jaw worked, but still he would not look at her. "I told him to talk to your brother." He paused. "He wants to marry you," he said in a gruff voice.

"What?!"

Hawk sat back, his expression guarded.

She shook her head. "No, I told him and the other four gentlemen that I only wanted friendship." She stood and started pacing. "I gave him no encouragement during that ride." She fisted her hands. "I knew it was a mistake to take a drive with him. But I couldn't refuse because I'd put him off. I didn't want to wound him."

She kicked a pebble. When Hawk said nothing, she halted and shook her finger at him. "You will not blame me. Maybe I should have refused to drive with him, but I didn't know he would take it into his head to propose."

Hawk rose. "You're not...in love with him?"

"Of course not." She drew in a breath. "And this does not count as my thirteenth proposal."

A smile tugged at Hawk's lips. "Since he hasn't officially asked, I agree."

"Damn it. Now I have to find a way to discourage him without injuring his tender sensibilities."

Hawk's shoulders shook with laughter.

"What are you laughing at?"

"You cursed," he said.

"I'll curse like a sailor if he goes down on bended knee."

"Would you prefer I tell him you aren't interested?"

"I don't know," she said. "I thought he understood. And now he'll hate me."

"You told him and the others you only wanted friendship," Hawk said. "Perhaps it would help if I told him your brother isn't likely to grant permission."

"No, I think he needs to know the truth," she said.

"Since he came to me, I will tell him that you're not ready for marriage yet. That will soften the blow a bit."

When she wiped her gloved finger under her eye, Hawk took out a handkerchief and dabbed at her face. "You did nothing wrong," he said. "Beaufort obviously didn't believe you. His pride will take a hit, but he'll recover."

She let out a shaky breath. "Thank you."

"Better now?"

"A little," she said.

Hawk took her hand, held it high, and twirled her round. Laughing, she begged him to stop. When he did, she staggered from the dizziness.

He caught her. "Whoa!"

She braced her hands on his chest. "Everything is moving round and round."

He untied the bow beneath her chin, removed her bonnet, and pressed her head to his chest. "Be still. The dizziness will pass."

She closed her eyes. Not long after, the world stopped spinning, but she lingered, inhaling his scent, a combination of starch, sandalwood, and him. He'd understood that she was truly overset about Beaufort.

He nuzzled her hair. "So sweet," he murmured.

She wanted to lift her face up to him in a silent plea for his kiss, but she feared what was beating in her heart would show on her face.

"Are you recovered?" he asked in a low rumble.

"Yes." She stepped back and held out her hand. "The bonnet, if you please."

He grinned and put it behind his back. "No."

"Hawk, give me the bonnet."

He wagged his brows. "You'll have to come and get it."

She ought to ignore his prank, but his boyish grin was irresistible. He backed up as she walked toward him. Laughing, she darted around him and almost snatched the bonnet, but he sprinted off.

Exasperated, she gave chase but lost him. "Rogue," she muttered, slowing to a walk so that she could catch her breath.

His arm shot out from behind one of the fat oaks. Her bonnet dangled from his hand. She considered how to best him, and then an idea occurred to her.

Lifting her skirts, she whirled around and ran as fast as she could toward his curricle. Oh, she'd get him when she drove his precious vehicle off without him. Granted, she had no idea how to drive, but how difficult could it be?

She grinned at the sound of his running steps far behind her. He'd regret teaching her how to be a hoyden all those years ago. Upon reaching the curricle, she lifted her skirts one-handed above her knees and hoisted herself up onto the wheel. She'd not climbed a tree in years, but at one time, she'd been a veritable monkey in petticoats.

"Minx," he yelled as she climbed over the seat to the driver's side. She was examining the reins when he leaped up the other side. He slid beside her, dropped the bonnet to the floor, and tickled her waist. She shrieked. This playfulness, the sheer joy of being the object of his teasing, all flooded her heart. This was what she'd missed the most.

When he grabbed her wrists and pinned them behind her back, she cried out, "Let me go—"

He swooped in and kissed her. As his tongue slid home, her heart blossomed, and she let him climb right back in. He slowed the rhythm as if he were savoring her. Her skin heated and her breasts felt full. She joined him in the kiss, tangling her tongue with his. Every reason she ought to protect her heart dwindled to nothing as he devoured her mouth.

Love me, love me, love me.

He shifted on the seat, causing the curricle to rock. The horses whinnied. He tore his mouth away, leaving her bereft.

No, no, no. Come back to me.

"Hush," he commanded the matched pair of grays.

They snorted.

Laughter gurgled in her throat. He regarded her with a wicked expression. "Now would be a good time to slap me."

She looked at him from beneath her lashes. "You'll have to release me."

His smile fled as he let her go.

She'd no intention of letting his guilt spoil the day. Julianne grabbed the sides of the curricle in order to leap to the ground. He caught her by the waist and hauled her back. She turned into his arms, meaning to be the aggressor this time.

The blasted horses whinnied again.

"Damn it," she muttered.

He guffawed.

"Stop laughing—you're making the horses nervous," she said.

"We'd best leave before my cattle mutiny." He grasped her bonnet, plunked it onto her head, and tied the bow. "Change places with me."

As he steered the curricle out of the park, he kept his eyes on the street. "That should not have happened."

"I only felt sorry for you."

"Really? Why?"

She sniffed. "Ever since I reformed you, I've noticed you've become irritable. I figured you were...frustrated. So I let you kiss me to alleviate your suffering."

He glanced at her. "It would take a lot more than a kiss to alleviate what's bothering me."

Hawk knew he should be horsewhipped for kissing her again.

He followed his aunt and Julianne through the receiving line at Lord and Lady Garnett's ball. His gaze strayed to Julianne. The netting over her blue ball gown sparkled in the candlelight. When she slid an impish look at him, he winked at her. Best to keep what had happened this afternoon light.

Once they entered the crowded ballroom, Hester hailed her friend Mr. Peckham and left them without so much as a by-your-leave.

Hawk shook his head. "Those two are thick as thieves."

"Hmmm," Julianne said.

Hawk offered his arm, and as he led her through the room, he noticed the avid stares directed at them. The devil. He knew he ought to make himself scarce to avoid speculation, but after what had happened earlier today, he couldn't make himself do it.

He'd felt a bit sorry for Beaufort late this afternoon after informing him that Julianne was not ready for marriage. Beaufort had taken the news hard at first, but Hawk had reminded him that Julianne had said she only wanted friendship from all of the cubs. Beaufort had admitted he'd hoped she wasn't serious.

Truthfully, he'd been relieved when Julianne had protested Beaufort's intention to propose. Hawk hadn't wanted her to know he'd worried she would accept Beaufort, so he'd resorted to teasing her. Lord, he'd never forget the way she'd scampered up the curricle. Or their slow, passionate kiss. The memory stirred his blood, but he must take care not to let his desire distract him—too much.

He should be sorry for kissing her, but he wasn't. If he'd thought he was setting expectations for a different sort of relationship, he would never have dared kiss her. But he knew she didn't want to marry yet. Well, he was fairly certain. After all, she'd told the cubs she only wanted friendship. He and Julianne were like two peas in a pod. Neither of them wanted to leap into the parson's mousetrap.

The only difference was that eventually she would wed, and he never would.

He shoved the thought out of his head. Tonight he meant to enjoy Julianne's company. He'd sworn to win her back as his partner in mischief, and today he'd succeeded. A voice deep inside whispered, *To what end? To the end of the season,* he silently answered. Long ago, he'd learned to live in the here and now. It had been the only way to keep from going quietly mad over circumstances he'd ceded control over to another man.

He'd had no choice.

Julianne waved. "There are Amy and Georgette. I'll leave you to your cards."

"You are throwing me over for your friends," he said in a theatrical voice. "I'm heartbroken."

"I'm sure you'll recover as soon as you meet up with your fellow rakes," she said.

"Your friends may need my help. Osgood is bearing toward them as we speak. Perhaps we'd better save them before he starts spouting poetry."

She gave him a warning look. "Don't poke fun at him. I believe he has developed tender feelings for Amy."

"Let us play matchmakers, shall we? They're both so timid that nothing is likely to come of it if we don't nudge them."

"You'll make a muddle of it."

He clapped his hand to his heart. "You have so little faith in me, but I assure you Osgood trusts my judgment about women."

"Liar. You only want to follow me about."

"No, it's true, but you mustn't let on. He asked for my advice."

Her eyes narrowed. "I hope you didn't put indecent ideas in his head."

He thought better of telling her Osgood needed no help with indecent ideas. "Come along. I'll encourage Osgood to ask Miss Hardwick to dance while you point out his positive qualities to her."

"Very well, but if you embarrass them, I'll make you sorry," she muttered.

"You can feel sorry for me anytime you like," he said.

"What?"

"How quickly you forget my suffering and frustration."

A rosy blush stained her cheeks.

He winked. "I'll be quite pitiful if you'll reward me for it."

She grinned. "Reward you? How?"

He wished to get her naked, but he kept that between his teeth. "Another memory lapse? Was my earlier kiss so forgettable?"

"Hush, someone might hear you."

When they reached Julianne's friends, Georgette regarded him with a smirk. He thought her reaction odd. She'd never made her dislike of him a secret, but now she acted as if she had something on him. Then that silly chit Sally Shepherd arrived. "Oh, goodness, everyone is talking about that pamphlet," she said.

"You mean *The Secrets of Seduction*?" Osgood said.

"Yes," Sally said.

"I heard about it in parliament," Hawk said. "Supposedly a lady wrote it."

Sally giggled. "All the ladies gathered at Lady Dunworthy's town house signed a petition to have it banned."

Hawk frowned at Julianne. "You said nothing about it."

She shrugged. "I didn't think you would be interested."

"Julianne nearly swooned," Georgette said.

Hawk noted Georgette's mischievous expression and regarded Julianne. "You, a wilting flower?"

"I was overcome by the subject matter," she said.

He laughed.

Osgood sighed. "I tried to purchase a copy today, but the bookseller had sold out. He promised a fourth printing."

Caruthers snorted. "Were you hoping to learn some secrets?"

Benton and Portfrey guffawed.

Georgette smiled slyly. "Mr. Osgood is a poet. Perhaps he wrote the pamphlet."

Amy Hardwick scowled at Georgette. "Don't tease him."

Hawk wondered if Amy was indeed smitten with the bad poet. He'd thought the girl had too much sense for Osgood, but Julianne seemed convinced the pair would suit.

At the moment, however, Osgood was making calf eyes at Julianne. She seemed oblivious to his moonstruck expression.

Hawk strolled over to Osgood and took him aside for the man-to-man talk.

The cub puffed out his chest. "I'm planning to ask Lady Julianne to dance—as soon as I can draw her away from Miss Hardwick."

Well, hell. He'd better find a means of dissuading Osgood. "Lady Julianne is in high dudgeon tonight," he said in low, confidential tones. "Beaufort wanted to offer for her, but she took a fit of the vapors as soon as I put the matter before her. Claimed she'd told all of you she wanted only friendship. If you ask her now, she's likely to put a flea in your ear."

Osgood frowned. "Damn Beaufort. I should have known he'd rush to claim her."

"Don't let her hear you say anything about claims on her person. She's liable to rip at you."

Osgood's face fell. "How am I to overcome her objections?"

"Dance with her friend Miss Hardwick. Julianne dotes on her. You'll impress her if you express interest in her friend."

Osgood drew closer. "But Miss Hardwick is taller than me."

"No, you're mistaken," he lied. "You've grown in the last fortnight."

"I hadn't noticed," he said, looking down at his trousers as if he expected to find them above his ankles, despite the foot straps.

Hawk managed to hide his amusement. "Go on and ask her to dance."

Osgood drew in his breath and walked over to Miss Hardwick. Hawk noted that Amy was frowning at something

Julianne said. The devil, this matchmaking scheme was proving a rather dicey business.

When Osgood approached Amy, his face turned bright red. He must have succeeded because Amy, who was indeed taller, took his arm. She didn't look any happier than Osgood about their impending dance.

Hawk strolled over to Julianne and offered his arm.

She wrinkled her nose. "I hope you're not insisting we dance."

He chuckled. "I thought you might wish to watch the couple we threw together."

Julianne brightened. "Oh, yes, that is an excellent idea. Afterward, we can remark upon how well they acquitted themselves."

"Right-ho," he said, leading her away.

She narrowed her eyes. "Are you funning me?"

"Julianne, men don't compliment other men on their dancing."

"Why not?" she asked.

"Because it sounds...Never mind. Just take my word for it."

She appeared to digest that information, and then a sly smile lit her face. "If you compliment him, I'll reward you."

"You're a cruel woman, but I'll make a bargain with you. If I say 'well done,' will that suffice?"

She sniffed. "You have to say it within my hearing."

"Done," he said. "Tonight, I get a kiss in my aunt's drawing room."

"I get to choose the time and place," she said.

"Tonight," he said.

"If your aunt is present, we cannot," she said. "Unless you're willing to settle for kissing my hand?"

"Oh, no, I want full payment—on the lips."

"There they are," she said as they neared the dance floor.

The dancers at the top of the line performed the steps. Eventually, it was Osgood's turn. He skipped forward and back, almost stumbling over his enormous feet. When he took Miss Hardwick's hands and turned, he rotated in the wrong direction, bumping into another couple in the process.

Hawk winced. "I don't think I can watch."

"Hush," Julianne said. "He made a mistake, but he'll recover."

When it was his turn to lead Miss Hardwick to the bottom of the line, Osgood managed to step on poor Amy's toes before parting to the opposite side of the line.

"Oh, dear God," Julianne said under her breath. "We cannot compliment their dance."

"I still get a reward," he said.

"No, you do not."

"You made me persuade him to dance with her. I deserve recompense for having to witness my cruelty to Miss Hardwick."

"If anyone deserves a reward, it's poor Amy," Julianne said. "I'll have to find her a decent dance partner to make up for it."

He looked at her. "All jests aside, you know as well as I do she'll not want to go anywhere near the dance floor after this disaster."

Julianne sighed. "I had high hopes for them. He's such a sensitive young man. I was sure he and Amy would make the perfect couple."

He led her away. "Even if it weren't for that horrible

dance, the two of them are ill-suited. They may be close in age, but she's far more mature than Osgood."

"I just wish...Never mind."

"What?" he asked.

She hung her head. "No one ever asks her to dance."

"I'll ask her," he said.

"No." Julianne swallowed. "She'll know I put you up to it, and it will humiliate her."

"I'm tempted to utter platitudes, but I know it doesn't make up for the cruelty of others. This much I do know. She's lucky to have a friend like you."

"Is she? When I try to put myself in her slippers, I think how I would feel if my friend danced every dance while I danced none. She ought to hate me for it."

"But she doesn't," he said. "Because she knows you care about her."

"I don't want her to end up alone and scorned," she whispered.

He laid his hand over hers and squeezed. "You won't let that happen."

He stood talking to a group of friends from his club. Unable to resist, he glanced at Julianne. When she smiled at him, he gave her a conspiratorial wink. She'd announced to the five cubs that she preferred conversation to dancing tonight. Then she'd drawn Amy into the conversation. There had been only one tense moment when Beaufort had asked Lady Georgette to dance. He'd purposely ignored Julianne, but she'd not let his rude behavior affect her.

Hawk had been so proud of her.

He returned his attention to the men surrounding him.

Archdale had joined the group and was talking about the pamphlet. Apparently, everyone knew about it. "Hot off the presses," Archdale said. "You'll not believe the title." He slapped his thigh. "*The Secrets of Seduction.*"

The other gents clamored to know where to purchase it.

"The Altar of the Muses in Piccadilly," Archdale said. "The anonymous author is listed as a lady."

"Harriette Wilson is the front-runner in the betting book," another man said.

Hawk glanced over at Julianne's friends. Based on Georgette's sly comments earlier, he had a feeling the ladies knew the author.

Archdale held his hand up. "Before you rush out to purchase a copy, you should know the author exhorts genteel ladies to ignore their mother's advice. The whole pamphlet is filled with advice on how to snare unsuspecting bachelors into the parson's mousetrap."

The laughter died.

Hawk shook his head and walked away. No doubt the publisher would make a fortune off fools because of the scandalous title. The lady was probably one of those reformer types who imagined herself the next Mary Wollstonecraft, that infamous woman who had called for the equality of the sexes.

He joined the crowd thronging around Julianne. As she returned his smile, his heart beat a little faster. He found himself unable to tear his gaze away from her. Something inside him shifted, and an odd feeling took hold of him, one he couldn't define.

Feminine laughter broke the spell. Hawk reminded himself to use care when they were in view of the rest of the ton. He couldn't afford to stir up speculation about his intentions—or lack thereof. What was between him and Julianne was no one else's business.

"I'll take you to the refreshment table for a cup of punch. If you wish," he remembered to add.

"I'd like that," she said.

As he led her away, she grinned at him. "Tell me what happens at a gentleman's club."

He laughed. "Why?"

"I told you a secret about ladies' retiring rooms. It is your turn to share," she said.

"There's not much to tell. We eat, drink, and gamble."

"What about the famous betting book?"

"Ah, that's a closely guarded secret."

"Then you must tell me," she said.

"Actually it's boring. Gents bet on stupid things such as which day it will rain. But yesterday, the bets were all about who wrote that infamous pamphlet."

"Oh?" she said. "And who is getting the most bets?"

"A courtesan, but I think it's likely some radical lady bent on making a bit of coin."

"Hmmm," she said.

They had reached the refreshment table. He handed her a cup of punch and procured one for himself.

She sipped the punch. Her eyes watered.

"The devil," he said after tasting his. "It's liberally spiked with brandy."

He took the cup away from her and set it aside. "Sorry."

The orchestra struck up the opening bars of a country dance. "Are you tired of standing? There are two empty chairs."

"I wouldn't mind resting for a bit," she said.

He led her to the chairs and stretched out his legs.

"That's better. Now we can watch everyone and make sport of them."

"You are bad," she said.

"I think we already established that."

"Will you teach me how to drive your curricle?" she asked.

"No."

"Why not?"

"Because you're liable to turn it over and kill us both."

"Not if you show me how," she said.

"You only want me to teach you so you can steal my curricle and my cattle."

She grinned at him. "I admit it crossed my mind this afternoon."

"Imp." He wagged his brows. "I did enjoy the view as you climbed up the wheel. Nice legs."

She lifted her chin. "You should not have looked."

"If you show me more, I might let you take the reins."

"Not a chance," she said.

He chuckled. "Well, at least you promised me another kiss."

"Hush, Georgette and Amy are headed this way," she said.

He sighed inwardly, knowing he dared not flirt with her in their presence.

"We are on our way to the retiring room," Georgette said. "Would you care to accompany us?"

She glanced at him. "I'll return soon."

He met her gaze, assessing her. Then he said the words he hoped would prevent her from disappointing him. "I trust you."

• • •

"Oh my goodness, I almost swallowed my tongue when I saw the way Hawk looked at you tonight," Georgette said as they ascended the stairs.

"Hush, Georgette," Amy said. "Wait until we reach the retiring room where we'll not be overheard."

Julianne did not want to discuss Hawk with them, but she knew Georgette would persist.

Upon reaching the retiring room, they sat together on a velvet bench. Julianne looked at the mantel clock and realized the midnight supper would begin in half an hour. Many of the ladies were departing, probably to avoid the worst of the crowd.

"Georgette, you must be careful what you say about the pamphlet," Amy said.

"I was only having a bit of fun."

"We all agreed to pretend ignorance," Julianne said. "Remember, our reputations are at stake."

Two giggling girls who had recently made their come-outs walked past. Watching them, Julianne realized that she'd changed in many ways over the past four seasons, but in some ways she was the same person. Was there a core-defining characteristic to each person? Were all people born with certain natures?

She realized she'd always thought of Hawk's charming ways as a natural part of his personality. He could win over anyone with a wink or a jest. She couldn't remember a time when he wasn't teasing others.

"Dear God, what is this dreamy look on your face?" Georgette said.

Julianne blinked. "Oh, sorry. I was lost in thought."

"You *are* different tonight," Amy said.

Georgette nodded. "Something has happened between

you and Hawk. He kept gazing at you. I almost felt as if the two of you were communicating without words."

She shrugged. "I've known him forever, so his habits are no mystery to me."

"We know you too well to accept that explanation," Amy said gently. "You've ranted about Hawk for weeks now, and tonight you're both suddenly in accord? It makes no sense."

"I suppose we just grew weary of fighting all of the time."

Georgette and Amy exchanged knowing glances.

Julianne said nothing. Not long ago, she'd admitted he'd kissed her, but she would say nothing to her friends about the events of this afternoon. What had transpired with Hawk should remain private. Even if she were tempted to reveal it, she didn't know how to explain his behavior and her confusing feelings. And there was a part of her that didn't want to examine too closely what had happened between them. She wanted to hold on to the bubbly feelings that had enveloped her this afternoon and again tonight.

"You know you can tell us anything," Amy said. "That is what friends are for."

Julianne looked at her clasped hands in her lap and decided to tell them just enough to satisfy their curiosity. "We had another row not long ago. He asked if we could be friends instead of enemies." She lifted her gaze. "I agreed."

"Julianne, you're not falling in love with him again, are you?" Georgette asked.

"We've always been friends. If he'd not become my guardian, we never would have been at odds." She'd tried to deny her feelings, but she'd never fallen out of love with him.

Georgette shook her head. "You didn't answer my question."

"Must you interrogate me?" she said irritably.

Amy gave her a worried look. "He hurt you terribly. We cannot bear to see you suffer heartbreak again."

"My mother said he's not the marrying kind," Georgette said. "My brother agreed."

Julianne bit her lip. She'd never said anything to Georgette about her despicable brother. Now she wondered if she'd done the right thing by keeping silent. But what good would come of telling Georgette about her brother's loathsome pursuit? She certainly could not tell her friend about the bad blood between Hawk and Ramsey, for Georgette would surely defend her brother.

"You are not one to keep your thoughts and feelings to yourself," Amy said. "I'm the one who weighs every word, but tonight you are saying very little. Has Hawk given you any sign he's formed an attachment?"

Yes and no. "He is my friend, as he has always been."

"If you meant to reassure us, you have not," Georgette said. "Would a true friend mislead you about his feelings and then call you his sister?"

A flush suffused her face. She stood. "I must go."

"I'm sorry." Georgette rose as well. "Please forgive me. I'm only concerned—"

Julianne held her hand up. "I know you mean well, but I don't want to pull apart my feelings at the seams like an old gown I've outgrown."

"We don't want to see you hurt again," Amy said.

"This is not between me and the two of you," Julianne said. "It's between me and Hawk."

They gasped as she turned and hurried from the retiring room. Her heated feelings had shown on her face, and still they'd persisted with their badgering. It had felt as if they'd seen her happiness and wanted to burst it like a soap bubble.

As she climbed the stairs, she realized her vexation stemmed from the fact that her friends had brought up her own fears. And she'd not wanted to face those fears today.

Upon reaching the landing, she caught Ramsey staring at her. She averted her gaze, lifted her skirts, and walked past him.

He caught up to her. "Lady Julianne, please wait."

"You can have nothing to say that I wish to hear."

"Even an apology?"

She didn't trust him. "This is another ruse."

"What?" His sandy brows drew together.

She turned her back, a cut direct. When she took a step forward, his voice froze her.

"I saw you with him at the park today."

Shock descended over her like icy pellets. She whirled around. "You spied on me?"

He visibly recoiled. "How could you make such an accusation?"

"You've given me every reason to mistrust and dislike you."

"I walk in the park in the early afternoon when it's deserted. The solitude helps me to think." His mouth twisted bitterly. "Ask my sister if you do not believe me."

"Your habits are none of my concern, and my life is none of your affair," she said. "You have continued to beleaguer me in spite of my guardian's wishes and my own, but you will not have another opportunity. This is our last conversation. From this moment forward, I will never acknowledge your presence again."

"I saw him kissing you." He held his fist to his chest. "I cannot even describe to you how I felt."

She saw the misery in his blue eyes and looked away. "If you were a gentleman, you would not have mentioned it."

"Open your eyes, Lady Julianne. He's persuaded you I'm the devil incarnate, but he bases his opinion on events that took place more than a dozen years ago."

Lady Boswood had said something similar about her son's youthful past.

Julianne wet her lips. "The animosity is between you and him. I am powerless in this matter."

"Before you cede more to him, you might want to consider what kind of man would refuse to shake my hand and let the past go," he said.

"You almost refused to shake his hand after your fencing match," she hissed. "So do not think to pull the wool over my eyes."

He met her gaze. "Why do you think I hesitated?"

Chill bumps erupted on her arms. "What happened to cause the bad blood between you?"

Ramsey shook his head. "The specifics are irrelevant now. He deserved to be angry then, but to hold a grudge for more than twelve years is beyond all reason."

"No one hates another without cause."

He hesitated. "My friends and I tricked him. He was much younger and fell for the scheme."

"There is something you're not telling me. I want the truth."

"You'll have to ask him. And for the record, I don't

hate him. I only hate that he stands between us and does it to get revenge."

"I don't believe you," she said. "You're slanting the truth to make yourself appear in a better light."

"You asked me what happened. Why did you not ask him?"

She stiffened.

Ramsey nodded. "You asked, and he refused to tell you, didn't he?"

She knew her silence confirmed his suspicion.

"Perhaps it's not me you should disbelieve."

She shivered as he strode toward the ballroom.

The double doors opened and a noisy crowd of guests spilled out. Hundreds of people emerged and headed toward the staircase. Julianne stepped back and found herself trapped against the wall. Panic gripped her.

She started gulping for air. She felt suffocated.

Hawk. She wanted Hawk. Nothing else in the world mattered. Because after everyone had warned her about him this evening, she needed his reassurance.

She made herself push into the crowd. "Hawk!"

Chapter Seventeen

A Scoundrel's Code of Conduct: The road to good intentions is paved with posies.

Hawk stood in the ballroom, craning his head trying to find Julianne. She'd promised to return promptly. He told himself something must have happened, but the denial made him angry. She'd manipulated him again.

He walked over to the nearly empty punch bowl, poured himself a cup, and downed it in two gulps. The brandy burned his throat. He set the cup aside and watched the crowd shuffle out the door. The laughter and din of voices grated on his nerves.

A stir erupted among the crowd. And her voice pierced through the hundreds of voices. "Hawk!" she cried.

He strode forward, pushing past people. "Julianne?"

Others were staring at him, but he didn't care.

"Hawk, where are you?"

The crowd parted a little. "Hawk!"

"I'm here," he called out, shoving past the other guests and ignoring their complaints.

She broke through. Her face was ghostly white. He threw his arm around her shoulders. "Let us pass," he said. "She is unwell."

A chorus of concerned voices erupted, but at last others stepped aside and let them pass. His heart was beating fast as he managed to withdraw her from the crowd. She was trembling.

He found an empty adjoining drawing room and took her to a sofa. Then he sat beside her with his arm around her shoulder. "Shhh. You're safe now."

"The doors opened. When all the people emerged, I got trapped against the wall."

He nuzzled her hair. "You must have been frightened."

"I couldn't stand it, so I pushed through the crowd. It felt as if I were swimming upstream. I caused a scene, but I wanted you."

I wanted you, too. "You were panicked, but it's over now."

"I wish I'd never left," she whispered.

He smoothed an errant wisp of hair from her cheek. "Where are your friends?"

"I left them in the ladies' retiring room," she said in a miserable voice.

"Did you have a disagreement with them?"

She shrugged one shoulder.

"Do you want to tell me?" he asked.

She wet her lips. "You know what it is like when well-meaning people offer advice and try a bit too hard to influence you?"

He thought of his mother and sisters and nodded.

"I didn't like it when they worked on me and persisted," she said. "They made me angry, but just because we are friends does not give them the right to pry and poke."

"I won't pry or poke, but if you wish to discuss the matter, I will listen," he said.

"No, there is a matter that is more critical," she said.

The fine hairs on his neck stiffened.

"One of the reasons I got trapped was because Ramsey waylaid me."

"He is spoiling for a fight," Hawk said between gritted teeth.

"I started to walk away, but he said he'd seen us at the park."

"What?" His heartbeat drummed in his ears.

She moistened her lips. "He claimed he walks there every day. He said his sister would confirm it, but I think he knows I cannot ask her without arousing suspicion."

He inhaled. "Did he see us kiss?"

"Yes."

He released her. God, he'd been an idiot.

"What can Ramsey do?" Julianne said.

"He can write your brother. Tristan will not take this lightly. I'm your guardian, for God's sake."

"Doesn't my brother know Ramsey's character? Tristan would not think well of a man who resorted to tattling like a schoolboy."

"If Ramsey does inform him, your brother will ask me. I won't lie to him." He paused. "I should not have kissed you."

"I should not have let you, but we've been partners in mischief for years." She tilted her head slightly. "It was a natural evolution."

It was pure lust, but he thought better of admitting it. "Nevertheless, I am your guardian, and it was wrong of me."

"Hawk, it was a kiss. We put our toes on the boundaries, but we didn't step over them." She paused and added, "If Tristan finds out, we will act sheepish and say we made a mistake."

"Your brother is likely to plant his fist in my face."

"I'll tell him not to be ridiculous. Besides, I suspect he and Tessa did more than talk all those times he called upon her."

Hawk kept his mouth shut, but he recalled the night he'd caught Tristan and Tessa alone in the dark library at Ashdown House. The memory gave him an idea. "I'll tell your brother I apologized profusely. He'll probably still try to beat me to a pulp, but I'll live."

"Don't worry. Tessa won't let him."

Hawk drew in his breath. "I apologize profusely for kissing you, but not for stealing your bonnet. There, it's official."

She laughed, but her expression sobered. "There is another matter Ramsey brought up."

Every muscle in his body tensed. "What did he say?"

"He said you hang on to a grudge against him for something that happened a dozen years ago. When I questioned him, he admitted that he and his friends tricked you."

He'd kill Ramsey if he'd told her about that sordid house party. "What else did he say?"

"He said if I wanted to know more, I should ask you."

His stomach clenched. He'd demanded honesty of her, but he could not divulge what had happened all those years ago.

She cupped his cheek. "Tonight, my friends badgered me, but I will not follow their example. Whatever happened to you long ago must have been awful or you would not despise him. I know you have scars, but the past is gone. No matter what transpired, it does not change who you are to me."

He covered her hand with his own. There were no words for his feelings. She believed in him unconditionally. "Ramsey manipulated me, but I am responsible for my actions," he said.

"You made a mistake when you were very young," she said. "It's time to forgive yourself."

How could he? Ramsey and his friends had tricked him, but he made the choice to stay. He could have walked away. Instead, he'd let them pressure him because of his damnable pride. He didn't like to think about that night. The consequences had been bad. His own father had denounced him and then set about paying a bloody fortune to save his sorry hide.

"Hawk," she whispered. "I can see you are haunted by what happened, but you cannot let this shadow you forever."

"I cannot undo the damage," he said in a hoarse voice.

"No, but you can prevent further damage—to yourself. The boy who made that mistake is now a grown man, a good man."

He scoffed.

"My brother asked you to be my guardian because he believes you are a good man," Julianne said. "And so do I."

He met her gaze. "My reputation is well deserved."

"Not any longer." She grinned. "I reformed you."

The dark clouds still hovered, but she managed to make him smile a little. He helped her rise. "We'd better go downstairs and find my aunt."

She squeezed his arm. "I cannot wait to return to Gatewick Park for the christening so I can tell your mother and sisters that I reformed you. They will be so delighted."

He didn't want to think about that house party, because when it ended, he would have to let her go.

Hawk felt a bit abashed and more than a little guilty as he set the two posies on the seat beside him and drove to his aunt's house.

He'd stayed away for three days, claiming parliament and estate matters called him. In truth, he'd needed time to think clearly about Julianne and the friendship they had reestablished.

She'd spoken of an invisible boundary and treated their kiss as if it were just another lark. Temptation had loomed, stronger than ever. He'd told himself flirting and stealing kisses were harmless enough.

That day at the park, she'd enchanted him. They had fallen into old patterns, teasing and taunting each other. He'd been so relieved when she'd refused Beaufort's suit that he'd not stopped to think about the implications. All he'd thought about was the moment. But when he'd kissed her, one word had echoed in his brain: *Mine, mine, mine.*

He wanted her badly, as a friend and a lover. She was never far from his thoughts or his erotic dreams. He realized she'd bewitched him, and that had put the fear of the devil in him.

She didn't understand, but he knew how easily a kiss could spark a fire that could rage out of control. He couldn't take any more chances with her, because he didn't trust himself. If he made a mistake, the consequences would cost him his oldest friend and rip apart their families.

He'd sobered the day after their discussion in that empty drawing room at the ball. She'd told him to forgive himself and called him a good man. But he knew differently.

Men like you never change.

His father had believed that it was bad blood passed on from his late, dissolute uncle's side of the family. Hawk knew it wasn't an innate character trait, but rather one bad decision, one stupid youthful mistake.

He'd pay for his transgression with a lifetime of regret, but he wouldn't add marrying a woman under false pretense to his list of sins.

If he were a different sort of man, he could walk away from his past and count himself lucky. Most men would go on with their lives and never lose a wink of sleep.

He'd lost a lot of sleep over the years, wondering and worrying because he had no control. No information. No contact at all. He'd signed the agreement more than twelve years ago. A devil's bargain. His life in exchange for staying away and keeping his mouth shut.

His aunt's square came into view. Today he meant to treat Julianne as his ward and avoid flirting. He must distance himself before he did something stupid—again.

When he steered into the square, he found carriages lining the street. Hell. Hester was entertaining. He finally found a place for his rig, jumped down, and grasped the posies. A few minutes later, he entered his aunt's drawing room to find a veritable crowd. To his surprise, Lady

Georgette and Miss Hardwick smiled genially at him. Usually, Georgette treated him with disdain, and Miss Hardwick regarded him as if he were Satan himself. Sally Shepherd had joined the group today and fluttered her lashes at him.

He ignored Sally and delivered the posies to his aunt and Julianne. When all the ladies made a to-do about it, his face heated. A maid arrived shortly thereafter with two vases.

At least he wasn't the only man present. Peckham and three of the cubs had called. Portfrey, Benton, and Caruthers were wolfing down cake. The dogs sat before them, whining.

Julianne brought Hawk a cup of tea and a slice of cake. When their fingers accidentally brushed, he inhaled. He called himself an idiot for letting a momentary touch affect him.

The dogs, having long ago decided he was a soft touch, abandoned the cubs and scampered over to him. To give himself some occupation, he held up crumbs, setting the spaniels off to barking.

"Marc, stop teasing them," Hester said. "Their barking is making an awful racket."

He devoured his cake and set the plate of crumbs on the floor.

Sally Shepherd fluttered her lashes at him again. "It's too bad you missed Lady Durmont's musicale last evening."

"Let me guess," he said. "Henrietta finally learned how to carry a tune."

Sally twittered like a bird. "Oh, no. One of the hunting dogs got loose, ran inside, and started howling."

"I laughed so hard my stomach hurt," Caruthers said.

"It was truly dreadful," Julianne said. "I almost felt sorry for Henrietta."

"Elizabeth threw a temper tantrum," Georgette said. "When she started wailing, her fiancé told her to clap her mouth shut."

"Mrs. Bancroft had to be revived with smelling salts," Portfrey said.

"But Hester came to the rescue," Julianne said.

Hawk regarded his aunt with lifted brows.

"I swatted my fan on the dog's rump," Hester said, "and Mr. Peckham chased him out."

He smiled at his aunt but said nothing. Keeping his distance from Julianne the past three days had been harder than he'd expected. But that had only strengthened his resolve. He'd be giving her up forever in the near future. Now was the time to ease back gradually, until he was no longer spending every afternoon and evening with her.

The butler arrived and announced Beaufort. A strained silence hung over the drawing room as the young man entered carrying a posy. He strolled over to Julianne and offered her the flowers. "Friends?" he said.

She smiled. "Friends it is."

After Beaufort took a seat near the other cubs, Hawk regarded the young man with respect. Beaufort had swallowed his pride and chosen to do the right thing. He was young and a bit cocky, but his father had obviously instilled good principles in him.

Once again, the beleaguered maid arrived with a vase. Benton followed her progress with his eyes and then turned to Julianne. "You're growing a regular flower garden today."

"I am fortunate to have so many thoughtful friends," she said. "The flowers remind me of our gardens at home. My brother kept the formal landscaping in place. It's not fashionable, but I love it, especially Mama's roses in summer."

The conversation drifted to the myriad parties and soirées for the upcoming week. "What entertainment are you attending tonight, Lady Julianne?" Caruthers asked.

"We're planning to attend the opera," Hester answered. "You are welcome to join our party. Mr. Peckham already agreed to accompany us as well."

Within a few minutes, all of Julianne's friends decided to attend. When she looked inquiringly at him, he drew in his breath. "I've other plans this evening."

He meant to visit the theater and proposition a willing actress. With any luck, he'd share his bed with a mistress at the love nest tonight and slake his lust. He would gradually return to his old life.

Julianne's smile disappeared. She rose and took her cup over to the tea tray. "May I refresh anyone's cup?"

Hawk felt like a devil. She'd expected him to attend. But he'd made up his mind. It was for the best. At the moment, what was for the best didn't set too well with him.

He'd decided to take his leave when the butler announced Charles Osgood.

Osgood strolled inside, leaving a stinky smoke trail in his wake. The ladies whipped out their fans. Ever oblivious, the bad poet went to sit with his friends.

"Egad, Osgood," Beaufort said. "Did someone try to set you on fire?"

"No, I got stuck at a book burning in Piccadilly."

Hawk seriously wondered how Osgood had managed to make it this far in life.

Mr. Peckham whipped his gaze to Osgood. "A book burning? Why, that is practically sacrilegious."

"Actually it was a pamphlet burning."

Julianne gasped.

Hester grasped her hand. "It is a shocking report, but perhaps there is some mistake."

Caruthers pulled a face. "Osgood, the proprietor was probably burning some moth-eaten tracts."

"No," Osgood said. "It was that pamphlet. *The Secrets of Seduction.*"

Hawk regarded his aunt and suspicion grew inside him. It would be just like her to pen some ridiculous advice for young ladies.

"What do you know about this pamphlet?" he asked her.

"Well, all the ladies gathered to discuss it recently," she said.

He narrowed his eyes. "I heard there was a petition to have it banned."

"It didn't work," Osgood said. "Lady Georgette, your brother was at the book burning."

"What?" Georgette cried.

Amy wafted her fan in front of Georgette's face. "I'm sure your brother was only curious."

"No," Osgood said. "He was shouting about trash. But then some folks brought buckets of water to put out the fire. A clerk from the bookshop came out with a full chamber pot and—"

"Osgood, there are ladies present," Hawk said.

"Oh, sorry, ladies," he said. "The smoke was awful."

Julianne still clutched Hester's hand. "Mr. Osgood, did they burn very many pamphlets?"

"Not as many as they wanted," he said. "All the commotion brought out a lot of curious people. The proprietor swore the publisher meant to print more. He looked rather pleased about it all." Osgood fumbled inside his coat. "I managed to rescue one. It's only a little charred round the edges."

"Well, that is good news," Hester said. "And I certainly think Mr. Osgood deserves praise for rescuing a copy."

Hawk gave his aunt a stern look. "I hardly think a scandalous publication such as this deserves rescuing."

Julianne glared at him. "No literature deserves burning!"

"Osgood, put the pamphlet back in your coat," Hawk said. Then he addressed his aunt. "That pamphlet is an outrage. Julianne is forbidden to read it."

Georgette made a choked sound. Amy elbowed her.

Mr. Peckham regarded Hawk. "No disrespect, Hawkfield, but how do you know the pamphlet is an outrage if you haven't read it?"

"I've heard enough to convince me it's salacious. The publisher probably hopes to make a small fortune. The title is meant to mislead the public. People will buy it expecting something far different. I'm not shelling out coin for that rag."

Julianne narrowed her eyes. "Perhaps you're afraid of what you'll read."

She was on her high horse today. "Julianne, I know how much store you put by novels and ladies' periodicals, but this is not art," Hawk said. "It's rubbish."

Hawk turned his regard to the others, only to find Caruthers reading over Osgood's shoulder. "Hah! The author failed miserably."

"What do you mean?" Beaufort said.

"She entrusts her female readers to keep the pamphlet from falling into the hands of gentlemen." Caruthers looked up and grinned. "Too late."

The other cubs laughed. Then they passed it round.

"I think I'll buy one for grins," Beaufort said.

"I shall purchase a copy as well," Hester said.

Hawk narrowed his eyes. "Aunt, you seem to know a great deal about that pamphlet. Do you know the author?"

"It is anonymous," she said.

He couldn't very well accuse his aunt in front of everyone. Lord knew he didn't want anyone to know his aunt had written it. "I don't want Julianne reading that pamphlet," he said in a stern voice.

"Read it before you pronounce judgment," Hester said. "And when you finish, we will discuss it."

"Since you insist, I will, but I don't expect to find anything of value in it."

After everyone left, Julianne paced around the drawing room. "Hester, they ridiculed the pamphlet. And burned it!"

"Yes, but all the attention is bound to draw more readers. The pamphlet is a sensation. All the outrage is bringing people to the bookshop."

Julianne halted. "Forgive me, but I wanted to hurl that scorched pamphlet at your nephew."

"Let us see what he has to say after he reads it," Hester said.

"He is already prejudiced when he has not read a word of it," she said.

Hester's lips twitched. "I did think it amusing when he insisted you were forbidden to read it."

"Well, at least my identity is protected. Goodness, everyone is talking about it," she said.

"That's the spirit," Hester said. "You have stirred up controversy, and now we will observe the various reactions. Some of them are likely to disturb you, but remember, you must be careful not to inadvertently give yourself away. As difficult as it may prove, you must say as little as possible."

"I shall be very anxious to hear the opinions of single ladies," Julianne said. "I'm sure it will be much discussed in ladies' retiring rooms."

Hester tapped her quizzing glass. "I was surprised my nephew did not insist upon accompanying us to the opera tonight."

"He despises the opera," Julianne said.

"But he has been distant lately."

"He has been busy with parliamentary and estate matters," she said. But deep inside, fear had taken hold over the last three days. She'd let him back into her heart, and she'd thought after their discussion about his past that they had grown closer.

"Hester?" she said tentatively.

"Yes, dear?"

"Why do gentlemen... Never mind. I already know the answer."

"To what, dear?"

She sighed. "It is of no great import." But she'd forgotten her own advice that night she'd spoken to him at Lady Garnett's ball. He'd been comfortable with her as long as she'd kept everything lighthearted, but after she'd brought up the very serious topic of his past, he'd put distance between them.

Nothing had changed. He enjoyed teasing her, but he did not entertain thoughts of marrying her. He was even abdicating his guardian duties. But why? He'd been so insistent until that night.

Because he'd sensed she had matrimony on her mind?

Her heart started pounding as she thought of what she'd written in the pamphlet.

However, you will note that most are in no great hurry to renounce their bachelorhood. In fact, they are, by and large, determined to remain single as long as possible. Why?

They do not wish to give up their drinking, gaming, and wenching.

A horrible suspicion gripped her. Had he taken a mistress?

"Julianne, you have grown pale," Hester said.

"I think I should rest. It's been a trying afternoon." She would say nothing to Hester, because Hawk was her nephew. And Julianne had no evidence. But she knew his reputation.

Like a fool, she'd fallen for him all over again. She'd let herself hope because he'd kissed her. Yet, he'd made his lack of romantic intentions clear when he'd asked for friendship, the same way she'd asked it of the cubs. And like Beaufort, she'd hoped for more.

She'd chased him at the park, kissed him back, and flirted with him. He'd taken freely what she'd so willingly given. But she'd made light of their kiss that night at the ball, because she'd feared his feet would grow cold.

She remembered what he'd said that day he'd taken her

to the park. *It would take a lot more than a kiss to alleviate what's bothering me.*

Her heart sank. He'd taken a mistress.

No, she was jumping to conclusions, when she had no evidence at all. She'd blamed him for staying away, but he was the earl, and he did have responsibilities.

He also had responsibilities to her, and he'd shirked them. There could only be one reason for his sudden disinterest in escorting her to nightly entertainments.

He'd found a hussy to warm his bed.

When she reached her room, she kicked the door shut. She would not wait for him to decide when to call on her. First thing tomorrow morning, she would send him a curt missive demanding his presence in Hester's drawing room. He'd get the shock of his life, but she would not back down.

That night, Hawk sat in his usual spot at the club, nursing a brandy and his bad mood. He'd gone to the theater as planned, but he never even made it to the dressing room. As he'd started down the stairs, two of his mother's friends had hailed him. They wanted to call on Lady Julianne and wondered if he would accompany them to Lady Rutledge's box. He'd been forced to admit they were not there. They had looked at him askance.

So here he sat all alone, wondering how many rakes were vying for Julianne's attention at the opera. No doubt they were ogling her bosom. He ought to go there straightaway and make sure she wasn't getting into trouble. But he'd spent too much time with her already. He was getting too accustomed to having her about.

The waiter brought him another brandy. He looked down at his empty glass, surprised that he'd drained it dry. The devil. He'd been right about one thing: guarding Julianne was driving him slowly mad.

He gulped his brandy and cursed himself for ever agreeing to be her guardian. She'd gotten under his skin. The last few days he'd stayed away hadn't done a damned bit of good. He thought about her constantly. Hell, she even invaded his dreams. Last night, he'd dreamed she'd stood before him naked and crooked her finger. He'd jolted awake, as hard as stone and frustrated.

He'd get drunk, and then maybe he wouldn't dream about her tonight. Maybe he wouldn't picture her lying beneath him. Maybe he would forget their hot kisses. Maybe he'd forget how sweetly she'd told him his past didn't matter.

She was too innocent. He swigged his brandy and swiped his mouth. She was too beautiful. He drank some more. She was too clever. He drained his glass and signaled the waiter.

His head felt light, but he didn't care. He meant to get stinking drunk so he could forget her. Forget her raspy voice. Forget her luminous complexion and her bright blue eyes. Forget the taste of her tongue.

The waiter brought another brandy. He shoved it aside, because even the brandy wasn't working. Nothing worked. He had a bad case of lust for her. And he couldn't have her. Not ever.

He wanted her.

Why could he not have her? Because he was bad. Because men like him never changed. Because she deserved better.

His head was swimming, but he decided he was thinking far more clearly. He wanted Julianne, and he would have her. But he'd have to marry her. Maybe she wouldn't marry him.

He'd kidnap her and race off to Scotland. One of his bad ancestors had kidnapped his great-great-great-grandmamma.

Grandmamma, he thought. It was all her fault. She'd decided to palpitate again. His nervous mama and flighty sisters had fled to Bath. They'd left him and his batty aunt Hester to look after Julianne. His family had taken leave of their senses.

He snorted and picked up his glass. A shadow fell over him. He looked up to find his least favorite brother-in-law, Montague, scowling at him. Hawk lifted his glass aloft, sloshing brandy.

"I might have known I'd find you three sheets to the wind and shirking your guardian responsibilities," Montague said.

"Have I told you lately how much I regret letting you marry my sister?"

"You're a disgrace," Montague said. "You had everything handed to you on a silver platter. But you thumbed your nose in your father's face. You broke your mother's heart by moving out. And then you set out to be the king of rakes."

"Montague, you're starting to bore me."

"I'm not half done here. You've abdicated your responsibilities to your brother. He's running wild on the Continent, and you're funding it. You don't give a damn about your family. I thought at the very least you would honor your responsibilities to Lady Julianne. You ought to be ashamed."

"Look in the mirror, Montague," he said. "You mistreat my sister."

"She is my wife, and you have no say."

"You think I don't know about your mistress?"

Montague stiffened.

Hawk stood. "Get rid of her, because if you don't, I will beat you to a bloody pulp."

After delivering that threat, he walked a bit unsteadily out of the room. He collected his greatcoat, dropped his hat, and managed to clap it onto his head. Somehow he got his sorry carcass into the carriage. When the driver asked for a direction, Hawk thought of the opera, but he was drunk. He told the driver to take him to his aunt's house.

Henderson looked more than a little alarmed when Hawk insisted on waiting for his aunt in the Egyptian drawing room. Once there, he refused Henderson's offer of strong coffee and decided to make himself comfortable on the sofa. His legs hung over the rolled arm, but he needed to sleep off the brandy. He fell asleep and dreamed Julianne was burning pamphlets.

Julianne's eyes nearly popped out of her head at the sight of Hawk draped over the sofa. Obviously he'd not gone to a mistress.

Hester put her hands on her wide hips. "What in the world was he thinking?"

Behind them, Henderson cleared his throat. "My lady, I believe he is drunk."

Julianne padded over to Hawk and shook his shoulder. He murmured something unintelligible. She bent over him and wrinkled her nose at the smell of brandy on his breath.

"Don't burn them," he muttered.

She straightened and looked at Hester. "Should we try to bundle him into his carriage?"

"We'd never get him down the stairs," Hester said. She told Henderson to send for a blanket and a pillow.

A few minutes later, Julianne managed to get the pillow under his head. He muttered in his sleep again. She draped the blanket over him. "I hate leaving him like this."

"He'll survive," Hester said. "Come along. It's late, and we're both tired."

As they climbed the stairs, Julianne looked at Hester. "I've never seen him drunk before."

"He's overset," Hester said.

"How do you know?"

"I know my nephew."

They had reached the landing. Hester groaned as she stepped up. "I'm getting old."

"You're just tired," Julianne said. She slowed her pace to match Hester's. As they reached her bedchamber, she turned to Hester. "What is wrong with Hawk?"

Hester smiled. "You."

Her answer startled Julianne. She wanted to ask Hester to explain, but Hester crossed to her room and closed the door.

Several minutes later, Betty helped Julianne disrobe and don a night rail. She snuggled under the covers, but she couldn't sleep. She kept thinking of what Hester had said, and she started worrying about Hawk. What if he got up in his drunken state and bumped into one of the side tables? He might trip over something in the dark.

She lay there thinking of a dozen excuses to check on him. Finally, she decided to listen to her inner voice and go. She found her dressing robe and slipped it on. Then she took her candle and crept downstairs. When she opened the drawing room door, she found him in much the same position. She ought to leave him be, but she set the candle on a side table and treaded over to him. She removed his shoes and set them aside. Then she walked over to his head and brushed his hair back.

He caught her hand. She stiffened, fearing she'd awakened him. When she tried to disentangle her hand, he pulled it to his cheek.

"Hawk," she whispered. "Wake up."

His eyes opened. "I'm still drunk."

"Yes, and you need to go home and sleep," she said.

"I don't have a home. I have rooms."

"I know, but your neck will ache if you spend the night on the sofa."

"Can't walk to the carriage," he said. "I'm drunk."

She sat beside him. "Why did you get drunk?"

"Dunno."

She cupped his cheek. "Hawk, what's wrong?"

"I'm drunk."

She laughed a little. "What else is wrong?"

"I'm bad."

"No, you aren't," she said.

"Men like me never change."

She frowned. "That's ridiculous."

"That's what my father said."

She inhaled. Why would his father say something so harsh?

"I don't care about my family."

"That's not true," she said.

"What Montague said."

"When did he say that?"

"Tonight at the club. I got drunk."

She kissed his cheek. "I should leave you so you can sleep."

"Don't leave me."

"I'll stay until you fall asleep again."

"Not ever," he said.

"You won't remember this tomorrow."

"I don't deserve you."

She frowned. "Hawk, don't say that."

"Truth."

Something was terribly, terribly wrong.

He closed his eyes. His breathing slowed. He'd fallen asleep again. She considered going back upstairs, but she didn't want to leave him like this. When she rose, his eyes opened.

"Hawk, I'll go to the other sofa and watch over you."

He curled onto his side, bending his knees. "Lie with me, like a spoon."

She hesitated but sensed he needed the comfort. They fit, just barely. He wrapped his arm around her and cupped her breast. Oh, dear, what had she done? His thumb circled her nipple. She caught her breath, knowing she should move to the other sofa. His fingers unbuttoned her night rail.

"Hawk."

"Shhh. I won't hurt you."

His hand delved inside and cupped her breast. He suckled her neck. Desire flooded her veins. But he was drunk, and she shouldn't let him. She felt him harden against her bottom. "Hawk, we shouldn't. Not like this when you're drunk and liable to regret it."

"You want me to stop?"

"I think I should move to the other sofa," she said, "so you can sleep."

"Yes, you better go, because I want to bed you. And we don't have a bed."

She laughed a little as she stood and buttoned her night rail. Then she kissed his cheek once more. It was a little scratchy from his beard. "Sleep."

She curled onto the other sofa, watching him in the wavering candlelight. He twitched once, but his deep breathing continued. She wondered if he would remember anything he'd said to her. Even if he did, he would probably feign no memory of it. She knew now that the clowning was a cover for deep wounds.

His father had told him men like him never change.

Her eyes welled with tears. She'd known whatever had happened all those years ago had been bad. But she'd not known his own father had condemned him.

He woke her before dawn. She sat up a little disoriented, and then all of it flooded her brain.

"I must go before the servants stir," he said, his voice a little hoarse. "Can you make your way upstairs again? I lit a new candle."

"Yes, I can."

"I'll return later this afternoon," he said. "I'm sorry."

"Don't worry."

"Julie? Thank you."

She stood and took the candle. "Wait. Look out the window and see if your driver is still there."

He did and cursed under his breath. "He's gone, of course. Poor man probably froze out there for hours."

"He knew you were drunk and probably left shortly after you arrived."

Hawk scrubbed his hand down his face. "I was roaring drunk."

"You don't make a habit of it."

"I said things."

"You needn't worry. I know you were soused." She provided him with the excuse so that he could save face.

"I touched you."

"You were a gentleman and agreed it wasn't a good idea."

"I've kept you from your bed. Go upstairs. I'll get the servants to find me a hackney when they're up and about."

She wanted to hug him but knew he would realize she'd heard too much last night. "I'll see you later, then," she said.

She trudged up the stairs. Despite her exhaustion, she found it difficult to fall asleep. He needed her, but she didn't know how to reach out to him.

Chapter Eighteen

*A Scoundrel's Confession: The path to reform
is fraught with temptation.*

He'd slept until noon. When he'd awakened, he'd bathed and drunk a dozen cups of tea dosed with willow bark. Last night, he'd reached a proverbial crossroad. He'd envisioned two paths. One involved going on as he had been, living day to day, refusing to look at the bleak future in which he remained the family scapegrace. The other involved letting go of the past and forgiving himself, as Julianne had said. It wouldn't be easy, but he'd ceded defeat a dozen years ago. Ever since then, he'd worn an invisible hair shirt and covered up the melancholy by acting the clown.

He'd made his choice, one that would free him from the past and open up a real future. One that would allow him to fully embrace his family and the incredible inheritance his father had left him.

His father had said a cruel thing to him that day so long ago. In hindsight and through the eyes of an adult, he knew his father had spoken out of anger and fear. Recalling his own fears that night Julianne had gotten foxed, he could imagine all too well how his father must have felt— only magnified a hundred times.

No father should ever have to face the possibility of his son dying in a duel.

He remembered how he'd felt. Scorned and scared. And full of bitterness. Tristan had said his father had been a good man. His father had been a hard man in many ways, because he'd felt Hawk didn't take his future responsibilities seriously enough. After Westcott had agreed to a payment in lieu of a duel, his father had been tough on him. He'd not given him any quarter nor had he sympathized.

Hawk suspected his father had wanted him to prove himself, but after hearing his father's denouncement, he'd felt he could never please his sire. So he'd set out to become the scoundrel his father had labeled him.

He couldn't turn back the clock and change his past. And he couldn't make contact. To do so would be a supreme act of selfishness, one that would condemn an innocent to scorn forevermore. His punishment would be to never know. And to always have an empty place inside his chest.

Today, he'd made his decision. He had chosen the right path, the one that meant doing his duty. No, it was more than duty and responsibility. He'd seen a glimpse of joy that day in the park with Julianne. That night at the ball, she'd shown him the way. She'd told him that his past did not define who he was to her, and she had said she would not pressure him to divulge his secrets. She had accepted him unconditionally. He'd not trusted that unconditional acceptance at first. He'd returned to old patterns, looking for a courtesan and drowning his sorrows.

Last night, she'd stayed with him. Any other woman would have turned away in disgust. But Julianne had stayed and told him not to worry about anything he'd said.

He'd always adored her, but never more than last night. He knew what she'd suffered as the unwanted child. Years ago, her vulnerability had touched him deep inside.

She was, and always would be, his Julie-girl.

He looked at the clock. It was time to go. He would not rush her. She deserved to be properly courted.

He looked in the mirror and laughed at himself for thinking he'd look different. His aunt would put a flea in his ear for choosing her sofa as a bed. She'd never let him live that down.

With a deep breath and one last tug on his cravat, he strode out to his new life.

Julianne sat in the drawing room, looking at the clock a little too often. She had some idea what to expect of him. He probably would make a great jest of it all. She would not let on how much his drunken confessions had disturbed her. He'd been worried last night about what he'd said, though she wasn't sure how much he would remember. She'd done her best to reassure him, but she felt at sea with him.

All these years, she'd thought she knew him. She'd learned that something bad had transpired involving Ramsey, but she'd never guessed that Hawk's father had condemned him in such a cruel way.

She'd only been thirteen when the late earl had died. All she remembered of Hawk's father was that he'd been a serious man, so unlike his son. She did know that Tristan had respected Hawk's father and had relied on his advice.

"Did he talk last night?" Hester asked.

Her voice startled Julianne. "A bit. He didn't make a great deal of sense." She didn't tell Hester that he'd revealed some disturbing facts about his father's treatment of him.

Hester set her novel aside. "How much do you know, dear?"

Julianne met her gaze. "Enough."

"I knew his father had covered up something. Marc was wild-eyed and tormented. His father said nothing to his mother, of course. But she knew and pretended not to notice. Louisa has a good heart, but she has always been one of those childish women who need others to take care of her."

Footsteps sounded on the landing. Hawk walked inside. "I told the butler I could see myself up."

Julianne rose. "I'll pour you a cup of tea."

"Thank you, but I've drunk enough to fill a bath." He looked at his aunt. "I don't know why I told the driver to bring me here last night. I suppose I've spent so much time here I've begun to feel at home."

"You are always welcome," Hester said. "Drunk or sober."

"Aunt, will you allow me to speak privately to Julianne?"

"Of course."

He helped her rise, and then he kissed her cheek. "Thank you."

After Hester left, he sat beside Julianne. Her stomach fluttered nervously.

"The things I said last night—"

"Don't worry. The spirits loosened your tongue," she said.

"It's true," he said. "I've thought a great deal about what my father said. He reacted out of fear for me."

Julianne swallowed. "You were in danger?"

"He paid a fortune to keep me from facing pistols at dawn."

She clasped her shaking hands hard. What had he done?

"When you told me I needed to forgive myself, I didn't think it possible at first. But you said something that helped me."

Her heart beat faster.

"You said no matter what transpired, it does not change who I am to you."

"Never," she said.

"You believe in me unconditionally?" he asked.

"Yes."

"I've chosen to bury the past," he said. "I've chosen the future instead."

She blinked back the threatening tears. "I'm glad," she whispered.

"I have to make amends with my family," he said. "While I haven't completely ignored them, I haven't fully lived up to my responsibilities. One of my biggest regrets is that I didn't look closely enough into Montague's character before giving my blessing to Patience's marriage. She has suffered for it."

Julianne reached over and clasped his hand. "I know

you feel responsible, but Patience chose to marry him. And she is stronger than you think. She doesn't let him run roughshod over her."

"When she returns, I will speak to her privately and ensure she knows I will help her and the children if the need ever arises.

"Ironically, Montague was right about me. I have broken my mother's heart by refusing to live at Ashdown House. And I did thumb my indiscretions in my father's face. I should have tried to make amends, but I let pride hold me back."

"But your father was equally guilty, if not more so," she said. "He should have begged your forgiveness for what he said to you. Words used as weapons have the capacity to wound."

"It cannot be changed now," he said, "but I am the head of my family. And I have shirked my responsibilities to my brother. William probably thinks I don't care about him."

Julianne squeezed his hand. "Why do you say that?"

"Because I let him run amok and put no restraints on him whatsoever. I didn't want him to suffer from an overbearing brother, because that was what I'd endured with my father. So I went in the extreme opposite direction and gave him too much freedom. It's time I called him home and spoke to him about choosing a profession."

She smiled at him. "You've made so many decisions in such a short period of time. Good decisions."

His eyes traveled over her face. "I have you to thank for it."

She had never loved him more than at this moment. "I'm proud of you."

He smiled and pulled her curl. "Will you allow me to escort you tonight?"

"Yes," she said breathlessly. Could it be possible? Did she dare hope that he loved her?

"Where are we going?" he asked.

"The theater." She laughed a bit nervously. "I don't even recall the play."

"Let my aunt know I'll call for both of you."

She rose with him. He kissed her hand. "Tonight," he said.

Her eyes welled with happy tears as he strode out of the drawing room. After he'd disappeared from her sight, she ran to the window for one last glimpse of him through the wavy glass. When he emerged from the house, she whispered, "I love you."

At the theater, Julianne felt as if she were living the dream she'd kept alive for four long years. Hawk sat beside her, and when the stage curtains opened, he reached over and held her hand on the seat beside her, where no one could see.

Hester and Mr. Peckham were engaged in a lively conversation. Julianne pretended to watch the play, but she could not concentrate. Excitement raced through her veins. She allowed herself to imagine returning home and announcing her engagement to Hawk. His family would arrive and exclaim over the happy news. Perhaps everyone would stay for an extra month while the banns were called. And then at long last, she would be Hawk's wife.

At intermission, Hawk released her hand. She felt unaccountably shy with him. It was silly, for she'd known him so long, but everything had changed.

When Hester suggested a round of champagne, Hawk begged off. "No, I think I'll avoid all spirits for a while."

"I don't care for any, either, Hester," Julianne said.

Amy, Georgette, and Sally entered the box. "Are we interrupting?" Georgette asked.

"No, of course not," Hester said.

Hawk helped Julianne rise and escorted her to her friends.

"We saw you from my parents' box," Georgette said.

Hawk bent his head. "Julianne, I saw a friend of mine on the other side of the theater. Will you mind if I call on him while you speak to your friends?"

She met his gaze, feeling as if she were dreaming. "Of course I do not mind."

"Ladies." He bowed and left the box.

Her friends drew her aside. "Oh my goodness," Georgette said. "The way he looked at you. I cannot believe you didn't melt into a puddle on the floor."

Her face grew warm as she lowered her lashes.

"You are shy tonight," Amy said.

"I don't know what has come over me." But of course she did. She was in love.

"Do you have an understanding?" Sally asked.

Julianne looked up and shook her head quickly. He'd made no promises, but he'd held her hand.

"Something has happened," Georgette said. "He looked very much like a man in love."

"We should not press her," Amy said. "I fear we have done so before."

Julianne regarded her gratefully. "Do you know what it is like to think a dream is about to come true, but you're afraid of hoping too much?"

"If he does not propose to you by the end of the season, I will be very surprised," Georgette said.

She bit her lip. "Please, I beg you say nothing to anyone else. I don't want rumors spreading before anything is decided."

"We will button our lips," Amy said. "But, Julianne, you deserve this happiness more than anyone I know."

A few minutes later, the five cubs called. They all exchanged greetings, and then Beaufort winked at her. "Have you heard the news?"

For a moment, Julianne thought he meant news about her and Hawk, but her common sense prevailed. No one could know. "I don't know what you mean."

"Do you recall that pamphlet?" Beaufort asked. "The newspapers are calling for a ban."

"Oh, this is delicious," Sally said, bouncing on her toes.

Julianne schooled her expression as she glanced at Amy and Georgette.

"I heard every copy sold," Caruthers said. "A fifth printing is said to be under way."

Julianne bit back a smile. Everyone was reading her pamphlet. She found it a bit difficult to keep her excitement a secret. But no one would ever guess she'd authored it. Part of her wished she could take credit for *The Secrets of Seduction*, but she'd known all along the necessity of hiding her identity. Still, she had so much to be pleased about tonight. All of the bad times made her appreciate her happiness all the more.

Caruthers grinned at Julianne. "Has Hawk read the pamphlet yet?"

She froze in place, recalling Hawk's disapproval. "I rather doubt it."

As the other gentlemen continued to speculate about the author, anxiety climbed in Julianne's chest. Had she written anything in the pamphlet that would tip off Hawk? She bit her lip. He'd asked for honesty. She couldn't lie to him, especially now that everything between them was perfect.

Maybe she would just forget to mention she'd authored *The Secrets of Seduction*. Drat it, she couldn't deceive him. She needed a better plan. He disapproved of the pamphlet, but he'd not read it yet. She would wait until after he read every word. Once he saw the merits of her work, he would not mind so very much that she'd masqueraded as the anonymous lady. Then again, perhaps she ought to wait until after the wedding. She would distract him with kisses and then admit what a naughty girl she'd been.

Delaying wasn't the same as lying. Was it?

Caruthers smiled at Julianne. "My parents wish to meet all of you. Will you come to their box?"

"Oh, what a lovely suggestion," Julianne said. "But perhaps I shouldn't leave. I'm sure the other girls would be delighted to accompany you." She wanted to wait for Hawk and speak to him about all his plans.

"They're especially keen on meeting you, Julianne," Caruthers said. "I'll not keep you too long."

How could she refuse without seeming churlish? "Let me speak to Hester."

When she reached Hester, she asked to speak to her privately. Mr. Peckham excused himself and said he would return shortly.

After he left, Julianne sat next to Hester and told her about Caruthers's request. "I would prefer to stay. Hawk will return soon."

Hester smiled slyly. "Gel, you don't want to appear too anxious. Go on with your friends. My nephew will appreciate you all the more if you make him wait a bit."

When Julianne hesitated, Hester tapped her with her fan. "Remember *The Secrets of Seduction*."

"Will you tell him where I've gone?" she asked.

"Yes, now go on. He'll be glad to see you when you return."

Julianne fidgeted during the long walk with her friends. While everyone else chatted, she kept silent. She hoped the visit would not last too long. Of course, Hester was right that she shouldn't appear too anxious. But after all the trials and heartache, she wanted to be near him as much as possible, especially tonight. Because today counted as the first day of their blossoming romance.

Caruthers led the way to his parents' box. Lord and Lady Frammingham welcomed the group enthusiastically. Julianne had to keep reminding herself to listen. She liked his parents very much. They thought it wonderful that the group of friends was sharing the season's festivities together. When his mother asked her about her brother and Tessa, Julianne told her about the babe and the impending house party.

The curtains opened for the next act. Her friends decided to stay a while longer. Julianne bit her lip. She didn't want to linger. "I had better go," she said. "I had a lovely time, but I promised Lady Rutledge I would return promptly."

Osgood rose. "Allow me to escort you, Lady Julianne."

"Oh, I do not wish to impose. Please stay. I can find my way back."

"I insist," Osgood said. "Hawk wouldn't like it if we let you go alone."

She knew it would be rude to continue to refuse. "Thank you, Mr. Osgood," she said.

As he led her out, she hoped he would not linger in the box. Then she felt awful for even thinking such a thing. Osgood was a nice young man, if a trifle thickheaded at times. She smiled, remembering how he'd traipsed inside Hester's drawing room, stinking of smoke.

He looked at her. "You look very pretty tonight."

"Thank you," she said.

He cleared his throat. "I hope I didn't offend you with that pamphlet."

"I took no offense," she said. "Did you read it?"

"Yes, I did. I was a bit dumbfounded," he said.

"Why is that?" she asked.

"I didn't know ladies played tricks on gentlemen."

"Tricks?" she said.

"It's not very nice," Osgood said. "The author tells ladies to plant flowers in her drawing room to make a gentleman think others have been there before him."

"You don't believe all is fair in love and war?" Julianne asked.

Osgood blinked at her. "I don't think it's fair to hoodwink a gentleman. It's not easy for men, you know. We have to get up our courage and risk rejection when asking a lady to dance."

Julianne winced. She'd not thought of it from a gentleman's viewpoint. To her, it had always seemed that men held all the power, but Osgood had pointed out that men risked humiliation every time they requested a lady's hand for a dance.

"I'm tempted to write a rebuttal and present a gentleman's guide to enticing a belle," he said.

"You're a poet," she said. "Writing a pamphlet should come easily to you."

"Do you think I should?" he asked.

She shrugged. "Why not? You have nothing to lose by trying."

"By Jove, I will. Thank you for the encouragement, Lady Julianne," he said.

"Thank you for pointing out the difficulties of courtship from a gentleman's perspective," she said. "I might never have known if not for you."

"You would never be cruel to a gentleman," Osgood said.

Not intentionally, but as she thought back over the past four seasons, she realized she had treated men as if they were toys to take out and put away at her pleasure.

"I say, there is Hawk by the stairwell," Osgood said.

Julianne craned her head. And then she saw him, standing with two sophisticated women wearing scandalous gowns. Their cheeks were painted with rouge. They stood on either side of him, clutching his arms.

Her throat closed. No. Oh, no.

"Lady Julianne, are you unwell?" Osgood said.

"Turn around," she said.

"Why?"

"Please, just do as I say."

He turned and started walking. "What is wrong?"

How could Osgood be so oblivious? "Please just keep walking for a little while."

Osgood remained quiet. She was glad of his silence, because she could not bear to speak right now.

Eventually, he halted. "I'm a blockhead."

She couldn't look at him. "No, you're a nice man."

"I'm sure it's not what you think," he said gently.

What else could it be?

"Do you want me to take you back to your friends?"

"No. Go on," she said. "Lady Rutledge's box isn't far."

The devil. She'd seen him with his two former mistresses.

Hawk strode after her. Bloody hell, he had to explain. They had waylaid him. He'd greeted them to be polite. But Julianne had seen them. He'd hated seeing the flash of pain on her face.

Osgood and Julianne stopped several feet away. Hawk saw the concern on the cub's face. And then he walked off. She'd probably told him to leave.

When she saw him, he strode faster, expecting her to evade him, but she stood there, glaring at him.

"It's not what you think," he said.

"I believed you this afternoon when you said you intended to start anew," she said, her voice shaking.

He shook his head. "I won't pretend I don't know them, but I only said hello."

"When is the rendezvous?" she said in a curt voice.

"What happened to your unconditional belief in me?" he said.

"I saw those strumpets clinging to your arms," she said.

"I spoke to them, and that is all."

"You were smiling."

"Either you believe in me unconditionally or you don't," he said. "If it's the latter, tell me now. I've spent too many years living under the shadow of my past. Yes, they are part of my sordid past. I'm not proud of it, but I can't change it. The one thing I won't do is walk on eggshells because you cannot trust me."

"You don't understand."

"Yes, I do. Last night when I told you my father said men like me never change, you said it wasn't true. And I believed you. But if you only meant to comfort me, if you believe I'm incapable of being a better man, then tell me now. Because this will never work if we can't trust each other."

"I'm afraid," she whispered.

"Of what?"

"I don't want to end up like my mother."

"Good-bye, Julianne."

"Don't you dare walk away from me," she said.

"You said you believe in me unconditionally, but it's not true. I can't have you judging me based on a past I can't change."

"I can't change my past, either, and it's made me scared. I'm vulnerable, too, but I'm willing to give this a chance."

"You want a chance? Fine, we'll talk, but not here."

He took her hand and strode off. When he reached Hester's box, he told the footman to inform his aunt that he and the lady were taking a hackney. Then he led her to the stairs.

Moments later, they strode through the foyer.

"My pelisse is in the cloakroom," she said.

"I'll send for it later," he gritted out. Then he instructed the doorman to hail a hackney.

As they waited, he gave her an icy stare. "No games tonight, Julianne. Just the raw truth."

Chapter Nineteen

A Scoundrel's Advice: If you bed her, you must wed her.

Julianne inched over in the hackney when Hawk climbed inside.

He knocked his cane on the ceiling and the hackney rolled off. When she tried to move to the other side, he caught her and hauled her back. "Afraid?" he said.

"I think you had better take me home," she said.

"That can be arranged, my dear. But not tonight. It's a long drive to Gatewick Park."

"I meant to your aunt's house," she said.

"Oh, no, we're going to have a look at my past."

"Don't do this, Hawk. You'll only regret it."

"No, I'm done with regrets," he said.

"You don't have to prove anything to me," she said. "I only wanted you to understand."

"Oh, I understand," he said, turning to her. "Earlier

today, you were willing to trust me, but when faced with the evidence of my past, you couldn't stomach it."

"I saw those women and assumed the worst. I made a mistake."

"Because you don't want to end up like your mother," he said bitterly.

"I spoke in anger."

"You told me the truth—it comes out when we're in stressful situations, you know. Like the day my father said men like me never change. He told me what he truly believed. He'd judged me based on my uncle's behavior and my own. My uncle was one of the worst libertines. Did you know that? He was the spare, my father's brother. My father bailed him out of trouble time and time again. But my uncle never changed. So when I found trouble, my father assumed I was cut from the same cloth. He told me the truth—as he saw it, based on his past experience."

"He was wrong," she said.

"Not from his perspective," Hawk said. "You're in a similar boat where I'm concerned. Your father was a notorious rake. He humiliated your mother repeatedly, and you witnessed it. So your greatest fear is marrying a man who will betray you. I'm right, aren't I?"

"Yes, but it doesn't mean I can't change. It doesn't mean that we cannot work together on our faults and make something better of ourselves."

"An interesting point. But here's the thing. You will always look at my behavior based on your past experience. You'll make assumptions every time you see me speak to another woman. Then you'll say you're sorry, and I'll forgive you, but I'll resent having to do it, because it won't happen just once. But if I make the mistake you fear the most, you'll never forgive me. Because you'll assume based on your past experience that it will happen again and again."

"You look at the situation fatalistically. But it is possible to change. I failed you tonight, but it doesn't mean that I will always."

"You say that, but you don't really know if you can. More important, I don't know if you can. So tonight is the test. I'm going to show you the hard truth about my past. If you're repulsed, I'll know and you will know that you cannot accept me unconditionally, sordid past and all."

Her heart thudded in her ears. "Where are we going?"

"You haven't guessed? I believe you expressed interest in it once before. It's apparently the talk of the ladies' retiring room."

He meant to take her to his love nest. Fear gripped her heart. She knew he meant to show her the bed where he'd lain with countless women. He meant to make her face his ugly past—and all those faceless women she'd hated because he'd taken them to bed.

"I can take you to my aunt's house if you're unable to stomach it," he said.

She lifted her chin. "I am my mother's daughter. There is nothing I cannot face with my head held high."

"We shall see."

He knew a moment of hesitation as he fumbled with the key. The better man would apologize and beg her forgiveness. But he'd spoken the truth in that hackney. Unless she saw the evidence of his past firsthand, neither of them would know if she could truly accept him unconditionally.

The door creaked as he pushed it open. He fumbled with the tinderbox on the hall table and lit a branch of candles. Holding it high, he said, "Behold, the love nest. I fear it is deserted." He smiled at her. "I dismissed the staff after your brother insisted I give up raking for the duration of the season. He didn't want you to be disappointed if you found out I was a notorious rake."

She put her chin up again and walked into the hall.

He followed her in order to illuminate the dark interior. "Notice the lack of marble floors, carpeting on the staircase, and pastoral paintings. Rather spartan, isn't it? I prefer it, you know. My rooms at the Albany are similarly utilitarian."

"You live in stark circumstances by choice to show you are not attached," she said.

"An astute observation, one I'd not thought of before. Come, let me give you a tour of the parlor. It's just past the stairs."

He'd expected her to tell him to take her home, but she marched past him and opened the parlor door. He followed her inside. "No fire, I'm afraid. I'd not planned on having a guest tonight, despite your earlier assumption."

"If your aim is to provoke me, save your breath," she said.

"Oh, I'm saving the provoking part for last," he said. "Notice the ugly mismatched furnishings. They came with the place when I let it years ago. I didn't bother to replace them." He flashed her a grin. "We don't serve tea and cakes at the love nest."

"You've never made the purchase. Permanence scares you."

"It's a love nest. Nothing is ever permanent here. I bring the women and send them packing when I tire of their demands. Temporary lovers suit me. I can change them out like an old coat." He knew he was being crass, but her cool demeanor brought out the worst in him.

"You dismiss them because you don't want to know them."

"I know them in the biblical sense," he said.

"You don't want to think too much about what drives them to accept your propositions. Because you know they need the money, and it troubles you."

Her razor-sharp observations unnerved him, but he'd be damned before he admitted she was right. "I pay them handsomely. They supplement their unsteady incomes from acting, make out like bandits, and move on to the next wealthy protector."

"To quote my friend Amy, it must be very frightening, and I would add degrading, to have to sell your body in order to survive."

"You imagine them as tragic figures, but I assure you they visit the same high-priced dressmakers as you do. Their jewels are courtesy of Rundell and Bridge. I know. I've paid the bills." He closed the distance between them. "As for degrading, you're wrong. They're performers, but if they're lucky, they find a protector who knows how to pleasure them."

She didn't flinch. "You say they are performers. I imagine an accomplished actress could convince any man he was a great lover—for the right price."

He chuckled. "Your innocence is showing, Julianne, but let us have a tour of the stage where these performances take place. You're under no obligation. I will certainly understand if the prospect offends your tender sensibilities."

"But you have a performance to complete tonight, do you not? You wish to shock me. Aren't you curious if you can succeed?"

"Oh, I know I can," he said.

"By all means, prove it."

He'd underestimated her. She was his best friend's sister, and he'd gone too far already. Taking her into that bedchamber would make him the worst sort of scoundrel.

"Having second thoughts?" She arched her brows. "Give me the candle branch, and I'll find my own way there."

She'd do it, too. He knew her pride was in it now, but if he backed down, nothing between them would ever be resolved.

He offered his arm. "Since you insist," he said, meaning to make it clear she'd made the choice.

But as he led her out of the ugly parlor and up the plain staircase, his conscience roared. They continued down the short corridor, and as he neared the door, he stopped. "Enough," he said.

"Finish what you started," she said.

He shook his head. "No, I'm taking you to my aunt's house."

She stepped past him and opened the door.

"Bloody hell," he gritted out as she walked inside.

He followed her. "Julianne, let us leave now."

She glanced around the room and then back at the bed with its crimson bed hangings and matching counterpane. "I confess I'm disappointed," she said. "I was expecting something gaudy." She regarded him. "I suppose you expect me to swoon after picturing you writhing in that bed."

He set the candle branch on the bedside table. "Imagine how many women have lain in that bed," he said. "Countless, and I literally mean countless. There have been so many I can't recall them all."

She walked to the bed and ran her hand over the post. "What? No notches?"

He admired her. She'd yet to crack, but he had another surprise for her. "Do you not wonder about preventative measures?"

She regarded him warily, and he knew she didn't have the faintest notion what he'd meant.

He walked to the bed and patted the mattress. "The performances that take place here can have consequences. Do you take my meaning?"

She swallowed. "Yes."

"Do you not wish to know how it's prevented?"

When she said nothing, he walked over to the bedside table and opened the drawer. "They're used for more than preventing pregnancy. I've an aversion to disease."

She met his gaze. "I understand now, but I doubt you do. My guess is that somewhere deep inside, you wanted me to see those painted women tonight. You sought a confrontation because you wanted to push me away."

He shook his head. "You're imagining things."

"No, I don't think so. You've been doing it since the night of the Beresford's ball."

He shut the drawer and folded his arms over his chest. "I have no idea what you're talking about."

"You tease and then you back away because you don't want anyone to get close enough to see the scars. You push others away before they can hurt you. That is the reason you choose to live in rented rooms rather than with your family. That is the reason you told everyone at that ball I am practically a sister to you."

He frowned. "I did it because I'm your guardian, and others assumed that waltz meant more than it did."

Her eyes welled with tears.

"What the devil?"

Her lips trembled. She ran toward the door.

He caught up to her and pinned her wrists against the door. "What did I say?"

A sob erupted from her.

He turned her around to face him. "Julianne, what is it?"

She fought him, trying to escape. He wrapped his arms tightly around her. "Stop struggling."

She raised her chin. "Take me h-home now."

"I don't know what I said, but I can't help if you won't tell me."

"No. I won't let you humiliate me again."

"I'm not letting you go until you explain."

She glared at him.

He looked at her tear-stained face and thought about the moment she'd broken. "The waltz?" he said, still not understanding.

She turned her head.

He thought about the way her husky voice had called to him like a siren's. He'd stupidly held on to her for far too long. So long that a crowd had gathered and burst into applause. All he'd worried about was preventing rumors of an impending engagement.

Then he'd confronted Ramsey, and she had grown very pale. He thought back to the heated words he'd exchanged with Ramsey, and then he felt as if he'd just opened draperies to a blinding sun. He stroked her hair. "It was because I said you were practically like a sister to me."

When she said nothing, he knew he'd hit the mark. "Julianne, I only said it so that others wouldn't make assumptions about us."

She pushed against his chest. "Take me home now."

"I think we need to talk."

"No, let me go."

He tightened his hold on her. "Is that the reason you escaped to the retiring room at the ball?"

"I planned to get foxed with my friends," she said.

Her voice trembled just a little.

"You had expectations after that waltz. My thoughtless words hurt you."

She struggled to break free. "I want to leave now."

"Calm yourself."

She fought him. He scooped her up in his arms and dropped her onto the bed. She reared up, but he pressed her back onto the mattress and pinned her wrists above her head. When she bucked, he used his body to still her. "I want you to answer me yes or no."

"How dare you?"

"I hurt you when I said you were like my sister. Yes or no."

"Let me go or I'll scream."

"There's no one but me to hear you. I hurt you by saying you were like a sister to me. Answer me. Yes or no."

She clamped her mouth shut.

"Answer me," he said.

When she still said nothing, he lowered his head to kiss her. She whipped her face aside. He kissed her cheek. "I never meant to hurt you."

She struggled underneath him again. "Don't you dare pity me. Don't you dare."

"I don't pity you. And no matter what I said, I never thought of you like a sister."

"Let me go."

"You don't understand. The entire time I waltzed with you, I was on fire. But you *were*—you *are*—forbidden to me. I'm your guardian. You're my best friend's sister. And I am so damned tempted by you I can't get you out of my head."

Her lips parted.

"Don't you understand? The sound of your voice alone makes me insane to have you."

She looked stunned.

"Remember the bad thoughts? I have them about you constantly. I sit beside you at the theater and fantasize about all the things I'm going to do when I get you naked and in my bed."

Her breathing grew as labored as his. He was as hard as stone, painfully aroused, and very aware of the dangerous situation. Hawk gritted his teeth, determined to get up and take her home.

She lay unresisting beneath him. Her blue eyes were languorous. She stirred beneath him. "I can feel you against my belly."

Get up, get up, get up.

"I have bad thoughts about you, too," she whispered.

Oh, God, help me.

"Kiss me," she said. "Just once more."

He almost said he wasn't made out of stone, but at the moment, he felt like he was. "I shouldn't, but I cannot resist you." He let go of her wrists. She wrapped her arms around him as he devoured her mouth, licked her lips, and tasted her in an unmistakable rhythm of what he really wanted of her. She kissed him back, sucking on his tongue and threading her fingers through his hair.

He rolled onto his back, taking her with him. Then he fumbled blindly with the buttons on the back of her gown.

"Sit astride me," he said.

She did as he asked, though her skirts hid her legs. He pushed her gown and undergarments down her to her waist. Then he cupped her breasts and circled his thumbs over her pink nipples. She arched her back. Pins fell onto the counterpane, and her long raven hair spilled over her shoulders. This was how he'd imagined her. He set his hands on the small of her back. "Lean toward me."

She didn't question what he asked of her, but she gasped when he took her nipple in his mouth and sucked. He pushed her skirts out of his way and his breath caught at the dark curls.

She reached between them and ran her hand over his rock-hard cock, measuring him through the tight fabric. When he felt her fingers on the buttons of his falls, he tried to make himself stop her, but the first touch of her soft fingers on his cock made him wild with lust.

He sat up. She wrestled his coat, cravat, and shirt off. He stripped off her gown and all her undergarments. After he removed his boots and trousers, he shoved the covers down and kissed her as he pressed her to the bed.

He slid his hands beneath her bottom, tilting her. Then he spread the folds of her sex and flicked his tongue against the sweet spot as he slid his finger inside her. She whimpered and arched her back. Within minutes, she cried out. The contractions sucked at his finger. Julianne opened her eyes as he rose up over her. She wrapped her arms around his shoulders, needing him, wanting him desperately. He had always been a part of her, and she was a part of him. Tonight, she wanted him to make love to her, because she loved him heart and soul, more than she'd ever loved him before.

He parted the damp folds of her sex again and inserted two fingers, stretching her, making her wild with need. And then she felt him pushing inside. She cried out at the flash of pain.

"Oh, God, I hurt you." The tension eased gradually, and he slid a little farther inside. "Still hurt?" he whispered.

"Not anymore." Her hands slid to his hips. He groaned against her neck. She arched up against him. "Mmmm."

He pressed inch by inch until he was fully seated. And then he took his time, entering and withdrawing with exquisitely slow movements. He wanted to make it last a long time, and most of all, he wanted to pleasure her. Eventually his control spun out. He gave in to the urge to plunge faster and faster. She wrapped her arms and legs around him. He knew nothing but the need to reach for the ecstasy. As the erotic sensations overtook him, he managed to withdraw at the last possible second.

Julianne could feel his heart pounding.

He lay atop her, still breathing fast. Her arms and legs were still wrapped around him. Deep inside, she felt a slight soreness, though that wasn't precisely the right word. The sensation lingered, as if her body held the memory of their joining.

His breathing finally slowed. She turned her head and

marveled that he could sleep after their lovemaking. He was heavy, but she liked being skin to skin with him. She'd never felt closer to him.

She'd failed him tonight. Her words had sliced open his wounds, and he'd reacted harshly because she'd voiced doubts about him. He'd made the decision to change, but her accusation had infuriated him. She knew he must have felt vulnerable and a little scared that he wasn't capable of changing. He'd needed her unconditional belief in him, and she'd let him down because of her own fears. But tonight he'd admitted how much he'd wanted her during their waltz. He'd said he'd been on fire for her.

She'd been on fire for him tonight. He already possessed her heart, but she'd decided to give him her body in the ultimate act of love.

A little voice in her head whispered that he'd taken her virginity in the bed where he'd slept with countless whores.

She refused to think of their lovemaking as sordid. In giving herself to him, in this bed, she'd forever banished the women who had only performed for money. There was no comparison, because neither of them had been performing tonight. He would not have made love to her if he didn't love her.

"I love you," she whispered. Then she kissed his cheek.

His eyes opened. He looked dazed, as if he couldn't remember where he was.

She smiled at him, waiting for the three words that would change their lives forever.

"Oh my God," he said in a hoarse voice. Then he rolled onto his back and covered his eyes.

Pain flickered in her heart, but she would not show it. *Please hold me. Please, please hold me.*

He sat up on the edge of the bed, his back bowed, and cursed under his breath.

Tears welled in her eyes, but she blinked them back. Then she touched his back. He stood and walked over to the wardrobe. When he opened it, he donned a robe. Then he reached inside and grasped a woman's robe. Searing pain wrenched her heart.

No, she would not wear it. She grasped the twisted sheet and covered herself. Of all the evidence he'd shown her tonight about his past, he'd managed to find the one thing that would tear her to pieces.

A stinging sensation shot up her throat, spread through her cheeks, and hurt her eyes. She would not cry; she would not.

He stood there and shoved the woman's robe back onto the shelf. Then he pulled out a voluminous man's dressing gown and walked over to her. He tugged the sheet from her hands, exposing her. The shock of cool air made her shiver. He took her hand and helped her rise. Her legs trembled. He was staring at the bed with a tormented expression. She looked at the sheets and saw the bloodstains.

He helped her into the robe and rolled up the long sleeves. He retrieved the candle branch. When he put his arm around her shoulders, she felt a bit better.

"There's a bathing room and towels, but there's no water."

She swallowed. Those were the first words he'd said directly to her. He walked inside and set the candle branch on top of a small wooden chest. When she stepped inside, the marble was frigid beneath her feet. She was shaking as much from the cold as from the significance of the mistake she'd made.

He brought her a towel. "You're shivering."

"I'll b-be fine."

His face contorted. Then he lifted her in his arms and carried her back into the bedchamber. He laid her on the bed and pushed the robe open. She tried to stop him, but he hushed her and applied the towel. Afterward, he sat on the bed, pulled her onto his lap, and hugged her so hard it hurt.

Please tell me you love me.

"I swear I'll make it up to you," he said, his voice hoarse.

She'd wanted his love, and all he'd given her was his remorse.

He'd wrapped his coat over her shoulders to keep her warm and held her during the ride back in a hackney. Cad that he was, he'd refused to let her get her pelisse at the theater. All he'd thought about was his own anger. He'd felt as if she'd stabbed him in the back when she'd said she didn't want to end up like her mother.

He'd asked her for honesty, and when she'd given it, he'd struck out. Because her fear of betrayal had unearthed his own fears that his father had been right about him. He'd treated sweet Julianne badly. But she'd stood up to him and said things that still shook him.

She reached up and wiped her cheek. Oh, hell, she was crying. He found a handkerchief and patted her face. "Please don't cry," he whispered. Then he kissed her cheek, drew her onto his lap, and held her tight in his arms. He'd hurt her, both physically and emotionally. How could he have done it when he'd always adored her? When he'd always, always thought of her as his Julie-girl?

Somehow, he would make this night up to her. He'd made her his tonight, but in truth, they had always shared a special bond. He couldn't explain it, but he knew that somehow they were meant to be. Or was he simply making excuses for the terrible way he'd treated her tonight? He tightened his hold on her, because he needed her now, more than he'd ever needed another soul.

The hackney rolled to a halt. He cupped her cheek. "I'll escort you inside."

"No, that is unnecessary," she said.

"Julianne, my aunt will guess." He'd had to warn her because her tumbledown curls and the love bite on her neck shouted what had happened to her. He kissed her hands. "I will call on you tomorrow, and I promise you there will be a new beginning."

She lifted her eyes and threw her arms around him. He hugged her. "Come along. I'll let my aunt know I'm calling tomorrow." He knew his aunt would rake him over the coals, as well she should. God knew he deserved far worse, but he'd spend the rest of his life making it up to his Julie-girl.

He kept his arm around her shoulders as he escorted her up the walk. The biting wind stung through his shirt-sleeves, but he figured he deserved it.

When he led Julianne into the great hall, his aunt stood at the top of the stairs. Her gray brows shot up. He shook his head once, a warning to Hester to keep her scathing comments between her teeth until Julianne was safely out of hearing range.

After he led Julianne to the landing, she handed him his coat. He kissed her cheek in full view of his aunt. What was the point in pretending when it was obvious he'd tumbled Julianne?

She fled up the next flight of steps. He stood there watching, wishing he could stay by her side and comfort her, much the same way she'd done for him that night she'd found him drunk and passed out on his aunt's sofa.

When she disappeared from sight, he met his aunt's gaze.

"In the drawing room," she said curtly.

He followed her inside and closed the door. "I compromised her," he said. "With your permission, I wish to call on her tomorrow."

"And?"

"I will propose," he said.

"You'd better do it up right," she said. "On your knee."

"Yes," he said.

"When you do, swallow your guilt. No apologies, no remorse. She doesn't want to hear it, do you understand?"

His ears grew hot. "Yes, ma'am."

"You will think of her, not yourself. Do I make myself clear?"

"Yes."

"If I had a switch, I'd take it to your backside," Hester said.

"I deserve worse," he said.

"I love that girl as if she were my own daughter," Hester said. "And I love you, too. But if you ever hurt her again, I swear I'll never speak to you afterward."

He swallowed, remembering the horrible things he'd said to her. "I plan to spend the rest of my life making it up to her."

"No, you will not. Hang your guilt. Spend the rest of your life treating her as if she were the sun and the stars combined."

"I will," he said.

"One last thing," she said. "Wait to announce the engagement until we travel to Gatewick Park. And under no circumstances are you to confess to Shelbourne. You'll only stir up a bee's nest and create lasting hard feelings. He doesn't need to know, and you'll only humiliate Julianne. All you need say is that you fell hard for her and can't live without her. I want your promise."

"I promise," he said.

"I know you regret what happened tonight, but you will never regret her," Hester said.

Something hot rushed up his throat and stung his eyes. He hoped to hell she wouldn't regret him.

Chapter Twenty

A Lady's Secrets of Seduction: The only thing that matters is three little words.

Hawk opened the jewel box. When he touched the silver locket, he thought of Julianne's blue eyes and his chest felt tight. He'd bought the locket to replace the one her father had given her. The one she'd shown him so hesitantly before that first ball. The one he'd not seen her wear since that first night. He'd bought her a new one, because he'd wanted her to wear his locket and know that he would always be hers.

He didn't have a miniature portrait yet, but he'd have one painted of both of them after they announced their engagement to their families. The devil only knew how Tristan would react, but he would take his aunt's advice to heart.

All these years, he'd believed himself incapable of being

faithful, but he would. He'd experienced the emptiness of lust-filled couplings with women he'd barely known. He was done with that life forever. Today, he would walk away from that cold life and begin anew with his sweet Julianne.

He straightened his neck cloth one last time. He remembered what his aunt had told him. *No regrets. No guilt.*

Think of her. He would keep his remorse between his teeth and spend the rest of his days making her happy.

He inhaled. After sleeping fitfully last night, he'd decided to set the tone of their marriage based on the life they had already shared and would continue to share. He wouldn't make solemn promises, because words were only words. Instead, he would spend each day of their lives together demonstrating through his actions that he was a better man because of her. But he felt certain she'd find it charming if he began with silly promises. He'd make her laugh and then he would kneel as he'd promised his aunt.

There was one issue that troubled him. He'd insisted on honesty between them, but he would enter into this engagement withholding a major fact about his past. She knew what his father had said about him, and she knew that he'd barely escaped pistols at dawn. But she'd not asked for specifics. She'd told him to let go of his past and forgive himself. And she'd said she would not press him to reveal more. The truth was she would never find out. Besides himself, only Westcott knew, and the man had been a key player in the cover-up. With good reason.

Hawk had kept silent all these years to protect those he'd injured. But today, keeping that ugly secret bothered him.

Last night, his aunt had told him never to reveal to Tristan that he'd compromised Julianne. She'd said he didn't need to know. The question of the need to know decided him. Telling Julianne would accomplish nothing. He'd told her he couldn't undo the damage, and it was true.

He blew out his breath, determined to put her needs first today and every day after. He swallowed hard, knowing he didn't deserve her, but he swore he would never hurt her again.

With one last tug on his sleeves, he strode from his rooms, prepared to do something he'd never expected to do. As he walked out into the bright sunshine, the hollow place inside his chest filled.

His heart beat harder, and all he knew was that he no longer felt empty. But he also felt a bit anxious, too. After the terrible things he'd said and done last night, he worried she would be afraid. But he couldn't let the doubts in. Not now. Starting today, he would demonstrate what she meant to him in a thousand little ways.

Julianne's stomach clenched as Betty dressed her hair. Today, Hawk would propose to her. No one had voiced the actual reason for his intended call, but she knew he felt obligated to offer for her. And it was that sense of obligation that deeply troubled her.

How could a marriage based on necessity thrive? And was it really necessary? She knew enough to realize he'd withdrawn before spilling his seed. There was no possibility of conception, but there was also the incontrovertible fact that she'd given her virginity to Hawk.

And he'd not once mentioned love.

Last night, he'd been consumed by guilt, but she had

encouraged him to make love to her. In the bed where he'd lain with more mistresses than he could count.

All these years she'd dreamed of this day, but those dreams had involved a declaration of love. He'd bedded her last night, but he'd never said he loved her.

Foolishly, she'd thought he would never have made love to her if he didn't love her. She loved him with all her heart, but she'd sworn never to marry a man who did not love her. Unrequited love was a miserable lot for a wife. She'd seen what it had done to her mother.

But would Hawk have made the declaration under such circumstances? He'd felt awful about taking her to bed in that love nest. He wouldn't want to propose to her in that sordid place.

Last night, he'd promised her that everything would be different today. Hope leaped in her heart. He'd wanted to wait until today to declare his feelings.

But what would she do if he didn't?

Betty finished and gave her the hand mirror. Julianne looked at her reflection. "Thank you, Betty. It's perfect."

A tap at the door startled her. Hester walked inside and smiled. "He is here."

Julianne rose. "I'm so nervous."

Hester enfolded her in her arms. "So is he."

She looked up. "He is?"

Hester nodded. "He's pacing about and very anxious to see you. Let's not keep him. I'll walk with you to the drawing room and close the door afterward."

"Thank you."

Her legs felt like jelly as she descended the stairs with Hester. With every step, she prayed this momentous day would end happily.

When they reached the open drawing room, she saw him stop and gaze at her. He'd worn a hunter green coat and for once his cravat was straight.

Hester leaned down and whispered, "Meet him halfway."

She took a deep breath and stepped inside. The door closed behind her. She kept walking, and when he reached her, he took her hands.

"I have something for you," he said.

She released his hands as he reached inside his coat and withdrew a jewelry box. Then he opened it. She caught her breath at the silver locket. She'd shown him the one her father had given her long ago before they'd left for the Beresford's ball.

She looked into his shining eyes and knew he meant to replace the other one as a sign of his love. He clasped the chain around her neck. "We'll see about miniature portraits later."

She touched it. "Thank you," she whispered.

He took her hands again. "I thought about making solemn promises, but it occurred to me that every day is a promise. It's not the promise that matters, but the doing does."

She nodded.

He grinned. "However, in honor of our many mischievous adventures, I will promise to steal your bonnets and your kisses."

She laughed.

"I swear to ply you with wine and bargain for your favors. But I will never let you drive my curricle. And I promise to interrupt your reading frequently because I'll want all your attention."

She knew she would always remember his silly promises.

"My adorable, sweet Julie-girl, be my sunshine and the brightest star in the night."

Her skin tingled at his romantic words. He kneeled before her. She held her breath, waiting for the three words that would complete her joy this day.

"Will you marry me?"

Her smile faded.

His lips parted. "Julianne?"

She knew then what she had to ask. "If last night had not happened, would you have proposed?"

His hesitation spoke louder than any words. She released his hands.

He stood and stared at her. "Julianne, it did happen, but I want us to go forward. I want to marry you."

She clutched her shaking hands.

"I know I hurt you last night, but today can be our first step toward a life together," he said. "I don't blame you for being scared, but I swear I'll make it up to you."

"It's not enough," she said.

"I made you mine last night. I cannot walk away from that, and neither can you."

"I won't enter into a marriage based on one night's folly."

"You would consign me to hell? You would send me away, knowing for the rest of my life that I dishonored you?"

"I won't consign myself to a marriage based solely on an honor-bound obligation. Because that would be a living hell for both of us."

He shook his head. "You won't even give me a chance to prove to you I can be a good husband."

Her eyes filled with tears. She wanted to say yes so badly, but he didn't love her. And if she married him, she would always know that he'd only married her out of obligation. "I'm sorry."

"You would marry another man after giving me your virginity?"

She winced. "I cannot answer for the future. But I can answer for now. I won't marry you just to assuage your guilty conscience."

"I won't accept defeat," he said. "When we arrive at Gatewick Park, I will go to your brother and ask his permission. And we will announce the engagement."

Tears streamed down her face. "Please don't do this."

He fisted his hands. "I asked for honesty between us, and you're making me pay because I won't pretend that last night never happened. If this is about your doubts, then tell me what I can do."

She'd spent the first eight years of her life trying to win her father's love. And the last four hoping Hawk would fall in love with her. She couldn't spend a lifetime hoping that one day he would grow to love her.

"I won't let you do this," he said. "When I take you home, I will announce our engagement."

When he strode out the door, she covered her mouth to stifle the sobs wracking her body.

He halted his curricle, barely remembering driving home. Every inch of his body was as cold as ice. He'd been honest with her about his reason for proposing, but if he'd lied through his teeth, she would have accepted.

He knew what it was. She was afraid he would betray her. She'd told him she didn't want to end up like her mother, but she wouldn't trust him. She wouldn't give him the benefit of the doubt.

There was no way in hell he'd let her do this to him. He'd suffered one bad mistake, one he could never redeem, but this one he could.

He walked past a hackney and strode up the stairs. She was probably paying him back for taking her to his damnable love nest. His aunt had advised him not to apologize, and he'd trusted that it was the right thing to do. But he would not let Julianne do this to him—or to her. She couldn't marry another man, knowing she was dishonored.

Damn it all to hell. She would make this as difficult as possible. After he put a wedding ring on her finger, he'd make sure she stayed out of trouble.

When he reached his door, he pushed inside and slapped his hat onto the hall table. His manservant, Smith, met him. "My lord, there is a young man waiting in the parlor. He's been here for over an hour."

Bloody hell. It was probably Osgood wanting advice. "Get rid of him."

"My lord, he came all the way from Eton in a mail coach and took a hackney here."

"Eton?" His nephews were too young for school. "It's some sort of hoax. Send him on his way."

"Begging your pardon, my lord, but you might want to speak to him first."

"Why?" he said irritably.

Smith hesitated.

Hawk frowned. "Out with it, man."

Smith took a deep breath. "My lord, he's the spitting image of you."

Chill bumps erupted all over his body. It wasn't possible. "What is his name?"

"Called himself Brandon, Lord Rothwell."

Hawk grasped the table with one hand. God Almighty. His son had found him.

"My lord?" Smith said.

"That will be all, Smith."

His heartbeat drummed in his ears as he walked toward the parlor. He paused at the open door. The boy sat on the sofa with a leather-bound book on his lap. He wore the Eton uniform—a blue coat and fawn breeches. When Hawk walked inside, Brandon jumped to his feet and looked at him. A shock of recognition gripped Hawk at the sight of his own golden brown eyes, high cheekbones, and full mouth. The devil. The boy even had the same unruly dark brown hair.

The room seemed to tilt for a moment. His son, the boy he'd never thought to see, stood before him. He inhaled, knowing he had to keep his wits for the boy's sake. "Brandon?"

The boy arched his brows, and Hawk nearly staggered. How could it be possible that the lad had the same mannerisms when they'd never met?

"She said I looked like you."

His heart hammered in his chest. "Your mother?"

"She died a year ago. Did you know?" His youthful voice held a challenge.

"I heard. I'm sorry for your loss."

"No, you're not."

The boy was angry, justifiably so. God, he felt as if the floor had dropped beneath him. "How did you find me?"

He held up the book. "I found her journal."

Goddamn Cynthia for leaving behind evidence. God-damn Westcott for not searching and destroying it. "My manservant said you traveled in the mail coach from Eton."

"Yes. I wanted to see you for myself."

He decided to deal with practical matters first, before tackling the difficult issues. "You must be hungry and thirsty."

"I can fend for myself."

He couldn't let him go. "You came a long way. I suspect you've got questions. I'll answer them. But there's no need to do it on an empty stomach."

Brandon's eyes flickered. "All right."

Hawk rang the bell. When Smith appeared, Hawk instructed him to set out an impromptu meal in the small dining parlor.

"This way," he said to the boy.

As he walked to the dining parlor, an unreal sensation enveloped him. But he had to stay calm for the boy's sake.

When they were seated, Smith brought in bread and sliced roast beef, oranges, and a jug of milk. Hawk watched the boy wolf down the food and drink two glasses of milk. He swallowed back the lump in his throat, thinking of the twelve years he'd missed. But then he'd never thought to ever see his son.

His son.

He had so many questions. Did Westcott treat him well? That was the part that kept him awake at night, wondering if his son was mistreated. But he couldn't ask directly—in truth, he had no right, for he'd given up all rights to his own flesh and blood more than a dozen years ago, before the boy was even born. And the day the letter had arrived, he'd wept as he read the news that Cynthia had delivered a healthy boy.

His father had snatched the letter away and thrown it on the fire. Burned the only news he'd thought to ever have of his son.

He'd known it was necessary to destroy the evidence, but at the time, he'd hated his father for his brutal words. *Stop sniveling. You're damned lucky to be alive.*

He'd been two months shy of his nineteenth birthday.

He forced the past from his head, because he didn't want the boy to see the torment on his face. "Do you want to talk here or in the parlor?"

"Makes no difference to me," Brandon said.

Hawk folded his hands on the table. "Let's start with a few practical matters. I take it your father doesn't know you left school."

"He went up to Bath to take the waters for his health."

That news alarmed Hawk. Brandon stood to inherit a substantial property. To the best of Hawk's knowledge, the elderly Westcott had no living relatives. There was nothing he could do about it. He had no legal rights, and worse, if he claimed Brandon as his son, the boy would lose his inheritance because he would be officially a bastard—scorned and mocked.

For now, Hawk needed to concentrate on the immediate problems. "You'll be reported missing," he said. "If you wish to write your father, I'll make sure the letter is delivered."

"I'll go back to Eton tonight."

He wasn't about to let the boy travel by himself again. "I'll take you in my carriage tomorrow."

"I don't need your charity," he said.

"You can have a clean seat all to yourself or you can be squashed between some smelly travelers who haven't bathed in a fortnight. You'll have a lot more stops along the way. I can make sure you get there faster."

"Maybe," he said.

"What do you want to know?" Hawk asked.

His mouth worked. "How did you meet her?"

He had no intention of telling the boy that his mother had lied to Westcott about her whereabouts to attend that raucous party. "Mutual friends introduced us."

"You knew she was married."

Hawk heard the accusation in the boy's voice, but he did not deny it. "Yes. It was wrong."

Of course, he couldn't tell the boy the truth, any more than he could tell Julianne. He could never tell her about the sordid events that still haunted him and about the woman who had made his life hell.

Cynthia hadn't been just a willing participant. She had been determined and had fawned all over him. Ramsey and his friends had thought it funny. Hawk had resisted her, because he'd known she was married.

The next night, Ramsey and his friends decided Cynthia needed a young lover to make up for her middle-aged husband. They'd supposedly put every man's name on slips of paper and drawn the *lucky* winner to warm Cynthia's bed. He'd been so green he'd never suspected that his name had been on every single slip of paper. They had heckled him and made sport of him. He'd let them bully him into going to her bed. She'd welcomed him with open arms. The next day, he'd overheard Ramsey and his friends laughing in the billiard's room over the great trick they'd played on him. But it was Cynthia's laughter that had infuriated him. She'd known about the trick and thought it a great joke.

Brandon glared at him. "She wrote you letters, and you never answered. You abandoned her after getting her with child."

The boy had clearly read that in her journal. Hawk chose his words with care. "She was married. I'd made a bad mistake and didn't want to sin again."

He'd burned Cynthia's letters. She'd wanted him to send letters to her friend, who would pass them on. The middle-aged Westcott grew suspicious when his supposedly barren wife of eight years was suddenly, inexplicably with child. After he'd intercepted one of Cynthia's letters, he'd sent word to Hawk's father demanding satisfaction.

"You were too cowardly to stand up in a duel of honor," Brandon said. "I was just your by-blow, rubbish."

He took a moment to compose his words. "I was eighteen years old and had a very strict father who made me do the right thing. The right thing was to pay your father for your support. I'd done a bad thing, but as my father told me, it would have been far worse to acknowledge you in any way. Because that would have put an ugly label on you, and that would have been unfair."

"Don't act like you care. I know you don't."

"I can see why you think that," he said. "But I suspect you have a good relationship with your father." He hoped to hell he was right.

"He's the best," Brandon said. "He's my real father."

Relief poured through him. "Yes, he is your father in every sense of the word."

The boy traced his finger over the condensation on the table left behind by the glass. "How would you like it if some man meddled with your mother and abandoned her?"

"I wouldn't like it at all."

"I read about you in the scandal sheets," the boy said. "You're an infamous rake."

Hawk ignored that statement, determined to keep the focus on the boy. "Do you play cricket at school?"

"Yes, I'm the team captain."

"I thought you looked athletic," he said. He'd been shooting in the dark, but he remembered how much he'd liked sports as a boy.

"I ought to be going. I need to get a room at the Claridge's."

He'd no intention of letting the boy travel alone in London. "You're welcome to stay here if you don't mind the sofa. It might be difficult to get a room. London is a popular place."

"I suppose so," he said grudgingly.

He realized that after tomorrow he would never see his son again. There was so little time, but he'd make the most of what he had. "Do you play backgammon?"

"Sometimes," Brandon said.

"Since you're stuck here for the night, we could play for a while. If you like."

"Might as well," he said.

Hawk smiled a little, wondering if the boy always spoke sparingly or if it was just the situation. He set up the game and asked innocent questions as they played. By the end of the night, he'd learned a great deal about the boy. He had two spotted springers at home and liked archery and fishing. He had two best mates at Eton who had visited him the previous summer. They toasted cheese over the fire at school. Hawk had confessed he used to do the same.

After several rounds of backgammon, three of which he'd let Brandon win, he persuaded his son to sit on the carpet with him, while they toasted cheese and drank chocolate. He remembered one Christmas when he and Tristan had toasted cheese at Gatewick Park. Julianne had wanted to join them. Tristan had balked, but Hawk had let her sit with him and help toast cheese. The bittersweet memory tugged at him. He feared he'd lost her.

When Brandon yawned for the third time, Hawk brought him a pillow and a blanket. He'd wanted to tuck him in, but a twelve-year-old boy wouldn't appreciate it, and in this case, the boy had plenty of reason to resent him.

Hawk put the game away, and when he came back into the parlor, the boy was sound asleep. He padded over to him and dared to brush the unruly lock of hair from his forehead. It was the first time he had ever touched his son.

At dawn, Hawk got the grumbling boy to awaken and persuaded him to eat a bit of gruel. He left a missive to be delivered to his aunt informing her he had to leave the city unexpectedly and that he would call when he returned.

Along the journey to Eton, they stopped twice at inns for tea and a meal and to change the horses. Brandon drank a good deal of milk each time. He was curious about the odd assortment of travelers and confessed his father didn't travel much, except to Bath for the waters. Again, Hawk worried about Westcott's health and the possible consequences for Brandon. Hawk's lack of power frustrated him. He thought of making discreet inquiries with an attorney, but he knew the consequences of exposing the circumstances of the boy's birth meant Brandon would lose his inheritance.

At one inn, Brandon had watched a couple of lads kicking a ball. When they invited him to join in, Hawk had encouraged him to play. His chest had tightened while watching his athletic son running about. Afterward in the carriage, Brandon had told him the two boys were brothers. Hawk told him stories of how he'd taught his younger brother to climb a tree. He didn't mention that he'd taught Julianne, but his chest had ached at the memory.

The boy slept curled up on the opposite seat for the rest of the journey. He was undoubtedly exhausted from his adventure. A few miles from Eton, Hawk woke him.

"We're almost there," he said.

When the boy rubbed his eyes and sat up, Hawk took a deep breath. "You might want to write your father and tell him you met me. If you do, ask him to write me. You probably shouldn't let on to your mates about me, just in case. It would wound your father if others found out." He didn't tell the boy that he would be the one to suffer the label of *bastard*.

Hawk thought a moment about the journal and decided the best course. "You might want to put the journal in safekeeping until you return home. I suspect your father will worry when he finds out you read it."

"I don't know if I'll tell him," Brandon said. "He's not in the best of health, and I don't want to make it worse."

"Perhaps you should put it back where you found it."

He glanced out the window. The round tower of Windsor came into view, signaling his time with Brandon was nearly over. Hawk drew in a deep breath. "I won't pretend to know how you feel. In your shoes, I'd probably be angry and shocked. But the circumstances of your birth aren't the most important thing. Focus on your father and your mates."

The boy frowned. "You're not what I expected. I thought you'd cut up nasty about me invading your life."

"I've no right to do so. You have every reason to be angry."

"Well, you're not so bad. You play a mean game of backgammon, and you sat on the floor to toast cheese. I've never met a grown-up before who was willing to do that."

His throat clogged, and he had to clear it before speaking. "Guess I missed being a boy last night."

"I bet you don't miss school," he said. "Latin is the worst."

"I hated it, too," he said.

When the carriage rolled to a halt, Hawk took another deep breath. "I won't get out because it would be hard to explain how I came to deliver you back at school."

The boy nodded.

Hawk's jaw worked. "You probably won't believe me, and I can't say as I blame you, but not a day has gone by that I didn't think about you."

Brandon frowned. "You feel really bad about what you did."

He swallowed. "Yes, but I'm glad I met you."

The boy held out his hand. Hawk grasped it.

The driver opened the door and started to let down the steps, but Brandon jumped. Hawk watched his son run to the steps until he disappeared.

When the carriage rolled into motion, he gritted his teeth and clenched his fists. His chest heaved. A hoarse sound came out of his throat. He wept for the first time since he was eighteen years old.

Chapter Twenty-one

A Scoundrel's Advice: There's no place like home.

Hawk spent the next week making arrangements.

He sent his aunt a letter, inquiring about Julianne and promised to call after he'd settled at Ashdown House. Then he gave up the lease on the love nest, found a new position for Smith, and packed his spartan belongings at the Albany. While sorting through his books, he found the notorious pamphlet and tossed it inside one of the trunks. As the servants carried away the last trunk, Hawk walked over to the hearth where he and Brandon had toasted cheese. He smiled a little, walked out of the refuge, and moved back home.

The first two days at Ashdown House, he'd felt a little at sea. He had a difficult time as he sat at his father's desk and sorted through the letters. He got rid of most of the papers, but he kept a magnifying glass his father used to let him look through when he was little.

After a great deal of trouble, he managed to locate William in Venice and informed him that he should return to England immediately so that he could attend the house party at Gatewick Park. Once Will was back on British soil, Hawk planned to have a discussion with his brother about career choices.

While dining with friends at the club, he ran into Montague. He managed to shock his brother-in-law when he said he'd taken his advice about Will and that he'd also moved into Ashdown House. Montague told him he'd gotten rid of the mistress. Hawk had been relieved.

He wrote his mother, who was ecstatic to hear he was moving home. Grandmamma said she would consider moving into Ashdown House now that Hawk had come home, but he doubted she would leave her friends in Bath.

One of the hardest decisions he had to make concerned Ramsey. In the end, he decided to pay a brief call on him. He shook hands with him and said he forgave him for that long-ago incident. Ramsey, of course, had no idea of the consequences of his trick, but Hawk thought better of him for apologizing.

While he'd half hoped to hear from Westcott, Hawk figured the boy had not told him that he'd traveled to London to meet his sire.

He'd completed all of his plans. There was nothing to keep him from calling on his aunt and Julianne. He dreaded the call, but he'd made a decision. He meant to tell Julianne that he would leave his proposal open in the event she changed her mind. As he climbed into his curricle, he told himself the first meeting would be the most awkward. But the season was nearing the end, and soon he would escort her home.

As he drove, he realized how much he'd missed her. He'd treated her badly that night at the love nest and couldn't see any way to make amends. She'd turned down his offer of marriage, and her refusal still stung. He'd hated the circumstances, but he'd thought they could be happy together. The part that made him feel the worst was that he'd taken her virginity. Her lack of virtue could have grim consequences for her, and he wasn't certain she fully understood that. Fair or not, husbands expected their wives to be virgins on their wedding day.

He was, he realized, back in familiar territory. He'd made another mistake he couldn't undo, not unless she agreed to marry him. And that seemed unlikely. He hoped he could talk to her today.

The hunt for the anonymous lady who had written *The Secrets of Seduction* was the talk of the town.

Julianne sat with Hester, the five cubs, and Amy, Georgette, and Sally in the Egyptian drawing room. She tried not to look as anxious as she felt, but she didn't like being the anonymous prey of every furious bachelor, rakehell, and wastrel in London.

Beaufort crossed his arms over his chest. "The latest theory about the author is ludicrous. I think Lady Elizabeth and Miss Henrietta Bancroft started the rumor about themselves being the twin authors behind the anonymous lady."

Amy huffed. "I cannot believe either of them could spell well enough to write a paragraph, much less an entire pamphlet."

Caruthers elbowed Osgood. "You were a good sport about the scandal sheets putting you up as the author."

"I'm planning to write one from the gentleman's perspective," Osgood said.

"Don't forget the stinky smoke," Portfrey said. "Attracts the prettiest ladies."

"Pay no attention to their teasing," Julianne said to Osgood.

"I won't let their ribbing get to me," Osgood said. "After all, you encouraged me to write the gentlemen's side of things."

Hester lifted her quizzing glass to her eye. "Most peculiar," she said.

Mr. Peckham shrugged. "I heard the publisher is looking for a similar pamphlet. The first one is selling so well he probably wishes to capitalize on its success."

While their talk of the pamphlet continued, Julianne sipped her tea. Her heart felt as heavy as a boulder inside her chest. She'd not seen Hawk for a week, and he'd directed his missives to Hester.

After refusing his proposal, her doubts had set in immediately. He'd been so romantic, but he'd not said he loved her. He'd spoken about truthfulness, and in retrospect, she realized that this truly meant he did not love her. He'd made an honest offer to atone for her loss of honor and his. She'd hated turning him down, hated the look on his face, hated that she'd spoiled his sweet, beautiful proposal.

Most of all, she missed him. Every single day and night. Nothing was the same. She missed bantering with him. She missed his jests and his beautiful brown eyes. And she missed his teasing as well.

Nothing had changed. She was still madly in love with him.

Almost as if she'd conjured him, Hawk walked into Hester's drawing room. Was it possible that he'd grown even more handsome since she'd last seen him? Her heart ached. She'd hurt him the last time he was here. Even though she felt she'd made the right decision, it still hurt very much.

"I told the butler I'd see myself up. Looks as if everyone is here."

The cubs wanted to know where he'd been, and Hawk said he'd had to take care of personal matters. He took his usual seat but refused cake and tea. The dogs regarded him with forlorn expressions—probably bemoaning the cake.

Julianne studied him. There was something different about him, though she couldn't put her finger on it.

Beaufort leaned forward. "I heard you moved out of your rooms at the Albany."

He nodded. "I've lived in bachelor quarters for many years. I'll be glad when my family comes home. It's easy to take your family for granted," he said. "But they're the most important people in my life. And that's as it should be."

Julianne looked at him. He seemed to have changed overnight, though she knew it had been a little over a week since she'd last seen him.

Mr. Peckham eyed Hawk. "Have you read the pamphlet yet?"

"Actually, I finally had time to read it last night."

Julianne held her breath. No doubt he would criticize it. She'd have to remember not to throw anything at his head or he might guess the truth.

"Well, what did you think?" Hester asked.

"There was something very familiar about the author's writing style." He shrugged. "I don't know why it struck me so." He met Julianne's gaze. "I found some of her phrasing quite lively and engaging."

"So you approve of the pamphlet?" Julianne asked.

"Oh, no. The exhortations on how to trap bachelors are ridiculous."

She sniffed. "What is so ridiculous about them?"

He held his hand up. "Here is a prime example of the nonsensical advice the author gives young ladies. She tells them to plant extra posies in the drawing room so that it will appear other suitors have beaten them to the door." He gestured with his hands. "This, according to the author, will make the gentleman jealous and wild to jump into the parson's mousetrap with his dishonest beloved."

When the other gentlemen guffawed, Julianne lifted her chin. How dare he make fun of her pamphlet? What did he know about the trials and tribulations of being a single young lady?

Beaufort frowned. "Julianne, you always had a regular flower garden in the drawing room."

Her heart thudded. "Oh, isn't that a coincidence."

"I have to give the author credit for her imaginative and spirited writing style." He looked at Julianne and winked.

She sucked in her breath. Oh, dear heavens, had she inadvertently written in such a manner that he recognized her as the author? Well, she'd never admit it even if he did accuse her. After all, he'd laughed at her pamphlet.

The butler strode inside. "An express letter for Lady Julianne. It arrived moments ago."

Chill bumps erupted on her arms as she tore the letter open. Her hands shook as she opened it. Then she gasped.

"Oh, it is news from my brother. Tessa was delivered of a healthy baby boy yesterday."

Everyone cheered.

Hawk was a bit more subdued in his reaction. "That's wonderful news. I know it's been a long nine months for Tristan."

"And Tessa," Julianne said. "She is the one who carried the babe, after all."

"I stand corrected," Hawk said.

Was she imagining a slightly melancholy look in his eyes?

"Have they chosen a name yet?" Hester asked.

"Oh, yes, how could I forget?" She scanned the letter. "Christopher George Gatewick. Tristan includes a note for you, Hawk."

When she handed him the letter, he read it quickly. "He wishes me to escort you and my aunt to Gatewick Park as soon as arrangements can be made."

Julianne bounced on the sofa. "Oh, I want to go tomorrow first thing."

Hawk regarded his aunt. "Can you be ready tomorrow?"

"Yes, of course," Hester said.

"We can make it in one day if we leave very early in the morning," Julianne said.

Hawk gave her a speaking look. "The journey takes ten hours. That's an awfully long time to be cramped up in a carriage, even with stops. It's especially hard on ladies, I think."

She realized he meant Hester. Julianne had noted she sometimes had to lean heavily on the stairwell. "Yes, I see your point. I'd forgotten how uncomfortable it can be on such a long drive."

"Julianne, you are officially an aunt," Georgette said.

"I am." She laughed. "I cannot wait until I can hold little Christopher in my arms."

Hawk rose and walked over to the window.

She kept the smile on her face, but something was troubling Hawk. Once before, she'd noticed he'd reacted oddly to discussions about the babe. She shook it off. The idea that he wouldn't be happy for her brother was bizarre, but it troubled her all the same.

He lingered in his aunt's drawing room, hoping he would have a chance to speak to Julianne alone. The cubs and her friends surrounded her, talking animatedly. His aunt walked out with Mr. Peckham. Hawk wondered if there was more than friendship between them, but he would not pry into his aunt's affairs. If she wanted him to know, she would tell him.

The cubs and Sally took their leave, but Amy and Georgette remained behind. Hawk idled about the drawing room while Julianne and her friends made plans to meet during the summer. Another ten minutes went by. He walked to the faux mummy and realized Julianne probably wanted to avoid discussing his proposal. She'd made her reasons clear for rejecting him. Nothing had changed.

He glanced over his shoulder. The three were huddled together on the sofa. Undoubtedly, they wished for privacy.

He'd wanted one last chance to let her know his offer of marriage would remain open in the event she changed her mind.

But she obviously did not want to hear him out.

Her husky laugh reverberated all along his spine as he walked out of the drawing room. He closed the door behind him and met his aunt's sharp gaze. "I will bring my carriage round at eight in the morning if that suits you."

"We will be ready." Hester took his arm and led him to the stairs. "Are you so easily defeated?"

He didn't pretend to misunderstand her meaning. "She won't have me. I'll not press when it is clear she does not welcome a renewal of my addresses."

"I know you've had regrets in the past," Hester said. "Don't let her be one of them."

"I don't regret spending the season with the two of you." Then he walked down the stairs.

Julianne walked around the bedchamber she'd occupied for one season. She trailed her fingers over the corner desk where she'd spent long hours writing the pamphlet. When Hawk had complimented the writing style in the pamphlet earlier today, she'd hugged her secret pleasure to herself. He'd winked at her, making her suspect he knew she was the author. She wasn't sure if she'd imagined a secret message from him, but she likely would never know.

She'd wanted to talk privately with him today, but she'd realized any further discussions about her reasons for refusing him would prove awkward for him and painful for her.

Betty placed the last shawl in the giant trunk that Tessa had lent her. All her gowns, shawls, bonnets, and underclothes were neatly packed.

"You might wish to check the drawers once more," Betty said. "I'll close it up in the morning after you're dressed."

"Thank you, Betty," she said.

After the maid left, Julianne walked over to the bed, remembering all the times she and Hester had spoken late at night. With a sigh, she opened the drawer of the bedside table. The locket her father had given her years ago lay inside. She picked it up, recalling how her friends had helped her to remove it when she'd grown panicked.

With a flick of her thumb, she opened the locket. She frowned at the miniature of her father's handsome face. Oddly, that miniature no longer held the power to hurt her. She'd never really known him. He'd died fourteen years ago, and though she'd felt his rejection keenly all these years, she realized he'd never really had any influence on her. Her brother and Hawk had always been the men who had cared about her.

She took the locket over to the trunk and kneeled before it. When she found the jewelry box Hawk had given her, she removed the locket, opened it, and looked at the empty ovals. Pain lanced her heart. She'd journeyed to London with high hopes he would propose to her. Ironically, she'd gotten what she wanted and had turned him down.

She'd hurt him.

The doubts returned. Would she always regret not giving him a chance? Her eyes welled with tears, but she blinked them back. She placed both lockets in the jewelry box, set it in the trunk, and stood. She was her mother's daughter and strong enough to face whatever the future held for her.

With her head held high, she walked to the bed, removed her dressing gown, and climbed onto the soft mattress. She looked at the spare pillow, tempted to hug it to her chest, but she was no longer the starry-eyed girl who thought wishing and hoping could end in happily-ever-after.

A tap sounded at the door. With a smile, she sat up in bed as Hester entered the bedchamber. "I knew you would come."

Hester sat beside her on the bed. "I'm feeling rather sentimental this evening."

"So am I," she whispered. "Thank you for everything."

"Oh, my dear, it is I who should thank you. I've very much enjoyed being your aunt for a season."

"I will always think of you as my aunt," she said.

Hester smoothed the covers. "I hoped you would be my niece by marriage."

She drew her feet up on the mattress and wrapped her arms around her shins. "I came here with girlish aspirations of winning his heart, but I leave as a woman with the knowledge that hearts are not won. They are given."

"Since this is our last night this season, I will offer a bit of wisdom if you are willing to hear it."

"I have always set great store by your advice," Julianne said.

"There are no certainties in life," Hester said. "Sometimes you must take a leap of faith. When you are in doubt, look into your heart. You will find the answer there."

Hawk was late as usual.

His aunt would probably put a flea in his ear for arriving thirty minutes late, but his spirits had risen this morning.

He'd received a letter from Brandon. Miraculously, it had not gone astray. The new tenant at Hawk's old rooms at the Albany had redirected the letter to Ashdown House. Foolishly, he'd folded it and tucked it inside his coat. He hoped to find a private moment during the long journey to read the letter again.

Brandon had said he thought it ridiculous for them to remain strangers. He'd admitted he'd been ready to plant Hawk a facer when he'd come to London, but he thought Hawk all the crack for sitting by the fire and toasting cheese. Hawk smiled. His son thought him all the crack.

He'd written to him immediately and warned the boy not to reveal the truth about their special relationship. And he'd told the boy it would be best to inform his father. Hawk knew he'd done the right thing, but he feared Westcott would try to put a stop to their correspondence. Westcott would likely cut up nasty, because Hawk had violated the terms of the agreement by answering the boy's letter. But Hawk had decided enough was enough. He'd spent twelve years in hell, believing he'd never see his own son.

He'd given Brandon his address in Richmond and let the boy know how to reach him at Gatewick Park. At the end of his letter, he'd told Brandon to contact him if he ever had the need.

Upon reaching his aunt's town house, Hawk directed the servants carrying the trunks. A year ago, he'd traveled with Tristan and his family to Gatewick Park. Lord, he still couldn't believe the now–dowager duchess had let Tristan and Tessa ride alone in that carriage. By the time they'd reached Gatewick Park, the pair had emerged from the carriage disheveled and flushed. Hawk had watched his friend court all those belles last season, and it had been obvious to him that Tristan was mad for his matchmaker.

Thoughts of his old friend troubled him. Tristan had entrusted him to guard Julianne, and he'd failed miserably. His conscience bothered him, but he couldn't undo his mistakes. In the end, Julianne had made her choice, one that still left a hollow place in his chest. He dreaded telling her good-bye after the house party ended. Because he would miss her. He already did.

The front door opened. His aunt and Julianne emerged, carrying the blasted spaniels. Hawk fisted his hands on his hips as they approached. "The dogs are not allowed in my carriage."

Julianne lifted her chin. "They will be miserable without Hester. Besides, they won't cause any trouble."

"They are dogs," he said. "All they want is food and a walk. The servants can look after them for a fortnight."

"Marc, I am bringing them, so save your breath," Hester said.

Caro wiggled in Julianne's arms and whined. "Oh, look, she wants you." Julianne dumped the dog into his arms. "She can keep you company."

"The devil take it," he muttered.

"Watch your language, Marc," Hester said. "By the way, you are very late. What kept you?"

"I had to respond to a letter."

"A likely tale," Julianne said. "You undoubtedly overslept."

"If those dogs cast up their accounts in my carriage, you're both going to answer for it," he said.

Ten minutes later, the carriage rolled off. Naturally, he got stuck with the dogs on his seat, because there wasn't room for them on the bench where Julianne and Hester sat.

They hadn't even gotten out of London when his aunt

pulled out the pamphlet. "Julianne, perhaps you could read to us."

Hawk schooled his features as he watched Julianne's eyes widen. He'd known the minute he started reading it that she'd written the outrageous tract. Lord, he could almost hear her speaking the lines. He folded his arms over his chest and decided to have a bit of fun at her expense. "Julianne, I forbid you to read that rubbish." That ought to make her blood boil.

"I'll read what I please," she said, opening the pamphlet. "And you have no say. I dismiss you as my guardian."

"You cannot dismiss me. I am your guardian until we reach Gatewick Park."

He couldn't resist bedeviling her and leaped up to snatch the pamphlet from her hands.

"Give that back," she cried.

He opened it. "Ah, here is one of my favorite passages." He grinned at her over the pamphlet, only to find her fuming with her arms crossed over her chest. Hawk read in a falsetto voice, " 'A woman who is assured of herself exudes a mysterious quality, one that makes her alluring to gentlemen. You need not have excessive beauty. It is said that Anne Boleyn was only moderately attractive, but her vivacity and quick wit drew gentlemen to her side.' "

He snapped the pamphlet shut. "Anne Boleyn, the most notorious woman in the history of our nation, is held up as an example to follow in this pamphlet. I am shocked, deeply shocked, that my ward and my aunt would admire such immoral and radical advice. As Julianne's guardian, I feel duty-bound to set an example. As soon as we reach the next inn, I shall toss this disgusting rubbish onto the fire."

Julianne gasped. "You will not burn my pamphlet!"

He clutched his chest. "*Your* pamphlet?"

Her attempt to look innocent fell far short of the mark. "Yes, that is my copy, and I demand you hand it back."

"I smell something fishy," he said, narrowing his eyes. "Now that I think about it, there is something familiar about the writing style. It has puzzled me for some time." He regarded his aunt. "Do the words not ring a chord of familiarity, Aunt?"

She grinned. "Scamp. How did you figure it out?"

Julianne gasped. "Hester, no. My reputation!"

"Will be in tatters if anyone ever guesses you were foolish enough to write and publish this pamphlet," Hawk said. "As for how I guessed, the advice about planting posies in the drawing room was one of the most telling clues. Aunt, I suppose you encouraged her."

She held her quizzing glass up to her eye. "I did."

"Your friend Mr. Peckham must have seen to its publication."

"Insolent puppy," Hester muttered.

Hawk laughed. "The day I lifted her restriction, I couldn't believe she wasn't chomping at the bit to escape the house." He looked at Julianne and shook his head. "Minx. You told me you were writing, and I thought you meant letters."

She sniffed. "I shall never tell. And I will never speak to you again if you burn my pamphlet."

"I won't burn it, but I highly advise you to keep it and your identity as the author well hidden," he said.

She rolled her eyes. "I'm not an idiot, Marc."

He stilled. She'd not called him by his Christian name since she was a little girl. He wondered if it meant something. Probably not, though he found himself wishing that things had turned out differently for them.

Chapter Twenty-two

A Lady's Secrets of Seduction: Love conquers all.

After an overly long journey that included far more stops than necessary, they had finally arrived at the Black Swan Inn. Now they sat in a private dining parlor adjoining their rooms after eating a plain but decent meal.

The spaniels pawed at his legs and whined. He glowered at them. "If you think I'm giving you treats, you're dead wrong."

"They are sweet little dogs," Julianne said. "And you shouldn't speak to them in such a gruff manner."

"Those *sweet* little dogs are the reason we arrived so late. I cannot believe how many times we had to stop for them to piss."

"Watch your language," Julianne said.

He snorted. "If I didn't know better, I'd swear they did it on purpose."

Hester yawned. "Could be. They know you're a soft touch."

He folded his arms over his chest. "I am not."

His aunt sighed and looked suddenly weary. When she rose slowly, he rushed over to help her.

"Don't treat me like an old woman, Marc. I may be, but I don't have to like it."

"You will always be young in spirit," he said.

"Well, my body is not so youthful. I am for bed. Julianne, you may stay with Marc if you're not tired yet."

"Oh, no. I should go to bed early as well. We have another long journey tomorrow."

As his aunt ambled off, Julianne regarded him. "I will ensure she rests well."

"Thank you." He didn't want to think about her aging. "I fear this journey has been too much for her."

"I will take care of her," Julianne said.

He looked down at her and saw the concern in her beautiful blue eyes. "You've grown quite fond of her."

"She's become like my own aunt."

She'd spoken with a hitch in her voice.

"Hester dotes on you. I know she's enjoyed your company this season." He paused, unsure if he ought to say it and decided to do so. "And so have I."

She laughed. "You obviously have a very poor memory."

He pulled her curl. "Imp."

She cleared her throat. "Good night."

He wanted to beg her to stay and discuss what was and what wasn't between them. Part of him still hoped there was a chance they could work through their differences. But she crossed the corridor to the room directly opposite his and disappeared without a backward glance.

• • •

He awoke, thinking he must have dreamed he'd heard geese honking. Then he heard the sound from across the corridor and winced. His aunt's snoring was unbelievably loud. He sat up. Poor Hester. She must be exhausted, and of course she couldn't help it. Poor Julianne. She wouldn't get a wink of sleep with that racket booming in her ears.

Well, there was nothing to be done about it. He yawned and turned onto his side.

Outside, a door creaked. Oh, Lord, now what?

Someone knocked on his door. "Hawk?"

It was Julianne. "Just a moment. He grabbed his banyan robe from the bottom of the bed and slid it over his naked body. Then he padded to the door to find Julianne standing there in her white night rail. Her long, jet braid hung over her shoulder.

"I can't sleep," she said.

"Come inside."

"I'm sorry to wake you," she said. "But I felt as if someone were blowing a trumpet in my ear."

"Poor girl."

"If you don't mind, I'll curl up on the sofa."

He shook his head. "I'll take the sofa. You take the bed."

"I'm smaller and will fit snugly there. You are too big to sleep on the sofa."

He took her elbow. "I insist." When she climbed onto the mattress, he pulled the covers over her. God, he'd give anything to crawl inside those sheets with her. But they weren't married and never would be. With a sigh, he took the other pillow and walked over to the small, lumpy sofa.

He didn't fit, not even curled on his side. For the first time in his life, he wished he weren't so tall. There was no help for it. He'd have to sleep sitting up. When he folded his arms over his chest and lowered his head, Julianne made an exasperated sound.

"This is ridiculous. I will sleep on the sofa. I insist you take the bed," she said.

"Julianne, believe it or not, I am a gentleman, and I'll be damned if I let you sleep on this lumpy sofa."

"Watch your language." Then she sat up and hopped off the bed.

"Julianne, get back under the covers. I am not letting you sleep on this sofa." He paused and then added, "It's probably got fleas."

She shrieked and ran back to the bed.

His shoulders shook. Lord, he enjoyed teasing her. But the room was growing colder, and he was uncomfortable. He gritted his teeth, knowing he'd survive.

She sat up.

"Julianne, lie down and go to sleep."

"I can't when you're shifting about and obviously uncomfortable. Come to bed."

"I think a flea just hopped on me."

"This is a big bed. We can share it."

"No."

"Don't be silly. We're rational human beings and can manage to sleep in this bed without doing something we ought not to do."

"Julianne, I'm not getting into bed with you. Look what happened the last time. Sorry but my self-restraint is limited."

"You hardheaded man. Come get in this bed right now."

"Will you please go to sleep?" he gritted out.

"Not until you come to bed."

Exasperated and more than a little uncomfortable, he strode over to the bed. "Just so we're clear, you invited me. If I try to do something stupid, you are to slap me. Do you understand?"

She snorted. "I don't know what difference it makes now. We've already breached that fortress."

He stilled. "Don't put ideas in my head."

"I'm sure they were there already," she said. "Get in the bed."

"I don't think this is a good idea," he said without much conviction.

"Get in bed."

He shrugged off the banyan.

Her eyes roamed over his naked body. "You're beautiful."

He slid between the covers. "Turn on your side and go to sleep."

She swirled her finger through his chest hair. "Let's think about this rationally."

"There's a very irrational part of me that wants to do all the thinking."

"I'm already damaged goods."

"Don't say that."

"Well, it's true. I'm not a virgin any longer, but it occurred to me, I might never find a man willing to marry me now that I'm damaged goods."

"Will you stop saying that? God, I feel badly enough for what I did to you."

"As I recall, I'm the one who issued the invitation. But we're digressing. The point is, I may never have another opportunity, and I already know you're quite skilled. So, if you're not averse to the idea, I would like it very much if you made love to me."

Good Lord. "Julianne, I'm not going to touch you."

"No one will know."

"I will." He inhaled. "I'm ashamed of myself, and now there's nothing I can do, because you've refused to marry me."

She cupped his cheek. "It was a beautiful proposal."

He swallowed hard. It still hurt.

"I wanted to say yes so very badly, but I'd sworn never to marry a man who didn't love me."

His heart started beating harder.

"This is the part that's hard to admit, but I wounded you, and I suspect you don't understand. I've always adored you, and I was infatuated with you for many years. I'll admit something that will probably shock you."

"What is it?" he asked hoarsely.

"I set out to win your heart. I've been planning this ever since you danced with me at my come-out ball."

"You're jesting."

"No, I'm not. I'm going to swallow my pride and hope you'll understand that the girlish me has very recently become a woman."

"I don't understand."

"I have fantasized about marrying you for four long years. I never let another man kiss me, because I wanted your kiss to be my first," she said.

Oh, God.

"That night at the Beresford's ball, I thought for certain that all my fairy-tale dreams were coming true."

"And I said you were like a sister to me."

"Don't sound so stricken. I'd built you up into this impossibly perfect romantic hero."

"And I didn't live up to your expectations."

"I was infatuated with the fantasy of you, but I fell in love with the imperfect and wonderful man."

She loved him. His heart gave an unmistakable leap.

"I thought you deserved to know, to understand, that the reason I turned down your sweet proposal was because you don't love me," she said. "A marriage where only one partner loves is miserable, Marc. I saw what it did to my mother. In public, she held her head up with pride, but at home it was another matter altogether. You see, like me, she tried to win my father over. And neither of us succeeded."

"He was an idiot, and a selfish brute," he said.

"I let his rejection rule over me, but yesterday, I finally realized that he doesn't matter. I never knew him, and he didn't deserve me, my mother, or my brother. And it wasn't as if I didn't have good male influence in my life. Because you and Tristan have always been by my side. And I couldn't think of two more honorable and overly protective men."

A little huff of laughter escaped him.

"I love you, but I knew that if I married you because you felt duty-bound, I would always feel inferior. I would always cover up my real feelings for you, because you don't return them. And I don't say this to make you feel bad—"

He put his finger over her lips. "My God, I'm a bigger blockhead than Osgood."

She grabbed his finger. "What does Osgood have to do with this?"

"Nothing, except I'm as oblivious as he is."

"You're making no sense."

His heart beat faster. "I am an idiot."

"Sometimes," she said.

"And blind because I—"

She put her finger over his lips this time. "Don't say it unless you mean it."

He caught her finger and drew both her hands into his. "I have been so miserable without you. I thought about you constantly, and I was so unhappy when you turned me down. I thought you hated me for what I'd done to you. I missed you, and I didn't understand what was tormenting me. But I could have avoided all that misery if I'd just admitted what I knew deep down. I am utterly, completely, hopelessly in love with you."

An impish smile curved her lips. "You're not just saying that so I'll let you make love to me, are you?"

"No," he said somberly. "I love you, and I don't want to live without you. But I don't want to propose in an inn bed."

"We'll wait until we reach Gatewick Park," she said.

"Does this mean I deserve a reward?"

"I think we both do."

He laughed. "What is your pleasure, my lady? Shall I lead or will you?"

"Well, you waltz divine, so I think I'll let you lead."

He unbuttoned the nightgown and drew it over her head. "You're beautiful. I wish it weren't so dark. After we're married, I want to make love to you in the daylight."

"I might let you," she said.

He kissed her lips. "I love you. And after we're married, I want to make love with you outdoors."

"That sounds naughty. I might let you."

He chuckled and caressed her breast. I love you. And after we're married, I want to make love with you in a tree."

"That sounds impossible and dangerous. Forget it."

He grinned. "I love you. And after we're married, I want to make love with you on the carpet in front of the fire."

"That sounds romantic. I might let you."

"I love you. And though we're not married, I want to make love to you right now. Because my heart is full and I thought I'd lost you forever." He kissed her deeply, slowly, savoring the taste of her mouth. Another miracle had happened. She loved him.

But there was something she needed to know. His stomach churned because he didn't want to ruin things between them, but he must be honest with her. "Julianne, there's something I must tell you."

"Tell me later." Her hand trailed down his chest, but he caught it.

"It's important," he said. "Before we go any further, I need to tell you something."

"Marc, darling, you don't have to tell me about your youthful mistake. I love you unconditionally. The past no longer exists."

"Everything changed the day you refused my proposal," he said. "When I got back to my rooms, I got quite a shock. Someone had found me."

Her brows furrowed. "What?"

He pressed her hand against his heart. "I was forbidden to ever see him. To ever write to him. To mention his name. I couldn't because it would have forever labeled him a bastard. I was eighteen years old when I signed the papers giving up my son before he was even born."

Her lips parted. "Oh, dear God."

"I never thought to see him, but he found me. Julie, he looks just like me."

"This is why your father condemned you?"

"It's an ugly story."

She held both his hands tightly. "You said someone tricked you. It clearly had to do with a woman."

He told her the abbreviated version because he could hardly stand to voice what had happened to him.

"Ramsey doesn't know about the boy, does he?"

"No, my father and Westcott covered it up."

"No wonder you hate Ramsey."

"I called on him last week, Julianne. And I forgave him."

"I knew I loved you, but I love you even more for doing the right thing."

"I did it for myself mostly," he said. "That sort of bitterness eats at your soul over time. And he couldn't have known the consequences. But I thought better of him when he apologized."

"I'm glad he did, though that doesn't entirely change my opinion of him. He ought not to have pursued me when you'd refused."

"He's done worse things than trick me, Julianne. Horrible, sordid things. That is the reason I didn't want him anywhere near you."

"His father is one of the most influential politicians in the nation," she said. "Why would Ramsey risk bringing scandal upon his family?"

"I don't know," he said. "Maybe he feels he can never measure up to his father. Or perhaps he's just a bad apple."

"Enough about him," Julianne said. "Tell me about your son."

"Julie, before I do, you need to know his father is likely to make trouble, but I won't give up my son again."

"Of course you won't. We'll weather the storm together."

"His name is Brandon." Hawk told her everything that had transpired that day. "When he mentioned that he and his mates toasted cheese over the fire, it brought back memories. Do you remember toasting cheese with your brother and me?"

She smiled. "Yes."

"I sat on the carpet to toast cheese with him, and now he thinks I'm all the crack because he's never seen a grown-up do it." He paused. "He sent me a letter today."

He told her briefly what Brandon had written. "Westcott is likely to threaten me."

"If he does, it will be because he's afraid his son will prefer you to him," she said. "But you and I will make it clear to Westcott that the boy's needs are the only priority. Brandon sought you out, and now he wants you to be a part of his life. He should have the opportunity to know you. There is no reason the boy cannot have two fathers."

"I am concerned. Twice, Brandon mentioned his father's health problems. I've no idea what ails Westcott, but as far as I know, Westcott has no male relatives to act as guardian to the boy. I've no rights, at least none that I can voice without labeling my son a bastard. He would lose his inheritance, and society would be cruel to him."

"Westcott had no other children?"

"No." He lifted his eyes to her. "You can imagine his humiliation upon discovering after eight years that another man had impregnated his young wife."

"Was he much older than she?"

He nodded. "Forty years."

"He's old enough to be the boy's grandfather, even his great-grandfather."

He nodded. "And apparently in bad health."

"Then we have even more reason to be involved in the boy's life. He needs a mother figure, and frankly, a younger father figure as well. As for fears about exposing the circumstances of his birth, all we need do is claim he is a distant cousin of yours. The aristocracy does it all the time. People may guess, but they will never openly question or scorn him."

"I keep thinking something will happen to snatch away my happiness," he said.

She kissed him on the mouth, a lush, slightly open-mouthed kiss.

His cock hardened. She reached for him, stroking him slowly.

He untied the ribbon of her braid. She sat up, shook her long, long hair back, and pushed him flat on the mattress.

"You wish to ride me?"

"That can be arranged, but I have another idea."

Her husky voice enslaved him. "Oh?" His cock stood at full attention now. He had to restrain himself from becoming the aggressor.

She slid between his thighs. "You did something very interesting with your mouth our first time. And it occurred to me you might like something similar."

Her hair trailed over his body. It was his favorite fantasy of her. Then she bent over him. As her tongue swirled round and round his cock, he groaned. "You're killing me."

Her wicked, husky laugh made him smile. He pushed her onto the bed and suckled her breasts and caressed her slick folds.

She wrapped her arms around him. "Make love to me."

"One question. Do you want to delay children?"

"No, I don't want us to delay another day of our lives."

He eased inside her, sliding in and withdrawing slowly. The whole time, he locked his gaze with hers. He reached between them, stroking her. Her back bowed as a single feminine cry came out of her mouth.

He lifted her legs over his shoulders. Then he drove into her faster and faster. As the sensations built to a fever pitch, a rough sound came out of his throat. He stilled, straining toward the pleasure, and when the throbbing burst upon him, he stayed inside her as his seed spilled. He lowered her legs and collapsed atop her, shuddering from the most erotic experience of his life. She locked her arms and legs around him. He kissed her cheek. "I love you," he said in a hoarse voice.

They slept, nestled like two spoons. She woke as he stroked her breast. He was aroused, hard against her bottom. He pulled her atop him. She rode him, leaning forward. He suckled her nipples, sending rivers of pleasure through her. When the ecstasy overcame her, he took her cry with his mouth and swept his tongue in the same rhythm as her body clenching him. Then still inside her, he rolled her to her back and pumped inside her, hard and fast as if he couldn't control his need. His ragged breathing grew even more labored, and then he was throbbing inside her.

He collapsed again. "Oh, my God."

She caressed his cheek, slightly scratchy with new beard. "Like that, did you?"

He rolled to his side, taking her with him, still inside her. "Can I say something really dirty?"

"Yes."

"Really, really dirty?"

"Do it," she said.

Even in the dark, she could see the glazed look in his eyes.

"I love you. And after we're married, I'm going to fuck you morning, noon, and night."

She laughed. "You prefer dirty words to euphemisms."

"I know lots of dirty words. I can say them in French if you like. Italian, too."

"International dirty words. Oh, my."

He grinned. "I'll call you into my study, presumably to complain about your dressmaker bills. Then I'll straddle you over my lap and cover up what we're doing with your skirts."

"Shocking," she said.

"I'll take you on a scenic tour of Ashdown House." He nibbled on her neck. "There are over one hundred rooms."

"I hope you're not planning to tour them all in one night."

He laughed. The room suddenly seemed a bit brighter.

"Damn, the day," he said. "Ah, hell, we won't be able to make love again at your brother's house."

"There are over one hundred rooms," she said. "We might get . . . lost."

"Egad, I can't do it in your brother's house."

"Then we'll take a long walk. The grounds are extensive at Gatewick Park."

He sighed. "I will be a gentleman and wait until after we're married. Four weeks to call the bans—ugh."

"I'm not above seducing a gentleman. And remember I know the secrets of seduction."

He guffawed.

She clapped her hand over his mouth. "Hester might hear."

He lifted his head. "She's still snoring." He grinned at her. "Once more? Please?"

"You're insatiable."

"Please?"

She opened her arms, but he pulled her atop him. She rode him and came quickly. He followed right behind and hugged her hard against his chest.

Afterward, he slipped her night rail over her, donned his banyan robe, and drew her to the door. "I'll watch as you sneak back into the room."

She blew him a kiss and scampered across the narrow corridor. When she disappeared inside, he shut the door and leaned his back against it. As the sun filled the room, he looked up at the ceiling and whispered, "Thank you."

Chapter Twenty-three

*A Reformed Scoundrel's Confession: A good woman
will make a better man of you.*

*W*hen the carriage rolled around the circular drive,
Hawk took a deep breath. He met Julianne's gaze. Earlier
at an inn, he'd taken her with him to walk the spaniels.
He'd warned her they would need to be careful in front
of her family. Then he'd told her he planned to ask her
brother's permission to marry her. He'd laughed when she
said she would do the proposing.

The carriage halted. A footman opened the door and
let down the steps. Hawk climbed out and helped his aunt
down. She leaned heavily on his arm. The journey had
been hard on her, but she'd never once complained.

When Julianne appeared, he forgot his own warning and gazed at her with his heart in his eyes. Then he
reached for her waist and swung her down. They turned
together. Tristan stood there, his brows arched.

Julianne ran into her brother's arms. He held her tightly, but he never took his hard gaze off Hawk.

He met his friend's gaze, unflinching, determined. *I'm going to marry your sister.*

Julianne leaned back and looked at her brother. "Where is Tessa?"

"Nursing Christopher," he said.

The dowager duchess walked down the steps to greet Hester. Julianne ran to her mother and hugged her. "I missed you all so much."

"Shall we go inside?" Tristan said.

The ladies walked ahead of them.

Hawk strode beside his oldest friend. "Congratulations on your son."

"He's a big, healthy boy." Tristan smiled. "I swear he's grown already."

"The duchess is well?" he asked.

"She tires easily, but she loves being a mother."

"I'm anxious to see him."

"I hope my sister didn't give you any trouble," Tristan said, eyeing him.

"Not too much," he said.

They walked inside. Hawk watched Julianne's bottom as she and the other ladies climbed the U-shaped stair-well ahead of them. He thought about their lovemaking all through the night, and slow heat swirled through his veins. Waiting to touch her again would frustrate him, but once they were married, he could have her anytime, any-place he wanted.

When they entered the drawing room, the ladies sat on the twin sofas. Tristan lifted his chin. "Come, let's drink to my son."

Tristan handed him a brandy. They clinked glasses. "To your son," Hawk said.

"Follow me to the window so we can talk out of earshot," Tristan said.

Uh-oh. He thought of his friend's hard look and resisted the urge to tug on his cravat. To hell with what Tristan thought. Julianne was a grown woman, and they were in love.

Tristan sipped his brandy and stared down at the formal gardens. "My mother kept something from me until after Christopher's birth."

Hawk sipped his brandy and said nothing.

"I'm glad you were there to protect Julianne from Ramsey. He's a dastard, and frankly, she's not ready for marriage."

Hell. "Julianne surprised me. She's far more insightful than I imagined."

Tristan scoffed. "She's flighty. All those beaux. How many did she turn down this year?"

He supposed he didn't count now. "There was one young cub who came to me. I told him I couldn't answer for you. When I put it before your sister, she wasn't pleased. She'd told the cubs she wanted only their friendship."

Tristan turned to him. "The cubs?"

"Five young men who called on her often. I was always there to supervise."

"Good Lord, man. I told you to guard her at balls and such. You must have been bored out of your wits."

"Believe it or not, I enjoyed visiting Julianne and my aunt."

When Tristan frowned at him, Hawk sighed. "Living alone is not all it's cracked up to be."

"My mother told me you moved back home. I never thought I'd see the day."

He met his friend's gaze squarely. "There are things I need to tell you."

"About my sister?"

"Yes, and something else. We'll talk later."

"There she is with my darling grandson," the dowager duchess said.

Tristan's eyes lit up. Hawk turned around to find Tessa walking into the drawing room with a blanketed babe in her arms.

Tristan strode over to his wife and kissed her cheek. "He's awake."

Hawk watched them and wondered if he'd gotten Julianne with child. He walked over to her and stood beside the sofa. When he looked down at her, she smiled at him with glistening eyes.

Tessa walked over to Julianne. "Would you like to hold him?"

"Very much." When she cradled the babe in her arms, Hawk's heart turned over. Someday she would hold their child.

"He's perfect," Julianne said.

Hawk bent down and touched the infant's hand. He grabbed Hawk's finger. He laughed. "Strong grip."

"Does he not look like Tristan?" Tessa asked.

Hawk thought he looked like a babe, but he grinned. "By Jove, I think he does look like you, old boy."

"Would you like to hold him?" Julianne asked.

He shook his head. "I might drop him."

"Sit beside Julianne," Tessa said. "Tristan was afraid to hold him at first, too."

"I was not," Tristan growled.

Hawk sat beside Julianne.

"Support his head," she said as she placed the babe in his arms.

He stayed very stiff at first. Baby Christopher opened his eyes and looked at him. "His eyes are blue."

"All babes have blue eyes at first," the dowager duchess said. "But he probably will have blue eyes. It is a strong family trait."

"Did you not ever hold your sister's infants?" the dowager duchess asked Hawk.

"No," he said. He'd kept his distance because their children reminded him of the son he'd given up. Hawk regarded his aunt. "Would you like to hold him?"

Hester cradled the babe and looked at Tristan. "I told you your duchess would bring your son into the world without mishap."

"You did, indeed," Tristan said. "Thank you for sponsoring my sister."

"I very much enjoyed having her." Hester regarded the duchess. "Your daughter is a wonderful young lady. I will miss her."

"Thank you," the dowager duchess said. Then she regarded Hawk. "You've been here for half an hour and not once have I had to tell you to behave. Are you ill?"

Hawk laughed along with everyone else.

"I reformed him," Julianne said.

"What?" Tristan said, narrowing his eyes.

Julianne laughed. "He was so busy guarding me he had no chance to engage in vice and depravity."

"Eh?" Tristan said.

"I wasn't about to leave her alone with every buck and blade sniffing round her skirts," Hawk muttered.

"He took his guardianship very seriously," Hester said.

Julianne looked at him. "He was ridiculously protective and lectured me constantly about flirting and men with bad ideas in their heads."

Hawk winked at her.

Tessa inquired about Amy and Georgette and all the other girls from last season's courtship. Then Tristan invited Hawk to join him in his study.

Hawk followed his friend downstairs. Once inside the study, he sat beside Tristan and stretched out his legs.

"Care for another brandy?" Tristan asked.

"No, thank you."

"You have something to tell me?"

"Two things, both of which may shock you." He inhaled. "I have a son."

Tristan's mouth opened, shut, and opened again. "The devil."

Hawk told him the story.

Tristan raked his hand through his hair. "I knew you'd gotten into trouble at a party years ago, but you never said a word."

Hawk leaned forward with his elbow on his knees. "I'd say it was because I was forbidden to ever speak of him. But the truth is I was horrified, scared, and bitter." He told him what his father had said.

"I'm stunned," Tristan said. "You're going to try to establish a relationship with the boy?"

"Yes, Brandon has indicated he wishes to stay in contact."

After Hawk told Tristan about Westcott's poor health, Tristan tapped his thumb on the chair. "Sounds to me as if you need to talk to Westcott and make him see reason. The boy needs security, and the current situation sounds precarious."

"It was your sister who suggested naming him a distant cousin. She's right; it's done all the time."

Tristan stared at him as if he'd grown horns. "You told my sister?"

"We've grown close."

Tristan bounded out of his chair, his eyes wild. "How close?" he said in a threatening tone.

Hawk stood and faced his oldest friend. "I want to marry her."

"No."

"I love her. And she loves me."

Tristan started pacing. His fists clenched and unclenched. Then he halted and glared at Hawk. "You compromised her."

He kept his gaze on his friend. "Whatever is between us is private."

"The hell it is," he shouted.

"I am a changed man because of her."

"You were to think of her as a sister."

"She is not my sister. She is going to be my wife," he said. "I hoped to have your blessing."

"I know too much about you and your women. She has no idea."

"She knows. But all of that is in the past. I gave up the lease on the love nest. There have been no mistresses. I decided to move back home so that I can embrace my family again. I love your sister."

"She's too young. She's infatuated with you."

"You think of her as young because she's your little sister, but she's a woman. We have both grown as a result of our relationship."

"Hawk, you are like a brother to me, but I can't approve of this match. Maybe in a few years, she'll be ready for marriage, but I know my sister. She is not ready yet."

He'd once thought the same thing. "You know her from your perspective as an older brother. Talk to her. And listen. You'll see."

Tristan narrowed his eyes. "Did you touch her?"

"Leave it alone."

"Damn you!"

The door opened. Tessa walked inside with the babe over her shoulder.

"Tessa, leave us," Tristan gritted out.

"Hawk, will you please close the door?" she said calmly as she padded into the room.

He did. "I love your sister, and I will marry her with or without your blessing. I hope it is the latter, because you are like a brother to me."

"I trusted you! And you touched my sister!"

The babe made a cooing sound. "Tristan, you will frighten Christopher," Tessa said. "Lower your voice."

"Tessa, leave us," Tristan said again.

"No, I will not, because you are being unreasonable. I told you before your sister left for London that she is in love with Hawk, but you would not believe me."

"Leave us, Tessa. I am going to beat him to a bloody pulp."

"No, you will not beat up your best friend. You will give your blessing, and you will not pry into their private affairs."

"Tessa, leave us."

"Tristan, you will never forgive yourself if you do not give your blessing to him. And I will never forgive you if you don't."

"He meddled with my sister. He's a rake!"

Tessa lifted her brows. "Must I remind you of your own bad reputation?"

Tristan's nostrils flared. "Sisters are forbidden."

"Men," she said, rolling her eyes. "Give your blessing now, and shake hands with Hawk."

Tristan fisted his hands. "I get one punch."

"You will not do violence to your best friend. He loves your sister. Do you think it was easy for him to come to you? He knew you would make this difficult. His family is coming for Christopher's christening. Hawk will be his godfather. Julianne will be his godmother. And soon they will marry, and we will rejoice in their happiness as they rejoiced for ours. Now give your blessing to Hawk and shake his hand."

Hawk regarded Tristan steadily. "I promise to be a good husband to her. She means everything to me. I am a better man because of her."

Tristan crossed over to him. Hawk steeled himself for the blow.

Tristan held out his hand. Hawk shook it.

"You have my blessing," Tristan said gruffly.

"Thank you. I'll make sure you never regret it," he said.

"Well, we might as well go back to the drawing room and announce it," Tristan grumbled. "Mama will swoon. Your family will never believe it. They will think it is another one of your one-hour engagements."

"Oh, I'd forgotten," Tessa said. "I once was engaged to

Hawk for the duration of breakfast. I was trying to evade your mother's matchmaking scheme."

Hawk cleared his throat. "I wish to propose to your sister first."

"Let us go upstairs," Tristan said. "I will close the door behind the two of you. You have five minutes. I will not leave her alone with you any longer."

"Ignore him," Tessa said. "Let us go now."

They trudged upstairs. Tristan muttered under his breath the entire time. Tessa told him to hush. The babe burped.

"Good boy," Hawk said.

"Men," Tessa said in a disgusted tone.

When they reached the drawing room, Tristan inhaled. "Everyone must step outside for five minutes, except Hawk and Julianne."

"Why?" the dowager duchess said.

"Hawk needs to propose to Julianne," Tessa said.

The dowager duchess held her quizzing glass up to her eye. "Is this another one of your sham engagements?"

"No, it is not," Hawk said.

"You will not engage yourself to my daughter for five minutes," the dowager duchess said. "Or for one hour. You are a scamp and a rogue. And your poor mother will go into a decline when she hears my daughter threw you over after only five minutes."

"I believe he is sincere," Hester said. "Look at him. He's lovesick."

"I am not sick," Hawk said. "But I am in love. Now, if you will all excuse us, I wish to make a proper proposal to Julianne."

Julianne rose. "Why should they stand outside the

door?" She walked over to Hawk and grasped his arm. "Come stand with me before the hearth."

"Julianne, I do not want an audience when I propose to you."

"You are not proposing," she said.

"What? I risked a beating from your brother and you are telling me I cannot propose?"

They had reached the hearth. "You are not proposing. I am."

"No," he said. "I am making a proper proposal to you, and you will listen and say yes."

She took his hands. "When I was a little girl, I knelt on my knee and proposed to you. You said I could ask you when I grew up. I am grown up." She tried to lower herself to one knee and wobbled.

He caught her by the waist and lifted her up. "Damn it, woman. Let me do this properly."

"Watch your language," the dowager duchess said.

Hawk's shoulders shook with laughter. Then he knelt on one knee and took her hands. "Julianne, I love you with all my heart. You have made me a better man. You also tried to steal my curricle, but I forgive you."

"You stole my bonnet," she said.

"This proposal is terrible," Tristan said.

"Hush," Tessa said. "I think it is sweet."

Hawk looked at everyone. "Will you let me finish?"

"Get on with it, Marc," Hester said.

He turned his attention to Julianne again and met her gaze. "Julianne, I love you, and I can't live without you. Will you marry me?"

"Yes, I will marry you."

He enfolded her in his arms and kissed her.

"Stop that," Tristan said.

Hawk decided his best friend deserved to witness him giving Julianne a thorough kiss. He opened her mouth and slid his tongue home. She kissed him back.

"Get your hands off my sister," Tristan growled.

Hawk broke the kiss and framed her beautiful face with his hands. "You have made me a very happy man," he whispered.

One week later

Hawk walked into Westcott's house in Devonshire. He'd had to make the journey because the old man was too frail to travel to Gatewick Park. Hawk wasn't sure what to expect, but when Brandon bounded into the great hall, Hawk ruffled his unruly hair. "Your trunks are packed?"

"Yes, sir. All packed. I've never been to a wedding before. Is it like church?"

"Sort of, except you'll see me make solemn promises to Julianne. And afterward, we'll have a wedding breakfast, with cake."

"I've never had cake for breakfast," he said. "I suppose I could get used to it."

Hawk chuckled. "Will you take me to your father?"

"This way. He keeps downstairs now."

Hawk schooled his features, but his son's words said it all. Brandon led him into a room with tall bookcases. The frail old man was reclined on a chaise with a blanket covering him. A servant eyed Hawk and walked into an adjoining room that must have once served as a drawing room but now held a bed. Hawk's insides roiled, imagining what would have happened if Brandon had not sought him out.

"Here he is, Father," Brandon said. The boy brought his father a cup of tea. The old man drank a bit, and then Brandon took it away to a side table.

Westcott broke into a coughing fit. Hawk was disturbed that it didn't even faze Brandon. He wondered if his son realized the old man was dying.

"Brandon, I'd like to have a few private words with your father," he said. "When I'm done, I'll call you inside. You can tell your father good-bye." He suspected it would be the last time his son saw Westcott.

When Brandon left the room, Hawk shut the door and took a chair over to the chaise. "I never had the chance to apologize to you. It's late in coming. I am deeply sorry for the pain I caused you."

He coughed. "He is my son, even if...he is not my flesh and blood."

"You have been his father, and from what I've seen, you have instilled good principles in him. I can bring him back to see you after the wedding."

Westcott coughed into a handkerchief.

Hawk winced at the bloodstains. He looked at the servant, who brought another handkerchief and took the soiled one away.

"I don't...want to let him go." Westcott breathed heavily for a bit. "But I don't...want to see me die."

Hawk struggled not to let his sorrow for the man show.

"When Brandon was born, you were the father he needed," Hawk said. "I was too young to be a fit father. I will take over the reins now and ensure he never forgets you."

"He is...a good boy."

"He will have a mother, the woman I am to marry.

He has cousins and uncles. A great-grandmother, a great-aunt, and my younger brother, Will. They have all accepted him, sight unseen. I will ensure his inheritance is protected until he is old enough to take over. And I will teach him what he needs to know about managing the estate. You need not worry. I love him."

"The papers... are on the table."

Hawk stood and walked over to the table. The papers assigning him guardianship were signed in a palsied hand. He put them inside the leather case and turned back to Westcott. "I will send him in now and give you privacy."

He walked out of the room. "Your father wishes to see you now."

Brandon looked somber as he walked into the room. Hawk strode into the foyer and directed the servants to stow the boy's trunks on top of the carriage.

An hour later, he escorted his son to the carriage. He sat across from Brandon. When the boy reached up to swipe his face, Hawk moved to the other bench and sat beside him. "You've every right to cry," he said.

He held his sobbing son as the carriage rolled away.

Chapter Twenty-four

*The Three Secrets to a Happy Marriage: Love,
Laughter, and Honesty.*

—*The Earl and Countess of Hawkfield*

The musicians struck up the opening bars of a waltz. Hawk kept his steps small at first as he danced with his beautiful bride.

All their family and friends stood on the sidelines watching their solitary waltz. Unbeknownst to him and Julianne, all the ladies had secretly planned to hold this ball to celebrate their wedding. Georgette had journeyed with Amy and her parents. Even the five cubs had attended.

Julianne's eyes were a bit misty. "You are keeping your steps conservative because you fear I will disgrace you."

"Is that a dare?" Before she could answer, he whirled her round and round in dramatic circles.

"I'd forgotten," she said. "That night we danced, I offered you a penny for your thoughts."

"And I bemoaned the fact that you thought my thoughts so worthless."

"What are you thinking now?"

He leaned down and whispered in her ear, "I want to bed you."

She laughed as he whirled her round and round again.

When the music wound down, he slowed his steps and held on to her until the very last note. Then he drew her closer for a thoroughly naughty kiss.

Thunderous applause erupted.

As he led her off the dance floor, he couldn't take his eyes off her. But others surrounded them. He sighed, wondering how long they must remain at the ball. It had been a long four weeks. He was on fire to make slow love to her.

Hawk looked about the ballroom and spied Brandon talking to the cubs and William. Brandon wrinkled his nose at something Osgood said. The cubs and William guffawed. Lord, he hoped they'd kept it clean for his son's sake.

He returned his gaze to Julianne and squeezed her hand. They had decided not to take a wedding trip until Brandon's summer holiday. His son had whooped upon hearing they would go to Brighton for sea bathing.

Tomorrow, they would journey with all his family to Ashdown House. Even Grandmamma had consented. She'd not had a single heart palpitation or sinking spell. But she had called for her smelling salts when Hester had read from Julianne's notorious pamphlet last evening. Neither he nor Hester had given away her identity. Amy and Georgette, whom he'd learned were in on the scheme, kept mum as well. The speculation about the author's identity went on for over an hour. Beaufort, Caruthers, Portfrey, and Benton announced it was written by Charles Osgood.

Tristan had taken Hawk aside and said he'd figured out the author. Hawk had nodded when Tristan told him it had to be Amy Hardwick. The girl was too silent, too secretive, he'd said. Hawk grinned at the memory. It was a good thing Tristan didn't know half the things that had transpired in London.

When Brandon approached, Hawk noted his glum expression and took him aside. "What's wrong, lad?"

"Will was all the crack until that redheaded girl arrived."

Hawk blinked. "You mean Miss Hardwick?"

"That's the one. She doesn't say much. I think that's why Will follows her around and tries to provoke her."

Hawk shut his gaping mouth. Will and Amy Hardwick? He shook his head. His rogue of a brother would have no interest in a shy little flower like Miss Hardwick. "Let's keep this under covers for now," Hawk said.

"Suits me," Brandon said. "I don't see what's so great about girls."

Hawk ruffled his hair. "You will someday."

"Oh, there are the gents." Brandon dashed through the crowd.

Hawk turned and took Julianne's hands. "At last we're alone."

"Not for long," she said as her brother and Tessa approached.

Tristan kissed Julianne on the cheek. Then he clapped his hand on Hawk's shoulder.

"I'll take good care of her," Hawk said.

Tessa's lips twitched. "Men. I daresay she is the one who will take good care of you."

"Duchess, I concede the point to you," Hawk said.

Tristan rolled his eyes. "Save the pretty lies for when you'll need them. Tonight's a sure thing."

Tessa swatted him with her fan. A cracking sound spelled doom for the ivory sticks. "You broke it," Tessa cried.

Tristan grinned. "Allow me to make reparations."

Julianne smiled as Tessa tugged her brother along the perimeter of the ballroom. Then Hester approached and eyed Hawk through her quizzing glass. "You could have taken her upstairs thirty minutes ago."

Hawk winced. "Hester, please."

"Go on now, while nobody's paying attention," his aunt said.

Hawk took Julianne's arm and they left the ballroom. He took her upstairs and left her in the care of a maid. Then with the help of Tristan's valet, Hawk undressed and donned a banyan robe. He sat on a chair, watching the clock, counting the minutes until he could go to her. He'd give her a half hour.

The connecting door opened. He stood and walked to the door. She fled into his arms and hugged him hard. Her hair was loose and flowing to her waist. He shut the door, lifted her in his arms, and took her to the bed where the covers were already turned down.

He tossed the prim night rail off the bed and started planting kisses at the top of her head and worked his way down to her feet. When he jiggled her toe, she laughed. He slid up her beautiful slim body, and she welcomed him with outstretched arms. Tonight would be slow, all for her.

She threaded her fingers in his hair as he suckled her breasts. He ran his tongue down her belly and slid his hands under her bottom. "Spread your legs for me," he said.

When he flicked his tongue rapidly along her slick

folds, she writhed beneath him. He slid two fingers inside her, and the sounds of moisture made his cock rock-hard. She was panting when he entered her. Then he pinned her wrists against the bed, because he'd remembered the glazed way she'd looked at him when he'd pinned her against his aunt's sofa. Her swollen lips parted and he took that as an invitation for his tongue.

He slid his cock in and out so slowly he thought he'd go mad with the need to pump harder, but he wanted it to last a long, long time. He reached between them and rubbed her high along her slick folds, and a little feminine sound came out of her throat as she shattered. He could no longer hold back and thrust inside her faster and faster. When the throbbing ecstasy overcame him, she locked her legs around him.

He collapsed and then rolled to his side, still joined inside her. "I love you, Julianne. And I promise to say that to you every night before we go to bed and when we awake in the morning."

"I love you, Marc."

They slept for a while, and then he woke her by pulling her atop him. He pressed her forward so he could suck her nipples while she rode him. The sound of her throaty moans pleased him. She came with a little cry, and he wasn't far behind.

He rolled them to their sides, and she grinned. "I can't believe I snared you in the parson's mousetrap."

"I'll get you for that," he said. When he tickled her, she shrieked.

They tussled about the bed, laughing and teasing as they'd always done. He made love to her once more and knew he couldn't have chosen a better wife.

Because she'd made him a better man.

Dear Reader,

My humble thanks to all who wrote to let me know how much you enjoyed many of the supporting characters in my debut historical romance, HOW TO MARRY A DUKE. *Many of you have requested stories for these characters, and I'm thrilled that readers adore my fictional friends as much as I do.*

I wanted to let you all know that Miss Amy Hardwick's book, HOW TO RAVISH A RAKE, *is coming soon. Amy starts out as a painfully shy wallflower in* HOW TO MARRY A DUKE, *but she is destined to undergo quite a transformation in her own story.*

Now, you may be wondering whom I would pair with this gentle flower of a lady, and I'm afraid to say that it is not a man Amy admires. In fact, she disapproves of his dissolute lifestyle. The gentleman who will bedevil her is none other than William Darcett, younger brother of the Earl of Hawkfield (a.k.a. Hawk). Will is such a notorious rake that the scandal sheets have dubbed him Devil Darcett.

The devil is the last man Amy wants to encounter, but circumstances conspire against her. A case of mistaken identity leads to a rather embarrassing moment for Amy, but she's determined to evade him. There's just one little problem: Devil Darcett has no intention of letting her escape.

For a sneak peek, just flip the page!

Cheers!

How to Ravish a Rake

London, 1818

"*Y*ou are *not* a spinster, and I will not let you marry that stuffy vicar," Georgette said.

Amy Hardwick drew in a steadying breath as she and her friend Lady Georgette Danforth minced about the Beresford's loud ballroom. "Mr. Crawford is sensible, not stuffy, and he has not proposed."

"Only because I snatched you away from certain doom," Georgette grumbled as she twirled a blond curl around her finger. "I saw the disapproval in his expression just before we left Hampshire."

"He was disappointed that I would be away all of the spring season," Amy said.

The day before she'd journeyed with Georgette and her family to London, Mr. Frederick Crawford had asked her if they had an "understanding." Amy had bitten her lip and looked at the ground, hesitating to make a commitment. He'd taken her arm and said he was glad she'd agreed. They were both practical people and well suited. For a moment, she'd wanted to reproach him for his presumption, but she'd swallowed the words. After five previous seasons, she could not afford to be anything but realistic about her marriage prospects.

Georgette halted beside a pillar. "Amy, I believe he means to propose. Will your parents try to persuade you to accept him?"

"They would never force me to marry anyone." But the day she'd told her mother that Georgette had invited her to spend the season with her in London, her mother had frowned. And then she'd asked Amy if she thought it wise to leave "just now." Her mother's question had left no doubt that her parents worried about her future. She'd known then that they held hopes Mr. Crawford would offer marriage.

Afterward, Amy had nearly sent her regrets to Georgette, but something inside her had rebelled. She would not give up the chance to see her friend based upon an understanding, one she'd never even agreed upon. But there was something else she wanted—for herself. One last chance to kick up her heels, because this, her last season, would be her only opportunity.

Of course, she'd never dared to flirt and tease the young men like the other belles. She wished she could be as glib as Georgette and match wits with the gentlemen. But in a large gathering, she always found herself tongue-tied and overwhelmed. This year she swore would be different.

"Amy, your gown is stunning!"

She looked up in surprise to find Sally, Suzanne,

Beatrice, and Priscilla approaching quickly. When they admired her white crepe gown over a satin slip, she thanked them.

"You must tell us who your dressmaker is," Priscilla said. "I simply must have something equally lovely."

"I agree," Suzanne said. "Your gown is bound to be all the rage."

"I love the emerald ribbons that flow all the way down the back of the gown," Sally said. "The pink rosebuds are a lovely touch as well. Whoever designed this gown is brilliant."

Georgette gave Amy a speaking look. "Will you tell or shall I?"

Heat crept into Amy's face, but she'd vowed to overcome her timidity. "I confess I drew the design and asked a local dressmaker to make it up for me." She did not tell them that she'd asked the dressmaker to make over her old gowns in order to keep the expense of another season to a minimum. While her father would have given her anything, she'd not wanted to burden her parents when this was her sixth season, and gowns in the first stare of fashion were costly.

The other ladies exclaimed over her talent and begged her to design gowns for them. Georgette told them all to call later in the week to discuss Amy's designs. Within moments, a crowd of matrons and single belles gathered round to inspect Amy's gown. When Hester, Lady Rutledge, joined them, she declared Amy the fashion darling of the ton.

Georgette's cheeks dimpled as she smiled at Amy. "I knew you would be popular this year," she murmured.

Amy kept smiling and nodding while the crowd kept

growing. As others squeezed closer and spoke louder, the cacophony of voices rang in her ears. She found it impossible to say a word when so many spoke all at once. Eventually, she could bear no more and turned to Georgette. "Please excuse me," she said. "I will return directly."

"Shall I come with you?" she asked.

Amy shook her head. "I only need a few moments of air," she said in an undertone.

"Very well," Georgette said. "I will look for your return."

Amy left the ballroom, meaning to go upstairs to the retiring room. But on the opposite side of the landing, a familiar-looking gentleman with dark, wavy hair stood whispering to a lady with rouged cheeks. With a wicked chuckle, the man leaned back against the railing. Amy nearly swallowed her tongue upon recognizing Mr. William Darcett.

Determined to evade him, she hurried downstairs. That man had tormented her last spring when she'd attended her friend Julianne's wedding. He'd taken to calling her "Red" because of her carrot-colored hair and had followed her about for his own amusement. Since then, she'd heard rumors that he'd raked his way across the Continent. He was a typical, dissolute younger son, with no ambition but to wench and gamble. The scandal sheets had even called him Devil Darcett.

Devil Darcett was the last man she wanted to encounter this evening.

At the bottom of the stairs, she turned right and treaded along an unlit, deserted corridor, hoping to find her way out to the back garden. But a slightly-ajar door to a dark room beckoned her. She looked left and right, but no one was about. Promising herself she would stay only a few moments, she slipped inside, closed the door, and waited for her eyes to adjust. Although the objects in the shrouded room remained indistinct, she could make out tall shelves along one wall. No doubt this was Lord Beresford's library. Upon seeing a sofa, she padded across the plush carpet and settled onto the cushion. Eventually the tension in her limbs eased a bit.

Perhaps she'd overreacted. After all, the devil had found an unscrupulous strumpet to entertain him. Of course, she needn't have worried at all if she'd stayed with her friends in the ballroom. She ought to have forced herself to remain. But no matter how hard she tried, she simply could not bear too much stimulation. She often spent hours in her room, because she needed to be alone in order to think.

Now at last she had a moment to contemplate her earlier conversation with Georgette. Though she typically shared almost everything with her bosom friend, there were things she'd not told her about Frederick.

At first, Amy had not realized that the young vicar's interest in her amounted to anything more than friendly regard. He'd approved when he'd seen her taking food baskets to the sick and elderly in the village, and he'd called her thoughtful when he found her setting flowers on the graves at the churchyard. Soon after, he'd begun calling on her father regularly. Then one day, he'd asked her to walk with him. Somehow, without her quite realizing the significance, he'd made a habit of calling and taking her for walks. One thing had led to another until he'd spoken of the understanding.

Frederick was a good man, a devout man, who had

devoted himself to the church. Marriage to him would secure her future. Deep down, she felt marrying for that reason alone was wrong, and she knew Georgette would disapprove. Yet, Frederick had never spoken of tender feelings for her. Instead, he'd clearly stated they were practical people and were well suited.

The problem was she didn't want to marry for practical reasons. Truthfully, she still yearned for the girlish dream of marrying for love, and it was so horribly foolish of her. With the exception of her participation in the Duke of Shelbourne's courtship two years ago, no gentleman had ever expressed interest in her, until Frederick had come along.

She had to think of her parents and their concerns about her future. If something happened to them, she would be in a precarious position, for she had no other living relatives. She tried to persuade herself that she could be content with such a marriage. At least she could look forward to having her own home and children. But all was contingent upon an understanding becoming an engagement—one that, ironically, she didn't want.

What she secretly wanted was to shed her wallflower reputation at long last. Then why was she in a dark library hiding from a rake who had probably forgotten her very existence? With a deep inhalation, she told herself to march back upstairs to that ballroom posthaste and mingle with all the other guests. She might be plain, but others had complimented her gown. Though she would never be beautiful, she could be elegant.

A light tap at the door froze her. As the door creaked open, she cringed. To her utter horror, a man walked inside and shut the door.

"Alicia, you're here," he said.

Oh, dear God. She knew that voice. It was the devil himself. He'd come here for an assignation—and found the wrong woman! As he walked forward, Amy held her breath. She thought of telling him he'd mistaken her identity but worried he would recognize her voice. If he knew, he would mock her, the same way he'd done last spring.

He stopped at her feet. "Why so silent? Is this a new game?"

She shook her head, hoping he would go away.

When he sat beside her, she tried to rise, but he caught her arm.

At her gasp, he chuckled. "Come now, you promised me a treat, and I'm famished."

Before she could utter a single protest, he cupped her cheek and trailed his lips lightly over her mouth. No man had ever kissed her, but she'd expected a rake like him to ravish her lips. Then he drew his tongue over the seam of her mouth. Her lips parted involuntarily, and then he swept his tongue inside. Shock kept her still, but as he slid in and withdrew repeatedly, she lost the ability to think of anything beyond the intimacy of his invasion.

When he lifted his lips momentarily, she inhaled. The scent of him curled inside her like a dangerous elixir, one that curbed her ability to listen to the voice of reason. He sucked her tongue into his mouth, and she felt strangely possessed by him. Or was it merely lust muddling her brain? Whatever it was, she couldn't find the strength to tell him he mustn't kiss her in this wicked manner—or at all, for that matter. Unfortunately, the wanton she'd never known existed inside her kept saying, *Yes, yes, yes.*

"You taste so sweet," he said against her mouth. Then he trailed damp kisses down her neck. He cupped her breast, plumping it up. She knew she ought to slap his hand away, but he pulled the fabric of her bodice down, exposing her naked flesh. When his mouth covered her nipple, her breathing shattered. As he suckled her, the most indescribable pleasure flowed through her veins. She was lost to the devil, lost in pleasure beyond her imagination, lost to everything but his sinful touches and kisses.

His hand swept over her skirt. When she realized he was bunching it upward and exposing her legs, fear brought her to her senses. She clamped her hand over his, knowing she must stop him.

He let go of the fabric, and she pulled her bodice up again. Though it was dark, she knew he was staring at her. He must have deduced that she wasn't the hussy he'd meant to meet in the library. When she stood, he rose with her. She was tall, but he was half a head taller, and for reasons that made no sense, that intimidated her.

"Who are you?" he asked.

Shaking her head, she took one step back, meaning to escape.

A quick rap sounded at the door. She spun around and covered her mouth.

He grabbed her hand and pulled her behind the sofa. Then he put his finger to his lips as she crouched beside him. Her legs trembled, but she mustn't move or her rustling skirts would give away their hiding place.

The door creaked open again. "Will? Are you in here?"

Amy squeezed her eyes shut and prayed for deliverance. If they were discovered alone in the dark, she would be ruined.

Footsteps padded across the carpet. "That sorry rake," the woman muttered. "I'll make him pay." Her skirts swished as her footsteps retreated. Then mercifully the door slammed.

He rose and offered his hand. She took it gratefully, because her legs felt a bit wobbly.

"Who are you?" he asked again.

She shook her head.

He squeezed her hand. "Tell me."

"You do not want to know," she whispered. Then she fled the library, closed the door behind her, and scurried toward the stairs. The entire time she prayed he would not follow her.

Upon reaching the ballroom doors, she paused to catch her breath. Then she smoothed her skirt and patted the curls by her ears. She wet her lips, hoping she didn't look as if she'd just been thoroughly kissed by a rake. But she had, and a terrible realization filled her with shame.

She'd betrayed Frederick.

What a lark!

Will stood behind the sofa, bemused at the thought that he'd had an assignation with an unknown woman. After his heated encounter with the silent lady, he knew three things about her. She was tall, had long legs, and did not want him to know her name.

Something about her seemed familiar, though he couldn't quite put his finger on it. Of course, he'd realized early on that she wasn't Alicia, who would have babbled nonstop—until he kissed her.

Because of her refusal to talk, he'd assumed he'd caught a married lady waiting for her lover. So, he'd decided to test her resolve by kissing her. She'd not tried to stop him, though she'd been rather passive. And that had made him even more determined to wring a response out of her. When he'd suckled her, she'd made a little feminine sound in the back of her throat. He'd felt triumphant—until she'd stopped his straying hand from lifting up her skirts.

He'd known a lot of women, but he'd never met one quite like her. Something about her was off, though he couldn't put his finger on it. He thought back over her reactions, and then he felt like a hammer had struck his head.

She'd not known how to kiss him back.

Good Lord, he'd dallied with an innocent. A shudder rolled up his spine. If anyone had discovered the two of them, he would have found himself snared in the parson's mousetrap. To a lady he didn't even know.

Will blew out his breath, relieved at his narrow escape. A pity about Alicia, though. He supposed she wouldn't be too eager for a tumble after he'd supposedly failed to show for their tryst. With a shrug, he rounded the sofa and noticed something on the cushion. Intrigued, he picked up the silk item. On a whim, he put it in his pocket. Then he strode out of the library, crossed the great hall, and climbed the stairs.

After he entered the crowded ballroom, he found himself looking for a tall lady. Then he recollected that Alicia had called out his name. Will tugged on his cravat, realizing he might yet be in danger if the innocent young lady decided to confess to her mama. Then again, the mysterious lady had refused to identify herself. Undoubtedly, she didn't want anyone to know she'd let a stranger kiss and touch her. Chances were he'd never discover her identity, and that was for the best.

On the other side of the rectangular ballroom, he saw

his brother Hawk and his sister-in-law Julianne. Shelbourne and his duchess were there as well. Will crossed the room, nodding occasionally at acquaintances.

When he reached the other side, he clapped Shelbourne on the shoulder. "Well met," he said. He bowed to his mother and the dowager duchess. Then he shook hands with the Marquess of Boswood. "Looks like a regular reunion," he said.

He caught sight of Boswood's daughter Lady Georgette and her friend, the tall red-haired lady he remembered from his brother's wedding. She glanced at him and turned away, not quite a cut direct, but close enough. Then he noticed something that nearly made him guffaw.

Will strolled over to the ladies and bowed to Lady Georgette. Then he stepped right beside Miss Amy Hardwick. A becoming blush suffused her cheeks. She unfurled her fan and wafted it.

He leaned closer to her. "I believe you've lost something."

She glanced at him from the corner of her eye. "I beg your pardon?"

A grin tugged at his mouth. "I found something that belongs to you."

"You are mistaken." She applied her fan faster.

"I'm quite sure." He reached inside his pocket and produced a pink silk rose with a stray thread. "I believe it matches the others on the back of your gown."

She winced as he set it in her palm.

"I hope you enjoyed our little interlude as much as I did," he said.

She closed her fingers over the silk rose. "Hush. Someone might hear."

"What? That I kissed you?" He was thoroughly enjoying her embarrassment.

Her green eyes flashed. "If you were a gentleman, you would not have dared."

"If you were a lady," he said, purposely letting his voice rumble, "you would not have let me."

Tessa Mansfield is having a problem
with the first rule of matchmaking:
Never fall in love with the groom.

Please turn this page for an
excerpt from

How to Marry a Duke

Available now.

Chapter One

London, 1816

The belles of the Beau Monde had resorted to clumsiness in an effort to snag a ducal husband.

Tristan James Gatewick, the Duke of Shelbourne, entered Lord and Lady Broughton's ballroom and grimaced. A quartet of giggling chits stood near the open doors, dangling their handkerchiefs as if poised to drop them. Determined to avoid playing fetch again, he strode off along the perimeter of the room.

With a long-suffering sigh, he conceded he'd contributed to this national disgrace. Ever since the scandal sheets had declared him the most eligible bachelor in England, he'd rescued twenty-nine lace handkerchiefs, five kid gloves, and twelve ivory fans.

If only he could have convinced himself to choose a bride based upon the inelegance of her fumbling, he might have wedded and bedded the most inept candidate by now. Alas, he could not abide the thought of spending a lifetime with Her Gracelessness.

He surveyed the crowd looking for the hostess of this grand squeeze, a useless endeavor. The crème de la crème swarmed the place like bees. The din of voices competed with the lively tune of a country dance, making his ears ring. He'd rather eat dirt than subject himself to the dubious delights of the marriage mart, but with his thirty-first birthday approaching, he could no longer pretend he was invincible. The dukedom had been at risk far too long.

Someone tapped a fan on his shoulder. He paused to find Genevieve and Veronica, two of his former mistresses. Seeing them together, he realized how alike the striking widows looked. Both were tall, dark-haired, and curvaceous. He canvassed the cobwebs in his brain and realized all of his past lovers had similar attributes. Well, those he could recollect.

Tristan bowed and lifted each of their hands for the requisite air kiss. "Ladies, it is a great pleasure to see you again."

"Were your ears burning?" Veronica said in an exaggerated boudoir voice. "You are the subject du jour."

"I am delighted," he lied. He'd grown increasingly frustrated with the notoriety the papers had whipped up. How the devil he'd ever find a bride in this circuslike atmosphere evaded him. But find one he must.

Genevieve tittered. "We were comparing you to all of our other gentlemen admirers."

He'd bedded more than his fair share of mistresses, but this situation was certainly unique among his experiences. "What did you conclude?"

Genevieve leaned closer and squeezed his arm. "We agreed you were the naughtiest of all our lovers."

He regarded her with a wicked grin. "Praise indeed."

Veronica glanced at him from beneath her lashes. "How does it feel to be England's most sought-after bachelor?"

High-pitched giggling rang out from behind him. He rolled his eyes. Not again.

Genevieve's shoulders shook with laughter. "Watch out, Shelbourne. A bevy of little misses are stalking you."

He grimaced. "Rescue me?"

The two women laughed, blew him a kiss, and drifted away, leaving him to the predators. When he turned round, the four silly chits he'd seen earlier halted and stared at him, agog. Given their youthful faces and puritanical white gowns, he surmised not one of them was a day over seventeen. He needed a wife, but he'd no intention of robbing the proverbial cradle.

When they continued to gape at him as if he were a Greek statue come to life, he took a step closer. "Boo."

Their shrieks rang in his ears as he walked off into the crowd. Ignoring the avid stares directed at him, Tristan squeezed past numerous hot, perspiring bodies, and not the kind one hoped to find naked and willing in bed. With more than a little regret, he banished thoughts of Naked and Willing in order to concentrate on Virtuous and Virginal. First he must locate Lord and Lady Broughton. Perhaps his hostess would introduce him to a sensible young lady of good breeding. Perhaps pigs would fly, too.

He might have avoided all this nonsense if his dear mama had cooperated. When he'd informed her of his bridal requirements a month ago, she'd swatted him with her fan and told him he had rocks in his head.

A loud bang nearly sent him ducking for cover. Feminine gasps erupted all around him. Alarmed, he sought the source of the disturbance and realized it was only the slamming of the card room door. The gentleman responsible for this discourteous act was none other than his oldest friend, Marc Darcett, Earl of Hawkfield.

Tristan hailed Hawk with a wave and walked in that direction. Intent upon reaching his friend, Tristan failed to notice the impending danger until something crunched beneath his shoe. A quick glance to the floor confirmed his worst fear—the thirteenth incident of a dropped fan. Damn and blast, he'd crushed it.

He lifted his gaze, expecting a devious mama and her blushing daughter. Instead, a petite young woman with honey-blond hair stood staring at his shoe. She said something that sounded suspiciously like *ashes to ashes, dust to dust*. With all the voices ringing in his ears, he assumed he'd misheard.

Though he was tempted to walk past her, he couldn't ignore the fan he'd broken. "I beg your pardon," he said, bending to retrieve the mangled ivory sticks.

"You are not to blame. Someone jostled my arm."

Her excuse was the worst he'd heard yet. He didn't even bother to hide his cynicism as his gaze traveled up her white gown. Blue ribbons trimmed her bodice, drawing his attention to her generous décolletage. He continued his perusal to her heart-shaped face. She watched him with twitching lips. Pillow-plump lips. He inhaled on a constricted breath. Lord, with that mouth she could make a fortune as a courtesan.

Her long-lashed eyes twinkled. "Sir, if you will return the remains, I will see to its burial."

Her witty remark stunned him. Belatedly, he realized he was grinning up at her. She probably thought he'd fallen for her ruse. Exasperated with himself, he grasped the broken sticks, rose, and placed the ruined fan in her small gloved hands.

He met her amused gaze again, noting she did not simper or blush. She was no miss fresh out of the schoolroom. "I apologize for the damage. Allow me to make reparations," he said.

"It is quite beyond repair," she said.

"I insist upon compensating you for—"

"My pain and suffering?" She laughed. "I assure you the fan's death is a relief to me. Look, you can see it is exceedingly ugly."

They'd not had a proper introduction, and yet, she'd invited him to come closer. He decided to oblige her and find out if her intentions extended beyond droll quips. While she chattered about a dim shop light and putrid green paint, he stole another glance at her mouth, picturing those lips damp and kiss-swollen. Slow heat eddied in his veins.

She continued speaking in an unreserved manner as if they were old friends rather than strangers. "Even my maids refused to take the fan," she said. "So I decided to carry the pitiful thing at least once."

A footman carrying a tray of champagne paused before them. She lifted up on her toes like a ballerina to place the ruined fan upon it. Pint-sized she might be, but her flimsy skirts outlined a deliciously rounded bottom. He liked voluptuous women, and his practiced eye told him this one had the body of a goddess.

His blood stirred. He wanted her.

A warning clanged in his head. She was probably married, and he never dallied with other men's wives. Then again, maybe she wasn't. He found himself hoping she was a willing and lonely widow, but he meant to do more than hope.

"Poor little fan. May you rest in peace." She pirouetted and gave him a dazzling smile. "There now, I'm done mourning."

She was exceptionally clever, but without the brittle artifice common among the ton. He caught her gaze, willing her with his eyes. "Now that the funeral is over, perhaps you would allow me to escort you to the refreshment table." And thence to a more private location.

"You are too kind, but I must return to my friends."

Triumph surged inside him. She'd said friends, but made no mention of a husband. "Will you allow me the *pleasure* of your company a little longer? I mean to persuade you to accept my offer."

"I have dozens of other fans," she said. "Your apology is more than sufficient."

She intended to play hard to get. Since he'd come of age, women had always pursued him. At the prospect of a chase, excitement raced through his blood. But he must proceed with caution. If he'd misjudged her, she would take offense. A smile tugged at his mouth. He knew exactly which card to play.

He reached inside his coat and produced his engraved card. "Take it. In the event you change your mind, send round a note." If she refused, he'd have his answer. But if she accepted, he'd have her name. And soon her.

When she started to reach for the card, he held his breath. *Take it, little charmer. I'll ride you to the stars all night.*

She hesitated and then peered at his card. Her doll-like eyes grew round as carriage wheels. She curtseyed, mumbled something he couldn't hear, and disappeared into the crowd.

Her sudden departure caught him off guard. He took two steps, searching for her, but the crowd had swallowed her. Obviously she'd not known his identity beforehand. But why had she fled?

"There you are."

At the sound of Hawk's voice, Tristan turned.

"I tried to save you," Hawk said, "but that dragon Lady Durmont waylaid me. So who was the latest clumsy belle to accost you?"

"I've no idea," Tristan said. "I take it you do not know her."

"I never saw her face." Hawk frowned. "What the devil were you doing engaging a strange lady in conversation?"

"I stepped on her fan."

Hawk made a sound of disgust. "Follow me."

As he walked with his friend, Tristan frowned, wondering how he could have misread her signals. Then again, the women who pursued him made no secret of their illicit intentions with their risqué innuendos. The mysterious lady had surprised and intrigued him, but she'd not taken the bait, so he dismissed her from his mind.

Hawk led him over to a wall niche displaying a winged statue of Fortuna, goddess of fortune and fate. "Old boy, you've got to be more careful," Hawk said. "These chits are desperate. One of them might trick you into a compromising situation."

Tristan huffed. "A cautionary tale in reverse. Lady Rake seduces unsuspecting bachelor."

"There are plenty of schemers on the marriage mart who would throw away their virtue to marry a duke."

"Ridiculous." He'd never fall for such tricks.

"Forget this bridal business for now," Hawk said. "You needn't rush to the altar."

"I've left the dukedom unsecured for thirteen years." With good reason, he silently amended.

Hawk released a loud sigh. "You're determined to wed."

"Determined, yes. Whether I'll succeed is debatable."

"As usual, you're making matters much too complicated. You're in luck. I have a brilliant plan."

"This ought to prove entertaining," he said.

"It's simple," Hawk said. "Choose the most beautiful belle in the ballroom, get an introduction, and ask her to dance. Then call on her tomorrow and propose. In less than twenty-four hours, you'll be an engaged man."

"You call that a brilliant plan?"

Hawk folded his arms over his chest. "What's wrong with it?"

He huffed. "Most of the beauties I've met are vain, silly, and clumsy."

"You want an ugly wife?"

Tristan scowled. "That's not what I meant."

"What the devil do you want?"

"A sensible, respectable, and graceful woman." He wanted more, but he wasn't about to confess his fantasies.

"If it's a boring and plain bride you're wanting, you need look no further than the wall," Hawk said, indicating a group of pitiful-looking gels sitting with the dowagers.

Tristan had started to turn away when he saw the amusing lady he'd spoken to earlier. His heartbeat drummed in his ears. She led two gangly young cubs over to the forlorn girls. The chandelier's soft candlelight illuminated her curly golden hair.

Within minutes, both cubs were escorting wallflowers toward the dance floor. The lady responsible for this turn of events clasped her small gloved hands. As she watched the couples, her plump lips curved into a dreamy smile, and her eyes softened. Transfixed, Tristan forgot to breathe. He'd last seen that expression on a woman after a vigorous bout between the sheets.

Then Lord Broughton and his new bride approached her. All signs of the temptress disappeared as the lady faced the couple. "That's her," Tristan said.

Hawk squinted. "Who?"

"The lady I spoke to earlier. She is standing with Broughton and his wife."

"Lord help us. It's Miss Mansfield."

Miss Mansfield? She was a virtuous, unmarried lady? The devil. He'd almost made her an indecent proposition.

Hawk laughed. "You've never heard about her?"

"You're obviously itching to tell me," he grumbled.

"She makes matches for every ugly duckling in London," Hawk said, wagging his brows.

Tristan scoffed. "You're funning me."

"I'm not jesting. She's not called Miss Mantrap for nothing," Hawk said. "The woman is a menace to bachelors. Good old Broughton is a prime example."

Good old Broughton gazed down at his pretty blond bride. The man looked as if he were suffering from unbridled lust, a term women euphemistically called love.

Hawk regarded Tristan with suspicion. "Why are you so interested in her?"

"Mere curiosity," he said with a shrug.

Hawk smirked. "Cut line. You thought she was available for dalliance."

He'd never admit it. No doubt she was as poor as a church mouse, without noble family connections. She probably found matchmaking preferable to taking a position as a lady's maid or governess. Most likely, she'd only received an invitation to the ball because she'd made Broughton's match.

He wished she'd not refused his offer to pay for the fan. But he understood her pride all too well, and though he thought her chosen career odd, he couldn't deny she'd made a successful match for Broughton.

Tristan's skin tingled. No, he would not stoop to hiring her to find him a bride. He could practically picture the news in the scandal rags. *The Desperate Duke has hired a matchmaker.*

He was not desperate. He was a bloody duke. With a mere crook of his finger, he could have any woman he wanted. The problem was he didn't want just any woman. He'd formulated requirements for his ideal bride.

All he needed was to find someone who met them.

He thought about spending week after week trolling for a wife in ballrooms. He thought about fetching fans, handkerchiefs, and parasols. He thought about his need for an heir. His chances of finding his perfect duchess seemed remote at best.

Tristan glanced at Miss Mansfield again and reconsidered. She needed money. He needed a bride. For the right price, Miss Mansfield would keep her involvement a secret from all but the chosen girl and her grateful family.

He frowned, realizing he was basing his decision on one example—Broughton. Hiring Miss Mansfield meant taking a risk, but if her efforts proved unsatisfactory, he could dismiss her. Truthfully, a larger risk loomed. Marriage was for life, and as matters now stood, he was in serious danger of tying himself forever to an unsuitable wife. Or no wife at all, at this rate.

Tristan sized up the situation and realized he had two choices: continue his haphazard search or hire Miss Mansfield. After weeks of pure hell shopping at the marriage mart, the matchmaker won hands-down.

Of course, he had no intention of enlightening his friend. "I'm off to pay my respects to Broughton and his wife."

Hawk snorted. "This marriage business has addled your brain."

"I fail to understand what you find so amusing."

"Miss Mansfield is a happily-ever-after spinster." Hawk clapped him on the shoulder. "Congratulations, old boy. You've just chosen the only woman in the kingdom who won't wed you."

Tessa Mansfield wanted to kick herself.

Heaven above, she'd practically flirted with that rake, the Duke of Shelbourne. She'd never seen him before tonight, but she'd heard about his reputation. The gentleman rake, they called him. Everyone said he didn't gamble to excess. They said he never seduced innocents. Every other female, however, was apparently fair game.

She prided herself on her ability to spot a rake at twenty paces. This particular rake had fooled her with his agreeable manner. But she knew rakes used their charm to disarm their intended victims. She recalled the duke's slow smile and could not deny she'd let his handsome face turn her head.

Tessa cringed as she recalled the way she'd chattered like a monkey. He must have thought she'd dropped her fan on purpose like all those silly girls she'd read about in the scandal sheets. Oh, how lowering.

She took a deep breath, reminding herself she was unlikely to encounter him again. Thank goodness.

"I am glad to see you, Tessa. I've missed you so."

Tessa returned her attention to Anne, her former companion and dearest friend in the world. "I missed you as well."

Anne's eyes misted. "I never imagined I would make such a happy marriage. You made all my dreams come true."

For nearly a year, Tessa had promoted the match between Anne Mortland and Lord Broughton. More than once, Tessa had feared all would come to naught, but true love and a dusting of luck had culminated in this fairy tale marriage.

Tessa glanced at Lord Broughton. "You both look well, my lord."

Broughton gazed at his bride with adoration. "I am the happiest of men."

Tessa's heart contracted with a yearning for something she could never have.

Anne clasped her arm. "Tessa, look quickly. You do not want to miss seeing Jane dance."

Tessa lifted up on her toes to see past the crowd. She caught a glimpse of her new companion, Jane Powell, but the fast approach of two fashionable and handsome gentlemen diverted her attention. As they neared, her heart thudded. She recognized the taller man with tousled black hair. It was the Duke of Shelbourne.

She turned round, hoping he'd not seen her. To her mortification, Shelbourne and the other gentleman approached Lord Broughton.

"Shelbourne, Hawk, this is an unexpected pleasure," Broughton said, rubbing his hands.

Tessa gazed up at the chandelier, wishing she could melt like the wax oozing from the candles. When she'd run away, he'd probably thought she wanted him to chase her. Belatedly, she realized her behavior only made her look guilty and a little foolish. She planted a serene smile on her face as Lord Broughton introduced her to the duke and Lord Hawkfield. Then she curtseyed and rose to find Shelbourne gazing at her. In the light of the chandelier, she could see his eyes were marine blue and fringed by thick black lashes.

"Miss Mansfield and my wife are friends," Lord Broughton said. "She is the one responsible for our happy union."

Lord Hawkfield raised his brows in an exaggerated fashion. "I say, a matchmaker? If only I had known of your skills when my sisters were single, Miss Mansfield. You might have saved me the trouble of finding them husbands."

His mocking tone vexed her. She'd encountered plenty of his kind before, always quick to ridicule her avocation. "I had no idea I had a competitor. Or do you only make matches for relatives?"

Before Lord Hawkfield could reply, the duke cut in. "His self-proclaimed talent is highly overrated."

She arched her brows. "Should I be relieved?"

"He never stood a chance against you."

His distinctive baritone voice sent an exquisite shiver along her arms. She mentally shook herself. *He's a rake, he's a rake, he's a rake.*

The music ended. Lord Hawkfield excused himself and disappeared into the crowd. The duke glanced at her, and then he closed the distance between them.

She looked at him warily. Could he not see she wished him to leave her in peace?

"I apologize for detaining you so long earlier," he said. "Without a proper introduction, I fear you might have taken offense."

He'd apologized in a gentlemanly manner, even though she was equally at fault, perhaps more so, since she'd done most of the talking. "No apology is necessary. The circumstances were unusual."

He inclined his head. Though he did not smile, there was a natural curve to his full lips. His was not the pretty face of a dandy, however. Oh, no, not at all. His thick brows, angular cheekbones, and square jaw were all male. Little wonder women reportedly swooned at his perfection. No, not quite perfect, she thought, detecting a faint shadow along his jaw and above his full upper lip. His valet probably had to shave him twice a day. Her skin prickled at this evidence of the duke's masculinity.

"There is something I wish to ask you." His voice rumbled, a sound as rich and irresistible as a cup of chocolate.

Her heart thumped at the low, seductive notes in his voice. She'd thought herself unsusceptible to such tricks, but evidently her traitorous body was not.

"May I call upon you tomorrow afternoon?" he asked.

"Your Grace, if this concerns my fan, I beg you to forget the matter." There, that should settle his concern once and for all.

"It is not about the fan," he said. "I have appointments early in the afternoon. May I call at four o'clock?"

She regarded him with suspicion. "Why not tell me now?"

"I prefer to discuss it in private, if you are amenable."

In private? Did he mean to make her a dishonorable proposal? Then her common sense prevailed. A handsome rake like him would have no interest in a plump spinster.

His mouth curved in the merest of smiles. "You hesitate. I can hardly blame you after I discomposed you earlier."

She lifted her chin. "I was not discomposed." What a bounder. She'd fled as if the engraving on his card read His Grace, the Duke of Devilbourne.

"I will of course abide by your decision." Then he gazed into her eyes with such intensity, she stilled like a rabbit in the woods. He drew her in, mesmerizing her with his arresting blue eyes. She felt the pull of his will like a swift current. And everything inside her said *yes.* "Very well," she said breathlessly.

"Thank you. Until tomorrow." He sketched a formal bow and walked away.

She let out her pent-up breath. Good God, he'd seduced her into agreeing.

Anne approached, using her fan to shield her voice. "What were you and the duke discussing?"

Tessa thought it best not to reveal his intended visit until she knew his purpose. "Nothing of consequence." But he wanted something from her. She suppressed a shiver.

"He spoke to you at length," Anne said. "You must tell me what he said."

"You make too much of the matter." Why had she let him turn her head?

"He looked at you like a starving wolf. Stay away from him," Anne said. "He is well-respected for his politics, but even Geoffrey admitted the duke has a notorious reputation with women. He probably has one hundred notches in his bedpost."

Tessa scoffed. "I'm sure he has no interest in carving one for an aging spinster like me."

"You are only six and twenty," Anne said. "Why must you always demean your charms?"

She ignored her friend's question. "Do not worry. I am in no danger of falling for a rake's wiles." Even if he'd persuaded her to let him call tomorrow, and she'd accepted against her better judgment.

Anne drew closer. "He has a reputation as a legendary lover. Women throw themselves in his path. I heard he can persuade a woman to do his bidding with his eyes."

Tessa gulped, knowing it was true.

Anne surveyed the crowd and grabbed Tessa's arm. "Look, there he is now by the hearth. Do you see that woman with him? That is Lady Endicott, a formerly respectable widow—until she met Shelbourne."

Tessa glanced in that direction. A tall, raven-haired beauty with jade feathers in her bandeau slid her finger along Shelbourne's lapel. Then the widow leaned against him and whispered in his ear. He turned his head and flicked her earbob.

Tessa gasped. Stars above. She'd invited that shameless rake to her drawing room.

His teeth flashed in a roguish grin. Then he winked at the lady and strode off.

"How could he engage in such brazen flirtation when his sister is present?" Anne said, her voice outraged.

Tessa swerved her gaze to Anne. "His sister?"

"Lady Julianne," Anne said. "She is dancing with Lord Holbrook."

The dark-haired young woman laughed as she skipped past her partner. Her complexion glowed with the radiance of youth, and her gold-netted gown set off her slender figure to perfection. A sliver of envy lodged in Tessa's throat. Long ago, she'd missed her own opportunity to have a season. Most of the time, she refused to dwell on the past, but once in a while, regret shadowed her heart.

Anne regarded Tessa. "Lady Julianne is purported to have declined more than a dozen marriage proposals since her come-out three years ago."

"She sounds very particular."

"Perhaps it is her brother who is particular," Anne said. "Some say the duke believes no man is good enough for his sister."

Tessa stilled. Did he mean to ask her to make a match for his sister tomorrow? No, surely he would rely on his mother's advice. Why then had he insisted on calling?

THE DISH

Where authors give you the inside scoop!

♥ ♥ ♥ ♥ ♥ ♥ ♥ ♥ ♥ ♥ ♥ ♥ ♥

From the desk of Vicky Dreiling

Dear Reader,

While writing my first novel HOW TO MARRY A DUKE, I decided my hero Tristan, the Duke of Shelbourne, needed a sidekick. That bad boy sidekick was Tristan's oldest friend Marc Darcett, the Earl of Hawkfield, and the hero of HOW TO SEDUCE A SCOUNDREL. Hawk is a rogue who loves nothing better than a lark. Truthfully, I had to rein Hawk in more than once in the first book as he tried repeatedly to upstage all the other characters.

Unlike his friend Tristan, Hawk is averse to giving up his bachelor status. He's managed to evade his female relatives' matchmaking schemes for years. According to the latest tittle-tattle, his mother and sisters went into a decline upon learning of his ill-fated one-hour engagement. Clearly, this is a man who values his freedom.

My first task was to find the perfect heroine to foil him. Who better than the one woman he absolutely must never touch? Yes, that would be his best friend's sister, Lady Julianne. After all, it's in a rake's code of conduct that friends' sisters are forbidden. Unbeknownst to Hawk, however, Julianne has been planning their nuptials for four long years. I wasn't quite sure how Julianne would manage this feat, given Hawk's fear of catching *wife-itis*.

After a great deal of pacing about, the perfect solution popped into my head. I would use the time-honored trick known as *The Call to Adventure*. When Tristan, who can not be in London for the season, proposes that Hawk act as Julianne's unofficial guardian, Hawk's bachelor days are numbered.

In addition to these plans, I wanted to add in a bit of fun with yet another Regency-era spoof of modern dating practices. I recalled an incident in which one of my younger male colleagues complained about that dratted advice book for single ladies, *The Rules*. I wasn't very sympathetic to his woes about women ruling guys. After all, reluctant bachelors have held the upper hand for centuries. Thus, I concocted *The Rules* in Regency England.

Naturally, the road to true love is fraught with heart-break, mayhem, and, well, a decanter of wine. Matters turn bleak for poor Julianne when Hawk makes his disin-terest clear after a rather steamy waltz. I knew Julianne needed help, and so I sent in a wise woman, albeit a rather eccentric one. Hawk's Aunt Hester, a plain-spoken woman, has some rather startling advice for Julianne. Left with only the shreds of her pride, Julianne decides to write a lady's guide to seducing scoundrels into the proverbial parson's mousetrap. My intrepid heroine finds herself in hot suds when all of London hunts for the anonymous author of that scandalous publication, *The Secrets of Seduction*. At all costs, Julianne must keep her identity a secret—especially from Hawk, who is determined to guard her from his fellow scoundrels. But can he guard his own heart from the one woman forbidden to him?

My heartfelt thanks to all the readers who wrote to let

me know they couldn't wait to read HOW TO SEDUCE A SCOUNDREL. I hope you will enjoy the twists and turns that finally lead to happily ever after for Hawk and Julianne.

Cheers!

Vicky Dreiling

www.vickydreiling.com

♥ ♥ ♥ ♥ ♥ ♥ ♥ ♥ ♥ ♥ ♥ ♥ ♥ ♥ ♥

From the desk of Jane Graves

Dear Reader,

Have you ever visited one website, seen an interesting link to another website, and clicked it? Probably. But have you ever done that about fifty times and ended up in a place you never intended to? As a writer, I'm already on a "what if" journey inside my own head, so web hopping is just one more flight of fancy that's *so* easy to get caught up in.

For instance, while researching a scene for BLACK TIES AND LULLABIES that takes place in a childbirth class, I saw a link for "hypnosis during birth." Of course I had to click that, right? Then I ended up on a site where people post their birth stories. And then . . .

Don't ask me how, but a dozen clicks later, my web-hopping adventure led me to a site about celebrities and baby names. And it immediately had me wondering: *What* were these people thinking? Check out the names these famous people have given their children that virtually guarantee they'll be tormented for the rest of their lives:

Apple	Actress Gwyneth Paltrow
Diva Muffin	Musician Frank Zappa
Moxie Crimefighter	Entertainer Penn Jillette
Petal Blossom Rainbow	Chef Jamie Oliver
Zowie	Singer David Bowie
Pilot Inspektor	Actor Jason Lee
Sage Moonblood	Actor Sylvester Stallone
Fifi Trixibell	Sir Bob Geldof*
Reignbeau	Actor Ving Rhames
Jermajesty	Singer Jermaine Jackson

*Musician/Activist

No, a trip around the Internet does *not* get my books written, but sometimes it's worth the laugh. Of course, the hero and heroine of BLACK TIES AND LULLABIES would *never* give their child a name like one of these....

I hope you enjoy BLACK TIES AND LULLABIES. And look for my next book, HEARTSTRINGS AND DIAMOND RINGS, coming October 2011.

Happy Reading!

Jane Graves

www.janegraves.com

♥ ♥ ♥ ♥ ♥ ♥ ♥ ♥ ♥ ♥ ♥ ♥ ♥ ♥ ♥

From the desk of Paula Quinn

Dear Reader,

Having married my first love, I was excited to write the third installment in my Children of the Mist series, TAMED BY A HIGHLANDER. You see, Mairi Mac-Gregor and Connor Grant were childhood sweethearts. How difficult could it be to relate to a woman who had surrendered her heart at around the same age I did? Of course, my real life hero didn't pack up his Claymore and plaid and ride off to good old England to save the king. (Although my husband does own a few swords he keeps around in the event that one of our daughters brings home an unfavorable boyfriend.) My hero didn't break my young heart, or the promises he made me beneath the shadow of a majestic Highland mountain. I don't hide daggers under my skirts. Heck, I don't even wear skirts.

But I am willing to fight for what I believe in. So is Mairi, and what she believes in is Scotland. A member of a secret Highland militia, Mairi has traded in her dreams of a husband and children for sweeping Scotland free of men who would seek to change her Highland customs and religion. She knows how to fight, but she isn't prepared for the battle awaiting her when she sets her feet in England and comes face to face with the man she once loved.

Ah, Connor Grant, captain in the King's Royal Army and son of the infamous rogue Graham Grant from A

HIGHLANDER NEVER SURRENDERS. He's nothing
like his father. This guy has loved the same lass his whole
life, but she's grown into a woman without him and now,
instead of casting him smiles, she's throwing daggers at
him!

Fun! I knew when these two were reunited sparks
(and knives) would fly!

But Connor isn't one to back down from a fight. In
fact, he longs to tame his wild Highland mare. But does
he need to protect the last Stuart king from her?

Journey back in time where plots and intrigue once
ruled the courtly halls of Whitehall Palace, and two souls
who were born to love only each other find their way
back into each other's arms.

If Mairi doesn't kill him first.

(Did I mention, I collect medieval daggers? Just in
case . . .)

Happy Reading!

Paula Quinn

www.paulaquinn.com

♥ ♥ ♥ ♥ ♥ ♥ ♥ ♥ ♥ ♥ ♥ ♥ ♥ ♥ ♥

From the desk of Kendra Leigh Castle

Dear Reader,

It all started with the History Channel.

No, really. One evening last year, while I was watching TV in the basement and hiding from whatever flesh-eating-zombie-filled gore-fest my husband was happily watching upstairs, I ran across a fascinating documentary all about a woman I never knew existed: Arsinöe, Cleopatra's youngest sister. Being a sucker for a good story, I watched, fascinated, as the tale of Arsinöe's brief and often unhappy life unfolded. And after it was all over, once her threat to Cleopatra's power had been taken care of in a very final way by the famous queen herself, I asked myself what any good writer would: what if Arsinöe hadn't really died, and become a vampire instead?

Okay, so maybe most writers wouldn't ask themselves that. I write paranormal romance for a reason, after all. But that simple, and rather odd, question was the seed that my book DARK AWAKENING grew from. Now, Arsinöe isn't the heroine. In fact, she's more of a threat hanging over the head of my hero, Ty MacGillivray, whose kind has served her dynasty of highblood vampires for centuries, bound in virtual slavery. But her arrival in my imagination sparked an entire world, in which so-called "highblood" vampires, those bearing the tattoo-like mark of bloodlines descended directly from various darker gods and goddesses, form an immortal nobility that take great pleasure in lording it over the "lowbloods" of more mud-died pedigree.

Lowbloods like Ty and his unusual bloodline of cat-shifting vampires, the Cait Sith.

Now, I won't give out all the details of what happens when Ty is sent by Arsinöe herself to find a human woman with the ability to root out the source of a curse that threatens to take her entire dynasty down. I will say that Lily Quinn is a lot more than Ty bargained for, carrying secrets that have the potential to change the entire world of night. And I'm happy to tell you that it really tugged at my heartstrings to write the story of a man who has been kicked around for so long that he is afraid to want what his heart so desperately needs. But beyond that, all you really need to know is that DARK AWAKENING has all of my favorite ingredients: a tortured bad boy with a heart of gold, a heroine strong enough to take him on, and cats.

What? I like cats. Especially when they turn into gorgeous immortals.

Ty and Lily's story is the first in my DARK DYNASTIES series, about the hotbed of intrigue and desire that is the realm of the twenty-first century vampire. If you're up for a ride into the darkness, not to mention brooding bad boys who aren't afraid to flash a little fang, then stick with me. I've got a silver-eyed hero you might like to meet. . . .

Enjoy!

Kendra Leigh Castle

www.kendraleighcastle.com